FULFILLING HER DESIRES

"I see I can expect no charity from you, Captain."

Frobisher came in close. "This isn't about charity."

"You dislike me. I think that's plain. I repeat, I want nothing from you."

"Oh, you want something from me, all right. And you don't even know yourself what it is. But I know. Yes, I know very well what you want from me, Miss Peartree."

"Tell me then, that which I don't even know myself." She raised her chin.

"This—" He snaked an arm about her waist and dragged her up against him. "And this—" He lowered his mouth and kissed her hard.

Frobisher wanted to shock her and frighten her, make her flee from him, back to Devon, back to Donald. He wanted to prove to her that there were some men you couldn't toy with and come away unscathed. *He wanted . . . he wanted . . .* He wanted her so badly that his whole body was wracked with the pain of it. He wanted to taste her and touch her, to trace his mouth over every inch of her beautiful skin. He wanted to take her, claim her and cleave to her forever. . . .

CASTAWAY HEARTS

NANCY BUTLER

A SIGNET BOOK

To Rafael and Daphne, Alexandre and the Baroness . . .
For seizing my imagination at an early age and never letting go.

SIGNET
Published by New American Library, a division of
Penguin Group (USA) Inc., 375 Hudson Street,
New York, New York 10014, U.S.A.
Penguin Books Ltd, 80 Strand,
London WC2R 0RL, England
Penguin Books Australia Ltd, 250 Camberwell Road,
Camberwell, Victoria 3124, Australia
Penguin Books Canada Ltd, 10 Alcorn Avenue,
Toronto, Ontario, Canada M4V 3B2
Penguin Books (N.Z.) Ltd, Cnr Rosedale and Airborne Roads,
Albany, Auckland 1310, New Zealand

Penguin Books Ltd, Registered Offices:
80 Strand, London WC2R 0RL, England

First published by Signet, an imprint of New American Library,
a division of Penguin Group (USA) Inc.

First Printing, March 2004
10 9 8 7 6 5 4 3 2 1

Copyright © Nancy J. Hajeski, 2004
All rights reserved

REGISTERED TRADEMARK—MARCA REGISTRADA

Printed in the United States of America

PUBLISHER'S NOTE
This is a work of fiction. Names, characters, places, and incidents either are the product of the author's imagination or are used fictitiously, and any resemblance to actual persons, living or dead, business establishments, events, or locales is entirely coincidental.

Chapter One

The Rook

*C*aptain Frobisher was late.

Lydia Peartree, unaccustomed to waiting for *any* man, paced the dock where his sleek black ship was moored. Sir Robert had distinctly said noon, and it was already fifteen minutes past the hour. The intense June sun beat down upon her, but she refused to open her parasol. A flock of harbor gulls, mewing overhead, seemed to mock her petulance.

The dock was deserted except for a scarred old sailor who sat cross-legged on a circle of heavy rope near one of the pilings. Her young maid, Tilda, hung back closer to the waterfront street, occasionally wrinkling her nose at the unpleasant odors emanating from the befouled fishing trawler opposite the *Rook*.

Lydia noticed the seaman squinting at her while he spliced together a sisal line. His face was striking, all hollow planes, with a narrow, high-bridged nose and wide cheekbones. Above and below his left eye a narrow scar—stark against his tanned skin—traced a course.

"Do you know Captain Frobisher?" Lydia asked him at last in exasperation. "Matthew Frobisher?"

"Aye," he said in a gravelly voice, tilting his head back to look at her. His eyes were that rarely seen shade of gray that in some lights appears to be no color at all. His hair, which hung loose to well below his shoulders, was a blend of jet black and silvery white. In spite of it, she realized with some surprise, he was relatively young—the angular face weathered more by sun and sea than by age.

Planting the tip of her parasol on the wooden planking, she leaned forward and said, "He is expected at his ship today, isn't he?"

"Aye." His head bobbed, and he began to sing a French sea chantey in a low, briery baritone. He continued to watch her over the rope he was mending.

She began pacing again in thinly veiled agitation, thinking she'd have done better to while away the afternoon in one of Exeter's dress shops than wait here, steaming in more ways than one.

Tilda crept forward timidly and stopped halfway along the dock. "Perhaps Mr. Frobisher forgot," she called out, not attempting to disguise her hopes that this was indeed the case.

"Do you know if he intends to sail out today?" Lydia asked the seaman.

He frowned, resentful at the interruption of his song. "Aye . . . but no use lookin' for 'im toward the end o' the dock." He spoke in the broad Devon dialect she normally found so musical. "He won't be comin' from down there. Whyn't you jus' go aboard th' ship?"

"Not until Captain Frobisher is here."

With an audible sigh, the sailor rose to his feet. He was tall and very lean, his shoulders wide beneath a white, open-necked shirt. His skin was tanned to a uniform deep hue, and since his canvas breeches fell only to mid-calf, his muscular legs and bare feet were displayed in a manner Lydia thought highly irregular.

He vaulted easily over the side of the ship, then bowed to her with an expression of barely contained mirth.

Her expression tightened as she took a half step back. "You? You can't be Captain Frobisher."

"Why not?" He set his hands on his hips and cocked his head. "Not what you expected?"

"I don't recall that I expected anything."

"Good. I've discovered it's always wisest in life to have as few expectations as possible. I probably have even fewer of you."

She started a little. "Of all the off-putting things to say! Whyever did you invite me?"

"Sir Robert," he said simply.

"Sir Robert Poole?"

"Aye. He pays my wages; I do as he says."

"But where is everyone else? Aren't some schoolboys from the Exeter Academy supposed to be sailing with you?"

"Aye."

"Stop saying that!" she snapped. "You must know it's very annoying."

He grinned. "Aye."

She wanted to spin away from his smirk and march off in dignified retreat, but he was holding out one hand from the top of the gangplank. Taking it begrudgingly, she stepped aboard.

"Thank you," she said in her chilliest voice.

He then motioned to Tilda, who was still hovering. "And won't you please come aboard, miss?" He'd spoken with the utmost gallantry, as though she were the lady and not merely the maid. Tilda mustered a determined expression and then went gingerly up the wooden plank.

There was a sudden commotion at the far end of the dock as a prosperous-looking older man herded seven boys toward the *Rook*. They appeared to range in age from twelve to fifteen, each of them carrying a bedroll tucked under his arm.

"Rowdy, Gilbert, Seamus, Tenpence, Oxer, Fripp, and . . . Jean-Louis," the man called out as they filed past him onto the ship.

"Well done, Hardy," Captain Frobisher said, leaning over the rail. "I see you managed to round them all up."

"Had to pry Rowdy away from the bake shop—as usual."

The captain stole a glance at one of the taller boys. "Ah, the baker's comely wife . . ."

"Excuse me," said Lydia, "but I thought this was to be an afternoon cruise at most. What are your boys doing with those packs?"

"Oh, we'll be back betimes," he said evenly. "The boys sometimes sleep on deck during warm weather. They'll be storing their bedrolls for later tonight." He then called over his shoulder, "Fripp, Tenpence . . . come show our guests around the *Rook*.

"The alpha and omega of my younger students," he added to Lydia under his breath. "Though I'll leave it to you to figure out which is which."

He then climbed into the web of ratlines that rose up from the ship's rail, shouting orders down to the boys as he moved easily up toward the sails. Lydia tried to keep her eyes on the deck but they kept straying up to the lean man in the rigging. He moved cat-like from mast to spar, sidling out to untie the lashes that held the sails snug.

"Why don't you help him?" she asked the tall, well-groomed boy beside her.

He raised his brows. "Captain Frobisher rarely lets anyone touch his sails."

"Aye," said the shorter, rather unkempt boy in East End Cockney. "Guards 'em like a virgin guards 'er virtue"

Lydia nearly smiled.

With a call of "Godspeed, Matthew," Hardy released the mooring lines. The ship slid away from the dock, moving into the River Exe. The wind caught at the staysail, then tugged and filled the foresail. As the breeze caught her up from behind, the narrow ship heeled over, her prow cutting cleanly through the water.

Lydia's two young escorts walked with her along the rail, explaining that the *Rook* was a hermaphrodite brigantine, built to the captain's own specifications.

"Square-rigged on the foremast." Fripp pointed to the front of the ship.

"Fore-and-aft-rigged 'ere on the main." Tenpence explained. "In a pinch, one man can sail 'er—the cap'n had 'er specially rigged for solo cruises. But we all like to try our hand at the wheel." He motioned to where a tall youth, dressed like their captain in simple sailor's clothing, stood at the ship's wheel. His hair in the June sun was an impossible shade of bright gold.

That must be Lady Monteith's brother, Gilbert, Lydia determined. He was accounted to be a budding Adonis. She studied him as he manned the helm, thinking it unlikely work for an earl's brother-in-law.

Once the ship reached the open waters of Lyme Bay, Tilda complained of feeling unwell, declaring faintly that God never intended for man nor woman to leave the safety of dry land. When she insisted on going below, Fripp and Tenpence offered to accompany her.

Lydia wandered to the stern, pulling off her straw bonnet to let the sea breeze tangle through her hair. A smile of pure pleasure lit up her face as she watched the coastline recede.

"You've sailed before, then?" The captain had come down from his canvas kingdom and was now leaning on the rail beside her.

"I have my own little sloop in Hampshire, the *Swallow*."

"Oh, lake sailing." He snorted dismissively, as though she'd boasted of sailing a toy boat in Hyde Park. " 'Tis nothing like this."

"Well, there's a tiller instead of a wheel," she agreed, attempting to be amiable. "But wind is just wind, as far as I can tell."

He squinted at her. She realized it was an affectation, rather than a result of his scarred eye. There were times when he'd looked at her quite normally. Apparently the narrow wound had marked his lean face but not affected the eye itself.

"What a daft thing to say. Wind is never just wind.

It's clear you've never been at sea in a storm. And there's more than wind to account for out here." He took her arm and rather brusquely propelled her to the starboard rail. "See that?" He was pointing to a long, dark shape, writhing beneath the surface of the water.

"Sea monster?" she asked, her eyes dancing up at him. She was never very well behaved when people tried to lecture her.

"Currents," he said portentously, slicking back his wind-tossed hair with one hand. "Tides, eddies, undertows, backwashes, whirlpools—all the things you'd never have to contend with sailing upon a lake."

"Water hyacinths," she said darkly.

"What?" He was squinting again.

"Snapping turtles, blue herons, noisy picnickers and romantic couples in rowboats." She folded her arms. "Those are the things *you* don't have to contend with here at sea."

He looked taken aback for a moment, then laughed out loud. "Quite perilous, Miss Peartree." His pale eyes appeared almost merry. "I had no idea."

"Especially the water hyacinths," she said, wrinkling her nose. "I can never keep my rudder from tangling in those long stems."

"A lady's always got to watch out for her rudder," he murmured.

Tenpence and Fripp reappeared at her side. "Your maid's not feeling at all the thing," Fripp pronounced.

"Shot the cat at least twice," Tenpence piped in.

"Oh, dear. Perhaps I should look in on her." Lydia had no illusions about her ability as a nurse, but Tilda *was* her responsibility.

"Let her sleep," said the captain. "By the time she awakens we'll be be beating back to Exeter harbor." He turned from her abruptly and went to tend something amidships.

His six young crewmen moved briskly about the deck, busy with their tasks, while the seventh held the

ship before the wind and kept the pennons on the
mast tops flying out behind.

At one point the captain approached a slender boy
with chestnut hair who appeared to be having trouble
with one of the lines. Frobisher removed the rope
from his thin hands, unsnaked the snarled line and
made it fast to a cleat on the rail.

"Ask, next time," he said curtly, "if you don't know
where something goes." As Frobisher stalked away,
Lydia couldn't help noticing the look of pained resentment in the boy's eyes.

Once the south coast of Devon had become no
more than an indistinct haze, the captain inquired if
Lydia would care to take some refreshment below.
Actually what he'd said was, "If you're starting to feel
peckish, Miss Peartree, I've some food in my cabin."

She followed him into the companionway, noting
how he had to duck his head to clear the entrance.
The main cabin, lit with the diffused light from a mullioned window, was not large but quite tidy. It was
furnished with a few serviceable items—a narrow
bunk with a sea chest beside it, a sturdy desk, several
chairs, and a sideboard with a brass humidor on top.
Bolted to the inner wall, a bookcase brimmed with
well-thumbed volumes. The cabin smelled like her father's library at home—of old leather and sweet
pipe tobacco.

The one note of discord in the cozy space was a
long, businesslike, silver sword, which hung above the
sideboard, dangling from a tooled-leather baldric.

Captain Frobisher motioned Lydia to a chair at the
front of the desk, then carried a tray of fruit and
cheese from the sideboard.

"Care for some wine?" He had already unstoppered
a dark bottle and was pouring her a glass. He drew
in the bouquet of the bloodred claret and closed his
eyes in pleasure. "It's a rare vintage, miss. Hardy still
has his connections with the Gentlemen."

"The gentlemen?"

"The man at the dock, Taunton Hardy, was once a smuggler with the Gentlemen of the Coast—until he married a lady of some property. Now he never so much as sets foot on a ship. I've known him since I was a lad; he helps me with my school."

"Neither of you looks like a schoolmaster," she remarked as he sat down opposite her.

"What, then?" He'd begun breaking the skin of an orange with his long, supple fingers.

"Well . . ." Lydia thought a moment. "Mr. Hardy looks like a London solicitor and you . . . you look like a pirate."

If she thought he'd be insulted, she was mistaken. He just chuckled as he handed her a plump segment of the fruit.

"You don't look much like the daughter of a princess," he observed, cocking his head to study her. "Oh, I suppose you're pretty enough, in that washed-out, redheaded way. Still, I thought you'd be more poised, more . . . well, regal. Not the sort of annoying chit who would throw a hissy fit on my dock because I wasn't setting off exactly on time."

He had crowded so many objectionable comments into that one sentence that Lydia didn't know where to begin addressing them. Her blue eyes flashed, and a flush of crimson rose to her cheeks. "I don't believe I heard you correctly, Captain."

"Sorry—was I rude?" he inquired amiably. "I'm not used to being in company with females. A man gets in the habit of speaking his thoughts aloud."

"It might interest you to know that Lord Byron himself composed a sonnet to my hair."

He studied the crop of bright auburn ringlets, which fell to just below her chin. "And what did perishing George write about your hair? Hmm, something like . . . 'Merely a touch of gold, more than a hint of red, fair locks that glow like copper, on top of her heavenly head?' "

"Did you just make that up?" Lydia was impressed in spite of herself.

"I am plainspoken, Miss Peartree, not stupid. Never could stand Byron, though."

There was a thudding footfall on the companion-way, and then the tall blond youth who had been manning the helm strode into the cabin. He sketched a salute to the captain.

"Rowdy's relieving me, sir." He bowed to Lydia. "I am Gilbert Marriott, ma'am, and most pleased to meet you at last."

Lydia gave him a wide smile.

"I understand you two have some sort of family connection?" the captain said. Gilbert nodded as he perched on the edge of the desk and proceeded to slice the wedge of cheese with a small knife.

Lydia elaborated. "Gilbert's sister Evelynne is wed to the Earl of Monteith, whose best friend is my first cousin, Arkady Pelletier, Marquess of Mitford." She'd spoken it like a catechism.

"There's a reasonable connection," the captain observed dryly.

"It's true," the young man stated, laughing. "We aren't related, Miss Peartree and I, but we know a great many people in common. Including Sir Robert Poole."

"It's a shame you and I were never at Levelands at the same time," Lydia told him. "My cousin Arkady adores your whole family. I've known Monteith for years, of course, and I've met your sister and brothers several times. But you've always been away at school."

"School?" Gilbert looked puzzled. "Oh, you mean here . . . with the captain. I never think of this as school. It's much too jolly for that." He popped a piece of cheese into his mouth.

"Jolly?" the captain echoed sadly. "I must be losing my touch."

"And what sort of things do you learn in this jolly school?" Lydia asked the boy.

Gilbert pondered a moment. "Fencing, shooting, seamanship, horsemanship, languages, mathematics"—

he made a nasty face—"umm . . . history, etiquette, picking pockets—"

"Picking pockets?" Lydia interrupted him. "That's rather unorthodox. And who teaches you to pick pockets?"

"I do," the captain replied.

"You? I don't believe it."

Frobisher reached into his pocket and withdrew a fine emerald ring. He twirled it under Lydia's nose.

"Th-that's mine," she protested, frowning at her empty right hand. "How did you—"

"Had it off you when I helped you aboard." He was looking at her with narrow-eyed amusement. "A parlor trick to entertain my guests." He drew her hand across the desk and slipped the ring onto her finger. The sudden warmth that rippled through her at the touch of his work-roughened hand was startling.

"A little sleight of hand is a useful skill for these lads to possess, all things considered."

"Useful?"

Gilbert leaned closer. "Sir Robert never told you? I mean, what sort of school the Exeter Academy is?" He looked questioningly at Frobisher. "Is it all right to tell her? She's practically family, you know." When the captain nodded, Gilbert said, "We are in training to become spies, Miss Peartree."

Lydia's eyes widened. *Spies?*

This cruise was turning out to be nothing like she'd expected.

A week earlier she had come to Exeter to visit the family of her fiancé, Donald Farthingale. Two days after her arrival, her betrothed had come down with measles, and his entire household had been quarantined. Even though Lydia had contracted the disease in childhood, she'd been sent to stay with Sir Robert Poole, the noted statesman and a longtime friend of her family. Sir Robert had squired her through Exeter until yesterday, when he'd been called away to London on government business. Knowing how much she enjoyed sailing, he had suggested she spend a day on board the *Rook* with the boys from the school he sponsored.

No mention had ever been made of spies.

In response to her perplexed expression, Gilbert explained, "Captain Frobisher was an intelligence officer for the Crown. When he left the service, Sir Robert thought it a shame to waste his talents and so he founded the school."

"We take in boys from all backgrounds," the captain added. "The only stipulation is that they be clever, observant and good at languages."

Gilbert continued, "The captain teaches us for three years—I'm in my second year now—and then we are sent off to school in Europe."

"Why not here in England?"

The captain quirked up his mouth. "Because, my dear innocent, they will not be asked to spy here in England. They've got to know a foreign country as though it were their own."

"This is all rather fantastic. You mean they actually decide which country they will work in?"

"I've chosen Austria," Gilbert said. "Now that Bonaparte is exiled, France isn't the opportunity it once was. I believe Vienna will soon become the hub of Europe, as Paris was for so long." He looked intently at Frobisher. "The captain spent ten years going in and out of France. Sir Robert swears we'd never have beaten Bonaparte without him." He motioned to the sword above the sideboard. "The Regent himself presented that to the captain for his services to the Crown."

Frobisher shook his head slowly. "I wasn't alone over there, Gil. Too many of those other fellows never came home to get credit for their work."

Lydia was trying not to gape at the man across from her. This unkempt seaman, with his bare legs and odd, nearly white hair, had been a Continental spy?

He must have read her glance; he squinted at her and leaned forward. "In my youth I was a bit more, um, presentable."

"In your youth?" Lydia objected. "You're hardly in your dotage, sir."

"Thirty-six this May," he said with a grin. "Time I did something with my life, don't you think?"

Before Lydia could respond, there was a clattering on the companionway, and a strapping, fair-haired boy burst into the cabin.

"Sir!" he panted. "You'd best come up. There's a squall blowing up off the south coast."

The captain rose immediately. "I'm coming, Oxer. Gilbert, you get back to the wheel." He turned to Lydia. "You'd best keep out of the way, ma'am."

"No," she said forcefully as she rose to her feet. "I want to see."

"You're not sailing on a lake now, Miss Peartree," he warned her. "The Channel can be worse than open ocean in a storm."

She set her chin and followed him onto the deck. The sky above was still a bright, hard blue, but to the north it was showing a swirl of dark, ominous clouds. The rising wind had set whitecaps dancing across the water, and the ship was noticeably picking up speed.

Gilbert went at once to the wheel, while the captain began issuing instructions to the six boys who had gathered around him.

"Should we head in, Captain?" Gilbert shouted over the rising wind.

"We'd likely run directly into the squall," he called back. "Let's take her farther out. It will probably pass in an hour or so."

The small ship beat away from land toward the center of the English Channel. The squall, however, possessed a capricious nature—instead of wearing itself out on the south coast of Devon, it seemed to be following them.

An hour later the wind had increased until it whistled through the sheets, the planks beneath Lydia's feet shuddering with each gust. In spite of the captain's frequent discouraging looks, she had stayed abovedecks, entranced by the wild beauty of the gray-green sky roiling above the waters of the Channel. They sped now before the storm with only the staysail and jib open to the wind. It occurred to her to check on Tilda, but then she decided it was wiser to let her go on sleeping. The sea and sky were not a sight for the faint of heart.

A stinging rain began to fall, and Lydia was just drawing her shawl over her head when Frobisher approached her.

"Here." He held out an oilcloth cape similar to the one he now wore. "If you won't go below, at least you can stay dry." As he draped it over her shoulders, his arms closed about her for an instant. Raising one hand to her damp ringlets, he murmured with some surprise, "Real curls. I had wondered." And then he was gone.

When the storm hit in earnest, it was as though a general had given the signal for an artillery volley. The sky grew dark as night and the wind's volume increased to a keening pitch that made speech nearly impossible. Thunder crashed directly overhead, while lightning blazed all around them, turning the gray water an iridescent green-gold. The rain was now a punishing wall of water.

Frobisher came toward her, a looming shadow in the eldritch light.

"You must go below now!" he roared into her ear. "I'm sending the lads down."

"Are we in any danger?" she cried. Lightning flashed off the port bow, and in that split second Lydia saw his face clearly—pale as death, his eyes like two burning brands beneath his dark brows.

"No, not if you go below." He seemed to be laughing at her. "Don't want you swept overboard. I've got to get back to the wheel. Now, go!"

He turned and went aft without waiting to see if she'd followed his orders. He took the wheel from Gilbert, who staggered his way to the hatch door.

Lydia clung to the rail, watching as Captain Frobisher fought the wheel. Huge troughs opened up in the sea before them, and the narrow brigantine dropped into each one and then bobbed up again, bowsprit raised to the sky. There was a primal beauty to the motion, like a rhythmic pagan dance. He held the ship secure, placing her exactly where she needed to be, to dip and rise with the cadence of the heaving waves.

Determinedly, she made her way toward the stern, hand over hand, clinging tight to the slippery rail. Frobisher didn't see her until she was nearly beside him. He opened his mouth to speak in anger, but before he could say a word, the ship dove into a deep trough. The deck swept out from under Lydia and she skittered sideways, arms flailing. She felt an instant of horror, certain she would be swept over the side. Then the captain's arms reached out, catching her securely about the waist.

With a curse he drew her up before him, encircling her with his arms as he wrestled the ship's wheel into compliance. "You're a damned, willful chit!" he growled into her ear.

She turned to face him and smiled exultantly. "I wanted to see!"

"You'll see plenty," he warned, tugging her back against him.

They stood as one before the onslaught of the gale. Captain Frobisher didn't speak again as he maneuvered his ship through the furious sea. Lydia could feel the warmth from his body against her back. His cape had blown open, and she leaned into the dampness of his shirtfront.

After what felt like hours, there was at last some surcease; the wind dropped noticeably, the pelting rain eased and the waves no longer broke full over the deck.

"Here, take the wheel." He placed Lydia's chilled hands upon the wooden spindles. "I'm going forward to check the staysail. I don't want it coming loose when things start up again. What? Don't look so alarmed, you said you could sail. Just keep her steady. And for God's sake, don't bring her about."

Lydia clutched the large wheel, sensing the vibration of the moving ship through her fingers. She held the course the captain had set, south-southeast, and watched him as he checked the lines in the bow.

When he returned, he didn't take the wheel from her.

"How does she feel?" He had taken a pipe from the pocket of his oilskin and managed to light it in spite of the stiff breeze.

"She feels . . . nimble," Lydia said. "The *Rook*'s a very responsive ship, isn't she?"

"That's why sailors like their ships better than they like their women." He drew on his pipe until the bowl glowed red hot in the gray light. "No arguments, no fuss, and they always follow directions."

"Still, she needs a strong arm to make her do your bidding."

"Like all females." He grinned around his pipestem.

Lydia knit her brow. "Captain Frobisher, what did you mean just now, when you said 'when things start up again?' "

His mouth tightened. "You won't like hearing this, but as one sailor to another, I might as well tell you. This is merely the eye of the storm, the calm center. We're in for more heavy going before it's all over."

"Oh." She turned the wheel slightly, adjusting their course. "I was afraid that was what you meant. Is this the worst storm you've ever sailed through?"

He tipped his head back, gazing up at the anthracite sky. "Lord, no. This is a baby squall compared to some I've been out in. I got caught in a hurricane once, near the Scilly Isles, and was blown off course for days. I thought I'd end up in Boston." He leaned closer to her. "The sea takes you on some remarkable journeys, Miss Peartree."

"Yes, I'd noticed. Where are we going to end up?"

"Not back in Exeter any time soon. I hope you

weren't planning to take tea with anyone this afternoon."

"Is it still afternoon?"

"Not much past five, as I reckon."

The rain started up again. The captain scowled as Lydia felt the ship lurch beneath them.

"Damn! The wind's shifted," he muttered as he pulled off his oilskin. "I've got to go aloft."

His rain-drenched clothing had molded to his lean body, intriguing Lydia in spite of herself. He was all dark skin and long, sloping muscle. How had she ever thought him a common seaman? There was nothing at all common about Matthew Frobisher.

"Watch the wheel," he cautioned as it slipped a little through her hands.

"Sorry," she murmured, head down, hoping he couldn't see her blushing.

He climbed into the rigging and released every sail on the foremast, moving nimbly from spar to spar. There was a polished economy to his movements that made it a pleasure to watch him.

"I must have water on the brain," Lydia grumbled under her breath, unable to tear her eyes away from the lithe figure above her.

She was a betrothed woman, she reminded herself, engaged to a man of wealth and accomplishments. A man who was her equal in every way. A man who . . . had contracted the measles. *Drat Donald!* What horrid timing. And here she was, cast adrift in the middle of the Channel with the most puzzling man she'd ever met.

"What are you going to do?" she asked the captain when he returned.

"Are you a gambler, Miss Peartree?" He was shrugging himself back into his cape.

She nodded tentatively. "Sometimes."

"Good. It's a bit of a risk, but I think our best bet now is to run before the wind. I'm going to give the *Rook* a chance to spread her wings and fly us out of this blasted storm." He nudged her gently aside as he took the wheel.

"It's warm," he said, rubbing the wooden spindle where her hands had been. "I think the *Rook* likes having you at her helm."

"You don't believe that women on board ship are back luck?"

He grinned down at her. "Not if they pull their weight." He eyed her slight form. "Everyone works on my ship."

"Except for my seasick maid," she pointed out.

He gave a soft chuckle. "There's nothing for it; we'll have to put her over the side."

Lydia's eyes danced.

"Go below now," he said gently, as he gave her a little push. "See how my boys are doing and check on your maid. And mind, if you come topside again, see that one of the lads fits you out with a rope. I don't want to answer to Sir Robert if you end up in in the briny deep."

Lydia left him, forcing her way through the rising wind to the companionway. She went only because he'd given her a reprieve—she was to be allowed back on deck later. She felt like a midshipman who'd just passed his first sea trial.

Tilda was still asleep in a small, stuffy cabin that bore the faint, sour smell of vomit. Lydia hung the dripping oilskin over the back of a wooden chair, then went in search of the crew. In the cabin opposite Tilda's, six boys lounged back on their bedrolls, their legs stretched out before them. There was barely space for Lydia to stand.

"Sit here, Miss Peartree." It was Gilbert who spoke, plumping up his bed roll. She settled herself there and then looked at the pinched faces of the boys clustered around her.

"I hate it when he won't let us stay on deck," said a lanky, dark-haired boy, with a snub nose and slightly chipped front teeth.

"Aw, Rowdy, you know the Cap'n can sail the *Rook* wivout anybody's 'elp," Tenpence responded.

"I'm sure Captain Frobisher is only thinking of your well-being," Lydia said evenly. "It's rather nasty up there." In truth, the ship had begun to pitch violently.

"He let you stay up there," Rowdy said peevishly.

"Well, he needed me to hold the wheel while he checked the lines."

"Gor! 'E let you sail the *Rook*?" Tenpence breathed.

"Faith, no woman's ever done that before!" This must be Seamus, red-haired and freckled.

All the boys gazed at her with open awe.

There was a boy she hadn't yet placed, one with dark russet hair and smooth olive skin. His age was hard to guess, though she thought he might be eleven or twelve. He gave the impression, even in the crowded cabin, of holding himself away from the other boys.

"I don't think we have met." Lydia smiled at him. When he looked up at her sullenly, she realized he was the one the captain had scolded earlier.

"That's Jon-Lewee," Tenpence said. "He's French. His English is not very good."

"Bonjour. Comment allez-vous?" she asked.

His hazel eyes brightened and he began speaking rapidly in French, telling her he was sorry her trip had been spoiled and that the *capitaine* would surely bring her along on another, better cruise.

"The captain prefers that he speak English, miss," Fripp said.

"I'm sure he'll forgive it this once. I think under the circumstances we need to put each other at ease." She thought for a moment. "Does anyone have a pack of playing cards?"

After several were produced, she formed them into two groups, and soon they were immersed in their games of casino. Even Jean-Louis seemed to relax. At one point Oxer, who had been operating the bilge pump, came in, and Rowdy promptly got up to relieve him.

Once she knew they were properly distracted, Lydia left them, promising to return soon. She fetched her oilskin and then went to the main cabin, where she cut up some fruit and cheese. Manning a ship singlehanded in the face of a storm was draining work, and she was sure the captain needed some sustenance by now. She found several coiled ropes in the locker. After tying the end of one about her waist, she secured the other end to the hatch door.

As she stepped onto the deck, her breath was knocked from her by the ferocious wind. The sky was full dark again, the rain coming down sideways in a barrage of stinging water. The *Rook*'s canvas was completely bellied out, straining tight against its lines as the ship flew across the water, hitting the waves head on and yet barely losing any momentum.

She staggered forward toward the stern, thinking she must be insane to leave the shelter of a warm, dry cabin. Too frightened to go near the rails, she hugged the deckhouse wall. Captain Frobisher, his long cape lashing out around him, was a ghostly silhouette at the wheel.

Lydia pushed away from the deckhouse and staggered to the mainmast, gasping and sputtering. She felt like she was drowning there above the water.

"You're mad!" the captain cried to her over the wind's shrill keening.

"I have a rope!" She held up her sodden train.

"You'd do better with a brain!" he called back.

With renewed determination, she let go of the mast and tottered like a drunken doxy toward the wheel. As before, he caught her just as she slewed past him toward the stern.

"Is it working?" She choked into his neck. "Are we outrunning it?"

"I'm still here." He clutched her oilskin with one iron hand and turned her to face the wheel. "That's about all I can report."

The ship was creaking and moaning all around them. She swore she saw the planks of the deck open and close, like the mouth of a soul dying in agony. The *Rook* was a demented creature racing to her doom, flying past every obstacle until the pit of Hades opened at her feet.

"You sail as if you have little regard for your life, sir!"

He bent his head to her. "There are worse places to die than at sea." His breath was a warming puff against her wet ear.

"Actually I wasn't planning on dying anytime soon!" she cried over her shoulder. "If you would just keep that in mind."

He said nothing but leaned into her, resting his chest against her shoulders. God, he must be exhausted. She braced herself to take his weight.

"I've brought you something to eat." She fished in her cape pocket. "Here." She turned and popped several pieces of cheese into his mouth.

"Thank you," he murmured.

After a while Lydia thought she spied a break in the clouds in the distance, a parting in the deep black giving way to a paler gray. She pointed it out to him.

"Yes, I see it. Now, if we can just hold together that long."

No sooner had the words left his mouth than a huge, barreling wind swept down upon the brigantine. It tore at the sheets, canting the ship over until the waves leaped high onto the deck. Suddenly there was a violent crack.

They both heard the brittle, wrenching noise that was a sailor's worst nightmare. The captain threw himself over Lydia and tumbled them both onto the hard, wet deck as the top half of the foremast came crashing down, pulling lines, cables, and canvas with it. The massive tangle landed only inches from where they lay. As it was, they were both covered with a snarl of rigging.

With no hand at the helm, the *Rook* yawed over, heeling far to starboard, tossing in the turbulent water.

The ship's wheel spun crazily, slamming left and then right.

Gilbert Marriott, a rope about his waist, came climbing toward them through the wreckage.

"Captain!" he cried, tugging at the entangling lines. "Miss Peartree!"

"The wheel!" Frobisher shouted from beneath the rubble. "Dammit, hold the wheel!"

Gilbert did as he was ordered, throwing his whole body onto the wildly spinning circle, trying to regain control. The ship righted herself slightly.

With a great deal of cursing and struggling, the captain managed to get out from under the rain-soaked ropes.

"Stay right there!" he barked to Lydia.

She was trying to sit up, but short of a hacksaw she didn't know how she was to free herself from the rigging that held her legs down.

Together the captain and Gilbert stilled the wild thrashing of the *Rook*. They brought her about, heading her for the ever nearing break in the clouds.

Fifteen minutes later, the *Rook* was sailing on relatively tranquil seas. The rest of the crew, white-faced and wide-eyed, came on deck now that the ship had stopped pitching. They immediately started to cut away the straining lines that still connected the foremast to her sister mast, threatening to topple it, as well.

After the captain had relinquished the wheel to Gilbert, he knelt beside Lydia.

"Are you sure you're all right?" he asked in a husky voice. He'd drawn a long knife from his belt and begun to slice his way around her trapped legs.

"I-I'm not sure." Her teeth were chattering so badly she could hardly speak.

"Tenpence," he called briskly. "Fetch Miss Peartree a blanket." The little Cockney shot away belowdecks and reappeared with a heavy woolen throw. The captain stripped off Lydia's streaming oilskin and wrapped the blanket around her.

"Did we make it?" She spoke through clenched teeth.

He stroked her wet hair, almost absently. "We did, but the foremast didn't. Don't fret, we'll have something rigged up in no time. Do you think you can stand?" He placed his arm about her waist.

"I don't think so." Lydia watched as the toes of her slippers moved back and forth. "My legs are working, but my brain is not cooperating."

"No mind." He gathered her into his arms and stood up with her easily, as if she were a thistledown.

"Cap'n," Rowdy called out. "I think I can see land far off to the east."

"The Channel Islands?" Gilbert ventured. "Have we been blown that far off course?"

No one on deck noticed the disheveled female figure that had tottered out of the hatchway, looking about with puzzled, sleepy eyes at the carnage of wood and rope that lay everywhere.

"No, not the Channels." Captain Frobisher tightened his grip on Lydia, as he said with a dry chuckle, "Welcome to France, lads and ladies."

"France!" Tilda squeaked, just before she pitched forward bonelessly onto the littered deck.

Chapter Two

Finistère

*I*t was now late night. True night, not the Armageddon darkness of the storm. The *Rook* had dropped her sea anchor a few miles off the northern coast of Finistère, that remote and rocky French province. Finistère—the end of land. Matthew Frobisher, with three centurie's of seagoing blood in his veins, had always loved the sound of that name.

Things had almost returned to normal aboard his ship. He and his crew had worked late into the night clearing the wreckage from the deck and lashing down the length of broken mast amidships. If no suitable lumber was available ashore, they'd have to rig it up again, at least to get them back to Devon.

Fortunately, the captain knew this stretch of the French coastline fairly well; during his time as an intelligence officer, it had been a favorite disembarking point. It wouldn't be a bad place to careen the vessel and replace the mast. If he'd had a full crew of able-bodied men, that was, and not a crew of seven lads—and two frail females.

One of the females was currently sleeping in his berth, tucked under several woolen blankets. The captain watched her from over his desk, drawing occasionally on his pipe, the lantern above him casting a wavering light on the angular planes of his face. He was supposed to be studying his sea charts and maps. Instead, he was studying her.

"Lydia Peartree." He'd said it aloud, but she didn't stir. How the devil did a Russian princess's daughter arrive at a name like Peartree?

Women were something of a mystery to Matthew Frobisher. They held secrets that no man, no matter how clever, could pry from them. And since his business, from early adulthood on, had been wresting information from the people around him, he mistrusted women with good cause. The workings of a man's mind could be assessed in an instant. Greed, lust, hunger for power—these were the driving forces that men heeded. Anticipating their actions was remarkably easy for a man of discernment.

Ah, but women's minds traveled along such oblique corridors that no one was ever quite sure what propelled them. Sometimes, not even they themselves.

Because of that, he had remained wary of the fair sex during his illicit excursions into France. Not that he'd exactly avoided their company; in his younger days he had even been something of a rake, as well acquainted with the perfumed boudoir as with the dockside brothel. It seemed he followed the old adage—keep your friends close and your enemies closer. He'd gotten quite close to a fair number of women. He'd even loved a girl once, long ago. But it had ended with . . . Well, suffice to say that it had ended.

Of late, he'd kept himself well away from females. He was engaged in other business now as a teacher of young men, and the responsibility rode heavy on his shoulders. There was no time for courtly pleasantries or idle amusements. Not that any woman worth her salt would give him even a second glance, he mused, with his scarred, weathered face and nearly white hair.

His previous occupation had taken a toll on him, emotionally as well as physically. He knew his ability to trust others had totally eroded over the years. He had become a cynic—caustic and jaded. It had helped him to survive, to prevail against his enemies, but at some cost.

It was only the presence of his young charges that gave him any reason to keep on. Sir Robert's idea for a special school had become his lifeline. Before that, he'd been passing his time in Exeter's numerous grog-shops, losing himself in the bottom of a mug of ale. Not a pretty retirement.

Still, if Sir Robert had bailed him out in that in-stance, he'd certainly gotten him properly into the suds in this particular case. In addition to looking after his seven young crew members, he now had to safe-guard this society chit and her less-than-stalwart maid.

His thoughts roamed back to that morning on the dock. He hadn't meant to be lounging in his oldest, most ragged clothing when his guest came along. Even if he'd been annoyed at Sir Robert's request that he take this petted darling of the *ton* out for an afternoon of sailing, he'd still intended to do the *Rook* proud—dress up in his nautical blues with his long hair tamed back in a ribbon, wearing a courtly smile upon his scarred face.

But he had lost track of the time, worrying over a problem that had long plagued him as he sat and spliced an old rope. And when he looked up at the sound of female voices, he realized his guests were prompt in arriving, and he'd been caught out. So he did what he had always done—what seemed like a mere fakir's trick to some, but it had saved his life innumerable times—he blended into the scenery.

If Miss Peartree chose to see before her an old, scarred seaman, then that's exactly what he made sure she saw. It wasn't acting or pantomime. He couldn't explain it—he just became someone else for a moment or a month . . . or for however long it took for him to accomplish his goal.

His unkempt appearance had been good camou-flage. It had given him a chance to examine Miss

Peartree while he went on endlessly resplicing the rope.

At first, he'd thought her vapidly pretty; all those fashionable ringlets laboriously curled and coaxed to cluster around her heart-shaped face bespoke a certain vanity. It wasn't until later—when she was drenched from the storm, and those same ringlets still danced about her face—that he realized it wasn't artifice. It was nature's own bounty.

Even before he'd seen her up close, he'd been impressed with the easy way she carried herself, almost like a loose-limbed boy. The freshening sea breeze had molded her muslin gown to her body, and he'd noted her figure with admiration—lush in some places, the good places, and quite slender in others.

Still, it wasn't until she drew near to him that Sir Robert's accolades over the girl became understandable. She was breathtaking. There was absolutely no getting around it.

She had the most beautiful skin he'd ever seen. Magnolia petals were harsh in comparison. Fresh cream . . . peaches . . . all the other trivial metaphors faded away. Lydia Peartree's face was a firelit window on a cold winter's night, a pale beacon glowing with honeyed light. Byron may have written silly poems to her hair, but he'd clearly missed her best feature.

This is not a prudent line of thought, he reminded himself. She was betrothed, he knew, to one of Exeter's first citizens—an amiable young man of wealth and consequence. Currently suffering from the measles, poor sod. Well, Farthingale's loss is my gain, he reasoned with a grin.

Lydia Peartree murmured slightly and fretfully pushed at her blankets. He crossed to her side and drew them back up, tucking them beneath her chin.

"Little Princess," he said softly, looking down with wonder at this fey creature. Willful and spoiled, he had no doubt. But with the heart of a lioness and— he sighed as he thought it—the very soul of a sailor. Were he a younger man, unmarked by the evils of the life he had led, he'd give Farthingale a proper run for her favor.

"No," he muttered to himself. At this juncture in his life it wasn't even an option. He had enough responsibility right now. He had his boys to look after, and one in particular to keep safe. And being marooned on the coast of France was not going to make that task any easier.

The captain pulled a blanket from his sea chest and curled up on the one upholstered chair in his cabin. Tomorrow they'd limp into harbor, into a small, secluded cove he knew of, and begin the difficult job of refitting the damaged mast.

He drifted into a troubled sleep, where he was beset by old enemies and where the only hope of safety lay in the warm light that glowed in the window of a snowbound house.

Lydia awoke to the sun streaming in through the aft window, which had been opened to let in the cool morning breeze. The ship was under way; she could feel the slight plunging movement through the base of the wooden berth.

She felt as though she had been trampled by a herd of wild horses. Everything ached. She was afraid to look at her legs, fearing she would see nothing but a welter of bruises. When she gingerly lifted the covers to assess the damage, her eyes widened.

She was wearing a thigh-length nightshirt. Had Tilda undressed her last night? She didn't recall much of anything after the mast fell. Still, it must have been Tilda who prepared her for bed.

As she was examining the trail of colorful bruises that traversed her right leg, she heard someone approaching the cabin, the captain by the sound of his tread. Drawing the blanket quickly to her chin, she lay back and feigned sleep. Once he was inside the cabin, she opened one eye slightly and saw with surprise that the unkempt seaman of yesterday had disappeared. He now wore crisp ankle-length cotton trousers and flat-heeled leather boots, with a short jacket of blue duck over his white shirt. His long hair had been neatly plaited and bound with a black cord.

From his desk to the sideboard and back again he paced, restless as a caged tiger. He toyed with a complex-looking metal instrument, knocking it several times against the desk, and then shuffled noisily through his charts. He coughed and hummed and scraped the legs of his chair against the cabin floor.

She realized he was making noise on purpose, to wake her up. She made a suitably sleepy murmur, stretched her arms over her head and yawned. When she opened her eyes, it was to meet the captain's amused stare. He was leaning against his desk, arms crossed over his chest.

"I was wondering when you'd stop pretending to be asleep."

"I wasn't pretending," she protested. "I always wake up slowly."

He narrowed his eyes. "And how do you fare this morning, Miss Peartree, after your first storm at sea?"

She didn't want to tell him about all the bruises, in case he felt it his duty to examine them. "Just a bit achy," she lied.

"I expect you're rather bruised . . ."

"Oh, no. Nothing to speak of."

"Well, I wish I could say the same." He gave a dry laugh. "I seem to have come out all in blues and purples."

Lydia recalled how he had protected her body with his own when the mast fell. He must be incredibly resilient to have bounced back so rapidly. She imagined she wouldn't be able to move faster than a crawl for a week.

"You're looking fitter than you did last night," he remarked. "I hope my shirt was comfortable for you."

"Y-your shirt?"

"I couldn't very well put you to bed in your wet gown."

"Tilda didn't look after me?" She felt her throat closing up.

He frowned and shook his head. "The girl's a total ninny."

It took all Lydia's resolve not to pull the covers up over her face, she was that mortified. He had changed her out of the wet gown *himself*.

"Don't gape at me so, ma'am. And don't flatter yourself. At the time, you put me in mind of nothing so much as a drowned rat."

After Lydia got past her shock, she grew a little miffed. He was certainly cavalier for a man who had been privy to certain aspects of her anatomy that other, more refined gentlemen, regarded as divinely out of reach. He didn't seem to account himself privileged in the least, however.

"Thank you for looking after me," she murmured.

"I look after everyone on my ship," he said brusquely.

"Are we really in France or was that something I dreamed?"

"No, you didn't dream it." He rolled his charts together and slid them into a leather tube. "We've been in French waters since the storm passed. I expect we crossed the Channel in record time. We're coming into land soon. It's a beautiful stretch of coast . . . if you like them bleak and rocky."

"Now what will we do?"

"We'll careen the ship, refit the mast and be on our way back to Devon."

"Will the French be hostile, do you think? I mean, Bonaparte's only just been sent off to Elba."

"It's a while since I've been to this part of Brittany. They're not so very political in these remote areas. But we don't really have a choice, do we?" He rubbed the back of his neck.

"I see you've dressed for the occasion." She motioned to his smart blue jacket. "I guess the French warrant more ceremony than my maid and me."

"Yes, well, it never hurts to impress the natives. Don't want them thinking I'm a pirate." He grinned and then studied her for a moment.

"What is it?" She gazed at him wide-eyed.

"I was just wondering . . . are you going to spend the entire morning lazing in my bunk?"

"I can hardly get up with you here."

"This is my cabin. Or had you forgotten?" He raised his dark brows. "If it pleases your maidenly modesty I'll turn the other way." He turned from her and began to fiddle with some ledgers in his bookcase.

Lydia threw back the blankets and stepped from the bunk onto a very old, very beautiful Chinese carpet. She found her underthings and her muslin gown laid over the back of a chair, clean and air-dried. She quickly pulled off the captain's shirt and slipped into her own clothing.

"Ahem . . ." She made a little noise.

"Yes?" he said over his shoulder. "Is decency satisfied?"

"Almost. If you would just call Tilda to come fasten up the back of my gown."

He turned to her with a look of irritation. "Your maid refuses to set foot outside her cabin."

When he approached her, she retreated until the backs of her knees hit the bunk.

"Here, let me." He spun her about and began doing up her buttons. "It's not the first time I've had to play lady's maid. Pray God, it's the last. There, done." He pushed her gently from him.

"I don't suppose there's anything for breakfast?" The tray on the sideboard held only the bare remains of yesterday's repast. Hunger was only one of the things she was feeling at this moment after Matthew Frobisher had played his warm hands along her spine, but it was the safest to focus on.

"We'll get provisions once we're ashore. Thankfully I keep some gold in my sea chest."

"Just like a pirate," she remarked, following him to

the cabin doorway. "But will they take English gold here in France?"

He stopped to let her precede him. "Gold is the one thing that doesn't seem to be affected by national boundaries or wars," he pronounced. "But some of this happens to be French gold. You forget my past history, Miss Peartree."

"Oh, the spy. Yes, I had forgotten. You do wear so many hats—"

As she emerged from the hatchway, Lydia was struck quite beyond speech by the stark beauty that lay before her.

The *Rook* was sailing parallel to a high, sweeping granite cliff. Treeless and austere, it rose up from the gray-green water, seeming to go on forever in either direction, a massive palisade without one visible break in its rocky walls.

"Finistère," Captain Frobisher murmured from behind her. "Land's end."

"It almost looks like *world's end*," Lydia said as she moved to the port rail. The cliff loomed above the small ship, and she could see terns and gulls huddled on narrow outcroppings. A few stunted, wind-bent bushes clung tenaciously to the rock.

"How long before we find a place to anchor?"

"Cap'n's got a cove all picked out." Tenpence had joined her. "Just—there." His small finger scanned the cliff face and then stopped where a vein of ocher stained the rock. For the life of her Lydia couldn't see an opening in the solid mass.

"Where?" She turned to the captain.

"It's a secret," he said with a wink.

"Oh, and I suppose you're going to blindfold me so I won't recognize it the next time I'm back here."

"Now, there's an interesting notion." He leaned toward her in mock threat, and she scurried away to where Seamus, Fripp and Oxer stood looking out over the water.

"Good morning," she said brightly. "I must commend you on how well your ship looks."

She'd not meant the compliment idly. They'd made a remarkable recovery after the chaos of last night. The only difference she could see, aside from the splintered mast lying amidships, was the sober expression that now lingered in the boys' eyes. This hadn't turned out to be the jolly day cruise they'd expected.

"Have you recovered, Miss Peartree?" Fripp inquired. "I was . . . we all were worried about you."

"She looks pretty fair to me." Gilbert Marriott came sliding down from the ratlines and straddled the rail. He was grinning at Lydia, his golden hair shining in the morning sun, his open face relaxed. He alone seemed to have escaped the hollow expression that afflicted his crewmates.

"Bottom's coming up fast, Captain," he called out. "I think you'd better take the wheel."

Frobisher nodded and strode aft, the breeze whipping his queued hair behind him.

"He's something, isn't he?" Gilbert's eyes never left the captain. "He'll see us safe home, never fear."

"I expect the worst is over," she responded. "How difficult can it be to replace a mast?"

"It's not exactly like changing horses, miss," Fripp explained. "We've got to find the right wood for a new mast."

"And careen the ship," Gilbert added. "Then get the old mast off her."

"We'll be needing a team of horses," Seamus piped in. "And a place to stay until the job is done."

Gilbert nodded. "And some able-bodied men to help out."

Lydia groaned inwardly. That didn't sound like an overnight proposition. What would her family and friends back in England think, once it was discovered that the *Rook* hadn't returned to her berth? It only then occurred to her—what had no doubt occurred to all the boys—that they were well and truly castaway.

"Do you think we can get word back to England, to let them know we are safe?"

"Cap'n knows some French smugglers," Oxer said. "Mayhap one of them can carry a message."

"If you like, Miss Peartree," Fripp said, "I will ask the captain to arrange transport for you back to Devon. There's no reason you should be stranded here with the rest of us."

Gilbert shoved Fripp playfully. "She's not as pudding-hearted as all that!" He turned to the other boys. "Think of how she rode out the storm yesterday, right next to the captain. You wouldn't desert us now, would you, miss?"

Lydia wasn't sure how to answer. Donald would be out of quarantine in a few days. Furthermore, there was to be a ball to announce their betrothal in a week's time. All of south Devon society had been invited.

"No, Gilbert, I am not so pudding-hearted." She wasn't sure how the words had gotten out. "I will stay with you and do what I can to help."

They gave a cheer, and as she grinned back at them, she realized there was someone missing.

"Where is Jean-Louis?"

"Below," Fripp said. "He's not very stout-hearted. He wouldn't even be part of our school if he wasn't the captain's ward."

Lydia perked up at this new bit of information.

"He was raised in a monastery," Oxer said. "With monks," he added, as if that would clarify things. "Somewhere in Switzerland."

"But why so far away if he was Captain Frobisher's ward?"

None of them had an answer to that. Lydia's interest was now utterly piqued. So, the somber lad was the captain's ward. She could think of several ways a man who'd spent years going in and out of France might have gotten himself saddled with a French child. Several very interesting ways. Had the captain been married while he was away on his spying missions? Could he possibly still be?

If she was to be marooned on this beautiful, desolate coast, she could at least pass the time trying to solve the mystery. She'd show the captain he wasn't the only one who could engage in intrigue.

The ship was now beating toward land, and to Lydia's untrained eye, it seemed as though the *Rook* was headed directly for the rocky scree at the base of the cliff. She marched aft to accost the captain at the wheel, where he was once again mastering the delicate dance of wind and water.

"Remember what I said during the storm, about not planning to die any time soon?"

He squinted back at her. "Yes, of course I do. You looked like a rain-soaked banshee when you said it."

"I was just wondering if you were keeping that thought in mind right now."

"What? You mistrust my navigation? Come stand behind me, then, and you'll see that I'm not going to run us up onto those rocks."

She placed herself at his left shoulder.

"See . . . ?" He whistled the word through his teeth.

She didn't see, not at first. Then a slight rift appeared in the cliff face beyond the bow. The water ran in a channel of lighter green, marking an opening in the palisade.

Frobisher guided his crippled ship deftly, tanned fingers barely nudging the wheel as he followed the liquid path. The *Rook* entered the channel where the granite cliff rose up close on either side, sheer and insurmountable. It seemed to Lydia as though she could reach out and touch the rocky walls.

"Will we fit?" she asked in a timorous voice.

"We should. The *Rook*'s of a narrower beam than Hardy's lugger. She draws less water, as well."

The channel was edged with large, jutting rocks, but the *Rook* took her time, like a dainty lady stepping through a littered alley. They might have been in a tunnel of stone, since the sunlight was almost totally blocked out, the sky a mere patch far above them.

Lydia was not aware that her hands had moved to the captain's arm or that she was holding onto him tightly. He was quite aware but kept his mind on his sailing.

Then the darkness shifted back to daylight as the

ship slipped out of the passage and into a small, serene cove, where the sunlight flickered upon the water, flashing like a million fireflies.

Lydia released her breath and then, with sudden awareness of her proximity to the captain, drew her hands quickly back.

"That was quite remarkable, sir," she said, still a little breathless. "I'm sorry I doubted your ability."

He turned to her with a flash of white teeth. "You do take a considerable amount of convincing, ma'am." He was looking at her with a strange expression on his tanned face. Something played behind his eyes, something that could have been masculine regard.

"Would you like to take her in, Miss Peartree?"

Lydia nodded eagerly.

"Bring her to the center of the cove and then we'll drop anchor." Once she had the spindles firmly in hand, he left her to gather up his crew.

She watched with a puzzled frown, as they pulled the tarp off the small skiff that lay keel side up on the deckhouse roof. Of course—they'd need it to get to shore. There was no dock in the cove for berthing the *Rook*. . . . In fact, there was very little to be seen at all.

A shingle beach, studded with patches of rough sea grass, ran in a crescent around the inlet. On the left side of the cove lay a number of weather-scarred huts, which had the look of long disuse. Beyond the abandoned village, a narrow trail, overgrown with gorse, led up and out of the cove.

The captain and Gilbert had righted the skiff and were now dragging it toward a hoist that angled out over the water. Lydia couldn't help comparing them, one a gilded youth, tall and broad-shouldered and the other a mature man, taller still, but lean, windswept, and weathered. Nevertheless, it was he who drew her eye, not the handsome blond boy. It was curious— she'd rarely found older men even remotely interesting.

Once Lydia had guided the ship to the center of the

cove, the captain motioned for her to come about. She gleefully spun the wheel, felt the ship resist and then pirouette upon the water. As Oxer released the anchor, the *Rook* tugged tentatively against her restraint and then was still.

"Happy now?" the captain called out to her.

"Well, it's not exactly Exeter harbor."

"Women," he muttered to the boys. "You see, they're never satisfied." He looked across at her in grinning reproach. "I told you I'd have you back on land in time for tea. It can't be much past noon."

There had been humor in his voice, but when he came to stand beside her she saw the concern in his eyes.

"I don't see any tea shops," she pointed out. "I don't see much of anything."

"No," he said slowly, his pale eyes scanning the deserted, tumbledown houses. "I hadn't counted on this. Ten years ago Evionne was a thriving little fishing village."

"What do you suppose happened?"

"Napoleon happened. *La Grande Armée* happened. And without men to go to sea, fishing villages are soon abandoned."

"What will we do now? I don't mean to be troublesome but I haven't eaten in quite a long while." She chided him gently, "It's too bad you don't keep food in your sea chest, instead of gold."

"We're all sharp-set, ma'am. I'll send Rowdy ashore to set some snares—he was a poacher's son—and Seamus grew up on Galway Bay, so maybe he can dig up some clams."

"Perhaps I can make some soup with seaweed. I've read about shipwrecked sailors who lived on it for years."

The captain winced. "I think hunger is preferable to that."

Lydia watched as Gilbert rowed Seamus and Rowdy across to the shingle beach, wishing she could have gone with them. The nervous feeling in the pit of her stomach was more than just lack of food. She wanted to feel the solid earth beneath her feet again.

As a distraction, she went belowdecks and tried to talk Tilda into leaving her cabin.

"They be devils in France, miss. My whole life I heared it, an' I do believe it is true."

"This cove is deserted, Til. There's no one here, devil or otherwise. You'd feel a lot better if you came up top. The boys are very pleasant, and the captain is, well he's—"

"He's a strange one," Tilda finished for her. "Them ghost eyes and all that white hair. He's like a dead man come to life, he is."

"Captain Frobisher has actually been very kind."

But the girl was adamant. Lydia gave up on her and went to look for Jean-Louis.

The boy wasn't in either of the larger cabins. Beside Tilda's cabin there was another door, to the storage locker. She opened it a crack and heard muted sobbing.

Jean-Louis was huddled in a dark corner, his arms wrapped about his knees. Lydia went inside, leaving the door ajar.

"Mon petit pauvre," she whispered, crouching beside him. English, she thought, he's supposed to learn English. "Don't take on so," she continued. "We're safe now."

"I am not afrightened," he sniffed. "The sea does not scare me, *non.*"

"Then what is it?"

He looked up with tears glistening in his eyes. "They hate me, those boys. And the *capitaine* . . . he makes me foolish to them."

"He makes you look foolish?"

"Oui. I am the laughingstick of this boat."

"It's laughingstock," she said, trying not to grin. "And you're not, I promise. Let me try to explain something to you. The captain is your guardian, yes?

And he cares about you. Yet sometimes we are harder on the people we care about than we are on others. *Comprends-tu?*"

"Non," he muttered. "He cares for no one, him."

She had a sudden inspiration. "Well, I care about you, Jean-Louis. I'm going to make us something to eat, but you must help me learn my way around the galley."

The boy untangled himself and stood up. He gave one last, choking sniffle. "Yes, I will help."

The galley was barely more than a closet—open shelves lined the wall and a coal brazier sat upon a wooden cabinet. There were pots and pans, a skillet, and a few jars of spices. Jean-Louis nursed the coals and finally got a small fire going. In a wicker hamper Lydia found a lump of lard, a bunch of carrots and three potatoes. She had not been in a kitchen above four or five times in her life, but she wasn't going to let a little thing like inexperience stop her. She chopped up the carrots and potatoes, then sent Jean-Louis to the main cabin for the jug of water.

The boy returned with the jug, plus the captain's bottle of wine and the remains of the cheese. After bringing the water to a boil, she added the vegetables, some sea salt and pepper and a liberal dose of wine. Jean-Louis scouted the shelves and came up with a packet of biscuits.

Twenty minutes later, they made their way topside. "Dinner!" she called out.

The boys immediately gathered around her. They were all seated on the deck, furiously wielding their spoons, when the captain appeared.

"What was that you said?"

Lydia looked up at him. "Dinner?"

He hunkered down beside her and peered into the pot. "I'll be dashed. You never said you could cook."

"I can't. Jean-Louis helped me. It's not very good, I'm afraid, but it's something warm."

He ladled the soup into a tin cup. "No seaweed?" he asked with a grin.

"No," she assured him, "that's for dessert."

When he was done, he set his cup down and studied her. "It occurs to me you'd make an excellent addition to my crew."

"Indeed she would," Oxer concurred. "If she can do this with bits from the galley, just think what she could do with real food."

"It wasn't only me," she protested. "Jean-Louis found the biscuits and the cheese."

"And the wine," he added proudly.

The captain's brow lowered. "You put my wine into this soup?"

The boy's face fell. Lydia could have boxed the captain's ears for his ill-spoken words. "A little wine is very restorative. You should know that, Captain."

He relented a little. "Yes, I suppose it is."

"In the abbey," Jean-Louis said, "we drink wine every day. We grow the grapes to make the wine. It is like magic, how the sour grapes make the sweet wine."

"How *do* you make wine, Jean-Louis?" Lydia asked. "I've often wondered."

He launched into a halting narrative and to their credit, the other boys let him speak. When he got onto the topic of raising sheep, Oxer, a farmer's son, was soon drawn into the conversation. Before long, the four boys were chattering away and Lydia turned to the captain with a smug smile. Her diplomatic skills were not restricted to the drawing room.

The smile drained from her face when she saw the look of almost tortured longing in his eyes as he gazed at the chestnut-haired boy. It was as though he saw a phantom before him, something that compelled him and broke his heart at the same time.

She touched his hand gently. His eyes focused back on the present.

"More soup, Captain?"

"No . . . save the rest for the boys who went ashore." He got up abruptly. "I want to check my maps. I seem to recall another village nearby, inland from here. I pray that one isn't abandoned as well."

With those encouraging words he left them.

As he moved to the hatchway, Jean-Louis's eyes followed him, devotedly, and yet with great sadness. Lydia felt her heart twist. Such a yearning between them, she thought, and yet so much distance.

Chapter Three
The Cove

*I*t was late afternoon when the three boys returned to the ship. While Seamus and Rowdy scouted for food in the cove, Gilbert had done a bit of reconnoitering in the abandoned village.

"Someone's been staying here," he reported to the captain. The two were seated on either side of the desk, while Lydia watched from the bunk. She'd insisted on being privy to their discussion, and the captain had finally relented.

"Fires have been lit recently in several of the outdoor hearths," Gilbert continued. "A stream runs behind the village—there were bootprints there in the mud. And hoofprints, from ten or twelve horses."

The captain ran his knuckles along his chin. "Smugglers, maybe, or brigands. I expect there are a lot of displaced soldiers about, now that Napoleon's army has been disbanded. Men who have taken to robbery as a means to survive. Well, with any luck, we will be away from here before they return."

Lydia felt a frisson of alarm. What he'd said was true. Even in England, many former soldiers had turned to crime once the army no longer had any use for them. Newgate was full of men who had once served the Crown. It was one of Sir Robert's favorite causes—finding respectable employment for those discarded souls.

"I think we can move into the huts while we careen the ship," Gilbert continued. "A few have lost their roofs, but the rest seem stout enough."

"Why can't we remain on board the *Rook*?" Lydia asked.

The captain exchanged an amused glance with Gilbert.

"Do you know what it means—to careen a ship?" There was patient tolerance in his voice.

Lydia pursed her lips. "I believe it means to repair it, to get it fit to sail."

"And how do we do those things while we are on the water?"

Lydia shook her head and shrugged.

"We don't, Miss Peartree. She has to be run into the shallows and dragged onto the beach. Then we'll tip her over, nice and gentle, so we can get at the places that need fixing."

"Oh," she murmured. "I don't suppose we can do all that ourselves."

"I'll go into Lempère tomorrow, see if I can hire some men. It's a bustling little town as I recall, with a proper marketplace and several inns."

"Will I be able to send a message from there, do you think?"

"You won't be joining us, I'm afraid. Until I get a fix on the political climate hereabouts, I'd prefer you stay in the cove."

"That's not fair," she said peevishly. "I don't want to stay here while you go jaunting off to town."

"Miss Peartree . . ." His voice held an ominous note.

"I'll stay behind with you," Gilbert volunteered.

"I'll tell you what," the captain said to her. "You can be in charge of our housing. Get the huts fit for us."

"Oh, cleaning and sweeping," she grumbled. "That's a right jolly job."

"You'll clean the huts, and that's an order. I warned you that everyone in my crew does their bit." He stroked his chin. "Now, if you want to be coddled and treated like a mere passenger, that's another story."

"Of course I don't. You must know that."

"Then do as I say." He spoke sharply and then added in a more even tone, "We have to keep things as normal as possible. Most of these boys are not long away from childhood. They are more frightened than they show. You and I have to set an example. Do you understand?"

She nodded and gave him a conciliatory smile. "Aye, Captain. Clean huts it will be."

"Good girl," he said. "And if you do a proper job, I'll bring you something nice from Lempère."

"Food would be very nice."

"Oh, that reminds me . . ." said Gilbert. "You'll be pleased to hear that Rowdy snared two hares and Seamus caught a sand shark from the beach."

"Ugh!" Lydia made a choking noise.

"You don't eat rabbit?" the captain inquired urbanely.

"Shark," she said with a grimace. "I never eat shark."

"Good. That means there will be more for us. But I'm afraid you will have to gut it and clean it. And the rabbits, as well." His eyes were fairly dancing now.

"I couldn't possibly—"

"He's only teasing you," Gilbert intervened gently. "The lads have already cleaned their catch. You do color up something wonderful when you're vexed."

Lydia crossed her arms. She felt a bit foolish for allowing herself to be baited. "I'll cook. But only if Jean-Louis helps me."

"Done," said the captain. "Now get topside and earn your keep."

"My keep?" She rose from the bunk, ready for a new battle.

"Just go," he laughed, waving her off. "We'll starve to death before you are through with me."

After she left, Gilbert noticed that the captain was still gazing at the doorway—like a hungry cat who'd just seen a plump mouse scamper away.

"She's going to be trouble," the captain said, almost to himself.

"You could send her back to England," Gilbert suggested.

"I could."

'There's really no point in keeping her here."

"No, probably not."

"She's recently betrothed, you know. My family was agog with the news in their last letter. My younger brothers adore her . . . You can see how she gets on with the boys. It's just that, well, perhaps she'd be safer back in Devon. So many things could happen to her here."

The captain raised one brow. "Are you taking me to task, boy?"

Gilbert blushed to the roots of his hair. "Sir? No, sir. I wouldn't presume to—"

"Then don't," he muttered.

Gilbert got to his feet and after a rapid bow made a hasty retreat.

The captain poured himself some wine and went to lie on his bunk. He stretched his long legs out before him and sipped slowly from the glass.

God, was it that obvious?

He'd always thought young Marriott an astute lad, but it had never occurred to him that he himself would fall under the scrutiny of those bright blue eyes. So Gil had the wind up did he? And Miss Peartree had herself a champion. *Well, well.*

Matthew considered himself properly warned off.

It had been a pleasant distraction, letting the chit play at being one of the crew. It gave the boys a sense of comfort, as he'd pointed out to Lydia. But playtime was over. He would no longer bait her, just to see the color rise on her velvety cheeks. He wouldn't offer her the wheel of his ship to sail into the wind. He wouldn't offer her anything.

He mused a little, thinking of how she had taken Jean-Louis under her wing. The boy had no heart, no spirit. . . . He was a sore disappointment. Yet Lydia drew him to her and was not put off by his feckless ways. It was most curious.

A woman's touch . . . maybe it was what the child needed. He'd spent most of his life surrounded by monks, and now he was always in the company of other boys. A woman's gentle touch. The captain grinned as he downed the last of his wine. Maybe it was what they all needed.

Lydia did the best she could with the food in the galley. She put the rabbits in a pot to braise and, on Jean-Louis's recommendation she fried the shark meat in the skillet. In spite of her initial repulsion, the fish smelled rather enticing as it sizzled in the pan.

She passed the time with Jean-Louis while she cooked, asking him about the abbey and Switzerland and about his life in Devon after he had come to live with Matthew Frobisher.

"The *capitaine*, he bring me to England in the winter. I do not want to come. I am happy with the good brothers. But I am too old to stay with them, they say. Unless I become *le moine*."

"A monk?"

"*Oui.*" He looked solemn. "The *capitaine* he is angry with them. I am to be a man, he says, not a shriveling monk."

"Sniveling,"

"*Oui.* Then he take me away. There are other boys in his house, those boys." He made a Gallic motion of disparagement toward the deck. "I miss *Frère* Pascal and the *Abbé*. They were most good to me."

"Had you met Captain Frobisher before . . . I mean before he came to take you away?"

He lowered his head. "I am not speak of it . . . not to those boys."

Lydia's eyes narrowed. "Surely you can tell me. Are we not friends?"

He nodded. "The *capitaine,* he come to see me each year. He ask me questions—how well I study, what I learn in the school. He never tells me why I am there in the abbey and not in my home in France."

"Do you remember your home?"

"Ah, *oui*, it was a most good home, in Provence. *Ma mère* was so kind. And pretty. But she died, *hélas*, while my father was away in Paris. The *capitaine*, he come one night and take me away. He was a stranger to me, so I do not want to go . . . but he makes me."

Lydia was taking the rabbits from the brazier, but at his last statement she nearly dropped the pot. "Oh!"

"Mam'selle," he cried. "You have burn yourself." He quickly rubbed a bit of lard on her fingertip.

"Thank you. I'm all right now."

Lydia's thoughts churned in her head as she stood nursing her reddened finger. Had the captain truly abducted this child from his home and then abandoned him in an abbey far from everything familiar to him? It was unthinkable, almost inhuman.

"What is your name, Jean-Louis, your family name?"

The boy shrugged. "I do not know. I was little when *ma mère* died. I remember she was named Marianne, and she calls Papa *le comte*. Beyond that, nothing."

Well, this was certainly a puzzle. She decided to mull it over a bit before she confronted the captain in the matter of his unhappy ward.

It was nearly dark by the time they finished cooking. The boys were lounging on the foredeck when she and Jean-Louis came topside with a tray of food.

Oxer appeared beside her as she served out the meal. "Cap'n said he'll eat in his cabin. I'm to take it down."

Lydia tried to hide her disappointment. Was he angry because she'd been pettish earlier? She had worked so hard at preparing this meal, and she wanted him to acknowledge her effort. She knew she could take his plate down herself but then thought better of it. She would not pander to him.

After dinner, the boys formed themselves into a loose circle, their soft voices the only noise in the still cove. Lydia, who was quite full to bursting with rabbit—and, yes, delicious, succulent shark—sat contentedly in the shadows, leaning against the deckhouse and gazing up at the night sky.

A trailing wisp of cloud laced over the waning sliver of moon, and the raised cliffs appeared, in the darkness, to be two giant arms encircling the little cove. The *Rook* rocked gently at her anchor, pulled by the outgoing tide. Laughter erupted from the group in the lantern light when Rowdy and Tenpence began to scuffle playfully.

There was a whisper of sound beside her as the captain edged himself up onto the roof of the deckhouse. He'd come noiselessly onto the deck. No wonder he had made such a good spy, she thought, if he could move so silently through the darkness.

The bowl of his pipe glowed and the scent of tobacco wafted out to mingle with the sea air. He sat there above her and said nothing. Lydia shifted slightly so that her head was almost against his knee. She said nothing either but somehow felt in communion with him.

When he spoke at last his voice was no more than a rough whisper. "I've reached a decision. I'm sending you back to Devon. As soon as it can be arranged."

She closed her eyes, trying to compose her thoughts. It was a logical solution. She had no reason to stay and many reasons to leave. Why, then, did the thought of leaving trouble her so?

"If you think it best," she said softly. Lateral resistance, she decided, was what was called for here. "It's a pity, though."

"Why is that?" He was leaning a bit forward; she could see his hawklike profile in the lantern light.

"Because I'd like to share this experience with you and your boys. All too soon, I fear, I'll be imprisoned."

"Imprisoned, Miss Peartree?"

"This is such a free life you lead. You must see that I'm drawn to it. And when I'm married—"

"Oh, that." He sounded dismissive.

"When I'm married, I know there will be very little freedom for me. This would be my one final adventure, staying here with the boys, with you . . ."

"And what if your betrothed finds it an unacceptable situation?"

"I suppose I would just have to take that chance."

"Yes, I daresay you would."

Lydia was smiling to herself in the darkness. Captain Frobisher was definitely coming around. "And you forget, sir, Tilda is here to lend propriety.

"Bah!" he growled. "Less than useless. You could be at the mercy of a ravening horde and she'd not budge out of her cabin." He slid off the low roof and settled beside her.

"What game are you playing at, Miss Peartree?"

"Game? I am bargaining for a stay of execution."

He gave a dry laugh. "It means that much to you?"

"It does." She leaned to him, pressing her hand on his arm. "Please don't send me away. You said yourself that the sea takes us on some remarkable journeys. Can't we just wait and discover where this journey takes us?"

He shifted away from her. "Beware, miss. You might not like where this journey takes you."

"I'll be with you, won't I? That's all I ask, for now."

His reaction to her words was startling. He surged to his feet, hoisting her up with one hand. Without a word to the boys, he propelled her into the hatchway, down the companionway and into his cabin. He shut the door firmly behind him.

"Now," he said, anger boiling just under the surface of his face. "You will tell me what the devil you are about."

She looked back at him wide-eyed. "I-I was only trying to make you see reason."

"With coquetry?" He laughed harshly. "Don't throw out your lures here, Lydia; they won't wash.

I'm not a drawing room dandy to be toyed with or some amusing fribble to be held on your leash. I'm not Donald Farthingale . . . thank God. He's to be saddled with you, and I say good luck to the fellow. He'll surely need it."

"Oh, that's an odious thing to say. Just because I enjoy your company and—"

"My company?" He loomed over her. "And that excuses your behavior up there? Touching my arm, leaning against my leg."

"I never did!" she protested.

"You most certainly did. You may play these games with the men in your circle, entice them with your body and your face until they are quite besotted. But it won't work with me. I am happily immune to your charms." He crossed his arms and turned away from her. "You may go now," he uttered over his shoulder. "I've said my piece."

Lydia fisted her hands. She wasn't going to run from him.

"Well?" He was looking at her now, scorn twisting one cheek.

"I have nowhere to go," she said. "Remember, I slept in here last night."

"And you expect me to give up my bed for you a second time?" One dark brow arched slowly.

"I see I can expect no charity from you, Captain."

He came in close. "This isn't about blasted charity."

"You dislike me. I think that's plain. I repeat, I want nothing from you."

"Oh, you want something from me, all right. And you don't even know yourself what it is. But I know. Yes, I know very well what you want from me, Miss Peartree."

"Tell me then, that which I don't even know myself." She raised her chin.

"This—" He snaked an arm about her waist and dragged her up against him. "And this—" He lowered his mouth and kissed her hard.

Frobisher wanted to shock her and frighten her,

make her flee from him, back to Devon, back to Donald. He wanted to prove to her that there were some men you couldn't toy with and come away unscathed. *He wanted . . . , he wanted . . .* He wanted her so badly that his whole body was racked with the pain of it. He wanted to taste her and touch her, to trace his mouth over every inch of her beautiful skin. He wanted to take her, claim her and cleave to her forever.

When he pulled back, after what seemed like an endless kiss, Lydia was clinging to him, her head pressed to his chest.

"I warned you," he breathed raggedly into her hair. "I warned you about this journey."

She threw her head back, a look of transcendent joy on her face. Her wide cheeks were flushed with carmine; her mouth was half open and rose red.

"Matthew," she sighed. "Oh, Matthew."

He shook her gently. "Little fool. You are supposed to be fleeing from me in horror."

She tightened her arms around his lean waist. "Make me flee then, if you can."

"I should beat you. Someone should have."

"Kiss me again, Matthew—"

"No." He was trying to untangle himself from her hands. "I'll not abet you. You are as good as wed."

"Donald never kissed me like that," she declared with a tiny pout. "Donald never kissed me at all."

"Well, that's what you get for hanging about with respectable folks. Lydia, I . . . I was just trying to teach you a lesson. Not to tease, not to use your charm to cozen men. I didn't mean . . . I don't . . ."

"What?"

"I don't want you." The words came out in clipped syllables, like a judge pronouncing a verdict.

Her arms dropped as stepped back from him. "No?" Her eyes sought his. "Truly?"

He shook his head slowly. "Not a bit. As I said, I was only trying to punish you a little." He shifted away from her and went to the sideboard, where he began to refill his pipe from the humidor. "I'm sorry if I distressed you," he murmured. "I warned you I was unused to the company of females."

"I'm not surprised they give you a wide berth." The disdain in her voice was blatant and cutting. "Since you obviously mislike women and have no idea how to behave around them."

"Don't I?" he said with a catch in his voice.

"It's clear to me you wouldn't know what to do with a woman, even if one were so unwise as to put herself in your path."

"You've already done so, my girl," he said as he abandoned his pipe and came toward her. "But you won't do it again on this voyage. I'll see to that."

"How?" she baited him. "With more kisses? You think I haven't been kissed before? And by better men than you? Real men! Not scarred old schoolmasters."

The expression that flashed across his face struck fear into her heart. She turned to flee, but he caught her halfway to the door. Fingers digging into her shoulders, he wrenched her around, catching both her arms behind her with one hand. With the other he grasped her tender throat and pressed inward.

"Do you have any idea whom you are dealing with? I could kill you this instant, if I chose. Do you know that?" His eyes were like nothing she had ever seen, unearthly, ghostly, smoldering with white heat. His taut cheekbones were sharp as two knife blades.

"This is just a reminder to you. Of who I was . . . and who I am. When you think to coquet with me or tease me with your body, remember this hand on your throat." He increased the pressure slightly just before he released her.

She stood, reeling a little, her eyes blazing back at him. To her surprise, his gaze fell. With a muttered curse, he went back to his pipe.

Lydia composed herself. "I'm sorry, Captain," she said in a low voice. "You are quite right. I *was* trying to cozen you. I've always believed that if you stray beyond what is permissible, at least you can take your knocks uncomplaining when things don't work out. And so I have no grievance against you."

This was an attitude that intrigued the captain, this woman with a man's sense of honor.

"I'd forgotten whom I was dealing with," she continued. "The men of my set are a bit more forgiving of my, ah, nature." She pushed her hair back from her eyes. "I had a falcon once who used to strike at me when I teased him with food. You are not unlike him. I will respect your wishes, Captain, and return to Devon. And I promise not to trouble you again—in any way."

She turned and made a dignified exit before he could gather his thoughts to reply.

"Move over, Tilda," Lydia complained, trying to shift the sleeping maid in her bunk. "Make some room."

"Miss!" Tilda sat up in the darkness, clutching Lydia's arms. "Are we being attacked?"

"No, silly. Go back to sleep. It's not the demon French. I've just discovered that the only devil we have to deal with is right here on this ship."

Chapter Four

Evionne

*T*he next morning when Lydia awoke, she and Tilda were both tangled in the blanket, and one of Lydia's bare legs was hanging completely off the narrow bunk. She tugged herself from the twisted covers, pulled her dress over her chemise and then tried to wake Tilda.

"Come on, Til. You've got to get up." She shook her forcefully. The maid roused enough to do up Lydia's buttons, then burrowed under the covers again.

Lydia was muttering to herself as she made her way onto the deck. The ship appeared deserted. The lines shifted and the rigging creaked in the sultry breeze. She couldn't see anyone on the beach or near the huts. Had they all gone off and left her?

She went to the opening in the ship's side and peered over. The skiff floated there, tethered to a cleat on the railing.

"Oh, there you are!"

The sudden sound of Gilbert's voice almost sent Lydia tumbling to the water below.

"Goodness!" she gasped, clutching the rail. "You startled me."

His keen blue eyes crinkled. "Sorry, miss. I was below collecting supplies with Jean-Louis."

"Where is everyone?"

"I rowed them to the beach first thing this morning. The captain's taking them into Lempère. I told him I'd stay here with you. Would you mind if we rowed over to the huts and started getting things sorted out?"

She wrinkled her nose. "Ah, yes, I remember. Cleaning and sweeping."

They found Jean-Louis in the storage locker gathering brooms, rags and pails. Lydia plucked up a torn cotton sheet to use as an apron and followed them onto the deck.

Once Gilbert had rowed them to the beach, Lydia walked along the row of crude, wind-weathered huts, shaking her head dolefully. Her father's horses had better quarters than this.

They found three huts which appeared to be habitable at the landward end of the village. The center one contained two rooms, and the boys designated it as the captain's. While Gilbert sliced up canvas for door flaps, she and Jean-Louis cleaned out the huts and poured buckets of water over the open hearth behind the captain's hut. Jean-Louis made a crude desk for his guardian using two battered barrels and a wide plank. As a finishing touch, Lydia put a spray of purple-gray wildflowers into an apothecary bottle and set it on the plank. Although Matthew Frobisher was definitely not in her good graces, it was hard to suppress her schooling as a lady of refinement.

It took several hours of exhausting labor, but by the middle of the afternoon they were able to survey their handiwork with considerable pride. There was little to do now except sit in the shade, nursing their hunger. Soon all three had fallen asleep—Gilbert stretched out on the dry sea grass, Lydia leaning against the captain's hut with Jean-Louis's chestnut head upon her shoulder.

The sound of hoofbeats ringing on hardpacked ground awoke Lydia. There was no one visible on the path yet, but since she wasn't taking any chances, she

instantly roused the boys. They were racing toward
the skiff, when Gilbert called, "Wait! It's the captain!"

Captain Frobisher and his crew were now pelting
down the slope, riding bareback on four heavy-boned
bay horses. With his long hair flying out behind him
and his lean, saturnine face, the captain looked more
freebooter than schoolmaster. Rowdy and Fripp followed a short distance back, and Oxer, with Tenpence
mounted behind him, brought up the rear.

They rode into the village, pulling up at the edge
of the water where Lydia and the boys stood.

"What do you think?" Frobisher called down to her.
"I leased them from a local farmer for more gold than
he'll earn in the next five years. They're hardy beasts,
if a little headstrong."

His horse reared up, its feathered hooves boxing
the air, but the captain laughed and stayed easily on
the beast's back. Lydia gazed up at him, an expression
of wonderment shining in her eyes.

"But where is Shamuse?" Jean-Louis called out.

"Seamus?" The captain appeared puzzled and
turned to Rowdy. "Did we leave someone behind in
Lempère?"

A raucous braying sounded from the top of the
path, and then a small gray donkey, hitched to a dogcart, appeared at the crest. Seamus had the reins in
one hand and a long stick in the other. He repeatedly
tapped the donkey's rump to keep him moving.

The captain was now staring down at Lydia.

"Yes?" she asked at last, when his scrutiny began
to make her uncomfortable. She feared what he might
read in her eyes.

"Soot," he said with relish. "You've got soot all
over your face."

"Oh!" she cried, swiping her hands over her chin
and cheeks.

"Ach, you're making it worse." He swung one leg
over the horse's withers and slid lightly to the ground.
"Here . . ." He scooped a handful of water up from
the cove, wetting the edge of her apron. He lifted the

dampened fabric and proceeded to gently wipe the smudges from her face. She could hardly credit that this was the same man who had threatened to throttle her last night.

She turned accusingly to Jean-Louis and Gilbert. "You might have told me!"

"It look *charmante*."

"Like Cinderella," Gilbert teased.

"Yes, well, I'm not likely to be going to any balls, am I?" She plucked at her grimy apron, and they grinned back at her.

After the captain had instructed Fripp and Oxer to rig an enclosure for the horses, Jean-Louis insisted he inspect the huts. Frobisher looked at Gilbert and started to say something, but then bit back his words.

"This is your cabin, *mon capitaine*," Jean-Louis proclaimed at the center hut.

When the captain saw the makeshift desk with the little vase of flowers upon it, he nodded. "You've done very well. Very well, indeed."

"I make the desk—"

"It's just what I require." He casually ruffled the boy's hair, and a beaming smile spread over Jean-Louis's face.

Seamus had finally gotten his stubborn beast down the path and was driving him toward the huts. The donkey took one startled look at the lapping waves and tried to sit down in his traces.

"He's the son of Satan, he is!" the Irish boy pronounced loudly.

"Donkeys, they are not horses," Jean-Louis said as he approached the cart. "You must make of them the friend." He held the animal's head and gently scratched him under his whiskery chin. The donkey's eyes closed blissfully. Jean-Louis had no trouble leading him the rest of the way.

"See, Seamus?" said the captain, trying to restrain a grin. "You can never *make* a donkey do anything. You've got to ask politely."

Seamus muttered a few very impolite words as he

climbed from his seat and began to unpack the cart. Lydia noted with relief that it was brimming with supplies—horse harnesses, wooden crates, and several packages wrapped in paper. She fervently hoped that there was food somewhere in the jumble.

The captain nudged Seamus aside and rummaged around until he produced a hefty sack.

"Miss Peartree, if you would do the honors?" When he handed her the sack, she nearly staggered under its weight. She dragged it to the shade and quickly undid the drawstring, revealing fruit and cheese, long loaves of bread and sticky buns wrapped in parchment.

The captain called out, "I also bought flour, eggs, bacon and sugar. And some fresh vegetables."

"Don't you want anything to eat?" Gilbert asked as he bit into a ripe plum.

"We, ah, ate while we were in Lempère." He looked a bit guilty. "The boys were pretty much done in after our long walk."

By twilight, they'd finished most of their chores. The horses were corralled beside the stream, the supplies had been stored in the back room of the captain's hut, and Jean-Louis had managed to get a fire going. Lanterns were lit in the three houses, the door flaps tied open to let in the evening breeze.

Lydia had sent some food for Tilda on one of Gilbert's trips back to the *Rook*. They would probably have to pry her bodily from the cabin before they could careen the ship. But she had more pressing problems than her maid's foolish hysteria.

The captain had called a crew meeting before dinner and had expressly excluded Lydia. She wandered now in the dusky light along the shingle toward the mouth of the cove. The little donkey had escaped from the corral and was grazing along the sparse grass of the shoreline. She reached into her pocket for a bun she had hidden there and held it out to him, calling softly, "Here, fellow . . . nice fellow."

He looked at her, sniffing the air with his upper lip

rolled back, and came trotting over on his hard little hooves. Apparently he understood the King's English.

She scratched his ears as she fed him the treat. His coat was matted and coarse, full of odd swirls and cowlicks. He licked the stickiness from her fingers, then leaned against her with a sigh. It was somehow comforting. And she definitely needed comforting just then.

She didn't know how it had happened. She certainly hadn't planned it. But from the moment the dark storm cloud had billowed up in the sky over Lyme Bay, it was as though her life's course had been altered, irrevocably altered.

There were no longer any thoughts of Donald Farthingale in her head. His image had vanished as if he'd never existed. Family and friends had likewise faded. There was now only the sea and the ship, the seven boys and the man who led them. *The man.*

There was no point in denying it any longer—she was falling in love with Matthew Frobisher. Intensely, frighteningly, in love. Against her common sense, against her better judgment, against every precept of the society in which she had been raised.

Lydia was not a green girl—she had passed her twenty-seventh birthday—and she had never before allowed her feelings to run away with her. Romantic attraction was something for schoolroom misses full of silly expectations.

In spite of her many suitors she had never considered marriage—her life suited her too well to encumber it with the restrictions of matrimony. Her recent betrothal to Donald Farthingale had come about only because she'd begun to feel the first whispering encroachments of age. Donald was amiable enough, even charming. It had been a prudent, well thought out decision, rather like choosing which entrée to serve at a dinner party. Lydia had reckoned herself quite immune to the tender emotions and so had not factored them into her choice of a future spouse—not because she was hard-natured, but because in all her encounters with men, none had ever affected her heart.

Until now.

Aboard the *Rook* she had felt something growing within her—blossoming in spite of her attempts to restrain it. She had turned uneasy and edgy, restless with the change that had come over her. She'd had no real idea what ailed her until that very afternoon, when Matthew Frobisher came galloping down the path with his long hair flying out behind him. He'd reared back on his horse with laughter in his eyes, and her heart had leapt up to greet him.

It was the culmination of everything she'd begun to feel for him—admiration, trust and a fledgling, but powerful, physical attraction. When he kissed her in his cabin, she had been stirred but hadn't counted it anything too serious. She had been giddy from kisses before.

Then they had spat harsh words at each other, and he had put his iron hand on her throat, letting her feel the strength and power he held in check. She had been stirred again, by his lean menace and his rapier eyes. But she hadn't leant much weight to that encounter either. They had merely been taking each other's measure.

It was only after a day spent without him, hungry and worn out with hard work, that she realized what Matthew Frobisher had come to mean to her. He was the anchor, the lifeline and the safe harbor.

Oh, it was fine to argue that these rash emotions had arisen only because of her predicament—that it was logical to seek the security of the captain's capable presence on this foreign shore. But her feelings for him were anything but logical. Though he made her feel eminently safe, he also aroused in her such a hunger, such a deep-seated yearning, that she could not steer her thoughts from him for more than a minute at a time. His every expression compelled her, his lithe grace fascinated her and his stern character, gruff and plainspoken to a fault, charmed her utterly.

What in blazes was she to do? The only solution she could think of was to put him firmly from her thoughts. She'd go back to Devon, back to Donald's chaste embraces, never to think of Matthew Frobisher again. She could do it; she had the fortitude of an oak.

The donkey nibbled on her fingers.

"What shall I do about him?" she asked him earnestly. "You look like a clever beast. What would you do in my situation?" He raised his fuzzy head and whickered against her neck. "Really? I'm not sure that wouldn't add fuel to the fire." The donkey eyed her quizzically and then turned his head as someone approached them.

So the meeting was over. Lydia had been so preoccupied she hadn't noticed the boys moving about the village again. When the tall, spare silhouette came out of the shadows, her heart swelled, and her pulse began a ringing tattoo.

So much for fortitude.

"I've been sent to fetch you for supper. Jean-Louis is making us a remarkable concoction."

Lydia, who'd been courted by English dukes and foreign princes, was suddenly shy in the presence of this sea captain. He, too, seemed a little reserved.

"I'm sorry I wasn't there to cook," she said. "I've been making a new friend." She tickled the donkey's forehead.

"It's of no matter. Our crew meeting only just ended."

"Ah, yes, the boys-only meeting."

"Don't get your hackles up," he said with a flash of white teeth. "I promise to tell you all about it after supper." He rubbed at his chin and then said haltingly, "I also need to say something to you . . . without the lads all around. It's about last night . . . I'm sorry I frightened you. I am not usually so easily roused to anger. You spoke no more than the truth—I *am* a scarred old schoolmaster." He laughed ruefully. "I suppose my own vanity had convinced me otherwise."

Her insides twisted, recalling how she'd let her temper get the better of her in his cabin, the cruel words she'd spat. She couldn't bear it that she had wounded him.

She took a step closer. "No, Captain, I also spoke in anger. And it was *my* vanity that suffered a blow, and rightly so. I'm far too used to getting my own way. I believe it's a good and proper thing that you share your knowledge with these boys. It was wrong of me to belittle you. To mock you. As for your scar . . . scars are considered quite dashing in London, providing they were honorably earned."

"I believe it was." His voice was a soft rasp in the darkness.

"Then I can find no fault with it."

"And my age?"

"Oh, pooh," she sniffed. "That's of no consequence. Spend some time with the Prince Regent's stuffy set and you'll fancy yourself a positive stripling."

He tilted his head. "Then I must thank you, Miss Peartree, for restoring my illusions." He held out one hand. "Will you come along now?"

Lydia took it and then, with great daring, pulled him toward her. She set her hands on his shoulders and laid her lips against his ear.

"They are *not* illusions!" she whispered fiercely— and sighed a whickery breath into his throat.

She dashed away then, down the beach to the huts, not sure if the sound that trailed after her was a man's puzzled laughter or the satisfied nickering of a little gray donkey.

Jean-Louis's concoction turned out to be an excellent omelette, garnished with peppers and onions. Everyone dined outside, sitting on pieces of driftwood or on the flat rocks that edged the water. The boys were less playful than they had been the previous evening. Lydia knew they'd all of them had an exhausting day. It never occurred to her that the lowering of their spirits might have had something to do with the crew meeting.

She feared that after her impetuous action on the

beach, the captain might not honor his offer to speak with her, but as she was dabbing up the remains of her omelette, his shadow spilled over her plate.

"I believe it's time for the lady and captain's crew meeting."

She smiled. He hadn't thought her a silly chit after all. She set her plate aside and followed him dutifully into his hut. He drew the canvas flap closed, then offered her the solitary chair.

"The first thing I want to address," he began in an ominously formal voice, "is the cleaning and sweeping issue."

"Yes?" She gazed at him intently. She knew they'd done a proper job of it.

"Miss Peartree," he admonished softly, "you weren't meant to do all this today. With nothing to eat since last night. I can't imagine what Gilbert was thinking. I expect my crew to work, but not on empty bellies."

"At least the work distracted us from our hunger," she pointed out.

"And there's another matter . . ." He disappeared into the back room and came out bearing several wrapped parcels.

"Presents," he announced with a grin. "After all, I did promise you something nice from Lempère."

Her eyes widened. "You didn't need to bring me anything."

"Ah, but I disagree." He took a fold of her makeshift apron between his fingers. "This is not a becoming garment, though you lend it as much charm as is possible." His eyes gleamed as he handed her one of the packages. "Open it."

Lydia tore at the stiff paper. "Oh!" she breathed as she drew a muslin blouse and cotton skirt from the wrapping.

"They won't suit you for Almack's, but I think they're quite dashing for Evionne Cove."

She held the white blouse up to her shoulders. It was

worked along both yoke and sleeves with flowers of colored thread. "I've rarely seen anything so lovely."

"Yes," he murmured, enraptured by the glowing blush on her cheeks. "Amazingly lovely. Though it's only peasant stuff. The Breton farm ladies save them for their Sunday outings. They look like a field of wildflowers all parading to church."

Lydia had risen, holding the dark blue skirt to her waist. She swirled around the little room, laughing.

"You're sure you like them?"

"Of course I do. If Marie Antoinette could go about dressed as a milkmaid, I don't see why I can't be a farm lady of Brittany."

A second parcel contained an apron of unbleached muslin, a hairbrush and a small hand mirror. She teased her hand through her tangled curls and grinned at him gratefully.

"I got you something else, as well." As he pointed to the the smallest parcel, his face tightened.

She pulled off the paper, surprised at how heavy it was, and then gave a low cry. It was a small pistol with a burled walnut grip. Hefting it in her palm, she looked up at him and said, "Why?"

He sighed deeply. "The news in Lempère was not good. There are still pockets of Bonapartists throughout the region, and the English are not held in much regard. Fortunately the boys are fairly fluent in French; we pretended to be a party of academics just off a ship in Brest—not far from the truth. When I bought the donkey cart and the supplies in the town, I mentioned we'd be heading south. It probably wouldn't be wise to return there."

"What of the horses? Didn't that raise anyone's suspicion?"

"I leased them from an old smuggling crony of Hardy's who has now taken to plowing fields. He'll keep quiet. Lord knows I gave him enough gold. He also agreed to find me some able-bodied men to help with the ship."

"But why the gun, Matthew?" She'd used his given name without realizing it.

He merely quirked one eyebrow at her lapse. "I truly intended to get you away from here. I thought there would be a packet boat or even a smuggler's ship. But the country is in turmoil, and there is no regular service to England from this coast. Even the smugglers are lying low. I'd send you by coach to the British embassy in Paris, but I don't think you and your maid should be traveling alone. I'm afraid you are quite irretrievably marooned."

She kept her smile of relief to herself. "And the gun?"

"More bad news. I visited with the local priest, gave him a letter to post to a merchant I know of in Paris who will see it reaches the British ambassador. While I was there, the priest warned me about a band of brigands who operate in this area. They've been holding up the diligences and robbing foot travelers." He paused and then added meaningfully, "It appears we are camped out in one of their favorite stopping-off places."

"Dear God!" Lydia breathed.

"Exactly."

"Can you take the *Rook* to another cove? Surely there are others along this coast."

"None that I have charts for. Still, I'm hoping the priest was being a bit melodramatic. This is a large area; the robbers might not be back for weeks."

"They could be back tonight."

"I'd prefer you stay aboard the *Rook* until she's careened."

"No!" she said forcefully. "I'm not running away. Show me how this thing works. Is it loaded?" She aimed the pistol menacingly at the doorway, and he gave a swift chuckle.

"Don't shoot yet. You'll scare the blazes out of the boys."

"The boys . . ." she murmured. "That's why they're

all so subdued tonight. You've told them about the brigands. I thought they were merely worn out."

"Yes, they're getting their training abroad a bit sooner than I'd anticipated." The captain paced a few times across the narrow space before settling beside her on the desktop.

"I've only ever come into France alone," he said softly. "I've only ever had to look out for myself. At the height of Bonaparte's power I was here and was rarely afraid. But now this, these boys, you . . ."

"Matthew," Lydia said intently. "I'm not afraid. Truly. And as for the boys—well, as you said, we'll set a brave example for them." Something occurred to her then, and she spoke the words before she gauged their prudence. "You could be away from here, couldn't you, if you weren't encumbered with the rest of us?"

He stood and turned to her with a look of thunder. "Just what is that supposed to mean?"

"Oh, no . . . no." She touched his shirt. "You misunderstand. It's just that it must be frustrating to be saddled with such responsibility in a country where you were used to moving about so freely."

"Hmm," he grumbled softly. "I'm not sure that's what you really meant."

"And I know you would never, ever leave your ship." Her eyes danced.

"Then you'd better stay near her, if you want to keep under my wing."

That's exactly where I want to be, Lydia thought. She'd stay close to the *Rook*, but she wouldn't hide out aboard her like some simpering damsel. She didn't have the blood of Russian princes in her veins for nothing.

The captain explained how the pistol worked. "We'll have lessons tomorrow. The boys will be armed from this time forward, and there will be someone on watch every night."

"Did you buy guns for the boys in Lempère? That must have really lulled the townspeople's suspicions."

"No, Miss Impertinence. Do you think I set to sea without arms? I've pistols a'plenty and several carbines on board the *Rook*. I . . . well, I thought you needed something more delicate than a man's gun. Pray God you never have to use it. But I'll sleep better knowing you can protect yourself, if it ever comes to that."

"Thank you, Matthew." She stood up and set her hands lightly on his chest. "I can't say it's the nicest gift anyone's ever given me, but it may be prove the most useful."

She raised herself up and swiftly kissed his cheek.

It took all the strength of thirty-odd years of discipline for Matthew not to draw his arms around her and return her kiss—with one that was not lightly given and most definitely not on her cheek. Her rosy mouth still beckoned him long after she had whispered a soft good night, gathered up her gifts, and slipped beneath the canvas flap of his door.

Lydia held the little pistol in the folds of her skirt and the other goods in the crook of her arm as she walked across to her hut. She wasn't sure which of the captain's gifts held the most portent. She'd think about it in the morning. Now she just wanted her bed.

Earlier, Gilbert had made up a bedroll for her, and the two of them had outfitted her hut with a makeshift dressing table and a wobbly stool. When she pulled aside the door flap, however, the only thing she saw in the flickering lantern light was the beautiful Chinese carpet from the captain's cabin, now on the floor beside her pallet. She had a glorious suspicion that its presence here had nothing to do with the devoted Gilbert Marriott.

She went and knelt upon it like a Muslim at the hour of prayer and knew the answer to her question. Matthew Frobisher had fed her, clothed her and armed her. But this piece of woven beauty was the most meaningful offering. It was comfort and warmth and caring. This truly was the best gift of all.

Chapter Five

The Demon French

"*Y*ou're to have your shooting lessons with Gilbert and Tenpence," the captain informed Lydia as they walked along the shingle the next morning.

The two boys were sprawled on the sand a little way beyond them.

"I've got too much to do on board ship," he added brusquely. He motioned toward the skiff, where Oxer awaited him at the oars. "Gil and Ten are both fair shots. You could do worse."

Lydia sighed in wistful frustration, disappointed that the captain would not be her tutor. She'd had a beau once who decided to teach her archery. It was amazing how frequently those lessons required him to put his arms around her. Surely the basics of marksmanship could not be so different. She gazed with barely disguised hunger at the captain's muscular arms as he strode away after delivering his verdict.

"I expect he's not very good with a pistol," Lydia said to Gilbert in a carrying voice. "I imagine he prefers a sword, since pistols have only come into fashion in *this* century."

The captain merely shot her an amused glance over his shoulder and continued toward the skiff.

At the base of the cliff Tenpence was setting up

practice targets on a long piece of driftwood. Gilbert
meanwhile had separated out the contents of a leather
pouch onto a cloth. He began to explain the rudiments
of loading a pistol to a noticeably inattentive Lydia.

After several minutes, he said with some irritation,
"Then you take the camel, attach it to the whirligig,
and churn up the pipestem . . ."

"What? Oh, Gilbert, I'm sorry. What were you
saying?"

He knew exactly why Lydia's attention had suddenly returned to him: the captain's lithe figure had
climbed up the *Rook*'s ladder and disappeared into
the belly of the ship. Gilbert's smooth brow furled
into a ponderous knot.

He had worshiped his teacher almost unreservedly
since the day he had arrived in Exeter to attend Sir
Robert's unusual school. Although Gilbert had had
his share of men to admire—his fiery older brother
Edgar, who'd been killed in the war, and his sister's
husband, the courageous Earl of Monteith—Matthew
Frobisher was something else entirely.

The tall ex-intelligence officer was a figure from the
pages of a boy's adventure story. He was fearless and
quick-witted, rode as well as any cavalry officer and
was a master of all the manly arts. He was a compelling teacher, inspiring enthusiasm for every subject,
even grim ones like mathematics and etiquette. Gilbert had never had even the slightest reason to fault
him. Until Lydia Peartree boarded the *Rook*.

Gilbert believed the captain to be an honorable
man, but he knew Lydia's presence among them had
stirred Frobisher from his usual sangfroid. The boy
was not at all happy with the way his captain's pale
eyes followed her and sought her out at every
opportunity.

Now Miss Peartree seemed afflicted by a similar
disorder.

Gilbert looked at Lydia, with her shimmering red-
gold hair and sparkling cornflower eyes, and his heart
ached. He knew quite a bit about calf-love. Back in

Exeter, Rowdy had become besotted with the baker's comely young wife. He'd had to put up with a great deal of teasing and had even bloodied Oxer's nose on one occasion when the ribbing became too much. No, Gilbert would keep his tender feelings for Miss Peartree very much to himself.

Still, that didn't mean he would not look after her. He knew she was in a precarious position, with only her foolish maid to act as chaperon. And from the look of open longing that had shone in her eyes as they followed the captain, she surely needed someone to stand guard. There were things afoot here that gave him an uneasy sense of foreboding.

"Maybe this is not a good time for lessons," Lydia sighed. "We all seem a little distracted."

"It's just the sun," Tenpence said, coming toward them. "Makes it 'ard to concentrate."

"No," Gilbert said, recalling himself to duty. "We've had our orders. Sit here, miss, and I'll show you again."

Lydia forced herself to pay attention. Tenpence lounged back a little way from them, a length of sea grass between his teeth. He gazed raptly at Miss Peartree's sun-kissed cheeks and her delicate white hands as she juggled the small gun. He may have been only twelve, but he wasn't beyond a little calf-love himself.

Once Lydia had mastered the loading process, the Cockney boy got to his feet.

"Give it 'ere. Let's see 'ow she fires."

He stood, thin legs apart, his narrow frame sideways to the cliff face, as he raised the pistol with a business-like expression. He'd laid out several old bottles, pieces of broken crockery and a battered wooden bucket on the log. He fired at one of the smaller bottles, which exploded into a hundred fragments.

"Oh, well done!" Lydia clapped her hands. *Little Tenpence was a crack shot!*

She recalled the captain's words when she had boarded his ship. "The alpha and omega of my younger lads," he had called Fripp and Tenpence.

She'd always assumed the well-spoken Fripp had been the "alpha" in question.

"Reload." Tenpence handed her the pistol.

Lydia carefully measured out the powder, shoved in the linen patch and then dropped in the ball, tamping it down with the small ramrod. She held the pistol up proudly.

"Not the speediest job ever," Gilbert chided her.

"Wait till she's got to do it with French brigands coming over the wall," Tenpence added.

"That's not fair. It's very time consuming. All that measuring and poking. I declare, it's worse than cooking."

"In the war," Gilbert observed, "our rifle brigades could fire four shots a minute. And that in the heat of battle."

"Oh, bother!" She struggled to her feet, took up a position that was a facsimile of Tenpence's and aimed at one of the bottles.

"Don't jerk the trigger. Squeeze 'er, nice an' easy."

"Umm . . . and I'd start with the bucket," Gilbert added helpfully.

Lydia pulled the trigger, the gun barrel flew up in her hand and one of the crockery pieces spun off the log. Gilbert and Tenpence rolled back on the sand, laughing and clouting each other on the shoulder.

Lydia turned in exasperation. "At least I hit something!"

"It only counts if you hit what you were aiming at," Gilbert said. "Here—" He rose and set his hand on her wrist, raising the gun with her. "Sight down the barrel. Take a breath . . ." He felt his own breath coming in uneven gasps—Miss Peartree smelled unaccountably of chocolate. "And fire as you exhale."

Gilbert pulled his hand back from her wrist; he was starting to feel a strong twinge of sympathy for Matthew Frobisher. If Lydia had this effect on a mere stripling, how must she be affecting a man who was full in his prime?

"Try again," Gilbert prompted, shifting back from her and moving out of range—in more ways than one.

Lydia sent the bucket careening off the log on her next attempt. This time the boys' laughter was of a more appreciative nature.

By noontime, Lydia could hit an object at fifty paces with some regularity. The captain had just returned from the *Rook*, and as the three passed his hut, he asked for a progress report—as if he hadn't been watching the entire exercise from the window of his ship's cabin.

Lydia replied cheerfully, "I can load two shots a minute and hit very small things. I hope the French brigands are very small, Captain. I haven't had any experience with large targets."

"I wouldn't worry. If you can hit the small targets, the large ones take care of themselves."

He watched her stroll off and felt almost relieved that she could joke about the French brigands. Her lighthearted banter wouldn't do the boys' morale any harm. He continued to be amazed at her good humor in the face of a rather trying situation.

He'd known after only one day in her company that she wasn't merely an idle ornament to London society. Oh, he probably would have wanted her as keenly if she'd been an empty-headed darling of the *ton*. A man could overlook a lot in a woman that beautiful. But with each passing hour he discovered more surprising facets to her character—her generous nature, her pluck and resourcefulness. She drew everyone to her like a magnet. Gilbert had spoken out as her champion, but he knew all of his lads would fly to her defense, even the callow Jean-Louis.

Frobisher shoved his hands in his pockets and went into his hut. There was no profit in thinking about her. No profit in lingering over the curious and highly inflammatory way she had nuzzled his throat on the beach last night. Absolutely no profit in recalling how lovely she had looked as she danced about his room with her new skirt or how sweetly she had kissed him to thank him for his gifts. There was nothing to be served by such thoughts and a deal to be stirred up if he didn't check himself.

That afternoon, the entire crew went aboard the *Rook* to strip her of every loose object. Lydia had been set to work abovedecks, neatly folding the unrigged sails into crisp squares. She looked up sharply when she heard a dull thud against the ship's side. No one else appeared to have heard it—or the low mutter of French voices. She jumped up, grasping the pistol in her apron pocket, and ran to the port rail.

A longboat had come alongside the *Rook*, six sailors sprawled in its belly. One spry fellow was climbing rapidly up the ship's ladder.

Lydia ran for the captain, who was just coming out of the hatchway.

"We're being boarded!" she cried breathlessly.

"It's all right." His hand gripped her shoulder reassuringly. "They've come to help us."

He raised a hand in welcome as the French sailor hoisted himself onto the deck. "*Allô*, Sebastian!"

"Monsieur Mattei!" the sailor called back.

"Not brigands?" Lydia gulped.

"Smugglers." The captain touched her nose. "Former confederates of Taunton Hardy. Apparently the farmer got word out fairly quickly."

The other sailors came aboard, each of them greeting the captain by name. They formed a colorful group with their brightly patterned shirts and silk kerchiefs tied about their heads as they chattered away in French. Even though Lydia spoke the language like a native, she drifted out of range. She was not in the habit of eavesdropping—especially since it was her physical attributes they were openly discussing. The captain said something quelling, and they all looked properly crestfallen—until their eyes fell on the ship's hatchway. Their gazes collectively brightened.

Tilda had finally been coaxed from her cabin by

Gilbert. Even with her rumpled dress and tangled, light brown hair, Tilda was a plumply pretty young woman. Sebastian's dark eyes gleamed as he beheld the maid, and he started across the deck toward her.

He was a handsome fellow, not tall, but muscular, with a cap of dark brown hair curling above his olive-skinned face. When he touched a hand to his forelock, Tilda, who was not immune to an attractive young man's regard, smiled back.

It was not until the he began to speak rapidly in a foreign tongue that Tilda realized the demon French had at last besieged the ship.

"No, Tilda!" Lydia cried as her maid's eyes rolled back in her head. "They're friendly!"

Gilbert leapt forward to catch her, but the sailor was there before him. He cradled Tilda's lifeless form against his chest, wearing a beaming smile.

"Put her over the side!" the captain barked out. "I've never seen such a woman for swooning." He turned to Lydia in irritation. "How did you ever come to employ such a creature?"

"She's very good with hair," Lydia said a bit lamely.

With a growl, the captain stalked away to the rail. "Put her in the longboat and take her ashore," he ordered Sebastian in French. "She'll never leave the ship willingly after this."

Sebastian heaved Tilda onto one shoulder and climbed nimbly down the rope ladder. Lydia watched anxiously as he placed the unconscious maid upon one of the wooden seats.

"Shouldn't one of us go ashore, to see that she's safe?" Lydia called to the captain.

"Why? Do you suppose he's going to ravish her?" His eyes gleamed wickedly. "It may surprise you to learn that even Frenchmen require a bit more, um, animation in their victims. I expect Tilda is as interesting to him right now as a piece of wet seaweed."

"Oh, no," Lydia protested. "I saw how that little sailor was looking at her. I think Gilbert should row me ashore."

"Oh, and who will protect *you* from the French sailors, *Mademoiselle*?"

"I have my pistol," she said, tapping her apron pocket.

"That's a wonderful prospect. I finally get some able-bodied men to help with the ship and you plan to shot them? And it might come to that. In case you hadn't noticed, those Frenchmen were quite taken with you. It must be the red hair, for you are quite commonplace in all other respects." He watched her bristle up nicely.

"Ah, yes," Lydia said in a challenging voice. "I'd forgotten I was not to your taste." She crossed her arms over her chest, effectively obscuring one portion of her person that was very much to his taste.

He studied her, eyes narrowed in amusement, and then tugged one of her curls. "Tilda will be fine, I promise you. Now, I can't stand here all day tossing you idle compliments. There's still a great deal to be done."

"Compliments!" she mouthed incredulously as he strode back to the hatchway.

Between the skiff and the French longboat, it took only three trips to ferry all the *Rook*'s furnishings to shore. The boys cleaned out one of the huts to use for storage, and another two for the French sailors. Evionne was turning into a thriving little community once again.

Lydia was one of the last to go ashore. By all reports, Tilda was still asleep in her hut, so Lydia busied herself by packing up the books from the captain's bookcase. It wasn't long before she was engrossed in his copy of *Robinson Crusoe*, one of her favorite stories from childhood.

When Captain Frobisher returned to the cabin, he found her sitting cross-legged on the floor in a tangle of muslin skirts, her little tan slippers peeping out from beneath her petticoats. She looked about seven. He leaned down and tilted up the book's cover.

"Hmm . . . Defoe. Now, there's an appropriate story. Shipwrecks, castaways, hostile natives . . ."

"Insufferable captains," Lydia murmured under her breath.

"Are you planning on staying aboard, miss? It may have escaped your notice, but everyone else has gone ashore."

"What? Oh." Lydia realized the cabin had been stripped of everything except for the final crate of books and the long silver sword. While she quickly packed up the remaining books, Captain Frobisher took the sword down and slung the leather baldric across one shoulder. He settled the rapier's hilt just below his hip.

Lydia really didn't want to look at him just then. She'd been courted by enough military men to know what the sight of a length of steel at a man's side could do to a girl's heart. She was glad she hadn't lived in the previous century, when gallants went about caped and booted, with their rapiers angled rakishly behind them. It would have been devastating.

He then hoisted the crate of books easily onto one shoulder, and Lydia followed him from the cabin. Through his cambric shirt she could see the long sloping muscles in his back. Where his rolled shirtsleeves ended, tanned sinews stretched in graphic relief as he balanced the heavy load upon his shoulder.

Lydia would have liked to believe that her attraction to Matthew Frobisher was cerebral in nature, but when presented with such a picture of raw masculinity, she lost all thoughts of prim regard and hungered for him like any tavern doxy. The sword was definitely not helping.

When he emerged into daylight ahead of her, Lydia had to clutch the doorframe to still the pounding of her heart. The long rays of the late afternoon sun swept over him, washing him with lambent light. His white hair and sword hilt both glistened like precious metal, and his shirtfront billowed open in the gentle wind, framing the wide planes of his chest. He looked like the very king of pirates now, with some captured booty raised upon his shoulder.

He turned to Lydia with an odd expression in his moonstone eyes. "Hard to leave her, isn't it? I know the feeling. She's a graceful, elegant bird today, my *Rook*, but tomorrow she'll be cast up on shore with her belly to the sky."

"She'll be very vulnerable then, won't she?"

Matthew was impressed by her acumen; many a captain had lost a careened ship—to fire or to shorebound scavengers or to any storm that battered the beach where she lay exposed.

"Aye. But she'll do," he said simply. "Come, now, off you go." He held one hand out to her. "I must be last off, you know."

Lydia left the shadows of the hatchway and took his hand. He was smiling at her, not his usual narrow-eyed smirk but a wide, teeth-flashing smile that betrayed a dimple in the folds of one cheek. Lydia was entranced. Stern, gruff, rugged Captain Frobisher had a dimple. A dimple and a sword. She was utterly done in.

He led her to the rail, setting the crate there while he handed her over the side.

"Matthew," she called up to him plaintively as she stepped onto the shifting rope ladder. "Do you truly find me commonplace?"

He looked down at her, at the glowing skin and wondrous hair that the sun had turned into a spun-bronze halo. He gazed at the lush body that haunted most of his waking hours and all his sleeping ones. There were no words for how he found her.

Lydia continued haltingly, "Because you are not the only one with illusions about yourself, if you must know. It's possible the gentlemen of my acquaintance have only been flattering me . . . Oh, you must think me horridly vain, but I was used to account myself rather . . . well . . . perhaps I'm really not so pre—"

He had leaned down and plucked her effortlessly

from the ladder with one arm, capturing her about the waist and swinging her onto the deck.

"Not so pretty?" he finished for her, holding her a hair's breadth from his chest. "No, you're not pretty, Lydia. Gentlemen may offer you Spanish coin, but surely your mirror does not lie." He knotted his hand in her ringlets and drew her head back, so that her white throat was bared to him. Her eyes were bluer than a Mediterranean grotto.

Lydia's face clouded with dismay. She'd feared what his answer to her artless question would be but had asked it regardless. She couldn't bear it if, after all the men who had been smitten by her beauty, Matthew Frobisher remained unmoved. Yet that definitely appeared to be the case.

Perhaps a walnut rinse for my hair? she thought in desperation.

"Pretty is a puny word to describe you, Lydia." His mouth was very close to her own.

"Puny?" she echoed.

"Aye." He leered at her. "Puny." He tightened his hold, bringing her up full against him.

This close, she could see the fine grain of his sleek skin. She quickly looked away from that enticing span of chest, up to his face. There was tenderness there and a certain diffidence in his expression. It put her in mind of someone else, though she hadn't the wit at the moment to sort out who.

Chiefly because he was kissing her.

He kissed her softly, delicately, running his mouth sideways along her lips, with gentle persuasion. She sighed and leaned into him. He increased the pressure on her mouth, and she opened it slightly beneath his languid exploration. She felt him shudder as his tongue invaded her. Her heart was pounding, tripping in a strange syncopation. She realized then it was his heart beating the counter measures.

"Matthew," she breathed, drawing his head down, feeling the fiery leap of his tongue as it explored her

soft mouth. *"Matthew . . ."* It was a name made for
silky murmurings.

His hand drifted from her hair and stroked down
her back, each finger pressing a separate caress. His
other arm was wrapped so tightly about her waist that
she could barely breathe. The hilt of the silver sword
pressed hard into her side. It was heavenly.

"I'm going to stop now." His voice was muffled, his
lips pressed against hers as he spoke. He set her body
apart from his, but still his mouth held her. It was
only when her shoulder brushed the crate of books
and nearly sent it tumbling to the water that he finally
released her. He dove for the teetering crate, setting
it on the deck, and then turned to her with a sheepish grin.

"Sorry, but a man does have his priorities."

Lydia leaned back against the railing, gazing at him
in awe. If this was how Matthew Frobisher sported
with a woman who wasn't his style, she wondered how
he would kiss a woman who was. It was more than
mere thought could encompass.

"Lydia—" He interrupted her dazed musing, tugging at one of her hands. There was earnestness and
confusion in his face, the cynical, bitter expression
had been wiped away. He looked youthfully ardent,
and she got an inkling of the beautiful young man
he'd once been, before age and experience had
scarred him.

He lowered his head and hid his face against her
palm. "We must go back," he said softly.

"No, Matthew." She drew his head to her shoulder.
"I don't think we can ever go back. Not from here."

"Where then?" He moved away from the warm
temptation of her muslin-clad bosom, and teased his
mouth against her ear. "Where shall we go, you and
I?" He slid an arm along her waist until his fingers
found the sweet hollow of her back. He pressed her
there until she was trembling in his loose embrace.

"Wherever the journey takes us," she said simply.

He stood holding her for a time, looking out over

the water, the freshening breeze mingling his magpie locks with her bright ringlets. He sighed. The boys and the sailors were probably getting an eyeful. Well, he'd told the Frenchmen she was his *chère amie* as a means of protecting her. Still, he hadn't thought to demonstrate the fact so blatantly.

"There may be shoals ahead and dangerous currents," he warned her.

"I don't care, Matthew."

He grinned. "Maybe even the dread water hyacinths."

She gurgled. "Don't mock me, sir. I'll take you sailing in the *Swallow*, and you can see for yourself how infuriating they are."

"Will you, Lydia?" He'd pulled back, frowning slightly, and his voice had lost its bantering edge. "Will you take me with you to Hampshire and introduce me to your family? The rough sea captain who protected you on the French coast. Somehow I don't think this journey will ever take us to Hampshire."

"I've said I would." Her eyes narrowed at his dubious expression. "There are so many things I want to show you. Won't you let me?"

He stepped back from her completely now, his arms at his sides, his gray eyes stark. He shook his head and said nothing.

Lydia hands clenched. "Why do you doubt my words? Do you have so little faith in me?"

He ran his hand along his chin and narrowed one eye, an expression she was rapidly coming to detest. "It's myself I have no faith in. Oh, I could kiss you, Lydia, for an eternity, I suppose. But I'm not daft enough to think I could hold you. There are younger, better men, who will come after me, who will entice you and woo you. Maybe you'll even return to your measly Donald Farthingale. That is where *your* journey lies. Mine lies somewhere quite different."

His mouth formed the rueful travesty of a smile. "And so I am sorry I kissed you. Sorry if I have given you the wrong impression." He sketched her an icy bow. "I pray you will forgive me my temerity." He knelt beside the crate of books, turning his back on her.

Lydia was speechless for all of thirty seconds. He was relinquishing her to younger, better men? He, who had become the very core of her existence, the one person who combined all the rare and admirable qualities she'd thought never to find in a mate. The man who took her breath away when the summer sunlight spilled around him. The man with the bright sword and the hidden dimple. The man with her heart.

When the shock of his words finally wore off, she was able to remind herself of one salient fact—at no time had he said he didn't want her. The opposite appeared to be the case; he wanted to kiss her for an eternity but didn't think himself worthy of her.

He was being noble, in a typically infuriating male way.

Back in Hampshire, Lydia had stalked the elusive bittern and had been rewarded to hear its strange booming call and to see it rise up from the marshes in breathtaking flight. She'd hunted after warier game than Matthew Frobisher.

Pushing away from the rail, she said lightly as she went past him to the ship's ladder, "Well, I don't forgive you. Because there is nothing to forgive. I've been manhandled at garden parties by lovesick mooncalfs who were a deal more presumptuous than you. You needn't bother yourself over my sensibilities." She went down the ladder and sat awaiting him in the skiff with an airy smile.

As he rowed her back to shore, she tried not to notice that his bleak, world-weary expression had returned. She would never forget the remarkable transformation that had occurred in his face when he'd kissed her—and she wondered that he could so easily turn from her now.

If anyone on shore had witnessed their rather public display on the *Rook*, there was no mention of it. Lydia went immediately to her hut to look in on Tilda. She was startled, but not surprised, to find Sebastian crouched next to her pallet.

"You will frighten her when she wakes up," she cautioned him gently in his own tongue. "She believes all Frenchmen are devils."

He raised his dark brows. "But I am not a devil. I wish I spoke English, so I could tell her myself. She is very pretty, this Tilda." He pronounced it "Teelda." It was quite charming. Not that Teelda would think so.

"I'll tell you what. When she wakes up, you can bring her something to eat. Then she will know you mean her no harm. But you'd better leave now."

Sebastian stood up with a sigh. He was a bit shorter than Lydia, but swarthily handsome. Tilda had acquired an admirable suitor.

Once he left, Lydia seated herself on the stool of her makeshift dressing table and proceeded to roughly brush the tangles from her hair. It was pointless to attack the tangles in her heart.

From early childhood on, she had been indulged in every way. The lone offspring of doting parents, she had been given free rein in all things. It was a wonder such lax discipline hadn't spoiled her nature. What it had done was give her a supreme sense of confidence and a proclivity for taking risks.

Her mother had been a noblewoman of the Russian court, the Princess Ivana Fokine. She had traveled to England to visit her cousin, the Marchioness of Mitford, and while staying in Hampshire, she'd fallen in love with a prosperous banker, Cyrus Peartree. Of course, the Fokine family had been scandalized. It was a highly unsuitable match—princesses did not marry tradesmen, however wealthy. But in spite of her family's disapproval, Ivana *had* wed him. After Lydia's birth, her parents led a semiretired life on their estate near Winchester.

Her mother suffered a slight complaint of the lungs, and so it had been Ivana's cousin, Nadia, the beautiful and ethereal marchioness, who saw to Lydia's coming out. It was only natural, since Lydia had run tame in her home, cavorting with her two cousins, Catherine and Arkady, since her leading-string days. When Lydia turned seventeen, Nadia took her to the Continent, introducing her to the bright European capitals that had not yet fallen under the hand of Bonaparte.

It was in these exotic cities that Lydia first learned of her power over men, how she could bring them to their knees with the slightest frown. It had disillusioned her somewhat to realize that even the most stalwart of males could be so easily led.

When she returned to London, the *ton* had greeted the dazzling young beauty with open arms. Lydia discovered that English men were even more impressionable than those on the Continent. Byron dedicated poems to her, Romney pleaded with her to sit for him, lords of every rank pursued her and even the Prince Regent himself sought her company. Lydia often felt as though there were no worlds left to conquer.

That was before she had met Matthew Frobisher. He had shaken her confidence to its core. All the masculine world waltzed to Lydia Peartree's tune, except for one Devon sea captain. She sighed as she set down her hairbrush. How imprudent to fall in love with such a man.

Lydia had an unsettling thought. Could it be that the captain's contrary nature was precisely why she had set her sights on him? He was certainly a challenge. It was he who called the tune for a change, and she danced her little feet off to please him.

"Oh, Matthew," she whispered into her looking glass. "If you would only love me back, then perhaps I should grow weary of you and leave you in peace."

What a peculiar notion. She sat upright and blinked. Was she really such a shallow creature? Did she want Matthew Frobisher merely out of pique?

And more to the point, did the captain view her overtures that same way? Did he see her as the spoiled child who desired only that which she could not have? Even if he cared for her, he must turn away from such self-serving love. *Especially* if he cared for her. How could he give his heart to a woman whose character he mistrusted?

Lydia pressed her hands to her forehead. It was bad enough he had undermined her faith in her beauty, but must he make her question her own soul as well? It was really too much.

Lydia had just come in from preparing supper with Jean-Louis and was trying to rouse Tilda, but all she got for her trouble was a few feverish moans. She stroked the hair back from her warm face, wondering if the girl was truly ill. When Tilda opened her eyes at last, they darted about the small hut.

"We're ashore, Til, in our own little house," she said soothingly.

The maid looked beyond her shoulder and then shrank back against the wall.

"They're here!" she uttered dolefully. "The French are here."

Lydia turned. Sebastian stood in the doorway holding a plate of food.

"Well, they live here, Til. It's their country." Lydia motioned him to enter. "This is Sebastian. He's brought you some supper. Sit up like a good girl, and try to eat something."

Lydia watched from the doorway as Sebastian knelt beside the girl and began speaking to her in his melodious voice. Tilda was at least woman enough to recognize the intent of his words, if not their actual meaning. She was almost smiling by the time Lydia left them and went in search of her own supper.

A merry group was sprawled around the stone fireplace, the sailors lounging beside the English boys. They were all speaking French, and Lydia was surprised at how well the captain's students had mastered the language. No, she shouldn't be surprised. Matthew Frobisher was an excellent teacher. It seemed he'd even taught her a few things that afternoon.

As the camp settled in for the night, Rowdy and

Nancy Butler

Gilbert were placed on first watch along with two of the sailors. Three of them patrolled the beach, while the fourth guard paced halfway up the cliff path.

Lydia lingered in her doorway, watching the long shadows the guards cast as they passed before her lantern-lit window. The *Rook* swayed against her anchor chain, a proud and sleek silhouette above the dark water. This was her last night of stately beauty before she was dragged up on the shore.

Finally Lydia blew out the light, struggled out of her dress and lay down next to Tilda on her own pallet. Another night of twisted blankets and tangled limbs.

"Sebastian's really ever so nice, miss," Tilda whispered. "He has a lovely smile and sat with me real proper like. You wouldn't know he was a foreigner, 'cept for the way he talks."

Lydia mumbled something noncommittal, despairing of sleep with Tilda's besotted prattle rasping in her ear. Then again, even that was preferable to thinking about Matthew Frobisher's disturbing kisses—or his repeated rejections.

Chapter Six

The Silver Sword

*T*he sharp reports of gunfire awoke Lydia.

One moment she was deep in sleep, the next she was awake and alert, quivering in the darkness. She was sure she'd heard the sound of shots. And men's voices shouting in the distance, and the cries of frightened horses. She didn't move, couldn't move . . . lay frozen in place, waiting, listening. But she heard nothing, only the lapping of the tidal waters upon the shoreline. Had it been a dream?

Lydia drew herself up on one elbow and peered around the dark hut. Tilda the Swooner slumbered peacefully beside her. Surely her fearful maid would have been roused by the noises—if they were real.

For several minutes Lydia lay there with her eyes open, waiting for the shivering to subside. It was only when she decided she'd been having a nightmare and rolled over with renewed determination to sleep, that a booming volley of shots sounded just outside her door.

Batting away the blanket, she struggled to her knees, groping for her apron in the dark—she had to find the pistol she'd hidden in its pocket. What an idiot she was not to have kept it beside her.

The door flap was wrenched back, and a tall, burly

man came striding in. He shouted over his shoulder in guttural French and then advanced on Lydia. She scuttled along the floor, seeking desperately for the pistol. The man caught her arm, jerking her roughly to her feet, just as her hand found the grip of her gun through the pocket.

Tilda was screaming now—sitting up and shrieking fit to wake the dead.

Another man barreled into the hut.

"Shut her up!" the man holding Lydia snarled. His companion halted to get his bearings in the dark, and then cast himself on top of Tilda. Lydia saw the glint of a knife in his hand. Without hesitating, she aimed her pistol at his broad back and pulled the trigger. He staggered to one side, then fell forward heavily.

Lydia's captor bellowed in rage and began to throttle her. She kicked and thrashed, pummeling his arms. He cuffed her hard upon the side of her head and dragged her from the hut, his hands again around her throat.

"The knife, Tilda!" Lydia wailed. "Get the knife!"

She could barely see—her vision clouded as the man's brutal hands cut off her air supply. All she knew was that their little camp had exploded into chaos. The dark shapes of men seemed to be everywhere, shouting as they ran. The acrid smell of gunpowder filled the air. Two panicked horses galloped past along the beach, and somewhere the donkey was braying out his fear in a high-pitched wheeze.

Lydia's last sight before the blackness engulfed her was a pale specter moving and darting through the melee, cutting down men to the left and right as he raced toward her, his white hair and silver sword glowing eerily in the dark.

Suddenly the pressure at her throat was gone and the night came back into focus. Matthew Frobisher, clad only in his canvas breeches, now had one arm around her. He braced her against the side of the hut as she gasped in the blessed night air. Her assailant lay in a dark huddle at their feet.

Two brigands now approached Lydia and the captain, their long knives held out before them. The captain thrust Lydia behind him and lashed out with his rapier. The nearest man staggered back with an oath, holding his shoulder, but the other closed in, grappling with the captain, seeking to get a hold on his sword arm.

With his free hand Matthew pulled a long pistol from his waistband, shoved the barrel against the man's chest and fired. Blood splattered everywhere; it fell like warm rain on Lydia's face and arms.

"Move!" Frobisher ordered her hoarsely, taking her arm in an iron grip.

"Tilda!" Lydia cried, trying to pull away.

"No!" He swung her away from the doorway, then roared across the camp, "Sebastian! *Viens ici!*"

Sebastian came at the run. He had blood on his face and carried both a sword and a pistol.

"Garde la femme!" He motioned to the hut with a jerk of his head, and then swept Lydia up over his shoulder. He carried her beyond the huts, toward the rising ground behind the village. No one impeded his progress. He stepped over the corpses of fallen brigands without altering his long stride.

Along the shoreline behind them, Lydia saw men locked in combat, their grappling silhouettes stark against the shimmering water of the cove.

"Stay here," Frobisher barked as he thrust her down onto the ground. Oxer and Seamus, both holding pistols, closed around her. Beyond them, in the shadow of the cliff, eight men huddled, trussed hand and foot. Tenpence stood guard over them, the stock of a carbine held against his hip. He grinned at her reassuringly.

As the captain turned back to the beach, Lydia threw her arms around his knees.

"No, don't leave me!" she keened. "Please stay!"

He laid one hand gently on her tumbled hair. "Princess," he said softly, and then melted back into the darkness.

It was Tenpence who had alerted the captain, long
after moonrise. He had crept silently into his hut, like
a proper little footpad. Matthew had just awakened—
it was nearly time for him to stand watch—and was
sitting at his desk in the dark, toying with one of Lydia's wildflowers.

"Sir," Tenpence whispered urgently, "they've
come."

The captain rose immediately and shoved two
loaded pistols in his belt. The silver sword was swept
from its scabbard, flashing in his hand.

"Tell me." He drew Tenpence to the side of the
door as he peered out. He heard nothing unusual.

"I couldn't sleep," the Cockney boy explained
quickly. "I was out by the 'orses, near the stream. I
saw the men at the far end of the beach. They didn't
come from the cliff path, so there must be another
way down. They struck down our patrols, sir, and I
think they killed one of the Frenchmen, stuck 'im with
a knife." He clutched at the captain's bare arm.
"They're out by the horses now, trying to get them
away. Eight of them I counted."

"Good boy, Ten. We'll trap them out there against
the cliff. Go and wake up the other lads, while I rouse
the French sailors. And no noise, mind." He saw Tenpence grin in the dark.

They slipped out into the still night, keeping close
to the shadows. The cove was quiet, and yet Matthew
sensed something was not right. He could see the
slumped figures of two of his patrollers on the shingle
some distance away. Pray God none of his boys had
been killed. These were practiced ruffians who struck
so swiftly and silently.

He thought to alert Lydia but then decided she
would be safest if she remained asleep. He had almost
reached the first sailors' hut, when a man leaped out
at him from beside it. Matthew pivoted, and his sword
snaked out. The man fell back, clutching the deep

wound in his belly, as his long knife went spinning away on the sand.

Matthew plucked it up, stuck it in his belt, and continued down the beach, his eyes wary, his sword angled out before him.

When he woke the sailors in the first hut, they responded immediately, pulling knives, guns and cudgels from their bedding. Matthew quickly explained his plan, to entrap the thieves before they could make off with the horses. He then slipped into the next hut and repeated his instructions. In less than a minute, all five sailors had joined him on the beach. They crept through the tall sea grass toward the improvised corral. Tenpence and the other four boys caught up with them by the stream, moving like wraiths in the near moonless night.

The brigands had tied rags over the horses' muzzles to keep them quiet, but the horses kept dancing and rearing. In spite of their numbers, the thieves were having a hard time leading the beasts away. Matthew counted eight men, all dressed in dark clothing. There was an occasional grunt as one of the panicked horses veered into one of the men, but the brigands made no other noise. Matthew was impressed in spite of himself.

The little donkey was cavorting in their midst, kicking the dust into a swirling cloud. When one of the brigands tried to throw a rope over his neck, all hell broke loose. The donkey went bucking and squealing down the length of the enclosure, braying raucously. The horses all reared up, screaming through the clothes that muzzled them.

At his signal, the sailors leapt up from the long grass, racing forward. The brigands, taken unawares, tried to stand their ground, pulling weapons from shirts and waistbands. Nevertheless, they were swept back toward the cliff face by the sheer force of the onslaught. The French sailors knew one of their number lay dead or wounded on the beach, and they were merciless. They fired with deadly intent and hacked with sword and knife, until the brigands were overcome.

Matthew whistled for his boys to come forward then, to hold the robbers at gunpoint, while the sailors restrained them with rope sliced from the corral fence. Once the men had been properly trussed up, he turned back to the village. His next order of business was finding Gilbert and Rowdy. He also wanted to reassure Lydia, since she must surely have heard the gunshots.

He looked toward her hut, a hundred yards away, and watched with stunned eyes as just beyond it the longboat scraped up on the beach. At least ten more men waded ashore, weapons at the ready as they fanned out along the shingle.

"No!" Matthew cried raggedly as he raced toward them. *God, no!* he wailed silently as he plunged head-long through the high grass. Behind him, the French sailors, who'd immediately recognized this new threat, followed in his wake.

He now knew what had troubled him earlier about the beach—the longboat had been missing. A group of the robbers had apparently rowed out to the *Rook* to look for gold. Gold that he had so carelessly flashed in Lempère. *Damn. Damn!* The sounds of the skirmish had doubtless drawn them back to shore to aid their companions.

Matthew slowed his pace as he came to the boys' hut and peered cautiously around the edge. A volley of shots whistled past his head, and he threw himself to the ground. Lying tense as a coiled spring, he watched in horror as one of the men entered Lydia's hut. Seconds later a sustained shrieking erupted from inside.

Before the brigands could finish reloading, Matthew leapt up and headed toward them at a jagged run. They surged forward to meet him. Another shot whizzed just beyond his ear. He raised one of his pistols, blowing a hole through the first man in his path, and then used the butt of the gun to knock away the man directly behind him. The brigands moved in, but Matthew never paused, laying about him with the long sword, slashing and thrusting, leaping over the bodies of fallen men as he moved inexorably toward Lydia's hut. One brawny fellow had pulled her through the doorway and had both hands about her throat. The white muslin of her chemise was ghostly against the dark wood of the hut.

He closed in on the struggling pair, and there was only death in his eyes as he ran his sword through her assailant's body. He thrust the dying man away from Lydia as he caught her about the waist. She clung to him weakly, her breath coming in ragged gasps.

He had never been more frightened in his life than in the thirty seconds it had taken him to reach her side.

Two more robbers challenged him and were swiftly dispatched.

By then, the sailors had spilled out onto the beach and the remainder of the brigands—those who had not already fallen under the captain's bloody sword— tried to escape in the longboat. They were quickly forestalled by the boat's rightful owners, who flowed over them with cudgels and fists.

The captain hoisted Lydia onto his shoulder, like the pirate she had once laughingly called him, and carried her to the safety of the cliff corral. She clung to him, crying for him not to leave her, but he had grim work ahead of him and could not afford to be distracted by her beseeching, frightened eyes.

He first went up the cliff path and nearly tripped over the fallen sailor, who was no more than a mis-shapen shadow on the rocky ground. The man was out cold, but his pulse was steady.

Matthew left him and went back down to the beach. The sailors had trussed the remaining brigands and were marching them off to join their brethren beneath the cliff. He slowly made his way along the shore, empty now except for the bodies of the robbers. Some distance beyond the huts he came upon the dead guard. The sailor had been neatly spitted.

Tried to put up a fight, poor devil.

Not far from the dead man, he found Rowdy. He'd been coshed on the head but was already returning to consciousness.

"You'll do, lad," Matthew said evenly as he helped him to his feet. He guided him back to where the sailors had gathered beside the stream.

"Auguste is dead," Matthew said softly in French as he coaxed Rowdy down. The men nodded somberly. "Pascal is up on the cliff path—I don't think he's too badly off."

Sebastian, who was sitting with Tilda's head on his shoulder, gently moved her aside and got to his feet. "I'll take my men and bring them back. Rest now, Captain. You must be very tired."

He shook his head. "No, I must find Gilbert."

Matthew scoured the long grass that verged the beach and roamed the banks of the stream, his eyes searching in the gray light for some sign of the tall youth. He thought to return to the huts to fetch a lantern, but it was nearly dawn and he knew his keen eyes would have spotted Gilbert. He hadn't gone back to his boys yet, hadn't wanted to alarm them, but he was nearing the end of his endurance. Perhaps it was wiser to wait and search in full daylight.

He followed the streambed back to the makeshift camp. Someone had built a fire of driftwood on the shaley ground, and three of the sailors were sitting beside it, passing around a crock of brandy. One of them held it aloft, offering it to him.

Matthew shook his head and then reeled slightly as the flames from the sputtering fire danced in his vision. He realized he was still clutching the long sword. With a bitter cry he cast it from him. It appeared he was much better at killing people than at saving them.

Gilbert . . . A piercing ache twisted inside his chest. *You were always the one after my own heart. Don't be gone from me now, you who were the best and the brightest.*

He was staggeringly tired, but knew he could not rest until he had at least determined that Lydia was unhurt. She had to be somewhere under the base of the cliff. Leaving the Frenchmen to their well-earned reward, he moved on to the huddle of brigands. Those who had been wounded moaned softly. Time enough in the morning to tend them, he thought vengefully.

Oxer and Tenpence, along with one of the sailors, sat guard over them. The boys looked up eagerly as he approached. Matthew gave them what he hoped was a reassuring smile and asked hoarsely, "Where is Miss Peartree?"

Tenpence motioned toward the base of the cliff. The captain moved off and soon came to Fripp and Seamus, who had fallen asleep among the tumbled rocks, looking like victims of a landslide. But of Lydia and his ward there was still no sign.

A frisson of alarm clutched at Matthew. Was he fated to lose all those he held dear in one night? No, he reasoned, they'd been safe when he'd last seen them.

He found them in a small, grassy clearing directly below the soaring cliff. The little donkey lay sleeping on its side, his rotund belly heaving with gentle snores. Between his outstretched legs lay Jean-Louis, his headed cushioned on the beast's furry shoulder. Lydia sat nearby, her chin resting on her drawn-up knees.

She looked up, her eyes drinking in the sight of him, and he feared what sort of figure he cut with blood and gunpowder streaking his face and chest. Without a word, she took his hand and drew him down beside her.

She had wiped the blood from her own face, but splashes of it had dried on the bodice of her chemise. Her eyes responded to his scrutiny by narrowing slightly.

"Soot," she said gently against his ear. "You have soot all over your face."

He drew in a ragged breath. She thought it was going to be all right. She thought she could tease him now; she believed they were all safe.

"No," he protested as she raised the edge of her chemise and began to tenderly wipe the grime from his face. "No, don't." His voice throbbed as he thrust her roughly away. The next instant he was grasping her shoulders, holding onto her as though she was the only stationary object in a wildly spinning universe.

"Lydia," he sobbed raggedly against her throat, his restraint almost at an end. "Lydia . . . I can't . . . Gilbert . . . he's gone. I can't find him. . . . Oh God It was for nothing . . . nothing."

He pushed back from her, trying to master his feelings.

Two tears had coursed their way down his powder-darkened cheeks, and Lydia was stirred to her soul at the sight of those pale marks. Whatever doubts she'd wrestled with that afternoon over the depth of her feelings for Matthew, they were swept away now. She knew she would do anything in her power to spare him such grief.

"Hush, Matthew," she crooned, pulling him back into her arms. "You are just tired and spent."

She recalled how he'd raced toward her on the beach, an unstoppable force cleaving his way through the brigands to rescue her from certain death. He'd been Fury Incarnate—and she would have been frightened by such unleashed carnage if it hadn't been carried out for her benefit.

Still, she was learning that men paid a heavy toll for such brutality, regardless of its justification. She had been blooded herself tonight, and it did not assuage her conscience one whit that she'd shot a man to save her maid. It was an unholy burden to be a bringer of death. The tears on Matthew Frobisher's face bore mute testimony to that.

She held him and comforted him until she felt his breathing even out. His head fell against her shoulder.

She thought he was asleep, when he startled her by speaking.

"Do you really think he's alive, Lydia?"

She nodded, pressing her chin into his hair. "Ten-pence saw them hit him. He told me they 'just plonked 'im on the 'ead, nice an' neat.' "

The captain chuckled softly.

"They haven't killed him, Matthew, I'm sure of it. He's got a very hard head."

"How do you know?"

"He's a male, isn't he?" Lydia said with feeling.

He smiled in the darkness. God, she was a proper tonic, his Lydia.

"He's probably just crawled off somewhere and is waking up now with the deuce of a headache. He'll be showing up here any time now, sharp-set and calling for breakfast."

"I hope you are right," he murmured. "Please God you are right."

When Jean-Louis awoke an hour later, it was to observe the two people he cared for most in the world sleeping in each other's arms. He'd heard them talking earlier; he knew Gilbert was still missing, and he resolved to do something about it.

He roused the donkey, and the two of them went quietly from the clearing. The boy skirted the trussed brigands, passed the sailors dozing around their fire and made his way onto the beach, the donkey trit-trotting behind him. He purposely looked away from the bodies that littered the sand. His *capitaine* was a demon with the blade. Foolish men, to go against such a one.

The sun was now visible over the high walls that surrounded the cove, the eastern sky slashed with bands of red and gold. The *Rook* floated serene and undisturbed in the gentle wash of the morning tide. Jean-Louis walked the perimeter, kicking at the scattered bits of driftwood. Small crabs scuttled away at his approach, pink and tan against the flinty shingle. As he wandered toward the far side, where none of them had yet explored, he thought he saw a very large crab among the rocks. It was pink and tan, just like the ones he had frightened away. But it was not precisely crab shaped. As he got closer, he realized it was most definitely Gilbert shaped.

Heart racing, he tore down the beach to the large boulders that marked the end of the cove. A small rivulet ran between those boulders from a hidden sea cave. It was into the mouth of that cave that Gilbert Marriott had crawled, spent and exhausted after a night in the water.

"Ghilbair," the boy cried, throwing himself down beside his crewmate. *"C'est moi, Jean-Louis. Oh, mon dieu! C'est terrible!"*

He clutched at Gilbert's water-soaked shirt, trying to turn him over, searching with his thin hands for a pulse, a heartbeat, any sign of life. The English boy opened his eyes, and Jean-Louis began to jabber away in a frenzy of Gallic thankfulness.

"English, you little scoundrel," Gilbert rasped. "Speak English. M' head's too tender for your damned French."

He pushed himself upright shakily, rubbing the side of his face with a sticky hand. Jean-Louis was gazing at him in pure delight.

"Don't look so pleased, *mon ami.* You have woken me from a rather nice dream. I was swimming with mermaids."

"Mer-mates?"

"Yes, mermates." Gilbert rolled his eyes. "Red-headed ones. And then *boom*, you started poking and pulling at me—and they all swam away."

Jean-Louis looked perplexed. "They are all most worried about you. The *capitaine*, he cry and—"

"That'll be the day," Gilbert muttered.

"—and there are many dead on the beach. French dogs, which I can say, because I am French myself, though not like those who come in the night to steal our horses . . ."

Gilbert set his hand over Jean-Louis's mouth.

"Enough. If they are worried about me, then we should go back." He tried to rise, but then sat down abruptly as his legs gave out.

Jean-Louis looked at the blond boy and then at the little donkey.

"Here, I help you to rise. And my *petit gris*, he will do the rest."

Gilbert looked doubtful, but he was eventually able to stand with Jean-Louis's assistance. The donkey did not seem to mind having the tall boy astride him. He carried Gilbert along the beach at a rapid, single-footed walk with Jean-Louis running alongside.

The sailors had just finished the grim task of ridding the beach of its half dozen bodies when they saw the missing boy riding toward them. As they reached the village, the men encircled Gilbert, cheering and calling out. Not one of them noticed when Jean-Louis slipped away.

Matthew was just leaving his hut; he heard the commotion and went swiftly across to Gilbert, his gruff voice masking his overwhelming relief. "Are you well, boy?"

"My head hurts a bit is all. And I'm afraid I can't walk very well."

Frobisher plucked him from the back of the donkey and carried him to the boys' hut, where Tilda was feeding breakfast to Rowdy and the wounded sailor.

"I've another lost soul here," he said, settling Gilbert on a pallet. "Fetch him some water."

"I want eggs, not water," Gilbert protested. "I swallowed a great deal too much water last night."

"What happened to you, Gil?" Matthew asked, crouching beside him.

"I'm not sure, sir. There were strangers on the beach. . . . Someone was struggling with Rowdy and I ran to help him. They must have hit me from behind.

I remember waking up and seeing the longboat in the water. I thought you were all abandoning me, and so I started to swim for the ship. I couldn't believe you would leave without me. . . ." His blue eyes clouded. "I swam and swam, but the *Rook* just kept sailing beyond my reach."

"Daft, lad," Matthew said fondly, stroking his brow.

"Did we trounce them, sir? The brigands, I mean? Did we?"

"Aye. These French smugglers know how to put up a good fight. And your crewmates were not too shabby either." He intentionally omitted news of the dead sailor.

"Miss Lydia?" Gilbert looked up eagerly. "She was not harmed?"

"No, she's just bit a ragged." Gilbert could draw his own conclusions when he saw the telltale purple bruises on Lydia's neck.

He left Gilbert in Tilda's care, still unable to credit the change in Lydia's hysterical maid. She had revived that morning and become a veritable dynamo of activity, preparing breakfast, bandaging wounds and helping to get the lot of them cleaned up. He suspected Sebastian had something to do with her miraculous recovery.

Lydia, on the other hand, had lost something.

When he'd awoken that morning, still held in her arms, she was staring off into space, her eyes distant and troubled. Though he had questioned her cautiously, she hadn't been able to tell him what ailed her. He had his own theory—a delayed reaction to the horrors of last night. He knew soldiers sometimes collapsed days after bloody battles had ended. Too many fearsome things had happened to her since they'd left Exeter. She may have been older than his boys but he suspected she didn't have their resilience. Nothing in her life had prepared her for violent storms or ruthless brigands.

It wasn't until he'd walked her back to her hut and seen the body on the floor—beside the apron with a powder burn on its pocket—that he understood what she was experiencing. He knew full well how it felt the first time you took a life.

He'd quickly led her to his own hut. Since she seemed unable to focus, he called Tilda to help her take off her soiled chemise, giving the maid one of his own shirts for her to wear. He wanted to burn that chemise, a bloodstained reminder of the night's carnage.

Afterward, she lay unmoving in his bed, her eyes following him. The dappled bruises where the brigand's fingers had bitten into her throat seemed to mock him. Hadn't he also placed his hands on her throat and threatened to do what the robber had done in fact?

It was no wonder women kept their inner hearts locked away from men.

"Lydia," he said softly. "You did what you had to back there. You can't regret it; it's foolish to even try. But I promise you, last night will soon be a distant memory."

"I'm fine," she rasped. "I'll get up in a bit."

"No, you need to sleep."

It pained him too much to see her, dazed and distraught, and so he'd left her. He was just stepping through the doorway, when he heard the sailors shouting—Gilbert had returned, salty, sticky, dazed, but alive. He knew he should go back and tell her the good news but he didn't know if he could face her hollow eyes again.

"Coward," he chided himself and headed back to his hut.

Lydia was lying exactly as he had left her. He told her that Gilbert had returned in one piece, just a trifle water-logged. He saw her try to smile and then wince.

He felt the pain as though it were his own. It was intolerable that he couldn't do anything for her. "Don't try to talk. Shall I bring you some sugared tea?"

She nodded.

Before he left, he picked up her bundled chemise, thinking to burn it in earnest. Tilda, who was scrambling eggs at the fire, snatched it away from him with a dark look.

"Your mistress is not faring very well," he said.

"I should think not," she said. "After the goings on here last night, it's a wonder any of us have our wits. Strange men in our hut. And my lady shooting in the dark. I was out of my head with fear, sir. Especially when the man she shot crawled into my bed. All I can say is, thank goodness Sebastian came in and finished off the wretch."

Matthew gaped at her. "He wasn't dead?"

"I just told you—Sebastian shot him."

With a crow of jubilation, he lifted her right off her feet and spun her around. "Thank you, Tilda!"

He went striding back to Lydia, leaving Tilda convinced that he was touched in his upper works.

"Princess," he said, taking up one of her hands. "Listen to me—you didn't kill the man who came into your hut. You were right about not being able to hit the large targets. You must have only winged him. He was attacking Tilda when Sebastian came in and shot him. Not you."

"I wanted to kill him," she murmured. "That's almost the same thing." She choked back a sob. "But I don't think that's what is troubling me."

"What is it, Lydia? You seemed fine last night. In fact *you* were comforting *me*. What's happened to you this morning?"

"I'm not sure. When I woke up I felt almost happy, as though the brigands were only a horrid dream. But then I saw the blood on our clothing . . . and I remembered that Gilbert was still missing. I knew then that our Robinson Crusoe adventure was over." Her eyes met his. "It isn't jolly any longer, Matthew. And it was jolly until last night. Even the storm was an adventure, exciting and stirring. It was easy for me to act brave, because I was never really afraid. You were there, and so what could I fear?"

"But I wasn't there for you last night when the brigands came." He'd uttered the words in a low, distant voice.

She touched his cheek. "You were, when it counted most. But what I saw last night showed me something . . . something I'd chosen not to look at before."

"What, Lydia?"

"The truth about the differences between us, Matthew. When I think of what you did on the beach . . . and then how you had to leave me . . . it makes me . . . it makes me feel so wretched inside."

She hung her head and fought back her tears. "Sorry . . . I know I'm not making much sense. And I'm not setting a very good example, am I? The boys must think me a total loss."

He stood up. "The boys are still a bit shaken. We all are." His eyes had hooded over and his voice had an edge of clipped politeness. She couldn't know that the meaning of her halting words had finally sunk in.

What I saw last night. Yes, she had seen an eyeful, he thought bitterly. A battle-crazed fiend with a bloody sword, a half-naked savage who had not once offered her a word of reassurance. Instead, he had abandoned her, afraid and in distress, to finish out the night's dirty work. It was a wonder she didn't shrink from him now.

"I think I need to sleep," Lydia said, tugging up her blanket. "Tell Gilbert . . . tell him I am so glad he has returned."

The captain nodded curtly and went from the hut.

Scovile closed up his small naval telescope and slid it into his shirt. He had seen enough from his perch atop the cliff overlooking Evionne Cove. More than enough.

His men were captured or dead. It was no more than the fools deserved for disregarding his orders and splitting up to search for the Englishman's gold. But it really didn't matter. The information he now possessed would earn him enough gold for a comfortable retirement in the temperate reaches of the Mediterranean. Hang Finistère with its neverending wind, its godforsaken granite cliffs and its whimpering peasantry.

He intended to take the diligence for Paris that very day. He would sell his watch to get there. He'd steal a watch and sell it to get there, if necessary.

He knew it might be wiser to conduct his business with a letter, considering he had once betrayed the man he would be seeking in Paris. But a personal interview would be so much more gratifying.

He licked his lips, thinking of the fine reward he would claim for imparting such valuable information— that he had seen a white-haired, scarred man striding along the beach below him, the living ghost of a man thought long dead. *Nightshade*. He shivered in remembrance. Six years had passed since he'd uttered that name aloud, and it still had the power to chill him.

But that was only part of the amazing discovery he'd made that morning. There was also the child, the chestnut-haired boy with an unmistakable resemblance to Marianne Dieudonne. His old friend in Paris would be doubly generous once he learned of this happy coincidence.

Scovile rose awkwardly to his feet and stretched. He was stiff and cramped from a night spent atop the cliffs. The brisk walk into Lempère would loosen his bones. And then on to Paris.

Chapter Seven
The Dark of the Moon

*T*hat afternoon the brigands were summarily carted off to Lempère, guarded by four of the sailors. Those too disabled to walk were loaded into the dogcart with one of the farm horses in the traces. The captain rode at the head of the procession.

The citizens of Lempère came out of their shops and homes to stare with amazement at the raggedy parade. These brigands had long been a scourge on their coast, and it was with great glee that they greeted Captain Frobisher when he pulled up in the town square.

Two days earlier, when he had come to their town to buy supplies, no one had suspected he was anything but a schoolmaster. The men had not noted his steely eyes or catlike walk. They'd seen only a spare, scholarly man with a troop of boys at his heels. The women had not sighed over his wide shoulders or imposing height; instead they had wondered at his scarred eye and his strange black-and-white hair.

Now that same man sat mounted before them, a silver sword dangling at his hip, his hair buffeting in the breeze and the look of eagles in his pewter eyes— and they couldn't believe it. This was no mere pedagogue, but a soldier, a warrior. The captured brigands, some twelve or so, who trailed sullenly behind him, bore mute testimony to that fact.

After the mayor had mustered his small militia to lead the robbers away, he offered the captain the hospitality of his home.

On a shady veranda, over wine and bread, they discussed the events of the previous night, and Matthew was well pleased when he walked from the mayor's garden. Men and supplies and seasoned lumber were his for the asking. For the man who had captured the brigands of Finistère, English or not, there was no boon too great.

After the body of the brigand had been removed, Lydia returned to her own hut. She'd wanted to get up, but Tilda told her it was the captain's orders that she remain abed. Tilda dressed her in the freshly laundered chemise and then bathed her throat with cool compresses. Fripp, Oxer, Tenpence and Seamus took turns sitting with her. Gilbert came in at dusk and played cards with her by lantern light. Oddly enough, Jean-Louis never made an appearance.

She wasn't surprised that the captain hadn't looked in on her when he returned from Lempère. Something had altered between them—he'd become suddenly remote with her that morning—and she'd spent the whole day trying to fathom it, trying to recall what she'd said or done to provoke him. It troubled her far more than the pain in her throat.

Lydia mulled over what had passed between them after the brigands were defeated. The first thing that came to mind was that he'd cried in her arms. She knew he had opened his heart to her last night, allowed her to see a part of him that most men kept hidden away, especially gruff, stoic men like Matthew Frobisher.

She had also cried and more than that, she had shown him her fear. Her fear of separation and of loss. She had never shared that part of herself with anyone. But was that what had driven him away?

She lay back on her pillow, musing over this complicated dance they were performing. The steps were all new to her.

He's feeling guilty, Lydia, a small but insistent voice proclaimed. *He thinks he failed you during the raid. He told you as much when he said "I wasn't there for you."*

Oh, that's unreasonable, she rebutted. He *was* there for her. Good heavens, he'd saved her life. He'd been magnificent and brave and—

There was a rustling in the doorway. The captain had drawn back the flap and stood on the threshold. He was dressed in his blue jacket and long trousers, quite a difference from the bloodied, bare-chested avenger of last night.

"I know it's late," he said, "but I saw your lantern was still lit. I won't keep you. Just wanted to make sure they've been taking care of you properly."

She nodded.

"Good, good." He turned to leave.

"Matthew, I'm sorry."

He took a few steps into the hut. "Sorry?"

"Yes, sorry . . . about what I said to you this morning. I garbled it badly, and I fear you misunderstood. You didn't fail me. After you rescued me, the reason I clung to you was because I was so frightened for *you.* Not for myself." She paused to gauge his reaction. His face remained impassive. "That is what I meant by the differences between us. You . . . most men . . . will always return to the battle. It's a woman's lot to sit and fret. I've never had to do that before, and I hated it, the waiting and worrying. Do you understand now?"

"Oh, I understand, all right." He bent his head toward her, his gray eyes dark with bitter knowledge. "You realized more than you know. It's not our stations in life that will keep us apart, Lydia, it is precisely that difference in our natures. Because, unlike me, you are not tainted."

"Tainted?" She sat upright with a frown. "And is your nature so unacceptable, then?"

"I'd say it was a bit more than that." His voice was like ice. "What you saw last night was only a fraction of my true nature. The word *base* might be appropriate, or *reprehensible. Loathsome, foul, detestable.* Shall I go on?"

"No, don't. Don't go on," she muttered fiercely. "I'm sorry you thought it was a foul and detestable thing to save my life. That it was loathsome to protect the boys."

"Why do you refuse to believe me?" He crouched down beside her. "There are things I have done that I cannot speak of. To you or to anyone. You must heed me when I tell you it is best for us to stay apart. Far apart."

"Then why are you here with me now?"

Her quiet question must have caught him off guard. He tipped his head back and drew in an audible breath. "Because I'm a fool . . . because I cannot bear having you nearby and not seeing you, not speaking to you or touching you . . ." His voice was strained by the naked honesty of his answer.

Lydia's heart leapt. He *did* care for her!

"—and that is why I've made arrangements for you to stay in Lempère until we are finished here."

"No!" she cried. "Please, no! Don't make me leave."

"We've had this conversation before. At least your reaction tonight is more honest. You tried to coquet with me last time." He ran his knuckles along his chin, and there was a hint of wistfulness in his eyes as he stood up.

"I'll say good night now. I won't see you in the morning—Oxer will be taking you to the mayor's home at first light. So I suppose this is good-bye, as well."

"Good-bye?" she croaked, holding one hand to her throat.

He looked at her ruefully from the doorway. "Aye," he said. And squinted.

She was off the bed and across the room in an instant, pummeling him in frustration.

"I hate you," she cried hoarsely as she flailed at him. "I hate your stupid nobility and your stubborn honor . . . and I hate your horrible squint."

"Stop now," he ordered gruffly, catching her arms and holding them at her sides. "You'll hurt yourself."

She could barely keep from sobbing as she gazed up at him. "And most of all I hate knowing how easy it is for you to walk out my door. How easy it is for you to send me away."

His cheeks narrowed. "Easy, Lydia?"

"Cowards always take the easy way out," she baited him.

He shook her gently. "Not easy, Lydia. Necessary."

She wrenched free of him and sank forward onto her knees.

"No, please don't." He tried to draw her up, but she pushed his hands away. She bowed her head, humbled by her need.

"It is absurd for you to think I could be repelled by you. You mean everything to me." She caught at his fingers, drawing them to her lips. "I know you think me willful and spoiled, and that I care for you only out of caprice. Maybe it was even true—until last night. Until you gave some part of yourself to me. You let me hold you and comfort you. I wanted so much to ease away your grief. You believed in me last night, Matthew; you trusted in me enough to lower your guard. . . ." She looked up entreatingly. "Please don't take that away. Please."

He was on his knees, his arms around her. "Ah, sweetheart," he murmured. "Of course, I trust you. And you did ease my grief. No one else could have comforted me as you did. I'm not sending you away because I don't care for you."

"Then why?"

He rested his head on hers and sighed deeply. How could he make her understand?

"Do you feel me trembling, Lydia? Do you feel my heart racing inside my chest? When I hold you against me like this, my whole body rises to meet you."

"I know," she whispered. "I quite like it."

He groaned. "Well, it's killing me. Because it's not only when you are beside me that I ache for you. It's waking and sleeping and all the damn time."

"It seems we both want the same thing." She smiled at him limpidly.

"Lydia," he said sternly. "I thought you a woman of the world. Do I have to school you in the notion that men and women never, ever want the same thing?"

She looked puzzled. "I want you to hold me and kiss me—"

"Yes, and love you and honor you," he intoned harshly, his fingers digging into her shoulders. "And shall I tell you what *I* want? Shall I?" His lips pressed into her ear. "I want to take you, ravish you like a damned brigand. On your bed or on the beach or up against a wall. I want to be inside you and have at you until you are screaming and pleading with me to stop. And crying out for me to go on and never stop." He drew a snarling breath. "There, that is what I want."

He pushed roughly away from her and stood up. She fell back against the dressing table, hugging her arms around her sides with a dazed expression on her face.

He pivoted and blew out her lantern.

"Good-bye, Miss Peartree," he said from the doorway.

Lydia knelt on the floor where she had fallen, shrouded by darkness. If a hundred robbers had descended from the cliffs, she couldn't have moved. She needed to keep still, needed to savor the multitude of shivery sensations washing over her. An inexplicable tingling radiated down from her head and up from her toes to meet somewhere in the middle with an ever deepening throb.

Matthew Frobisher had done this to her. With words.

She wondered how she would react if he actually carried out any of his threats. She would surely fly into a thousand delicious pieces.

Once her body began to inhabit itself again, it occurred to her that it was quite late and that Tilda was not back. Was she off somewhere with Sebastian? Was he kissing her? Was *he* making her cry out for—

Heavens! She must be mad. Tilda would never do anything like that. She was only seventeen.

"And I'm twenty-seven," Lydia muttered as she rose to her feet. "And I'm dashed if I'm going to wait one more minute before I learn what my seventeen-year-old maid probably already knows."

She marched out her door and crossed the fifteen feet of shingle that separated her hut from the captain's. The moon above the cliffs was at full wane; it appeared only as a deep gray orb in the night sky. The whole cove was an inky landscape, the water nearly indistinguishable from the land.

Lydia slipped under the captain's doorflap into his darkened room. She was halfway across the floor, when she heard him growl ominously, "You'd better be a brigand. Because if you're who I think you are, you're done for."

She felt his hand on her upper arm and a point of cold steel against her breast.

"Then I'm a brigand," she whispered, gingerly removing the blade tip from her chest.

"God, Lydia, no," was all he had time to utter, before she cast herself upon him.

She tangled her hands in his long hair, finding his mouth in the darkness. He threw the sword from him, then locked his arms around her. Together they tumbled onto the low bed, Matthew cushioning her fall with his body. His mouth devoured hers, biting and sucking at her lips. She opened her mouth for him, inviting him to taste her. His tongue answered, plunging deeply inside her, again and again.

"Stop," he finally managed to gasp out. "This is madness."

But she was too busy trailing her hands down his bare chest to pay him any heed. She was fascinated by the contrast of the soft mat of hair with the hard expanse of muscles. Her mouth found the side of his throat and she bit him there, sucking on the taut skin until he was groaning beneath her.

He raised her up by the shoulders, as effortlessly as if she were a doll, then pulled at the muslin of her chemise with his strong teeth until the fabric tore. "Lydia," he crooned just before his mouth caught her bared breast and closed over it. She shivered and cried out as he drew her in. His tongue probed her like the steel tip of his rapier, and she felt herself swell and burgeon under his assault. Her whole body seemed to expand and burst away from that one place where his hungry mouth suckled.

"Matthew . . . *Aaah*," she keened as she arched away from him. His mouth followed her retreat, not releasing the fevered tip. She wanted him to stop, to halt this overpowering onslaught, yet she never drew herself so far back that his heated mouth could not reach her.

He released her at last, turning his head away, and she felt his halting breath against her dampened skin.

"Princess," he said hoarsely, "you are more beautiful than any dream."

Lydia propped herself on his chest. "Are you a cat, then, that you see me in the dark?" She thought she could make out the pale gleam of his eyes.

"No, but I can taste you and touch you."

Yes, those were his eyes, glowing even brighter now. She drew her mouth along his cheek, savoring the taste of him, a salty tang laced with the heated musk of desire. "I've wanted to touch you, Matthew. Wanted to feel your skin beneath my hands."

"Brazen wench," he muttered. "Here, then . . ." He was guiding her hand along his body, from chest to hip and then along his rock-hard thigh. Everywhere she could feel his awesome strength, the raw power held barely in check.

Lydia heard his gasp as her hand strayed to his groin. He was wearing cotton breeches, the same ones she'd thought unseemly that first day. They had clung to his thighs and showed off a good deal too much muscular leg. Now they clung to another hard, muscled part of him. As she laid her hand over his swollen manhood, something surged through her—heat and desire and a strange, tender caution. Here was her power. Not beauty, not witty conversation. Her power was to make Matthew Frobisher live again, to reawaken him to love and joy. She must go carefully now, she must—

With breathtaking swiftness he had rolled her onto her back and now loomed above her.

"I won't take you, sweetheart," he murmured. "But let me touch you. Please God, let me touch you."

His hand was already between their bodies, under her chemise, stroking warm against her thigh. She gasped as it drifted up to caress her hidden core, playing against her delicately. Waves of sensation flowed over Lydia as she blossomed under his provocative fingers. She was nearly beyond conscious thought when he stopped.

He was sitting up, a hazy shadow in the dark room. "No more," he said hoarsely. "I'll have your maidenhead in a minute."

Lydia was panting, burning, balanced at the edge of a high precipice. She needed Matthew to fling her far, far over the edge. He'd said he wanted to be inside her. She wanted it now more than anything.

"Take me, then," she said breathlessly

"I don't think—"

"Sssh." She put her hand to his lips. "We both think too much, Matthew. It's deadly. Please take me."

"No. I'll not take anything I can't pay for properly."

She sat up in shock. "What did you say?"

He chuckled softy. "Now it's you who've misunderstood me. I meant I can't give you what you deserve in return for such a gift, Lydia. It's not within my power to offer you love . . . or a future . . . or any of those things women cherish."

"I don't recall asking you."

She felt him shrug.

"And yet you want me?"

"Oh, yes."

Lydia was overcome by a combination of confusion and mortification. Apparently she was greener than she knew. "I don't understand," she said weakly. "How you can want me so desperately, yet feel nothing more?"

His arm snaked around her. "I feel a great deal more, Princess. I said I can't offer you more."

A sudden horrid notion struck her. "You're not married?"

"No . . . but I could remind you that you are betrothed."

"I intend to put an end to that the instant we reach Exeter," she declared. "It was a mistake in judgment."

He gripped her by the wrists. "No, not on my account, Lydia." His hands eased and slid up her arms, pulling her against him. "God, you're making this so difficult. Don't you know that a man can desire a woman, even care for her enormously, but understand in his heart that . . . circumstances will keep them apart?"

She touched his cheek tentatively. "You can tell me if you're in love with someone else."

He muffled his face in her throat. "No, there's no one. Perhaps that's the problem. Perhaps I've forgotten how."

Lydia smiled in the darkness. "So you're not completely averse to the notion of loving me?"

He laughed softly. "I once called you a damned willful chit. I fear I understated the case."

She sighed and nuzzled his chin. "Just leave the door open for me, Captain Frobisher. That's all I ask."

His arms tightened around her for an instant. "I have a feeling that even if I don't, you'll find some way to break it down. And now will you go? Before I forget all my good intentions. You've got the damnedest mouth, Miss Peartree—I'll be up all night just thinking about it."

"You won't send me to Lempère, will you?"

He blew out a breath. "That was an idiotic notion. All the men for twenty miles would be at the mayor's door trying to court you, and I've no intention of fighting them off. No, I'm not letting you out of my sight."

She slid from his arms and stood beside the bed, reaching out to draw her fingers through the long strands of his hair. He took her hand and kissed the palm softly, caressingly. "Good night, my Lydia," he murmured. "You've danced with the devil and lived to tell of it. There are few who can claim that."

"You're no devil," she said.

"No?" He smiled against her fingers. "Just wait until you see all the hellish barricades I erect against you."

"I'll be waiting, Captain," she said, slowly drawing her hand away.

As she drifted dreamily back to her hut, Lydia smiled only once, but it fairly lit up the darkened cove.

Chapter Eight

The Gypsy

*T*he mayor of Lempère was as good as his word.
The next morning half the village appeared in
Evionne Cove carrying food, hauling carpentry supplies, driving teams of horses. There was even a caravan of traveling players. Two longboats full of sailors
rowed into the cove to help with the careening.

The visitors set up cook fires and rigged canvas aw-
nings. Hawkers strolled through the crowd selling trinkets and meat pies and lemonade, while one of the
actors, a towheaded giant with a monkey on a leash,
juggled for a circle of onlookers. The entire cove soon
took on the atmosphere of a merry country fair.

Lydia walked along the edge of the beach, lifting
her skirts away from the lapping waves. In honor of
the occasion she had donned her new clothes, the
beautiful lawn blouse and the wide blue skirt. Tilda
had repaired her torn chemise that morning, shooting
dark looks at her the whole while.

A fine one to be casting such looks, Lydia thought,
since it had been near dawn when the girl crept back
to her bed.

Lydia had not yet spoken with the captain. He was
out in one of the longboats, directing the placement

of ropes on his ship. She could see him across the water, shirtless and bronzed in the midst of the sailors. Last night's encounter had not lessened her appetite for him one bit. If anything, it had whetted it to a painful degree. She only prayed the feeling was reciprocated.

Gilbert and Rowdy approached her, each brandishing a skewer of roasted chicken. The other boys were mingling with the crowd, delighted by this unexpected holiday. All but the French boy, who was again conspicuously absent.

"Have either of you seen Jean-Louis?"

"He's bound to be about somewhere," said Rowdy.

"Have you looked in the sea cave?" Gilbert tore off a chunk of chicken and chewed thoughtfully. "That's where he found me yesterday. It looked just the sort of place a young boy would find intriguing."

Lydia smiled at his superior tone.

"It's down there." Gilbert was pointing to the far end of the beach, where a tumble of jagged boulders lay in the surf. From that distance it was impossible to see the opening. Lydia looked doubtful until a little gray donkey appeared, emerging from the very rocks it seemed, and went trotting along the beach.

"He's there," Rowdy proclaimed. "That beast is never very far from him. Jean-Louis rescued it from the brigands, you know. One fellow was trying to slit its throat, and our little French lad bashed him with a rock. Don't tell the captain—we were supposed to hang back till the fighting was over. But Jean-Louis saw what was happening and just leapt into the fray."

"Surprised us all," Gilbert added. "He's never shown much grit before."

"He's, ah, not quite like the rest of you," Lydia said. "He's very sensitive, but that doesn't mean he has no spirit. You might do well to remember that."

Both boys lowered their heads. Heaven forbid they should find themselves in Miss Peartree's bad books.

"And remember, you all volunteered to attend the

captain's school. Jean-Louis didn't have a choice. He was plucked from the only life he'd ever known. I'm not surprised it's taken him a while to adjust."

"I don't think he's a bad fellow," Gilbert said earnestly. "But the captain has no patience with him."

Lydia gave a little snort. "Then perhaps he's the one I should be lecturing. Oh, Gil, Rowdy, look!" She purposely distracted them. "That man has the dearest monkey. It's dressed like a tiny sailor."

"He looks like Gilbert," Rowdy chortled. "Only smarter."

Lydia grinned as he darted off along the beach with Gilbert in pursuit. They were the eldest of the captain's crew, but even they had been infected with the day's high spirits.

It was closing on noon when the *Rook* was finally hauled to shore. The longboats drew the ship toward the beach until her hull scraped against the sloping bottom. The ropes were then transferred to three teams of horses. The teamsters cracked their whips, the horses dug in until their knees knuckled over and the heavy ship came wrenching up out of her watery home and onto the shingle. As the onlookers held their breath, she tipped slowly over onto her larboard side. For a few seconds there was only the sound of spars and beams groaning as they settled, and then a cheer went up from the crowd.

Lydia's cheer died in her throat. Matthew stood in the bow of the longboat, a bleak expression narrowing his face. She knew it must have been difficult for him to see his ship in such a state, a sleek lady turned into a wallowing matron.

As his boat neared the shore, he leapt out and strode through the waves.

"Damn!" he said, coming right up to her.

"And good morning to you too, Captain."

"It's her bottom," he said.

"Pardon?"

"Fouled," he said. "There's more than a week's work here. More like a fortnight's. It's my own fault for not keeping an eye on things the last time she was overhauled. And her rudder's not in the best fettle either. Damn!" He started to walk past her, caught a whiff of something chocolatey and spicy, and instantly recalled, with a familiar twinge in his nether regions, whom it was he was about to snub.

"Lydia—" He turned back to her. "Sorry. I'm all sailor this morning. Not very courtly, I'm afraid." His glance shifted from side to side. "You know I'd kiss you if there weren't a hundred people around us." His voice lowered. "No, I'd do more than kiss you. Don't blush like that, lass, they'll think I'm saying rude things to you."

She laughed and hid her face behind her hand. "I like it when you're all sailor, Matthew. You're really something to watch. Ever since that first day, when you went up the rigging and I couldn't take my eyes off you. I was very impressed."

"Were you really? I admit I was showing off a bit. Not that I had any interest in you or anything." His eyes taunted her. "Just entertaining the passengers."

Tenpence came running up with the captain's shirt. To Lydia's disappointment, he quickly slipped it over his head, obscuring the tanned expanse of his chest.

"I fear I look quite shabby next to you. That is a very becoming outfit."

"Oh, this? It was a gift from a gentleman admirer."

"Hmm? I didn't know there were any gentlemen hereabouts."

"If you want the truth, he is one of those stubbornly noble gentlemen that drive women to distraction . . . but I'm working on him."

Lydia realized Tenpence was taking this all in, wearing a savvy expression on his impish face. She sometimes forgot these boys were trained to listen and observe. Apparently their teacher had forgotten as well.

"Tenpence," she said. "Will you fetch me a cup of lemonade? Oh—" She turned to the captain. "I don't have any money."

"I believe our credit is good. Run along, Ten. And get one for each of us. I need to drown my sorrow over the state of my ship's hull."

She and Matthew strolled through the crowd, stopping to watch the various entertainments. At the edge of the throng, a brawny young man was taking on all comers in a makeshift wrestling ring. Gilbert and Oxer stood in the line of men waiting to challenge him.

"Oh, no," Lydia said. "They're sure to be hurt. He's twice their size."

"You'd be surprised what those young fellows can do."

"And what about you, Captain? Care to take him on?" She raised one eyebrow.

He looked aghast. "He's nearly half my age, ma'am. I am in my dotage—or had you forgot." He took her arm and led her away before he was tempted to have at the fellow just to impress her.

He stopped a hawker who was selling trinkets and bought her a bright blue ribbon for her hair.

"Shall I have a scarf as well to cover my bruises?" She put a hand to her throat.

"No, I think not." The last thing he desired was for her to hide her beautiful neck and white shoulders. "Here, let me tie it for you."

She turned her back to him so he could lace the strand of satin through her curls. From his vantage point he had a remarkable view of her bosom, swelling above the scooped neckline of her blouse. No, definitely no scarves for Lydia.

As the village priest wandered by, his long soutane flapping in the breeze, the captain forestalled him. "Father Boniface!"

He turned to them with a smile. "Captain Frobisher."

"This is Miss Peartree, Father. She is one of my castaways."

"Dear lady." The priest bowed as he raised Lydia's hand. He was a courtly old gentleman with a narrow face and a hawk-nosed profile, not unlike an etching of Cardinal Richelieu she had seen in her cousin's library.

"We owe the good father a debt of gratitude," Matthew explained. "He's the one who told me about the brigands."

"Thank you, Father." Lydia smiled. "It was kind of you to forewarn us."

"Praemonitus, praemunitus," the priest quoted. "I am glad you had the sense to be forearmed. You must come and take tea with me, my dear. These days I so rarely get a chance to entertain."

"I'd like that very much. And perhaps I will bring a few of the boys along."

He bowed from the waist before moving on.

"He's a bit of a mystery," the captain said. "A cultured Parisian hidden away here in this little outpost."

"I though him quite charming."

Moments later the captain was called from her side by the mayor. She decided it was time she located Jean-Louis. As she made her way toward the end of the beach that Gilbert had indicated, the noise of the merrymakers faded to a pleasant din. When she reached the tumbled rocks, the donkey trotted up to her expectantly.

"No treats," she said. "You are growing quite fat."

She scrambled over the boulders until she came to a small stream that trickled out into the cove. At the base of the cliff beyond her, a narrow cleft opened in the granite, the height of a man's head and no wider than an armspan. She followed the course of the stream to the mouth of the cave.

Inside, the bright sunlight was filtered to a soft, amber glow. A small pool shimmered in the center of the space, its water an exotic aquamarine. A thousand prisms of light danced off the surface and reflected up onto the high, arched roof. The pool was fed by a small cascade that trickled down the back wall.

It was the most beautiful place Lydia had ever seen, an enchanted home for water sprites and sea sirens.

Jean-Louis was lying on his stomach at the edge of

the pool, gazing into the water. He looked up, startled, as she approached.

"Oh, it is you, *mam'selle*." He sounded displeased.

"Why aren't you on the beach, Jean-Louis? The people of Lempère have come to help careen the ship, with food and jugglers. . . . It's all quite festive. The other boys are out there."

He wrinkled his nose. "Me, I do not like to be festive. You go. Go off with those boys." He resumed his contemplation of the pool.

She knelt down beside him, gazing into the water. Tiny silver fish darted beneath the surface, above a white sand bottom studded with anemones and starfish and narrow fronds of kelp.

"I was very sad that you didn't visit me yesterday," she said gently. "I wanted to hear about your adventure with the brigands."

He scrambled to his feet and set his hands on his narrow hips. "No one cares about my adventures," he proclaimed, a look of bitter resentment narrowing his angular face. He reminded her unaccountably of the captain at that moment. "So why should I tell you? This donkey, him I save. You do not care. That Gilbert, I find when he is lost. You do not care. I get hit on the head, I get killed, then maybe you care, eh?" He stalked past her out of the cave.

"Jean-Louis!" she called out, rushing to her feet. "I *do* care; we all do."

She caught up with him and pulled him toward her. He was rigid in her arms.

"*Non*," he said, thrusting her away. "Let me go."

"Please," Lydia entreated. "I'm sorry no one praised you. I'll tell the captain how brave and clever you were. He will be so proud."

"Do not!" he snapped. "He is nothing to me, that one. I will not go back to England with him. This is my country, and I want to stay here. I want to go home to my papa. To Provence." There was a throb in his voice. "I will go away and you will never see me again."

Lydia was rapidly discovering that this callow child had a core of steely stubbornness. She felt a moment of panic—suppose he did run away? They had enough worries without having to scour the countryside for a lost, homesick boy.

Gripping him by the shoulders, she cried, "No! You must promise me that you will not leave. There must be some way to find your father. I will help you. But you cannot do this thing alone. Promise me." She leveled her sternest gaze at him until at last he nodded.

She hugged him. "Good. Now, come along. Don't you want to see the dancing monkey and the juggler?"

"Later," he said. "I will come later." His tight smile did not reach his hazel eyes.

Lydia was lost in thought as she made her way back. The grievances of children were often exaggerated, she knew, sometimes far out of proportion. But this boy wanted so much to be acknowledged and yet had such a hard time earning any recognition. Was she the only one who ached for him? How could Matthew not have praised him for finding Gilbert? Even with all the turmoil in the aftermath of the attack, couldn't he have taken the time for a little kindness?

The captain came toward her from the edge of the crowd and immediately caught up one of her hands. "What's amiss, Lydia?"

"Why, nothing at all." She gave him her most dazzling smile. Sorting out Jean-Louis's problem required a quieter, more private place.

The mayor had climbed onto the back of the caravan and was giving a short speech, commending Captain Frobisher and his brave crew for apprehending the bandits. He waxed on about the end of the war between their two countries and how all sailors were brothers under the skin.

"Politicians," the captain snorted. "They're the same the world over."

"Shhh," she admonished, pinching his arm. "He's complimenting you. Have a little respect."

Afterward, a group of musicians struck up a tune,

and the crowd parted to make room for dancing. Lydia and the captain watched from the sidelines as couple after couple whirled past them. Then Gilbert came up beside Lydia and, without so much as a by-your-leave, tugged her into the dance.

"I almost beat that fellow in wrestling," he announced as he slid his arm about her waist. "If I hadn't been hit on the head the other night, I could've taken him easily. The captain's taught us some really capital moves, and I'm his best student. . . . You can ask any of the others."

"You're also quite a good dancer," she observed, trying not to grin at his boyish bravado. "Did he teach you that as well?"

He made a face. "No, of course not. My sister Evelynne taught me. She said I had to acquire some other skills besides sailing and spying."

Wise woman, Lydia thought.

When the dance ended, the captain claimed her from Gilbert, who seemed a little breathless.

"My turn," he said gruffly. The musicians were playing a slow country tune, and he guided her in measured circles around the sandy floor. He danced as he did all things, with supple grace. Lydia closed her eyes as she relaxed against him, letting his strong arms lead her.

"Not going to sleep are you?" he drawled.

"No," she said dreamily, "just enjoying it all. I wish it could go on forever."

"It's only just begun," he said huskily.

Her eyes opened in bewilderment.

"Us," he whispered against her ear. "It's only just begun for us."

Sudden relief flooded over her. He was being cryptic, as usual, but she had an inkling he'd just stopped holding her at arm's length. She sighed and let him draw her closer until the dance became an intimate, fluid embrace.

When the music ended, he propelled her through the crowd muttering, "Dangerous, very dangerous."

"What are you talking about?" She was laughing

up at him when he finally drew to a halt in the shadow of the careened ship. "What is dangerous?"

"You are." He also sounded a bit breathless. "I need to swim a few laps across the cove after dancing so close to you."

"Well, you could kiss me," she said hopefully.

"Fuel to the fire, my dear. And besides, we have an audience."

She followed his gaze to where Seamus and Fripp were having their fortunes read by an exotically dressed old woman. She had lit a fat candle in a brass saucer even though it was hours until sunset.

Matthew approached her blanket. "Tell them only good things," he cautioned, winking at the gypsy.

She tipped her head back. "You are the one, sir. The one I have been waiting for." Her dark eyes narrowed. "Here, give me your hand."

The captain looked at Lydia, who nodded in encouragement. *This should be interesting.*

Matthew crouched down as the boys made way for their master. Lydia stood directly behind him, leaning one knee against his back.

The gypsy ran a clawlike finger along his palm. "I see several lifelines here . . . many different lives you have lived." She spoke under her breath in an odd French dialect. "Your heartline is severed. But it knits, just here." She stabbed at the base of one finger. "I see a child with hair like autumn leaves. I see betrayal and loss. I see death."

The sky seemed to darken, and the air grew heavy and still. Lydia felt a shudder ripple across the captain's back.

"The purple flower is blooming again," the gypsy intoned. "Its poison will spread." Matthew was positively tense against Lydia's knee. "The white blossom can heal, if you let it. Otherwise you will lose everything." The old woman closed his fingers over his palm. "I can see no more."

Thunder rumbled off in the distance; Lydia felt light-headed from lack of air.

"Thank you." Matthew's voice was a monotone. "Shall I give you silver as is customary?"

The gypsy shook her head. "Save your silver to buy trinkets for your lady. All I ask of you is this. . . ." She leaned forward and whispered into his ear.

"Yes," he answered. "It's a strange request, but yes."

Under Lydia's curious gaze, the woman drew a small knife from the pouch at her waist. She reached forward and severed a white lock of the captain's hair, twining it into a loop before placing it in the pouch.

"Thank you. 'Tis a fine talisman. And heed what I said, sir—you are the one."

Matthew got up, brushing past Lydia as though she wasn't there. She ran to catch up with him. "Matthew?" she cried. "What was that all about?"

"A damned lot of hoodoo. Purple flowers, white blossoms . . . Bah!"

He was striding along, weaving though the crowd.

"Stop!" she pleaded, taking hold of his arm. "Something has surely upset you."

"It's nothing." He halted and scrubbed the back of his hand along his brow. "Come away from here, Lydia. We need to talk."

He led her back to the deserted huts. It looked as though rain was imminent, and some of the townspeople had already started up the cliff path, but no one had yet returned to their camp.

He drew her into his hut and closed the door flap.

"Sit," he ordered, turning the chair away from the desk. She eyed his bed longingly, then sat down with a deep sigh.

"Now," he began, "I'm going to ask something of you."

"What the gypsy said was true, wasn't it?" Lydia said, unable to keep still. "You *have* led many lives, and there is a boy with hair like autumn leaves—Jean-Louis."

Matthew was frowning. "Listen to me, Lydia. You must not ever question me about my past."

"What?"

"I mean it. If we are to be . . . well, if there's any chance of a future for us, you must promise not to poke around in things that don't concern you."

"But everything about you concerns me." She twisted her skirt between her fingers. At the moment, Matthew seemed like a stranger to her. The strained expression had not left his face, but for once she didn't want to comfort him. She almost wanted to run from him.

"No, my past does not concern you. It's dead and gone. Let it be."

"If it's dead, it can't harm you. And if that's the case, why won't you talk about it?"

"You think the dead can't harm us?" His mouth tightened. "They can strike at us as surely as the living."

"Stop it!" she cried. "You are frightening .ne."

"You should be frightened. I warned you last night to heed me." He paced to the window and stood gazing out. "I was a fool to think we could ever be together. Only one day has passed and you are already discovering the truth about me."

"What is the truth, Matthew? Tell me, please."

"Every word the gypsy said was true," he stated grimly. "Betrayal and loss and death."

"Those are only vague phrases, Matthew. Fortune-tellers excel at vagueness. We've all suffered those things at some time." She was trying to sound reasonable, but her heart was racing out of control. "It was her mention of Jean-Louis that upset you, wasn't it? Please tell me who he is. Just that one truth between us, and I will ask for no more."

He turned from the window. A soft rain had begun to fall. In minutes his crew would be back from their revels on the beach.

He knelt before Lydia and took up both her hands. "I told you last night that I trusted you. You needn't remind me that I've just now behaved like a damned hypocrite. But this subject . . . it is very difficult for me to speak of."

"I know. But I think you must." She leaned her cheek against his brow. He smelled of sea spray and lemons and some indefinable masculine scent. She breathed him in and sighed.

"Here—" He slid onto the desk behind her, straddling her chairback. She felt his hands light on her shoulders. "It's easier if I can't see your face."

She touched his fingers reassuringly.

"Twelve years ago," he began in a low voice, "I was on a mission in Paris, posing as a gentleman of the provinces. I met a young woman there, the daughter of an old French family recently returned to power by Bonaparte. She was called Marianne. Even though she was being courted by a wealthy nobleman, I made sure she became infatuated with me. I needed to get close to her brother, you see, who was a deputy minister of the army. I was prepared to use her, Lydia, for my own devious ends. Unfortunately, I also fell in love with her. When it came out that several of her brother's papers had been stolen, he hanged himself—"

"Oh, no." Lydia clutched his hand.

"He had become my friend, and I think remorse would have destroyed me . . . if I had been responsible. But I was not the one who took the papers. You see, I had determined not to act against Marianne or her brother. They were patriots, idealists, who thought Bonaparte would bring France to glory.

"But by some twist of fate, another got his hands on those papers and sold them to the English. But Marianne, my Marianne, believed I was responsible. She betrayed me to the French authorities and I was taken prisoner."

Lydia wanted him to stop. It was all so tragic. It had never occurred to her that spies came to know and care for flesh and blood people . . . or that the term "enemy" was best applied to the faceless masses.

Matthew went on. "Two days before my execution, I was rescued from prison by a stranger, a young Englishman. No one in the Foreign Office had any idea who he was. I went underground in Paris for another year and then spent the next five years scouting military operations in the countryside. I did learn that Marianne had married, only days after I was arrested. She wed her noble suitor, a man of unsteady character— a jackal, in fact. It was he who arrested me." He paused for a breath. "A year later she bore him a child."

"Jean-Louis," Lydia whispered.

"Mmm. The boy lived with her in Provence, and when she died, I went to her chateau and took him away—in the dead of night while the household slept."

"You took him from his father?"

"He had no father. The man was dead by then. Killed in a tavern duel over a whore."

"Jean-Louis believes his father is alive," she said softly. "He has hopes of being reunited with him. Shouldn't you tell him his father is gone?"

"Bah! The boy is a dreamer. I've told him more than once. Jean-Louis has no close family left. That's why I brought him to the abbey in Switzerland—so he'd be part of a community. Anyway, I'd had a bellyful of spying by then and decided it was time I returned to Exeter."

"Why didn't you bring the boy to England with you?"

He gave a humorless laugh. "At the time, the last thing I wanted was to be saddled with the jackal's brat."

"He was Marianne's child, as well."

"Ah, the woman who betrayed me. It still cuts deep, Lydia. She loved me, and so for her sake I turned my back on England . . . and yet she laid evidence against me that would have sent me to the guillotine."

"Has it occurred to you that she might have been a pawn of that man you called a jackal?"

He shrugged. "The fact remains that I had no time for children. There were grogshops and brothels to be explored, all in pursuit of blessed forgetfulness. I did a rather good job of it. I almost forgot who I had been. Almost."

"What happened?"

"Sir Robert bloody Poole happened. He picked me up out of the gutter, gave me a large sum of money and ordered me to start up a school to train boys in espionage. I hated the idea at first. I wasn't so lost to decency that I could face turning innocent lads into what I had become. But these are different times, Lydia. Spies are not lurkers in the night any longer. And God knows, England still has need of them.

"So I had a new vocation. And the man who didn't want any children on his coattails found himself saddled with seven or eight at a time. When Jean-Louis turned eleven, the abbé suggested he study for the priesthood. I realized then that I hadn't given him much of a life. So I fetched him back to England."

"What was his father's name, Matthew, his family name? Jean-Louis should know that at least."

"No, it's better he should never learn of his despicable patrimony."

Lydia worried her lower lip and said nothing.

The captain rested one hand on her shoulder and muttered wearily, "God, I haven't spoken this much in twenty years. I'd give a guinea for another glass of lemonade."

"How do you feel now, Matthew?"

"Better, I think. Yes, much better. That gypsy gave me a turn, if you must know."

"Yes, I do know. She gave me one as well. I wonder how she came to be on the beach. Her accent was very strange."

"It was Provençal," he said. "It's not unlike Jean-Louis's accent."

"Matthew," she turned in her seat. "Will you do one more thing for me?"

"I've poured my heart out to you, and you dare ask for more?"

She was relieved at the teasing note in his voice. "Yes, I dare, because it's not for me that I ask. It's for Jean-Louis. Didn't you notice that he wasn't on the beach? He spent the whole day in a sea cave. And he never came to visit me yesterday when I was ill. I think he may have been upset by the attack, but you haven't spared him a moment since the brigands came." She added intently, "If you really sat down and talked to him, I think he might surprise you."

Matthew purposely looked away from her. She could see things in his face that his well-trained lads could not begin to fathom. He had been neglecting his duty to Jean-Louis for a very long time. For six years at least.

There was the sound of cat-calling and laughter outside the hut. His crew had returned from their holiday. Tomorrow they would begin the difficult task of removing the mast, but for tonight they could sleep off their sweetmeats and honey cakes and dream of monkeys dancing on the sand.

"Find him, Matthew." Lydia tugged on his shirt.

"Oh, aye. You've distracted me long enough, Miss Peartree—from all my duties." He rose and pulled her up after him. "Just tell me, why does knowing all this matter so much to you?"

Lydia's brow formed a delicate furrow. "Because," she said at last, "I don't like secrets, and I hate mysteries. And I—Why are you laughing at me, Matthew?"

"Because you have saddled yourself with exactly the wrong man. Come, kiss me, Lydia, before those infernal boys start traipsing in here. And then I'll be off to find our truant."

He drew her against him, his palms flat on her back.

She looked up at him wistfully. "Matthew, the gypsy woman said your heartline was broken. After Marianne betrayed you, have you ever cared for anyone else?"

"No," he said, gazing deep into her clear blue eyes. "I have had no thoughts for anyone else."

He saw the look of sadness cloud those eyes. It wasn't fair to torment her this way. He laid his mouth over hers, pressing a lingering kiss upon her sweet, parted lips.

"Until now, Lydia," he murmured. "Not until I met you."

The rain had turned to a heavy downpour, and Jean-Louis found himself stranded in the sea cave. He and the donkey sat in the opening, watching the water stream from the cliff above them.

The *petit gris* had been grazing all afternoon, but he, Jean-Louis, was most hungry. Through the scrim of water, he watched the last of the wagons crest the top of the cliff path and thought longingly of honey cakes.

It wasn't only the rain that kept him from going back to camp. He had been very rude to the *mam'-selle*, and he was ashamed. None of his troubles were her fault.

He wanted to blame Matthew Frobisher, but it was difficult to mix accusation with adulation. He worshiped the *capitaine* and sought only to please him. But he knew he could not stay with him. His failure to live up to his master's expectations was a constant knife in his heart. He must find his own people. Perhaps they would not ask so much of him.

The dark, caped figure came abruptly through the wall of rain. Jean-Louis scrambled back in alarm until he realized it was Captain Frobisher, clad in his oilskin.

"You've found yourself a nice hidey-hole, I see," he remarked, sweeping the wet cape from his shoulders. He crouched down beside the boy, brushing water droplets from his hair. "Quite nice." Even in the diffused, rain-washed light, the cave kept its aura of enchantment.

"It is a secret," Jean-Louis said sullenly. *That Gilbert must have told everyone.*

"Well, I can keep a secret. The English government used to pay me a great deal of money to do just that. How do you think I was able to buy the *Rook*?"

"Sir Robert, he own the *Rook*," Jean-Louis said, crossing his arms.

"The devil he does. She's mine, free and clear. For what she's worth now, all hove up on the beach. Did you watch the careening, lad?"

"*Non*, I do not care to watch such things."

Gad, something had put the boy's back up. Lydia was right. Matthew examined him. His olive skin looked almost sallow and his chestnut hair was tangled at the crown, as though he had been sleeping on his back.

"Miss Peartree is worried about you, Jean-Louis. You should have a care for her."

"She is *très belle*," he said, then added wistfully, "I think sometimes that she is very much how *Maman* looked."

"Ah, Johnny," the captain said softly.

The boy turned to him in surprise. The *capitaine* had not called him that since he was living at the abbey.

"I knew your mother. Did I ever tell you that?"

"*Non*. You say when you take me from my home that you are a friend. I think you must know my papa. He had many friends in Paris."

"Yes, I knew both your parents. But before your mother married your father, before you were born, I was, well . . . I was in love with your mama. Do you know what that means?"

"*Oui*, of course. It is to be most happy with a person. Why did you not marry *Maman*? I do not think my father had a love for her. He went away from us so many times."

"He loved her. Perhaps in a different way than I did. He loved you both." He toyed with a pebble under his boot and hoped Lydia was happy. This was the most difficult conversation he'd ever had in his life.

"You look very much like her, Jean-Louis. Do you know that? She had hair like yours, the color of a marron, and her eyes were green and gold, just as yours are."

"I cannot remember," he said sadly. "I would wish to have a picture of her."

The captain set his arm around the boy's shoulders. "I know. There were times I forgot what she looked like. Until I found you. Now I will never forget." He tightened his hold on the boy and was rewarded when a small hand slid into his own. He couldn't recall ever feeling that sort of warm, rising pleasure.

"Tell me," he asked gently. "Were you frightened when the brigands came? It's all right if you were. We were all rather shaken."

"Not you, *capitaine!*" The boy's eyes widened.

Matthew smiled ruefully. He was getting weary of being a demigod to striplings.

"Vraiment."

"Non, it is a thing impossible. You rescue *mam'selle*; you kill the French dogs. How are you afraid?"

"Soldiers are always afraid. Or they are fools. Do you understand that? It is not wrong to be afraid. It's only wrong to run from your fear."

Jean-Louis grappled with this concept. "I was afraid when the robbers came. But I hit the man who try to kill the *petit gris*, even so."

"You did? You little rogue. How did I not hear of this?"

The boy fidgeted. "We were not to be in the fighting. I disobeyed you, *capitaine*. But the donkey, he lives, *enfin*, so I am glad."

"Another rule, Jean-Louis—a clever soldier knows when to disobey an order."

"You think I am clever then?"

"Yes, I do. And beyond that I don't know what to think. Except that I should get you back to camp. You must be starving." He bundled the boy in the oilskin, wrapping it twice about him. "And I promise to keep the secret of your cave. But tell me, how did you discover it?"

"Oh, this is where I find Gilbert when he is lost. He was swimming with the mermates."

"God in heaven, Johnny!" the captain uttered as he swept the boy out into the deluge. "You amaze me. Now, run, lad. Run!"

They pelted along the beach together, the man keeping pace with the slight boy. Matthew Frobisher could have flown, had he a mind to. The boy had finally shown some mettle—he might just turn out to be his mother's son after all.

Chapter Nine

The Comte

Paris had changed a great deal since Scovile had last been there six years earlier. The Corsican was gone now, off to his island kingdom. His absence had left the city sadly lacking in spirit. The reinstated king did not have the backing of the people, only the support of England and her allies. Paris had lost her vital, beating heart.

For himself, Scovile had borne no great love for the Little Corporal. He had served Napoleon because it suited his purse. Unfortunately he'd made an enemy of the Comte de Chabrier, who was in his own way as powerful as the emperor. Perhaps even more powerful now with the Corsican gone. Somehow, the comte had weathered the radical transition in government; he was now a valued servant of the new regime.

Chabrier was the canny cat who always landed on his feet. "Napoleon may own France," he used to joke in his sinister, unsmiling way, "but I own Napoleon." It now appeared that Chabrier owned Louis XVIII as well.

Scovile had found lodgings the night before in a respectable boardinghouse near the Tuileries. He hadn't needed to sell his watch after all to get to Paris. Most of the citizens of Lempère had gone off to the town square to goggle at the Englishman; it had been no trouble at all to break into one of the shops and rob the till.

Scovile's appointment had been set for early that afternoon. After spending the morning purchasing a decent suit—he dared not appear down-at-heels lest the comte fob him off with a pittance—he set out for a street near the Place de la Concorde, where Chabrier lived and had his suite of offices.

The comte's secretary met him in the foyer of the office wing. Scovile didn't give his name; he merely said he was there to furnish information on a certain François Mattei. It was enough. Scovile knew how to bait his hook better than most.

The secretary returned for him in less than ten minutes.

He was escorted down a long corridor where guards clad in Chabrier's distinctive gray-and-yellow livery stood along the walls. Scovile was starting to sweat by the time they reached the heavy oak door that led to Chabrier's private office. It was carved with writhing, demonic figures and might well have had the legend "All hope abandon ye who enter here" inscribed above the lintel, for such was the man's reputation in Paris—and in most of France.

The secretary bowed Scovile into the room and then left. Chabrier was seated at his desk, a massive affair with lion's paw feet and a leather-inlaid top. Behind him a large mullioned window let in the sunlight, yet in spite of it the spacious room was chilly and shadowed. Bookcases lined the walls, and a marble bust of the deposed emperor stood upon the mantel of the cavernous fireplace.

"Sit, sit." Chabrier motioned with his hand without looking up from his papers.

Scovile took this opportunity to assess him. His thick hair, which had been jet black six years ago, was graying now. He appeared to have put on very little weight—fortunate for a man who'd been stocky to begin with. The face was much the same, that of a country-fair pugilist, square, rough-hewn, with a large, blunt nose and heavy lips. It was not an unattractive face; it merely carried the Bourbon physiognomy to an extreme. Scovile recalled that the comte's paternal grandfather had been Louis XV. If only his father had not been born out of wedlock, he might well be sitting on the throne. Scovile knew Chabrier's base ancestry had rankled him his whole life.

When the comte at last looked up, directly and with no surprise whatsoever, into Scovile's eyes, he was smiling.

"I thought it might be you, my old friend. Who but Scovile has such an interest in François Mattei?"

"Except for Chabrier," he purred back.

"Ah, then, we find something in common after all this time. Will you take some wine?"

"Only if you drink from the same bottle, my old friend. I haven't forgotten what a neat hand you are with poison."

The comte raised one gray brow and looked dismayed. "What a thought. I wouldn't think of poisoning such a well-remembered associate."

At least not until he has my information, Scovile reflected.

The comte rose from his desk in a leisurely fashion and went to an inlaid table, where he poured them each a glass of claret. "To our memories." He held his glass up to Scovile's.

To your bank account, Scovile toasted silently with an anticipatory grin.

The comte resumed his seat and began to toy with a glass paperweight. "Now, tell me what you have discovered."

Scovile leaned back in his well-upholstered chair and drank deeply from his glass, letting the heady wine infiltrate his senses. It was almost like old times.

"I have been engaged in some business in Finistère," he began.

"You've been leading a pack of brigands. Go on."

"A disabled ship came into one of the coves re-

cently. Near Lempère. A party of Englishmen, with
two women aboard. They had gold and horses and so
seemed ripe for a night raid. Someone had warned
the ship's captain that we were about in the neighbor-
hood, however, and my men were taken by surprise.
I was able to escape up the cliff, along a secret path.
But when I got to the top, the men who had been
holding our horses had fled."

The comte made a moue of distaste. "A shoddy
operation, if I do say so."

"Well, it turned out all to the good, as you will
hear. I had no horse and so decided to bide my time
on the cliff until morning. When I observed the English camp by daylight with my spyglass, I made an
amazing discovery. François Mattei was the English
captain. He was there below me, sleeping beside one
of the women."

"The man is dead. I saw the body myself."

"But it was badly burned. You cannot be sure."

"So why do you insist this man is Mattei?" The
comte seemed to be losing patience.

"You must remember Mattei's hair—it was starting
to come in white even twelve years ago. It's almost
completely white now. He wears it long, past his
shoulders. He wore it long back then."

The comte made a dismissive motion. "So, two men
with long hair gone prematurely white. I am not
amazed. What else was there to convince you so
thoroughly?"

"The scar," Scovile responded.

"You could see the scar from the cliff top?"

"It's a good little spyglass. I had it off a German
traveler. He didn't require it any longer—he was
dead. But, yes, I could see the pretty scar you gave him over
his left eye. Listen to me, Chabrier . . . he was Mattei's
height, he had his walk, his manner. I'd know him in
the dark—especially in the dark." His companion still
looked unconvinced. "My God, he defeated eighteen
of my men with a handful of sailors. Who but Mattei
could put up such a fight?"

The comte closed his eyes halfway and rubbed the tips of his fingers together. He appeared quite catlike at that moment.

"So Nightshade lives. And is again in France. I'd not thought to have my reckoning with him in this lifetime. I've hunted his ghost in my dreams. . . . Now I can hunt him in earnest."

"There's another thing you should know. I believe he has the boy with him."

"Jean-Louis? Well, that certainly whets my appetite." It was not the most paternal of statements. "I assumed it was Mattei who abducted the child, but then when the Englishman's body was found so soon afterward here in Paris, I feared I must be wrong. I hate to be wrong, Scovile, as you know."

"I'd could almost swear it was Jean-Louis. He was also below the cliff; I saw him quite clearly. He had the look of your wife, her coloring, her features."

"This is delightful, my friend. You have brought me good news. Mattei in France again and with Marianne's whelp in tow. Quick now, tell me about this woman he was with."

"She was red-haired, quite pretty . . . English, I'm certain. Didn't look at all like a doxy. She slept right beside the captain, so she must mean something to him. When he led her back to the huts at first light, he was very attentive."

"Excellent." The man behind the desk rarely smiled. He was smiling now. "The man, the boy and the red-haired woman. I always prefer things in threes."

"Will you go to Finistère?"

"Not if I can help it. I'm far too busy here. Treaties, councils, keeping the king happy. You know how it is. I've got several correspondents in Finistère, though. I'll write to one of them and set things in motion. Nightshade *will* come to Paris." He sighed. "It's really much more gratifying to hunt in one's own backyard."

He rose and came around to the front of the desk.

"I am greatly in your debt, Scovile. There will be something very nice for you when this business is finished."

"I need to be away now." Scovile rose. "There is nothing to hold me in Paris."

The comte's hand shot out and closed over his arm, like an iron band tightening on his sleeve. "I disagree. There is a great deal to keep you here. Your greed for one thing. And I may have need of you. I'm surprised you don't want to be in on the kill."

Scovile twisted away from him with a grunt. "Unlike you, I never want to set eyes on François Mattei again."

"Afraid, my friend?" the comte purred.

"Prudent. The man led an enchanted life. I don't want to tangle with him. Just pay me for my information, and I'll be gone."

"No, you'll stay. And you'll keep your prudence to yourself, if you know what's good for you. I'm the one you should be afraid to tangle with, old friend. I am Minister of Police. And what is Mattei? A sea captain. Think who shall make you the worst enemy."

Scovile bowed his head. He had been beaten. He refused to leave Paris empty-handed, so he would stay on and face the dark avenger again. "You will pay me when Mattei is dead?"

"Only then. But be assured you will get all that is owed you when the time comes."

Scovile walked from the room, shutting the carved door firmly behind him. He had never noticed before that one of the laughing demons carved into the wood looked uncommonly like François Mattei. It gave him a very unsettled feeling as he made his way toward the foyer. He couldn't help wondering which of them, Chabrier or Mattei, would eventually get the last laugh. It certainly wouldn't be Scovile.

The comte immediately composed a letter to his contact in Lempère, thinking himself fortunate that his enemy had chosen that part of Brittany to refit his ship. He gave the note to his secretary with instructions that the messenger was to wait for a reply.

Afterward, he sat staring into space, mulling over Scovile's news. He was aware that his powerful position in the government made him appear almost invincible. And it was true that few men had crossed him over the years with any success. His gaze strayed to the clear glass paperweight with the delicate purple flower at its center—his memento of the one man who *had* crossed him and gotten away with it. It served as a constant reminder to never take anything for granted. He knew he was not invincible—only clever and very, very cautious.

He thought back to that time twelve years ago when he had first encountered the man called François Mattei. Scovile had been Chabrier's trusted confederate then, not the brightest of fellows, but capable, eager to take on the less savory duties of policing the city.

The comte had met Mattei at a ball at Marianne Dieudonne's home, where they'd been introduced by her older brother, Armand. Chabrier had been at the point of offering for the beauteous Marianne and so he was surprised to find that in Mattei he had an apparent rival. Marianne was clearly bewitched by the pale-eyed young man with the distinctive, silver-streaked hair, and the fellow appeared equally smitten with her.

Chabrier, who had not yet achieved his current lofty position, was then a deputy minister, but he'd already created a network of informants throughout France. It was natural that he look into his rival's background. His sources discovered that there was indeed a François Mattei from Rouen. But they also reported that the young man in question had recently returned from Holland and was living on his father's estate. Further investigation revealed that a man of Mattei's description had earlier appeared in Lyon society—and had disappeared with some critical military affidavits.

In spite of his flawless French and courtly manners, François Mattei was an English spy.

Chabrier arranged for the theft of several of Armand's war-committee documents, intending to incriminate the knave beforehand. Unfortunately, Armand caught Scovile leaving his study. When he discovered the missing papers, he immediately challenged Chabrier, accusing him of being a traitor.

It was very sad. Scovile had been forced to strangle him. They had hung him in his own stable with a forged suicide note to Marianne, blaming Mattei for the theft and insisting that, if honor would be served, she denounce him to the Consulate.

Chabrier himself had made the arrest. Mattei had resisted, of course. He was a fiend with a sword and managed to wound Chabrier twice before his guards restrained him. It was as they held him back, writhing and cursing, that the comte had sliced his eye with the tip of Mattei's own sword.

"Not such a pretty face now, my friend," he had snarled. "You'll need to pay for your ladies after this. Not that there will be any ladies where you're going."

The guards had led him away, a marked man in more ways than one—the comte had already signed his death warrant.

Two days before Mattei's execution, a man posing as a lawyer visited him in prison and apparently aided his escape. Chabrier was angry but unalarmed. He had gotten what he wanted, the gracious daughter of an old French family who would give him sons to carry on his line. He'd wed Marianne while Mattei was still imprisoned. She hadn't objected to the hasty marriage, and Chabrier hoped, now that her lover was proven a traitor, she would again turn to him. But circumstances soon forced him to send her away to his chateau in Provence.

Over the next year, the comte found himself beset by unsettling incidents. Important papers disappeared from his desk; military documents were intercepted in transit. His whole carefully nurtured network of spies and informants had been infiltrated. After each episode, Chabrier received a letter, a blank sheet of paper inscribed with a curious insignia—a small purple flower. A nightshade, a botanist from the Sorbonne informed him, a common, poisonous weed.

It was only after Scovile was attacked one night that the identity of Chabrier's nemesis became known. As he lay gasping on the cobblestones, Scovile saw his assailant turn to look back at him near the lit doorway of a tavern. It was François Mattei.

Chabrier's fingers closed around the paperweight. It was odd, he mused, how directly after the birth of Marianne's son, Nightshade's depredations ceased. The comte knew Mattei had never been anywhere near his wife in Provence—she was heavily guarded. Yet somehow Mattei must have learned of the child and for his own reasons ceased his vendetta.

For five years Chabrier had been blessedly free of him. But then, a month after Marianne died of a fever, the boy disappeared—whisked out of his nursery despite the maid sleeping in the next room. The comte was certain Mattei had taken him.

Less than a week later, his certainty was shaken when his informants brought him news of a man who'd burned to death in a boardinghouse fire—a tall man with black hair streaked with white.

When he investigated the fire-gutted room, he found books in English and on the title page of one volume, a drawing of a small purple flower. Chabrier barely gave the charred body a second glance. He had thought to see Mattei in hell—it appeared at the time the man had gotten there well before him.

"Clever, clever fellow," he murmured. "If you are alive in Finistère, Monsieur Mattei, then who was the dead man in Paris? I commend you and your wily British colleagues for furnishing me with such an effective red herring."

He had lost his Marianne, not to the fever but to the ghost of her lover, whose memory had haunted her for the duration of their marriage. He had then lost the child of her body. He had never, however, lost his desire for revenge. It was a dish best served cold, the Italians said. If he could look upon the scarred face of François Mattei just once more and see terror quivering in those pale eyes, then it would have been well worth the wait.

Chapter Ten

The Sea Cave

*F*or three days the work went forward on the careened ship. The ragged base of the foremast was removed, and the scraping of the hull commenced. The sailors built rough ladders to scale the sides of the ship or hung on ropes from the canted gunwale. It was gritty, sweaty, time-consuming work.

On the fourth day, the captain rode inland with Gilbert to look over some lumber for the new mast. The tall, straight trees that shipbuilders required were rare on this windswept coast. Matthew had warned Lydia not to expect him back until nightfall.

She was sorry now she'd told him she liked it when he was all sailor. He'd carried that behavior to an extreme these past days. She was rarely in his company, and even when she was, he was either dirty, sleepy or hungry. And not hungry for her, either.

The only bright spot was that his relationship with Jean-Louis had improved. She often saw them laughing together as they worked on the ship. It pleased her that he was making time for his ward; she only wished he would spare a bit of it for her. She couldn't help fretting that he had changed his mind about leaving the door open for her.

To distract herself, she'd taken to spending her

mornings teaching French to Tilda. Her early after-
noons were occupied teaching English to Sebastian,
when the workers rested out of the midday sun.
They'd better name their first daughter after her, for
all the effort she was making.

That particular afternoon the sun was more blaz-
ingly hot than ever. The workmen broke early, and
Sebastian disappeared with her maid. Apparently
Tilda was going to give her own English lessons today.
Lydia watched them stroll off arm in arm and wished
her own beau hadn't ridden off somewhere to look at
masts. Why hadn't her mother or Nadia ever warned
her not to fall in love with a sailor?

She plucked at the neckline of her blouse. Gad, everything was sticking to her in the heat. She would
have stripped off her clothing and swum in the cove
if there hadn't been at least fifteen interested males
lounging nearby.

She pulled off her slippers and trudged barefoot
along the beach, hoping the lapping waves would cool
her. A pity there wasn't a more private place for bath-
ing. It wasn't until she was almost at the end of the
cove that she remembered Jean-Louis's cave.

Hiking up her skirts, she waded around the barrier
of rocks until she came to the narrow stream and then
followed it into the mouth of the cave. It was as beautiful as she remembered, a cool, shadowed sanctuary.
She quickly shed her skirt and blouse and stepped
into the pool wearing just her chemise. The water was
delightfully cool, the sandy bottom silky against her
bare feet.

She lay on her back and floated blissfully, the slight
currents fanning her hair away from her head. Drifting
aimlessly, she kicked gently away from the shallows,
back and forth across the deepest part of the pool,
barely encumbered by her chemise. Above her, the
cave narrowed into dark eaves. She wondered idly if
there were bats up there and decided that if there
were, they were fortunate to live in such a magical
place.

There had been a lake at Levelands where she and her cousins had learned to swim, but it was full of pickerel weeds, bullfrogs and other squirmy things. This placid pool was the antithesis of her cousin's lake.

"Mmmm," she mused aloud. "It's wonderful, no weeds, no turtles . . ."

"And not a water hyacinth in sight."

The gruff voice sounded unexpectedly in the quiet cave. Lydia shrieked and almost went under.

"H-how long have you been there?" she sputtered at the captain, who was crouched at the edge of the pool, backlit by the cave's opening.

"Long enough," he drawled.

"What are you doing here?"

"Watching you. I thought that was obvious."

"Well, you shouldn't be here. I'm having a bath."

"In your chemise?"

"Yes—and a good thing too."

"No, it's rather more a pity. Not that wet muslin leaves much to the imagination."

"You are supposed to be inland," she chided him, paddling backwards. "Looking at masts."

"As it happens, we met a fellow in Lempère who wants to give us a mast, a shipbuilder from Brest whose sister lives near here—her farm was robbed twice by the brigands, so he's offered to deliver it by way of thanks."

"That was very decent of him—W-w-what are you doing now?" He'd tugged off his boots and shirt and was wading into the water still clad in his breeches.

"Lydia, I'm going to lose all regard for you if you keep asking me such nonsensical questions."

She tried to swim away from him, but he caught her at the center of the pool. His arms closed around her and turned her into his embrace.

"Matthew! I'm all wet." She struggled against his hold. This wasn't how she wanted him to see her, not with her sopping gown plastered to her and her sodden hair trailing down her neck.

"We're both wet now, sweetheart." His eyes shone

with mirth, but they darkened as his arms tightened. "God, Lydia, it feels an age since I've held you."

"I really don't think you should be here. What if one of the boys comes along?"

"Gilbert's had his orders. Short of French cavalry charging over the cliffs, no one is to disturb us. Have you lost heart, Lydia? Is that what this is about?" He searched her face.

When she made no response, he released her, moving to the shallows. He pulled himself up onto the sand and sat, one arm upon his bent knee, regarding her with narrowed eyes.

Had she lost heart? No, of course she hadn't. His timing was just a little off. Three days off, to be precise. She was miffed by his inattention, and now he was miffed by her peevish behavior. She didn't know which one of them was more prickly.

She swam a few strokes closer, unsure of how to heal the breach. He was still watching her intently.

"Jean-Louis said there were mermaids in this pool," he murmured. "I thought he was imagining things until I saw you swimming here. You *are* like a bewitching siren." His voice was lulling away her doubts. "Don't swim away from me, back to your home beneath the sea. Stay here on land . . . where a mortal man can touch you."

He leaned forward, holding out one hand to her. When she reached for it, he pulled her right up from the pool, water running in rivulets all down her body, and locked his mouth onto hers.

It was as though they'd never been apart—as though they were again on his bed—the sensations returned to her that quickly. His mouth, hard and insistent, his hands caressing her body. The fire that had simmered inside her for over three days quickly ignited.

He was kissing her neck . . . sucking on the skin . . . moving his head back and forth until she wanted to cry out with the pain of it . . . only it didn't hurt, but she wanted to cry out anyway . . . and then he was

running his teeth over her shoulder, which was bare,
because he had stripped her of her damp chemise . . .
and, oh, god, he was pulling at her breast with his
mouth, tugging at it . . . and again, the pain-that-
wasn't-pain washed over her.

"Matthew . . . ah . . . Matthew," she panted.

He lowered her onto the sand, his hand drifting far
down her belly, stroking heat against that hidden
place, until she gasped and struggled to sit up. He
kissed her deeply, drugging her with the taste of him,
the feel of him, taming her so that she lay back, moaning and mewling, certain she was going to die.

He quickly tugged out of his breeches, then cast
himself on top of her, pinning her arms above her
head, his hands hard on her wrists, the long slick of
his naked body holding her down. His eyes were
fierce—full and potent—as they bored into hers. When
she met that gaze boldly, a sizzling spark leapt between them.

"Now," he rasped. "*Now.* And God help you if you
cry out, for I shall never stop then, never."

She did cry out as he entered her, from the stinging
pain, and then soon after from the wonder of feeling
him deep, deep inside her. She groaned when he
pulled back from her. He was waiting, watching to see
if she would take him again, to see, even in his moment of driving passion, if she was ailing or hurt. Her
eyes reassured him, and so he thrust again inside her,
reading her low gasps now as pleasure and desire.

Matthew knew it had been a long time, too damn
long since he'd had a woman, and never, never had
he taken a woman like this. His Lydia, flushed and
burning for him, skin and face aflame with passion.
He'd give her small pleasure this time. She was too
hot and wet and, God, so tight, and he was . . . he
was . . . *God . . . ! No!*

Lydia tightened her hold on Matthew's waist. She
thought he must be asleep, he was so still in her arms.
As long as she lived, she would never forget the look
in his eyes when he had taken her. There had been an

eternity of hunger in them and a world of vindication. Afterward, he had kissed her tenderly and murmured, "It'll be better next time, sweetheart."

Whatever could he have meant by that?

She trailed her fingers from the small of his back to his nape, savoring the hard, sleek surface. A lock of his damp hair clung to one shoulder, and she smoothed it back. There was something there beneath the silver-black skein of hair, a small tattoo. As if he sensed her scrutiny, he shifted against her and then leaned up on one elbow, his mouth curved into a lazy smile.

"Hello, Princess. Did you have a nice nap?"

"I didn't sleep. I've been looking at you while you slept."

When he grimaced, her eyes narrowed. "Matthew . . . why do I get the feeling you believe I care for you in *spite* of your appearance?"

"You'd have to. Not much here to recommend me." He twined his hand through her ringlets. "Especially compared to the present company."

"How can I make you understand how much it pleases me to look at you? Your body is so beautiful to me, the muscles and the skin, so smooth and hard. And your face—"

"Ah, no." He squinted, and she slapped him on the arm.

"Stop it. You have a remarkable face—intelligent, compelling, heroic, even. I should think women would stop and stare at that face."

"In my youth perhaps. Now women mostly stare at my fetching scar."

He looked at the unguarded adoration in her face and could not comprehend it. "I wish I was more things for you, Lydia. Richer, maybe. Younger, certainly. I wish I had some stature I could share with you. You give me so much."

"Me? I'm a foolish gadabout with no other purpose in life than to look pretty."

"Well, you do that rather effortlessly. You are also

intrepid, frighteningly brave, good-natured, generous, and warmhearted, and you amuse me more than any woman I've ever met."

Her eyes glowed. No man had ever called her intrepid before, or generous.

"And," he added with a glimmer of humor, "you kiss like a waterfront doxy—high praise coming from a sailing man."

"Matthew!" She launched herself at him in mock outrage. He fended her off, laughing and kissing her all along her throat.

"Come now, we've got to be getting back. Stop trying to have your evil way with me." He released her and pulled on his breeches. She reached for her chemise, wrestling the damp folds over her head. He had started to tug on his shirt, when she stopped him.

"What is that?" She touched the mark on his shoulder, tracing the purple and black device.

"Nothing. A tattoo."

"I know it's a tattoo. But what is it? It looks like some sort of flower."

"You don't find it off-putting?"

"No, not a bit. Though you're the first man I've ever met with one."

"Then you don't hang about much with sailors."

"Not until very recently," she said with a dry look. "But what is it?"

"It's a nightshade."

"Isn't that a poisonous plant?"

"Yes, deadly nightshade—part of a witch's brew, no doubt, for bringing on warts or boils."

"Then why did you chose that flower? Why not a rose or a snapdragon?"

"Does it matter?" He wasn't sure he liked the direction this was leading them.

Especially when her eyes widened and she exclaimed, "It's the purple flower! The one the gypsy spoke of. Oh, you must tell me, Matthew; what does it signify?"

He shrugged and said matter-of-factly, "It was my

code name while I was on assignment in France. Intelligence officers use a simple, distinctive cartouche for sending messages. I chose Nightshade.''

''Weren't you afraid someone in France might see the tattoo and discover your secret identity?''

''I hadn't got it yet. I told you I spent a lot of time in grogshops once I left the service. One night after a real head-pounder, I found myself in a tattoo parlor. I sketched it for the fellow.''

''*Were* you deadly, Matthew? Is that why you chose that name?''

''It was just a caprice. It's not something I want to talk about.''

''It's just that I saw how well you handle a sword and—''

''I was protecting you, if you recall,'' he said tersely.

''And you've probably had to put people . . . out of the way.''

''That's a nice drawing-room way of saying I killed them.''

''I s-somehow thought when you said you'd done base things, it was more like breaking into people's homes, stealing important documents . . . Oh, I don't know what I thought. It doesn't matter. I know you don't want to talk about it.''

It was too late. He'd shifted back from her, his eyes wary and hooded.

''If I'd been a bonny soldier, if I'd ridden off to war with a regiment and killed a hundred Frenchmen from an honorable distance, you'd have applauded me. But since I sometimes took lives at close quarters, with a knife or a sword, you find me questionable.''

''No,'' she protested. ''I—''

''Don't deny it. I see the look in your eyes. Dismay, distaste, perhaps even disgust.''

''No, never—''

He had risen to his feet, knocking the sand off his breeches with brisk strokes.

''Matthew,'' she cried, dragging him back down beside her. ''Don't you dare tell me how I'm feeling.''

She took his face between her hands, but he refused to meet her eyes. His arms were braced stiffly on either side of her, the corded muscles stretched taut in his throat.

"It's no good, Lydia." He tried to shake off her hands, but she held firm.

"Matthew, look at me."

"No . . . a drowning man closes his eyes to the sky."

"You are not drowning and I am certainly not the sky. Please look at me."

He did look, in spite of his resolve. One glimpse he'd allow himself before leaving her. She was gazing at him with a puzzled, yearning expression.

"You always were too forward, Miss Peartree. 'Tis a sad failing in a lady."

"It's a good thing one of us is forward, Captain, or we'd not have gotten this far."

He broke her hold and wrenched away from her. "We'll go no further. I wish I could say I'd left you as I found you, still a maid. But you'll survive, I think . . . and you can't say I didn't warn you about my past. And now I've got work to do."

He rose and stood there, weaving slightly. Standing away from Lydia was the hardest thing he'd ever done. God, it seemed as though he was always doing it.

Lydia didn't speak until he was at the mouth of the cave.

"I love you, Matthew." The words were uttered with all the intensity she could muster.

He halted and turned to her. The bright sun was upon him now, his arms and chest darkly bronzed, his hair a spill of silver and ebony. She thought he had never appeared more vital. With his patrician cheekbones and unearthly eyes, he might have been a fallen archangel. It was only the hawklike profile and strong, jutting chin that turned the beauty of his face to something stark, rugged and masculine.

"I said I love you."

"Love," he echoed blankly. "What can you know of love?"

"Only what is in my heart," she said. "Is that not enough?"

"Love is never enough." He made no attempt to disguise the bitterness in his voice.

"It would be, if you loved me. It would be enough."

He took a step toward her. "*If* I loved you? Are you a fool then, that you would seek the love of such a man?" He circled the pool in three strides and pulled her roughly to her feet. "Is this what you want to love you—a lurker, a deceiver, a destroyer of other men's souls. I told you about what happened in Paris. I told you about the death and the betrayal. I thought you would flee from me then. But you didn't. I can make you flee now, Lydia."

She set her chin defiantly, but she was trembling before his cold fury.

"Let me not mince words. I was called Nightshade for good reason. I went to France to do a dirty business; I went to spy and, when necessary, to kill. I have been an assassin more than once. Is that what you want? A man who treads softly in the night and steals a life. A man who traded his soul fifteen years ago to keep England safe."

He took her trembling hand and pressed it to his scarred eye. "Is this creature who is halfway to perdition what you desire? Is this what you love?"

Lydia knew that if she gave vent to her tears, he would read them as horror and be lost to her forever. What she was feeling was horror of a sort—the horror of discovering just how deeply he had been marked by the dark work his country had sent him to do.

"No." She controlled the vibrato in her voice by sheer will. "That is not what I love."

"I thought not."

She wanted to box his ears for being so pigheadedly contrary. "You must think me very shortsighted if I cannot see past who you were to what you have become. I . . . I admit that loving you is not the wisest thing I've ever done, but—"

"Ah, you begin to show some sense."

"Hush, let me finish. My misgivings have nothing to do with your other life. It's just that it's very difficult to love someone who is forever pushing me away. I am twenty-seven years old and have never been in love before now. Oh, I have flirted and had my infatuations—"

"This is no more than that—a badly timed infatuation."

"I don't think so. I quite disliked you when we first met. No, this feeling has come from a deeper part of me, and I must heed it."

"Then I am sorry for you. These feelings of yours have no foundation."

"I don't blame you for thinking that, knowing what you do of my frivolous history. But I'd hope you would discount my past when I tell you that I love you with everything that's inside me."

He felt his resolve begin to falter. Never in his wildest imaginings had he thought to hear those words from her lips.

"And would you have me discount *my* past, as well?"

"It's your future I'm more concerned with." A wry smile curled her mouth as she raised his hand to her lips.

"Don't!" He snatched it back. "There can be nothing between us."

"No. Not if you don't love me." Her eyes probed his face, keen as a surgeon's blade.

He knew what she was doing: she believed he couldn't lie about his feelings for her—and she was right. As low as he'd sunk in his life, there were some things he would not do.

He sidestepped her implied question.

"Love has nothing to do with it, Lydia. Nothing can redeem me. Not love, not trust. What is damaged inside me cannot be mended by pretty words or delicate sentiments. Ah, I see you are still not attending me. Shall I put my hands on your throat again to remind you of the foul thing I once was?"

"Only if you plan on finishing the job," she shot back. "Because short of killing me, you will not be rid of me in this lifetime." She took a step closer. "Well?" she challenged. "I'm waiting."

"If I kill you," he mused, losing himself in the blue intensity of her eyes, "you will doubtless haunt me."

"No, Matthew," she said softly. "I don't think you have room for any more ghosts."

He smiled slowly, tipping his head forward until their brows met. "Aye," he said. "Too many ghosts. Perhaps it's time I laid them to rest."

"Yes, my love." She raised a hand to his cheek and was rewarded when he leaned into her palm.

"Lydia," he breathed. "Will you, can you, take me as I am? Scarred, poisoned—"

"Honorable, brave," she countered.

"Ah, you are quite daft."

"Yes," she smiled. "Hopelessly."

"Shall I tell you that I love you? Will you believe me?"

"You've never lied to me before."

He winced inwardly. "Ah, but I've lied to myself, and often."

"Then tell me when you believe it yourself."

He caught her by the shoulders, his hands almost painfully possessive. "I can tell you this, sweetheart . . . that I could no more let you go than I could stop breathing. That you are more precious to me and more fine than all the riches of the known universe." His palm drifted over the rise of her breast. "And that I will desire you, and only you . . . till the heavens rip asunder and the world is turned to dust."

Lydia's throat had closed up; she could barely speak from the wonder of his words. "It's enough," she managed to get out. "Oh, Matthew, it's more than enough."

This time Lydia slept, and Matthew observed her. He had made love to her again—slow, languid, honeyed love—beside the aquamarine pool. He'd kept her at the edge of her pleasure until she had begged him to free her. Only it hadn't freed her—it had bound her to him, he knew, in ways he could only try to comprehend.

One thing he did know—he would never willingly part from her. All her bounty and her beauty were indelibly entwined within him. Her every cry and moan of pleasure was an ancient song that raced through his veins and fired him anew. Her laughter and grace brought back vivid traces of a happier time in his life. Every gift she offered completed him. Every token she bestowed enriched him. No woman, not even his beloved Marianne, had ever filled him so totally.

He looked down at her, cradled against his chest. Her beauty frightened him at times. Was it a burden, he wondered, to carry such loveliness out into the world? Men had surely judged her on those looks alone and rarely seen the fine character and deep warmth that lay beneath the gossamer surface. But he had seen and valued her for them. He had seen and loved. Without her beauty, Lydia Peartree would still be an amazing woman.

She made him feel as though he could be whole once more. No, he was whole. He felt the tendrils of trust working their way gently but inexorably back into his soul.

"Princess . . ." He whispered a kiss against her ear. She made an inarticulate noise deep in her throat and turned slightly, her head seeking the hollow of his shoulder. She had one long leg angled across his thighs, and her breasts were pressed against his chest. He had remained inside her after his shuddering release, loathe to sever the sweet connection. Now the clefts of their bodies were still touching, fused no longer but joined by a constant, thrumming awareness. He felt himself stir and begin to grow hard again. God, she *was* going to kill him.

He eased his way out from beneath her, bundling his shirt to pillow her head. She groaned softly as he drew away, seeking, even in her sleep, for the reassuring warmth of his body.

He made a shallow, arcing dive into the pool and then floated, as Lydia had done, gazing up at the vaulted ceiling. The cool water was having a properly quelling effect on his ardor.

His crew were probably done with their break and back working on the ship. He had an uncanny feeling that all but the youngest of them could guess exactly what he and Miss Peartree were up to. Gilbert, he knew for a fact, had not been happy to watch him saunter off to meet her.

Matthew believed he'd set the boys a good example of gentlemanly conduct, kept to the code that insisted women be treated with respect. Until now. He'd have to set things right—and quickly. Perhaps he could even wangle one more favor out of the mayor of Lempère.

Lydia slid into the pool behind him with a soft splash.

"Mmm," she murmured into his nape. "It's colder now. It feels wonderful." Her hands moved lower in the water, running along the hard, flat contours of his stomach. "You feel wonderful."

"You are quite shameless," he chided, turning in her embrace. "Sometimes I think I must have invented you."

She gave him a smug, feline grin. "I feel the same way about you."

"Listen, Lydia, we've whiled away the afternoon here and—"

"I know. You're going to tell me we should be getting back. It feels like we've been here for days."

"That's not precisely what I was going to say." He drew away from her and stood up, the water lapping just below his naval. He slicked his hair back and turned to Lydia, who was perusing him with great interest. "Stop staring, you wicked girl. Come on, we do have to get back." He tugged her from the water and then dried her off with his shirt.

"What were you going to say?" she asked as he coaxed her into the damp chemise.

"I'm afraid there's a forfeit to pay for shirking our duties this afternoon." He had pulled on his breeches and was tightening the laces.

"You weren't shirking, Captain. Not that I could see." She wrinkled her nose at him and then danced out of range as he tried to pull her hair.

"Maddening wench," he muttered. "So we weren't shirking. But there is still a price to be paid. Will you be serious a minute, Lydia?" She was drawing hearts in the sand with her bare toes.

"Oh, all right." She plumped down at the edge of the pool. "What is this forfeit? I have an uncanny feeling I'll be the one to pay it. You're the captain—you never have to do anything disagreeable." She threw her head back dramatically. "What are you going to do? Force me to walk the plank? Hang me from the yardarm? Make me eat seaweed?"

"Marry you," he said.

She blinked once before she uttered, "No."

"Yes, Lydia." He hadn't expected her to refuse him so abruptly.

"I mean, no, will you really?" A blush of joy suffused her cheeks.

He lowered himself beside her. "Yes," he said gruffly. "If you will have me."

Have him? Was he mad? She'd never wanted anything so keenly in her whole twenty-seven years. He wasn't going to send her back to amiable Donald, who had never even tried to kiss her. Oh, dear, sweet, wonderful Matthew.

She gripped his shoulders urgently. "You're not just saying this because you and I . . . because we . . . ? Oh, Matthew, tell me you're not being stupidly noble? I don't want you to marry me just because you think it's proper."

He lowered his head to her throat and laughed silently. Only Lydia, his glorious, complex, infuriating Lydia, could accuse a man who was holding her nearly naked body against him of being too proper. What was he to do with her?

"Next week, in Lempère, before the mayor, I intend to make you my wife." There, that was a declaration that would set any maiden's heart to throbbing.

She was still looking at him dubiously.

"Because," he said with a deal more tenderness, "I can't think of spending a day without you beside me. Not just this way—" He brushed his lips across her mouth. "But in every way. You have my heart, little jade, and my soul as well. You have all my love."

She leaned her damp head into his shoulder. She was choking softly. "Thank you, Matthew. Thank you."

He pulled her head back, astonished by the tears coursing down her cheeks. "Ach, don't cry, Princess. It's not such a gift."

"Oh, it is. It is to me. Your words just now—they are everything to me."

He was confounded. "And just what do you think I've been saying for the past hour—telling you I will want you forever, that I can't bear to be parted from you. Did those words mean nothing?"

"I've heard that kind of talk from men before. Those were words of passion, not loving words or marrying words."

"I'm not quite sure I understand the difference."

But he did. He understood how relatively easy it had been to tell her he would desire her until the world turned to dust; it had taken a lot more fortitude to tell her how he felt.

"God, I do love you, Lydia." It was easier spoken the second time. "You must know it, sweetheart."

"I do now," she said softly.

"There will be no turning back from here. My moods, all my self-doubts, will no longer color my behavior. That I promise. I will not ever let you go."

"Never, Matthew?" She gazed at him raptly.

"Never while I live."

Chapter Eleven

The Web

*C*habrier reread the letter on his desk, needing to savor it again. His correspondent in Lempère had been thorough—there was a great deal of information contained on the sheet of vellum that lay beneath his hand. As he studied one name in particular, his face curved into a grim, unlovely smile.

Matthew Frobisher—a Devonshire schoolmaster, of all things.

He pondered whether he would have carried his blood feud to the green coast of Devon if he'd had this name sooner. No matter. Frobisher was in France now and likely to remain for some time. Forever, if the comte had his way. Buried in a pauper's grave with no one to mourn him save the scavenging rooks.

The woman was a bit more problematic.

He went to his bookcase and pulled out his Debrett's. The pages were well-thumbed, many of the names crossed out with crisp pen strokes. Soldiers, sailors, spies—any Englishman of aristocratic birth who had fallen victim in the war with France. It was Chabrier's tally book; he often read it at night when he couldn't sleep. It reassured him.

"Cyrus Peartree, Baron Meade," he read. "So created 1791. Wife, Princess Ivana Fokine, daughter of Prince Alexander Fokine of St. Petersburg. Daughter Lydia Anastasia, born 1787."

His brows rose. The Devon schoolmaster had rich taste. The daughter of a princess, no less.

Out of idle curiosity he looked up the name Frobisher. He was surprised to learn that the captain's family was a collateral branch of the Frobishers of Yorkshire, who had given the world the Elizabethan sea dog Martin Frobisher, hero against the Spanish Armada. It appeared Nightshade had some decent forebears after all.

That gave the comte something to look forward to—two bodies in a pauper's grave, two names inked out in his tally book.

As he began to compose a letter to his contact in Finistère, a stray beam of sunlight struck the glass paperweight on the desk, blinding him momentarily. With a soft curse, he got up and drew the heavy draperies across the mullioned window, then continued his missive in the shadowed darkness of his office.

It was a bright, clear morning. Lydia was sitting on the rocks near the beach, watching the captain and his men prepare the new mast, which had been laid over a half-dozen sawhorses. He'd promised her they would be heading home to Devon within days if the mast proved sound.

She couldn't wait to see Matthew's reaction when he finally saw her properly gowned and coiffed. Not that her present tattered appearance had affected his ardor. They'd mastered the art of stealing kisses. Still, England beckoned—especially after Matthew described the wide tester bed in his house in Exeter . . . and whispered all the things he could do to her on a plump feather quilt.

She started out of her daydream when a dark shadow fell over her. Jacques, one of the sailors from Lempère, was standing there, his eyes shifting uneasily. He quickly slid a letter into her hands, a creamy, heavyweight paper addressed to her in an elegant, spidery script.

Lydia thanked him and pocketed it in her apron.

So Father Boniface had at last deigned to answer the letter she'd written more than a week ago. She had all but given up on hearing from him. The day after the careening she'd smuggled the note to Jacques, asking him to deliver it to the priest. It seemed a small disloyalty to Matthew at the time and was the only thing she could think of to help Jean-Louis locate his family. Who better than a priest to respect a confidence?

Lydia paced across the shingle to her hut, where she quickly broke the seal and scanned the note.

"Miss Peartree," it began. "It would be greatly to the boy's benefit if you would bring him to me this afternoon. I have some answers to the questions you posed in your note. As this is a matter of some delicacy, however, it is imperative that you come only with the boy. I must insist on this, if you wish to receive the information I now possess."

She thought the priest's wording a trifle melodramatic. It appeared all men were the same—layman and cleric alike—all hankering to enliven their lives with intrigue, real or imagined. She'd play along with Boniface, and gladly, if it meant Jean-Louis would finally learn about his family. She *was* in full accord with the priest on one thing—she had no intention of revealing her true mission to the captain.

When she strolled up beside him as he worked a plane over the new mast, he raised his head with a smile. It turned to a frown when she told him she had been invited to take tea with the priest that afternoon.

"I'm afraid I can't spare the time today." He motioned to the ship, where his workers toiled, shirts off and muscles oiled with sweat. "Tell him maybe later in the week if we haven't sailed."

She pouted slightly but then said in a reasonable voice, "I certainly don't expect you to stop work to visit with a priest. I'll drive myself in the donkey cart. Jean-Louis can come with me. I think he could do with a little civilization. We both could."

The captain's mouth twisted. "So all this rough living's finally gotten to you, eh?"

"You know that's not the case. But I do think having tea in a priest's garden sounds like heaven."

His expression darkened. "No, heaven or not, I don't like it."

Lydia's brow furrowed as her temper stirred. She always got testy when she was feeling guilty. "Are you forbidding me? I could remind you that I am not one of your students to be ordered about."

He drew her away from the canted ship. "Easy, lass. It's just that I don't like having you out of my sight. You've already had a taste of how quickly things can turn ugly."

"I'm not made of glass, Captain. And I somehow doubt Father Boniface is secretly in league with the brigands."

He fetched a heavy sigh. "Oh, very well. But I insist you take Gilbert with you. He can buy supplies in Lempère while you're playing the grand lady in the priest's garden."

She wondered if the devoted Gilbert would be able to peel himself away from her. "Can you spare him?"

"I've no choice. I don't want you traveling alone—you never know what ruffians might be lurking along the road."

She was grumbling as she marched off. "I think they're all here working on your ship."

A briny, seaborne wind played over the high track that led to Lempère. Lydia brushed her hair back and raised her face to the warming afternoon sun. She had donned her Breton outfit for the occasion but it offered little protection from the stiff breeze.

The donkey was taking his time, ambling along in a halfhearted fashion.

"Can't that lop-eared furball go any faster?" Gilbert called down from his horse.

Jean-Louis shot him a look of annoyance. *"Avance, mon ami!"* he cried. At the sound of that favored voice, the donkey immediately quickened his pace.

"It's a marvel," Gilbert observed. "The little beast heeds him like a doting spaniel."

"It is because I save his life," the boy explained. "Donkeys never forget."

"I think you mean elephants," Lydia interjected.

"Elephants *and* donkeys," he amended.

"Elephants, donkeys, and *some* people," Gilbert said. "Especially the captain. He caught me in a lie once, covering up some foolishness of Rowdy's, and I don't think he's ever forgotten."

"But he forgave you, didn't he?" Lydia inquired with more than a little anxiety.

"Aye, he did. But I had to scrub floors for a month." Gilbert wrinkled his nose. "He's as fond of dishing out penance as that starchy old priest you're going to visit."

The village of Lempère soon appeared below them, the shops and houses that lined the cobbled main street sitting in a haze of yellow dust. The ancient church of Saint Christophe, its granite wall weathered and mossy, lay at the near end of the town. Recessed from the road, it was reached by a narrow lane with a graveyard on one side. A two-storied stone rectory fronted the main road.

Matthew had pointed out the priest's home several days earlier, when they had ridden to Lempère together. They had not stopped at the priest's that morning, however, but had gone on to visit the mayor. It had been a glorious day, she recalled with a sigh, the bright sun beaming down on the two of them—

"Look—" Gilbert was pointing to an elegant traveling coach drawn up in the lane. The body was a gleaming, polished black, the wheel spokes and fretwork picked out in yellow. "Someone important must be visiting the church."

"Probably religious pilgrims," Lydia said. "That

church looks old enough to possess a few interesting artifacts. Maybe even the toenail of a saint."

Gilbert chuckled, while Jean-Louis muttered darkly that it was bad luck to make light of saint's toenails.

"Do you want to come in for some tea and cake?" Lydia asked Gilbert, praying he would dislike it above anything.

He didn't disappoint her, screwing his face into an expression of distaste and reminding her he had errands to run. "There's an inn at the other end of town, so you needn't worry I'll starve."

Lydia sighed as he went trotting off toward the shops. Beside Matthew, the astute Gilbert was the last person she wanted to intrude on her meeting with the priest, but his departure left her feeling a bit hollow. She was of a mind to drive after him, to ask him to stay close by, but Jean-Louis was already tying the donkey's reins to the branches of a lilac bush.

The priest must have been watching for them; he came out his front door before they'd crossed the yard.

"Ah, Miss Peartree—" He held out both hands. "And Jean-Louis, is it not?"

"Yes." The boy nodded, and then bowed. "How do you do, Father Boniface. Thank you for inviting us to your house."

"Ah, my humble home. I hope you will not be disappointed."

Jean-Louis shook his head. "We have not been inside a proper house for many weeks. Only ships' cabins and fishermen's huts."

Lydia was surprised at his easy rapport with the rather austere cleric. Then she remembered he had been raised in a monastery. This must feel like a homecoming to him.

"You are quite welcome here, Jean-Louis, you and Miss Peartree both."

Jean-Louis gave him a wide smile, but then his expression tightened as his noticed the rows of headstones beyond the stone wall. "But are you not frightened to live beside a graveyard?"

"Ah, no. They are at peace, those souls," Father Boniface assured him. "The dead do not haunt us, my son."

The priest's eyes raised suddenly to Lydia's, and she realized she had gasped. He had inadvertently reminded her of Matthew's bitter proclamation . . . *The dead can strike at us as surely as the living.*

Lydia shook off an involuntary shiver and smiled evenly. "He has a vivid imagination."

"Most children do." The priest leaned down to Jean-Louis. "Our resident cat has just presented us with five new kittens. They're back in the barn, if you would like to see them."

Lydia gave his shoulder a slight nudge. Jean-Louis didn't hesitate but took off at an ambling trot toward the barn.

"A fanciful boy," the priest remarked thoughtfully. "I hadn't expected that. Now, if you will come inside, we can discuss your note."

Lydia nodded, fighting off her lingering feelings of guilt.

"I promised the child I would help him trace his family," she said as they passed into the hall. "Captain Frobisher told me you still had connections in Paris, so you seemed like my best resource."

"The boy is not from Paris, though. His speech is quite provincial," the priest observed as he ushered her into a room paneled in dark wood. Bookcases, maps and several fine paintings adorned the walls, and a small pianoforte stood in one corner. It was the elegant study of a man of culture and refinement.

Boniface motioned her to a chair and then went to his desk, where a tea service sat on a silver tray.

"He was from Provence originally," she said. "But his father spent most of his time in Paris. I wrote all this in my note."

"I am just clarifying, my dear." The priest poured

the tea into delicate porcelain cups. "Now, tell me, how came the child to be Captain Frobisher's ward?"

"I really couldn't say," Lydia demurred as she took the cup he held out.

The priest shook his head regretfully. "Miss Peartree, I wish you would trust me. Your note intrigued me, and I want to help. But I cannot assist you if there is no trust."

"I do trust you, Father. But by the same token, I cannot betray another's trust. I *can* tell you that Jean-Louis came to Captain Frobisher as a young child and cannot remember his family name. If the captain knows it, he has not revealed it to me."

"He is a man of secrets then?"

Lydia almost chuckled. "He keeps his own counsel," was all she permitted herself to say.

Though his mouth pursed, Father Boniface appeared to accept this. "Now, about your request. I wrote to one of my correspondents in Paris to inquire about the boy. I'm pleased to say my investigation was successful." He opened his desk drawer and drew out a sheaf of papers. "These arrived only this morning."

Lydia set down her teacup and stood up. This was more than she had even hoped for.

The priest had spread the papers over his blotter—five or six newspaper clippings, several flyers, and a pencil sketch of some sort, half hidden by a handbill.

A broadside, dated six years earlier and yellowed with age, caught her eye. It advertised a large reward for the capture of a man who had kidnapped a child from Provence. Something about the wording bothered Lydia. Why was the reward not for the return of the child himself? she wondered as she read the smaller print, which was a description of the missing boy.

"The child's hair is of a chestnut color, thick and straight," she read aloud. "He is medium complected, the eyes a greenish-brown. He is slender and bears a scar in the shape of a half-moon behind his right ear.

"It could be Jean-Louis," she murmured. "His coloring, the scar on his neck . . . He hates that mark; he's always tugging his hair over it."

The cleric sat down and steepled his fingers. "Read on, Miss Peartree."

There was also a description of the person suspected of the crime, a tall, spare man, it said, with pale eyes and graying hair. It was odd that they had been able to describe Matthew so clearly—he'd been so sure no one saw him take the boy.

"And does that description resemble anyone?" the priest asked softly.

"It could fit many men, Father." She smiled archly. "Even you."

She was heartily beginning to regret enlisting him in her quest. It had been foolish to think she could keep Matthew out of any investigation of his ward's past.

"It does rather bring to mind one man in particular. Captain Frobisher is a tall, spare man."

"If he took the child—and I am saying this only as a conjecture—then I am sure it was with good reason."

The priest tapped the papers with a narrow finger. "There's more here."

One by one, Lydia picked them up and scanned them. Most were newspaper clippings worded similarly to the broadside. There was also an article which seemed unrelated to the boy's abduction. It told of the brutal murder of a lace merchant named Macanée. His body had been found near the Seine, stabbed repeatedly.

Lydia held it up with a puzzled frown. "What has this to do with Jean-Louis?"

"Macanée swore he knew the identity of the child's abductor," Father Boniface explained. "He had boasted to his friends in a tavern that he would claim the reward. It's not a stretch to think that someone killed him to keep him silent."

Lydia felt herself starting to sweat. "I don't understand," she said. "There is no mention of murder in this story. The merchant could have been the victim of footpads."

"My correspondent assures me that Macanée was a threat to the man who abducted the boy."

"There's another thing," Lydia went on doggedly, trying to disregard the ripples of alarm spreading down her spine. "Children go missing every day. Why was there a nationwide outcry over this particular boy? I understand the concern over any lost child, but I can't comprehend the extent of this search—all these broadsides and advertisements. And how is it that, six years after the fact, someone in Paris was able to lay their hands on these documents?"

The priest shrugged. "I was equally surprised that my colleague was so prompt and so thorough. But now that I know who the child's father is, I am not amazed. No, not amazed at all."

"Who was his father?"

"Not *was*, Miss Peartree, *is*. Jean-Louis's father is the Comte de Chabrier."

Lydia could not prevent an audible gasp. Chabrier was a highly placed French minister and, if Sir Robert was to be believed, something of a wily snake.

"It was he who furnished these documents," the priest went on. "Who else but the father would have kept such grim mementos? I assume you have heard of Chabrier, minister of police under Napoleon . . . and now under our beloved Louis. Whoever stole his child struck very high."

"He is dead!" Lydia cried, still unable to face the ramifications of Boniface's chilling revelation. "The boy's father is dead. I explained that in my note. Killed in a tavern brawl—over a trollop, if you must know. I only wanted to discover Jean-Louis's family name, to learn if he had any other relations left alive. There *is* no father." She repeated it because she needed desperately to believe it, to believe that Matthew had not lied, had not told her such a despicable untruth.

"Jean-Louis's family name is Chabrier," the priest

recited patiently. "He is the only son of Lucien, Comte de Chabrier, and of his late wife, Marianne Dieudonne."

Marianne . . . the same name Matthew had spoken. And Chabrier . . . minister of police, the man Matthew had called a jackal. There was now open distress in her face.

"Come, my dear, compose yourself. You should be glad that this has worked out so favorably for the child. He has a very bright future with such a man."

"The captain *did* tell me one thing—he said the boy's father possessed an unsteady character."

The priest shrugged. "Men of power are often targets for slander. Besides, any dutiful Englishman would be bound to say that of Chabrier—when he was Napoleon's right hand, he plotted your country's defeat."

"I tell you this is a mistake!" she cried, her hands gripping the edge of his desk. "There must be another child."

"Mam'selle?" Jean-Louis peeked into the study. "Father Boniface?"

The cleric smiled, motioning him inside. "Did you enjoy those kittens? Are they not God's own little imps?"

"Yes, they are very bad kittens." Jean-Louis's gaze swung to Lydia. *"Mam'selle*, you are unwell?"

"I'm fine." She gave him a swift, forced smile. "But I think it is time we were going."

"Ah—" The priest held up a hand, and she saw that his fingers were twisted with arthritis. "There is one additional piece of evidence."

"You sound like a lawyer," she said scornfully.

"Yes, well, that was my previous profession . . . before I was touched by the hand of God." He crossed himself and looked solemn for a moment before he picked up the sketch she had noticed earlier.

"It can make no difference," she proclaimed.

As if in defeat, he let the paper drift from his fingers. It fell onto the carpeted floor at Jean-Louis's feet. The boy bent to retrieve it.

"Here, Father . . ." He held it out, glancing down for an instant—and his mouth twisted into a rictus of shock. *"Maman!"* he cried. "Oh, *Maman!"*

The priest stared at Lydia, eyes burning with relentless intent. "I believe you have your answer now, Miss Peartree."

With a dazed expression, she sank back into her chair.

"And so, we must decide what is best to do. The comte is most eager to see his son. He even had the forethought to send his own coach with these papers. My orders are to leave for Paris at once with the boy."

"My father is in Paris?" Jean-Louis asked in a hushed voice.

"Yes, he is alive." The priest touched his russet hair. "And only awaits your return."

"Then I must go to him." A tremulous joy colored his cheeks and brightened his eyes. He turned to her questioningly. *"Mam'selle?* Is it not right that I go?"

"I don't know what you should do." This was happening too fast. She needed time to think. "I . . . I believe we must ask the captain."

The boy's eyes dulled slightly. "The *capitaine* . . . he told me my father was dead. I did not think he would ever lie to me."

The priest's thin mouth tightened. "You may do as you see fit, ma'am. But I am leaving for Paris today . . . with the boy."

"No," she cried, rising again to face him. "He is my responsibility. You can't just take him away. This is not why we came here." She nearly sobbed.

"It is, alas, why I invited you. To put right a very serious wrong. I have a duty to this child."

"I have a duty as well—to see him returned to Evionne Cove."

He shook his head. "You are completely at liberty to return. But I have a sacred commission, before God Himself, to reunite this child with his father."

"No," Lydia said, and again, "no." But her resistance was faltering. It was hard to stand firm against a man who so easily invoked the name of the Lord.

"There can be no further argument, I think. In your woman's heart you know I am doing the right and just thing."

Jean-Louis, who'd been watching this exchange with anxious eyes, now gripped her hand. "Is this not what you wanted for me? Is this not what you promised?"

"No . . . I mean, yes. Yes, I wanted you to find your family. But Paris is so far away . . ."

"Then come with me, *mam'selle*. Oh, please." He swung to the priest. "May she come with us? Please say she may."

Father Boniface reflected a moment. "The child's father sent enough money to cover your expenses, Miss Peartree. But I would not coerce you."

Would you not? she thought wrathfully. He had to know she couldn't let Jean-Louis go off with a complete stranger, regardless of his holy calling. And short of bashing Father Boniface over the head with the fat volume of Homer on his desk, she had no idea how she could physically prevent him from carrying out his plan. Especially since Jean-Louis himself seemed more than willing to accompany him.

Gilbert would have aided her, she knew. He was probably sitting down to a late luncheon at this moment. By the time she reached him, Father Boniface and the boy would be long gone.

She had a distressing vision of Matthew's face when she confessed to him that she had lost his ward—through her own misguided intentions, no less. It was not to be borne. There was only one way out of this untenable situation she had unwittingly created. It was the only way that would serve Jean-Louis. Because, Lydia acknowledged, *she* also had a duty to see to his welfare, one of longer standing than the priest's righteous claim.

"You leave me with no choice, Father. I must go with you."

"A wise decision," he murmured.

"Ah, thank you, *mam'selle*," Jean-Louis cried.

"I will need a shawl or a cloak of some kind." Her voice was dull, emotionless.

"Of course. I will see what I can find."

Boniface gathered up the documents from his desk and disappeared into the hall. Lydia and Jean-Louis glanced at each other, but there were no easy words between them. Lydia knew her face did not invite confidences.

The priest returned carrying a faded black bombazine cape with a wide hood. "My housekeeper's Sunday best. Not new, I'm afraid, but it's clean."

He draped it over her shoulders, smoothing down the hood with one hand. She nearly shrank away from the whispery touch of his twisted fingers.

"We must leave a note," she said.

"That is not a good idea. I am loathe to remind you of this, but that *gentleman* we spoke of earlier"—he cast a quick look at Jean-Louis—"has already disposed of one man who tried to interfere. We dare not risk it."

"I am at no risk certainly," she protested.

His pale eyes probed her face. "Search your soul, my dear, and tell me if you honestly believe that."

The words Matthew had spoken in the cave came rushing back to her. *I have done unspeakable things . . . I went to spy and, when necessary, to kill. . . . I have been an assassin more than once.*

She swallowed thickly and then nodded. Before Lydia could make any more protests, Father Boniface bundled her and the boy out the front door. He raised a hand to the coachman in the lane, who mounted the box and brought the coach around to the gate. Lydia was hanging back, desperately trying to think of a way to stall until Gilbert came to fetch them. Mindless of her obvious distress, Jean-Louis climbed eagerly into the coach.

"Miss Peartree?" Father Boniface was holding the door wide.

Her heart lurched. "Oh, no! I've . . . I've left my

reticule inside," she stammered in confusion, hiding her purse in the folds of the cloak. "Please wait."

"Make haste," the priest hissed.

Lydia ran back to the study, her heart pounding. Dear God, how had things come to this pass? She knew she had to go with them, but how could she leave Matthew with no explanation? Even if she wasn't sure he deserved one, she couldn't put him through such anguish. Jean-Louis was not the only one she had made promises to.

She had vowed to love Matthew in spite of his past. Yet how could she love a man who stole a child from his father? A man who killed ruthlessly to protect his anonymity? A man who deceived her and then took her in his arms and kissed her? She must be lost to all hope, she thought, because even if he were all those things—kidnapper, assassin and liar—she would love him till she died.

As her eyes filled with tears, she tugged her handkerchief from her reticule. The monogrammed scrap of lace had been misplaced aboard the *Rook*; Matthew had discovered it that morning in the storage hut and had presented it to her with a flourish.

Matthew . . . It was unthinkable to leave him without a word. She was certain he would search this house, and so she hefted the copy of Homer's *Iliad* from the desk, quickly thumbing through the illustrations bound into the front until she came to the one she sought. She placed her handkerchief over the edge of the drawing and closed the book.

When she heard Father Boniface in the hall, she quickly set the book on the spinet's music stand and went forward to meet him.

"I found it," Lydia said, holding her reticule up by its woven cord.

The priest made no response as he hurried her down the path. One of the coachmen was holding the door open. He coughed and spat as they approached, and Lydia had to dodge out of range.

It was not an auspicious beginning to their journey.

Chapter Twelve

The Priest's Secret

*G*ilbert was sitting in the *Chat Noir*, staring into the amber depths of his ale. He had completed his errands and should have been enjoying his meal, but something was troubling him. He worried at the vague disquiet as if it was a bit of undercooked mutton.

The black coach, he realized suddenly, was at the root of his misgivings. Though it had been parked in the lane that led to the church, it had been drawn up closer to the rectory. Wealthy pilgrims did not leave their coaches to walk along dusty country lanes, not if they didn't have to.

Damnation. He couldn't let it rest. Matthew Frobisher had taught him that it always paid to heed those insistent inner voices, and right now his intuition was pricking him like a burdock seed.

Gilbert swallowed the last of his ale and then set the mug down with a determined thump. The captain would have his hide if anything happened to Lydia.

The rectory was overtopped by a wide chestnut tree; at this hour of the afternoon it lay in deep shadow. As he pulled up beside the donkey cart, Gilbert could see no light from within—and the black coach was gone.

The first tug of real anxiety twisted in his belly.

He ran to the door and banged on it. He waited and then hammered again even harder. *Was the man deaf?* After a minute of fruitless knocking, he tried the door. It was locked. Gilbert muttered an oath of frustration as he headed toward the church. It was possible they were merely touring the sanctuary. As he entered the eerie, musk-scented darkness, he noticed a covey of old women kneeling before the flickering candles at a side altar.

"The priest? The English lady?" he asked rapidly in French. "Have you seen them?"

They shook their heads in confusion.

"What about the coach? Do you know who was traveling in that black coach?"

Again they could offer no help.

When he stepped out into daylight, the hair on the back of his neck was standing full on end. They had disappeared, as if into the very air.

Gilbert returned to the town and canvassed every shop along the main street. No one had seen the priest, the English lady or the chestnut-haired boy. Only the baker had seen the black coach. "It arrived here late this morning. And I think I heard it going past some time ago."

"Which way was it headed? Did you see who was inside?" Gilbert asked.

The baker gave an infuriatingly vague Gallic shrug. "Who can say? I mind my dough, young rascal, not the comings and goings of coaches."

Gilbert was already out in the street, running for his horse. Captain Frobisher would sort this out. He would know what to do.

Matthew was enjoying his pipe, sitting at the water's edge on a high, flat rock. His gaze kept straying to the top of the path; Lydia and the boys should be back any time now. He had missed her that afternoon, especially since they'd parted in ill humor. In truth, he missed her when she was out of sight for more than ten minutes.

Finally, he shifted to look across the cove to the entrance of the sea cave. They had returned to it only once, in spite of how things stood between them. The weather had cooled significantly, and so the workers' afternoon breaks were abandoned in order to move ahead with the ship's repairs. He and Lydia had been forced to content themselves with yearning looks and the occasional stolen kiss.

That was until yesterday, when the mercury soared again, tempers frayed, and the black sides of the *Rook* took on the texture of boiled pitch. Lydia had gone with him eagerly to the sheltered pool, and they had swum for an hour. Afterward, he had made love to her, slowly, wonderingly, their passion languid and honeyed in the severe heat.

He sat now, lost in his thoughts, his pipe neglected on the rock beside him. The sky above was a pale azure laced with billowing white clouds, but he did not note it. His reverie was hued with radiant copper, bright blue and glorious apricot—Lydia' hair, Lydia's eyes, Lydia's sun-kissed skin.

He thought back to the first time they'd been together in the cave, when he'd drawn his bewitching siren from the water. Gad, he'd argued with himself endlessly before seeking her out. He'd set the terms himself, Lord help him, and so if he went to her, if he took her there on the white sand, he knew precisely what it would mean—that he had acceded. No, accepted was a better word. It meant that he had at last accepted Lydia into his life.

It was perhaps the wisest thing he'd ever done. The gnawing ache inside him was at peace for the first time in twelve years. His tangled thoughts and complex, contrary feelings had sorted themselves out. All at the hands of one woman.

It seemed a startlingly simple equation: he loved and was loved in return.

He looked off to the west and felt a jolt of homesickness. They'd have a proper wedding back in Devon, see if they didn't. With his boys and Hardy in attendance. And every society Adonis that Lydia had thrown over would be there wearing the willow.

Matthew was not above a little vindictiveness.

Afterward, he would find a separate house for the boys, because as much as he cared for his crew, he'd been wishing them at Jericho these past days. And he was certainly not going to share his home, now that—

"Captain! Captain!" It was Gilbert's voice, echoing across the cove. He heard the cry before he saw the rider come racing over the crest at a headlong gallop. The next instant, he was up and running.

He caught Gilbert as he tumbled from the saddle. "Steady, lad, steady. Catch your breath."

"You m-must come, sir," Gilbert stammered, clutching at his jacket. "To Lempère. She's gone. I think she went with the priest. Took the boy, sir. She took Jean-Louis." He sagged to his knees as the captain eased him down.

Matthew glanced up at the path, a terrible understanding etched around his eyes. The priest. The Parisian priest.

God, how could he have let her go to Lempère alone?

The boy told him in halting sentences what had transpired in the village. "No one knows where they were bound. No one has any idea."

He crouched beside Gilbert, rubbing his shoulder. "You did well, Gil. It's nothing you could have prevented. But we'll get her back, and Jean-Louis as well."

The other boys were gathered about them now, their faces anxious.

"Tenpence, Rowdy," the captain barked. "You'll ride with me."

Gilbert got to his feet and stood weaving. "I want to come."

"You're worn through, lad. And your horse is nearly lame. We've only three horses left."

"I can ride behind Rowdy," Tenpence volunteered. "Let 'im come, sir. He was that fond of her."

They raced toward the village, passing the actors' caravan at the side of the road, not pausing when the troupe waved at them. When they reached the rectory, Matthew's frail hopes sank. Every window was dark. They left the horses behind the barn and moved silently back to the house. Tenpence climbed through an unlatched window in the kitchen, and soon all four of them were inside.

At the captain's command, they dispersed throughout the house. Gilbert went up the narrow staircase to the priest's bedchamber, while Rowdy searched the parlor, and Tenpence scoured the kitchen. Matthew made his way to the study.

Lighting a candle with his tinderbox, he went first to the desk, where he pried open the locked drawers with his pocket knife. He sifted through Boniface's papers—sermons, homilies, butcher's bills. The man ate a considerable amount of meat for such a stick. More sermons, letters to the mayor, letters from the mayor. He looked through every drawer twice, but found nothing.

He scanned the bookcases next, praying he wouldn't have to search through every volume. It would be better if they could locate—

"A safe!" Gilbert rasped from the doorway. "In his bed chamber."

Father Boniface's bedroom was all that was proper for an elderly cleric with an aesthetic bent—a spindle bed with a woven coverlet, a chest of drawers holding a mounted crucifix, a small bookcase rife with ecclesiastical reading. Over the bed hung a painting of the Virgin, by Titian, if the captain was not mistaken. Father Boniface's vows of poverty clearly did not extend to the acquisition of art.

Gilbert pointed to the side of the fireplace, where three loose bricks had been pulled away to reveal an iron plate. Frobisher held his candle in close. A complicated lock protruded from the center of the plate. "Ten," he said over his shoulder. "This looks like your sort of work."

The boy peered at the device. "Piece o' cake," he chuckled, reaching into his pocket for the tools of his trade.

After what seemed like an hour to his breathless audience, there was a sharp snick, and the whole metal plate slid forward, revealing a strongbox cleverly recessed in the mortar of the fireplace. It was stuffed with papers.

The captain settled on the floor and studied them. They were legal documents for the most part, dealing with the disbursement of various properties in Brittany. He was beginning to despair of finding anything incriminating, when he lifted a note from the pile. It was oddly worded, offering a blessing upon the recipient for his continued support to all those who were no longer on the roads of France. There was no signature.

He held it up to the candlelight, marveling at the rich vellum paper, a sharp contrast to the soldierly scrawl on its surface. Something whispered, cold and urgent, against the back of his neck.

"What is it, sir?" Gilbert asked.

The captain passed it over. He scanned it and then looked up, perplexed. "Why would he keep such a foolish thing in a safe? Why would he keep it at all?"

"A memento," Frobisher said softly, "from his deposed emperor."

"Napoleon?" echoed Tenpence. "Gor!"

Matthew tucked the note into his shirt. He swore the paper burned against his skin.

So, the good father was a Bonapartist. Things were beginning to make sense now. He reexamined the real estate documents, noting the names and cities. These, then, must be Boniface's local contacts, other men who continued to plot against the government in hopes of returning the emperor to power. Matthew gathered them up and then returned the safe to its cubby hole.

He led the boys back to the study, thinking there had to be something more, something that would connect Boniface to Frobisher's old enemy in Paris. Why else would he have gone off with Lydia and the boy? He sat at the desk, his head in his hands, and thought furiously.

"Tenpence," he asked at last. "Did you find anything in the cookstove?"

"Just some charred rubbish. The fire was still smolderin'. I couldn't get close enough to see."

"Rowdy, fetch me anything that wasn't burnt."

Tenpence looked downcast, and the captain grinned. "Ten, give it up. It's simply a matter of physics. His arms are longer than yours, so he has less chance of getting burned."

Rowdy returned with a kitchen tray littered with bits of charred paper. The captain poked through the ashen debris with an ivory letter opener. There were the remains of newspaper clippings, nearly unreadable, and some sort of handbill, printed on heavy paper. He could just make out the letters *R-E-W-A-R* at the top. There was also a handwritten letter, in two blackened fragments.

"Bring the candle closer," he motioned to Tenpence.

The words danced before his eyes and he blinked. *". . . and you must make certain she accompanies the child."* The paper crumbled in his fingers, melting into a pile of black scales. No matter, he'd seen enough.

Tenpence leaned toward the captain. "Did the priest abduct Miss Peartree, do you think?"

"She wouldn't have gone with him willingly," Gilbert protested.

"I doubt the good father had the strength to coerce her."

"Why else would she have gone off, sir? Away from us . . . from you?"

"I believe he offered something to Jean-Louis that the boy has been hankering after. And she went along, well, because she felt it her duty. And because she's Lydia, after all, and never sees danger even when it's under her nose."

They continued to gaze at him with dark, troubled eyes.

Matthew knew he was behaving in a remarkably calm manner, all things considered. The boys couldn't know what it cost him to maintain that serene exterior or how his heart lurched whenever he thought of the peril Lydia would encounter. The man she would face.

Nevertheless, all his training had come back to him. You stayed calm, aloof from your emotions. You schooled yourself to pragmatism and even cold-bloodedness. Anything less and you left yourself open to bad judgment—and that could very well be fatal.

No, if he loved Lydia, he would keep his head. Perhaps that was the only way she would end up keeping hers.

He rose and turned toward the door. "Come, lads. We've a deal to do before morning."

Gilbert lingered near the spinet. "Sir," he asked musingly, "is there music in the *Iliad*?"

"Only the music of Homer's verse—why?"

He pointed to the book on the music stand. Matthew went past him and picked it up. It fell open to the page where Lydia's lace handkerchief lay, demure against the bold etching of a classically-featured Greek man carrying off a woman in a white robe.

"What is it? What does it mean?" Tenpence jostled Gilbert and Rowdy to see over their shoulders.

"It's a drawing of the abduction of Helen of Troy," the captain explained, tucking her token into his shirt next to the note from Napoleon. "And I believe it's a message from Miss Peartree."

His clipped voice disguised his relief—she hadn't left him without a word after all.

His eyes gleamed with appreciation at her cleverness as he easily identified the Greek youth in the drawing.

"It's as I suspected—they've gone off to Paris."

Gerardone's singing kept everyone awake that first morning. He sprawled on the wide seat of his brightly painted caravan and bellowed out an Italian aria in a surprisingly good tenor.

"For his size, I'd have thought him a baritone at least," the captain muttered to Gilbert, who was curled up beside him in the commodious belly of the wagon.

"Do you think he's going to sing all the way to Paris?" Oxer asked with a grimace.

"We'll be deaf if he does," Rowdy moaned. "I've never heard such caterwauling."

"It's opera," Fripp said. "Not to everyone's taste."

The captain crept to the front of the swaying caravan, and pulled back the canvas sheet that separated the interior from the driver's perch.

"Mr. Gerardone, we are having a hellish time sleeping with all your noise. I am as fond of Mozart as the next man, but we have been up all night. So, if you could just keep it down a bit."

The large Frenchman rubbed one hand against his impressive nose. "I am creating a diversion. All who pass by will say, 'What a fine fellow that is, with such a voice.' They will not think, ah, here are seven English rascals sneaking into Paris."

"That is a clever plan. But since no one can see us in the wagon, perhaps less diversion and more driving would be a better plan?"

Gerardone launched into a Basque lullaby. Matthew sighed and went back to his crew. They settled down again and within minutes were sound asleep. Matthew lay with his hands beneath his head, watching the copper pots and woven baskets swaying above him. This was the moment he feared most, when activity ceased, when he was left to face his own troubled thoughts.

He had been in constant motion since Gilbert came galloping down the cliff path.

After they'd searched the priest's home, they had been heading back to the cove when they came upon the players' caravan—and he had been struck by a very timely inspiration.

He'd sought out the troupe's leader, a tow-headed giant from Gascony.

"My politics?" Gerardone had answered his question with a brittle laugh. "I am an actor, Captain. My politics are all in my purse. These have been lean times for those who display their art upon the stage. With Napoleon gone—surely the king of actors—the people have lost their taste for drama and display."

"Then perhaps we can strike a bargain," Matthew said. When he finished elaborating his plan, the Gascon looked questioningly at his troupe. They all nodded eagerly. He spit on his hamlike hand and clasped the captain's in the time-honored gesture that closed a deal.

When the captain returned to the cove, he took Tilda aside. "Miss Peartree tells me you are quite good with hair," he remarked silkily, guiding her into his hut.

When he emerged, the boys had been openly amazed. He had donned a proper suit of clothes and fine leather boots. Most significantly, his long hair had been neatly barbered, leaving only a stylish crop of white locks. The man who'd gazed back when Tilda held up Lydia's hand mirror might have been a courtier from the previous century.

It wasn't long before the caravan came trundling down the cliff path. The boys hefted their bedrolls into the wagon, and he and Oxer loaded his sea chest and a crate of arms.

It had been an ideal solution, he now mused, the perfect camouflage to get them into Paris undetected by Chabrier's spies. Inside the caravan, packed in wicker hampers, were costumes and greasepaint and innumerable props. They had left the five actors behind on the beach, pockets bulging with coin, but their leader had insisted on accompanying them. Gerardone's troupe had performed in Paris only three months earlier; he would be able to guide them through that city, where Matthew had not set foot for many years.

But in spite of his good fortune in winning over Gerardone, misgivings began to cloud his thoughts. They would arrive in Paris perhaps a day behind

Lydia. It was too much time. A great deal could happen in twenty-four hours. His greatest hope was that she'd gone to the British embassy. With the might of Britannia holding her safe, she could possibly stay beyond the comte's reach. Maybe. He doubted if even that bastion of British might was without Chabrier's informants.

Matthew was not a devout man, but he prayed that morning, prayed that a benevolent deity would hold Lydia in the palm of His hand until the caravan reached Paris.

His other worries had to do with his crew. They'd insisted on going along with him. It was precisely what they'd been trained for, they argued—infiltration, observation and stealth. It was too dangerous, he warned them, the city was unfamiliar, and the man he was going up against was ruthless. Their youth would not make them exempt from his revenge.

"Don't you have faith in us, sir?" Gilbert countered, while the other boys muttered their assent. "Haven't we proven ourselves to you here in France?"

In truth, he couldn't have been prouder of them. He wanted nothing more than for them to be beside him in Paris—his eyes and ears in the teeming capital. But he refused to place them in the way of that monster. Bad enough that Lydia and the boy were heading straight into his clutches.

"No," he said implacably. "You are to stay behind and work on the ship."

There was a murmuring of dissent, and Tenpence got to his feet, bristly as a bantam cock. "You need us, sir. Oxer, 'e's as strong as a grown man, Fripp speaks French like a Parisian, Gilbert has eyes like an eagle, and Rowdy can cozen secrets out of any lady. Seamus is good with his fists, and me"—he waved his thin fingers in the air—"I've got the best hands in Europe for pickin' locks and pockets. And I can shoot, sir. We all can. Straight and true, like you taught us."

"This is not some lark," Matthew said. "There's a man in Paris who is my sworn enemy. Men—skilled, trained men—have died at his hands. If anything happens to even one of you, I couldn't face myself."

"We are making this decision for ourselves," Gilbert said. "Accept that, Captain. We're not the same crew you left Exeter with."

He watched them now as they slept. The Gascon's little dancing monkey lay tucked under Tenpence's arm. They were an ill-assorted group, to be sure. Yet he'd back these lads for spirit and grit even in the face of Chabrier's hired ruffians.

There were few forces in the world, as the French had recently discovered, that possessed the power of good English pluck.

Chapter Thirteen
The Jackal

*L*ydia's head throbbed during the first hours of their trip. She wondered groggily if the priest had drugged her tea. If only it were true, then she might have some meager excuse for allowing herself to be forced into making this rash journey.

There had been no need to drug Jean-Louis, however. His initial enthusiasm never flagged. He prattled endlessly, conjecturing on his new life in Paris, how he would have a fine pony and many wonderful toys, how his father would take him driving in the city and show him many wonderful sights. Lydia vowed if she heard the phrase "many wonderful" one more time, she would throw herself from the coach.

The priest also seemed to be in high spirits—regaling Lydia with the beauties of Paris. She had never seen the city, for the simple reason that England and France had been at war since before her come-out. She had eagerly looked forward to visiting there one day, but in her present predicament, she felt no sense of anticipation. All she could muster was a vague reassurance that she was acting in Jean-Louis's best interests. When her deeper misgivings floated to the surface, her response was to seek the oblivion of sleep.

It was not surprising, then, that she spent most of

the journey in a fitful doze, her head lolling back against the upholstery. Yet even when she slept, her dreams were full of Matthew's perfidy. The questions continued to plague her—Why had he taken another man's son? Was it because the Frenchman had arrested him or because he'd married the woman Matthew loved? Was the captain so determined on revenge that he'd lashed out at the child to hurt the father? It was a scoundrelly sort of behavior, whatever his reasons, and nearly impossible to attribute to the Matthew Frobisher she had fallen in love with.

Adding to her worries was the unsettling suspicion that something was not right with Father Boniface. She wasn't sure when she first began to doubt him. His refined cordiality never waned, but she was disquieted, nonetheless. For one thing, he had a pouch of money, which he kept hidden in his soutane. Once, while she was in a half-doze, Lydia had watched him surreptitiously counting out a large number of coins. She knew Chabrier had sent money for their journey, but it was unlikely he had sent quite so much. Lydia was unaccountably tempted to ask Boniface if all thirty pieces of silver were accounted for.

When they were less than a day's journey from Paris, Jean-Louis's enthusiasm seemed suddenly to vanish. He was silent all morning. When they stopped for luncheon, Lydia waited until the priest left their table, and then she accosted the boy.

"You were very quiet this morning. I hope all this traveling has not made you ill."

He shook his head and said in English, "No, I am not sick. But I am not so good, either. I have the sadness for the *capitaine* and the boys."

She set her fork down and said a bit sharply, "But I thought you didn't like those boys."

He shrugged. "I work with them, study with them. They begin to be special to me. More now that they are gone. I don't understand it, but it is how I feel, *enfin*."

"I thought you were very happy now that you will be with your papa."

"My papa . . ." His gaze drifted out the grimy window of the inn. "You will think it most foolish, *mam'selle*, but I keep thinking about what my master said, that Papa was dead."

"It was a mistake, Jean-Louis. Who else but your father would have sent the picture of your *maman*?"

He touched his shirtfront where the folded drawing lay. "I want to believe it. But I . . . I still cannot understand why the *capitaine* would lie to me."

Lydia winced. She'd asked herself the same question a thousand times.

"You must be very angry with him over that," she said gently.

His eyes narrowed thoughtfully. *"Non,"* he said. "He would not lie without a reason, that one. He told me once that a clever soldier knows when to disobey an order. I think this lie he told me, it was like that. He did a wicked thing, but I think he was being a clever soldier. *Comprenez-vous?"*

Lydia clenched her hands to keep from giving him a good shake. She had gotten them both into this situation because she believed him to be grieving over his lost family. To her eternal regret, and against his repeated admonitions that she leave it alone, she had stirred up Matthew's dark past. In her efforts to aid Jean-Louis, she had given up more than his child's mind could ever begin to fathom. And now he was waxing nostalgic over the captain and his boys. The disembodied doubts that had troubled her since they left Lempère begin to solidify.

"Do you want to return to Evionne? Speak quickly before Father Boniface comes back. We are not without resources—I can sell my ring."

He looked across at her, startled. "I don't know, *mam'selle*. I hear the innkeeper say we are only hours from Paris. We are so close. I do want to meet my father, but I am also a little afrightened. He will be like a stranger to me. Will you stay with me when we are in Paris?" His hazel eyes beseeched her.

"If you like," she said with a sigh.

The boy had held out a reprieve to her and then snatched it back. So they would see the business to its end. And she would remain in Paris as long as he needed her. She really had nowhere else to go, no reason to rush back to England. Donald Farthingale was ancient history now. And Matthew—Lydia felt her insides twist—Matthew would most likely refuse to ever see her again.

He might lie and plot, scheme his little schemes, but she knew he would deal harshly with anyone who repaid him in like coin. It wasn't fair, but it was his nature. "Our natures will keep us apart," he had said. What truth those words now bore. Marianne's betrayal still cut him like a blade, twelve years after the fact. She wondered desolately how many decades it would be before he forgave *her* for turning against him.

It was full dark when the coach pulled up before an imposing mansion in a wealthy quarter of the city. Father Boniface handed her out and then drew the sleepy Jean-Louis onto the pavement beside a guarded wrought-iron gate. After the priest had spoken a few words to the guard, they were led along a pebbled path in a courtyard planted with dwarf fruit trees. Off to their left, Lydia saw the sweeping entrance to the house—twin staircases rising on either side of a balustraded porch. Doors of a dark metal were stark and forbidding against the pale stone of the facade.

The guard led them to the opposite wing and knocked at an ironbound door. A tall, broad-chested man with grizzled hair opened it. He was not in uniform but wore a dark suit tailored to his heavy frame.

"Ah, we have been expecting you, Father." He motioned them into the foyer, then without another word, he led them down a long paneled corridor where armed guards stood at attention. Jean-Louis's hand crept into Lydia's.

Their guide paused when they came to a heavy oak door. Human figures had been deeply carved into its surface; in the sparse light they appeared to be writhing in agony. Lydia had only a moment to note this oddity before their escort ushered them into the room.

The man seated behind the sprawling desk was perhaps fifty. His dark hair was graying at the temples yet he gave the impression, with his barrel chest and thick neck, of great physical strength. He wore a fashionably cut black coat, and his neckcloth held a large, brilliant diamond.

"Thank you, Scovile." Rising to his feet, he dismissed the man with a wave. He was of medium height, but again, as he approached them, Lydia got a sense of great power held in check.

"I am Lucien, Comte de Chabrier." He nodded briefly to Lydia and then to the priest.

"Father Boniface of Lempère, my lord. And this is Miss Peartree. She accompanied me from Finistère to look after the boy."

Lydia performed her best court curtsy.

"And this is Jean-Louis." The priest urged him forward, but he hung back and would not look at the comte.

Chabrier took Jean-Louis's chin in his hand and tipped his head back. The man's eyes were jet-black, and they glittered almost feverishly as he gazed upon the face of his son.

"Say 'good day' to your father," she coaxed with a hand at his shoulder. She could feel the tension in his thin muscles. "You have been raised better than this, Jean-Louis."

"Papa?" Jean-Louis said at last in a reedy voice. "It is me. I am come home."

Lydia's heart almost broke at the plaintiveness in his voice.

The comte smiled as he knelt and put his arms around the boy. "Yes," he murmured. "You have come home." He looked up at the priest, his smile widening. "Thank you, Boniface, you've done very well. You have brought me exactly what I have been praying for."

Jean-Louis was crying now, sobbing in a muted way. The comte rose and stepped back from him. Lydia had the fleeting impression that Chabrier did not want his son's tears to mar the perfection of his shirtfront.

He fiddled with his cuffs as he observed the boy. "He has the look of my late wife."

In truth, Lydia could see little of the burly father in the narrow form of his son.

The comte turned to Lydia. "Please excuse me a moment. I must speak privately with Father Boniface."

Lydia settled beside the boy on a small couch as the two men went into the hall.

"Tell me," Chabrier asked quickly, once the carved door was shut. "Does the Englishman know they have come to Paris?"

"If he is as clever as you claim, he will find the partially burned papers in my stove. They should tell him all he needs to know."

"Good. We don't want to leave too obvious a trail. He'll suspect a trap, otherwise."

He motioned toward the room behind them. "The woman is even more than I had hoped for. He'll come after her; who can doubt it? Few men could resist such a one as that." He leaned forward and said softly, "And then my English friend will meet his fate at last . . . and all for a pair of pretty blue eyes."

"Rather like Samson and Delilah," the priest added. "Beauty will surely bring down the mightiest of men."

"Exactly. But tell me, are you sure there was nothing left behind in your house that might implicate you in our other . . . ah, activities?"

"I assure you, sir, the Englishman will find only what I intended him to find."

"Excellent. Now I must see to my . . . guests. Your service to the emperor has been compounded by your very gratifying efforts on my behalf. You will find we are both most grateful."

"It is my pleasure to serve," the priest murmured, a barely contained smile of satisfaction pursing his thin mouth. As Boniface made his way down the long hall, Chabrier motioned sharply to Scovile, who was waiting beneath a recessed archway.

Lydia looked up as the comte entered the room with the grizzled man hard at his heels. She had been passing the time observing his palatial office, wondering why, if he was now a trusted servant of the king, there was a bust of the deposed emperor on his mantel. She had also been trying to imagine what the comte needed to say to the priest that could not be said in front of her and Jean-Louis.

"Father Boniface has gone to seek his bed in a nearby hospice," he explained. "I expect he is weary from the journey. The boy also looks as though he could do with some sleep. Go along, child. Monsieur Scovile will take you to your room."

"Please, Papa," Jean-Louis whispered urgently. "I want Miss Peartree to stay here with me."

"I was planning on going to the British embassy," Lydia put in quickly.

The comte laid his hand on the boy's hair. "She will not leave this house, you have my promise. We will talk in the morning, you and I. You will have a pony, if you like, and some fine new clothes and many wonderful things to eat."

Lydia heard the familiar phrase and nearly smiled. Perhaps the boy took after his father after all.

"My chef makes delicious bonbons," Chabrier was saying. "He was once confectioner to the Emperor Napoleon himself."

"I do like bonbons," Jean-Louis murmured half-heartedly.

"Then I will see that some are specially prepared for you."

When Jean-Louis turned to her to say good night, she couldn't resist tugging him into her arms. "I'll come up and tuck you in before I retire," she whispered.

He smiled at her then, the first really joyful emotion he'd exhibited since they left the coach.

As Scovile led the boy from the room, Chabrier moved to an inlaid sideboard. "Will you have some wine?"

Lydia, rapidly nearing the end of her reserves, gratefully took the glass he held out. The comte resumed his seat and began to toy with a clear glass globe, never lowering his eyes from her face. She feared she did not present a very inspiring picture with her hair in disarray and her Breton skirt and blouse travel-worn and wrinkled.

Finally, he relaxed his scrutiny. "I was sorry to hear of your misadventures on our coast. A disabled ship, an attack by brigands. Most unfortunate."

"We managed to come through relatively unscathed. Our captain is a man of some resource."

"Ah, that would be Captain Matthew Frobisher."

He was certainly very well informed. But then information was Chabrier's stock in trade.

"The same," said Lydia. "He is a schoolmaster in Devon."

"Odd work for such a man of action."

"That was all a very long time ago." Lydia almost bit her tongue. Subterfuge was clearly not her long suit. She had to make sure she said nothing that would connect Matthew to the young man who had courted Marianne Dieudonne.

"He was formerly a captain in the navy," she lied, bold-faced. "Something of a hero, as I recall."

"And how came my son to be in his keeping?" the comte asked softly.

Lydia realized she should have spent less time on the journey dozing and more time concocting a suitable explanation.

"It was through Sir Robert Poole, the statesman. You must know of him. He discovered the boy in an English orphanage and sponsored his entry into the captain's school. Sir Robert has a very philanthropic nature."

"I'm quite sure," the comte purred.

Lydia again fidgeted under his probing eyes. "Perhaps we could continue this conversation in the morning, my lord. I too am fatigued from the journey, and I want to look in on Jean-Louis before I depart."

She set down her glass as she rose. The comte did likewise, replacing the globe on his desk. Lydia could make out a small device set in its center.

"You study my paperweight, Miss Peartree. I had it made up to a specific design." He hefted it again and then offered it to her. "Have you ever seen its like?"

Lydia took it, turning it toward the light. She prayed she hadn't gasped in surprise when she recognized the glass flower. It was identical to the tattoo that Matthew wore on his shoulder—the purple nightshade.

"Just so," the comte said in a low voice. "I see you are familiar with that particular flower."

"It is a common enough weed in England," she replied lightly.

"Oh, no. I would say there is nothing at all common about this variety."

"You speak in riddles, sir. And I fear my wits are too addled by weariness to engage you." She put up her chin. "It would be better if we spoke again in the morning."

He removed the globe from her hand. "Please be seated. I'm afraid our conversation cannot wait until morning."

"They are expecting me at the embassy," she said as calmly as she could. "I sent a message ahead to alert them. If you would have a carriage brought around . . ."

The comte retook his seat, observing her obliquely, his hands clasped, his chin resting on his knuckles. "Don't fence with me, ma'am. You will find yourself at a disadvantage."

Lydia laid one hand on his desk and leaned forward. "I don't need to fence, *Mr.* Chabrier. I am a British citizen. Paris is in the hands of England and her allies.

Napoleon is exiled . . . or had you forgotten?" She cast a meaningful look at the bust on the mantel. "I am also the daughter of an English baron and a Russian princess. You do not trifle with me, sir, or it is you who will find yourself at a disadvantage."

A gleam of appreciation shone in his eyes. "Mattei has again proven himself a connoisseur of woman. And always the red hair. It is most curious."

"I don't know any Mattei," she muttered.

"That is unfortunate. You are only of use to me if you are acquainted with the man."

"I came here to return your son. Is this how you repay me, with vague insinuations?"

"My son?" He gave a brittle laugh. "The boy was only a ruse to bring you to Paris, Miss Peartree. He is no longer of any use to me."

The boy's father was a jackal . . . Matthew's words came back to Lydia like an icy slash through her heart. Dear God, what had she done? Had she truly delivered herself and the child up to this creature, who sat watching her hungrily with the hooded eyes of a jungle beast.

"What do you want with me?" Her voice quavered in spite of her resolve to stay calm.

"When a man seeks a very large fish, he must use impressive bait. And you, dear lady, are most impressive. It's a pity, really, what awaits you. But I dare not let you go, not if I am to have my reckoning with Mattei."

"More riddles!" she berated him. "What have I to do with anyone named Mattei?"

"A great deal. You know him as Matthew Frobisher, but when he was spying in France twelve years ago he called himself François Mattei. I take it you've learned something of our history, his and mine."

Her eyes gave away nothing.

He continued on as though she had assented. "So knowing how he served me then, you will understand why his death is mandated now."

"His death? Mandated?" she cried in disbelief.

"In payment for his crimes."

"But the war is over. England and France are at peace."

"Not all his crimes were against France."

She glared at him. "Why should you wish for his death? You gained everything he sought. You married the woman he loved. You fathered a child with her as he was not fated to do. You rose to power, while he sank into virtual obscurity. And he . . . he has looked after Jean-Louis as if he were his own. What, I beg you, has Matthew Frobisher done to inspire such lasting hatred?"

Two deeply etched lines had appeared at the edges of his mouth. "I am relieved you are done with prevaricating. A naval hero, indeed! Matthew Frobisher never wore the uniform of the British Crown. His was a darker disguise. As for my hatred, suffice to say it is a matter of honor. He stole something from me all those years ago, and though it can never be returned, I can and will take my restitution. Beginning with you."

He barked out a command, and Scovile came in, leading a company of six guards. The comte took a paper from his desk drawer and held it up. "This is an order for your arrest and execution. For crimes against France and against myself."

"No!" Lydia nearly shrieked the word. She drew a breath to steady herself. "This is ludicrous. Father Boniface knows the truth. He will not let you act on these wicked lies. And Jean-Louis . . . Is he not my best witness, the son I brought safely home to his father?"

The comte looked at her with amused disdain. "How sad that you should place your faith in a doddering old priest and an overwrought child. Now, Miss Peartree, you will be taken from here to a city prison. At the end of the week you will be sent to the guillotine. It is so written."

Lydia fought off the swoon that threatened to engulf her. "Matthew will come for me," she whispered fiercely, her eyes raking him. "He has bested you before, Mr. Chabrier. We English have all bested you. He will save me, and you will face his anger and his sword. And may God have mercy on you then."

Lydia had the pleasure of seeing the imperturbable Chabrier turn pale. Beside her, Scovile crossed himself. She smiled grimly.

"Just take her away," the comte hissed. "She wearies me with her chatter."

Scovile's fingers bit into her arm, drawing her from the desk. After tying a cloth over her eyes, he pulled her cloak tight about her and raised its hood. When he prodded her forward, she heard the guards fall into ranks behind her.

"He *will* come for me," she repeated, almost to herself, as they marched her out the door.

"I am counting on it," the comte responded softly.

Her seven captors escorted Lydia through the warm Parisian night. Her feet felt like they were made of lead, but her back was straight and her chin was up. Scovile held her by one arm, to guide her along the pavement. She thought it curious that they'd needed to blindfold her. If she was to be imprisoned, what did it matter if she saw where they brought her? It was not as though she had the means to tell anyone.

After fifteen minutes or so, Scovile knocked at a door. She heard the rasping of a key in a lock and the sound of masculine voices. A man with a nasal wheeze greeted Scovile by name. "So this is the comte's prisoner. Tasty. Very tasty."

Scovile must have made a threatening motion—the nasal voice took on a note of supplication. "Just making an observation, Scovile. I have my orders. The lady is not to be tampered with."

"See that you remember that, Redon."

The gravel underfoot changed to a paved floor as Scovile guided her down a flight of stairs and along a corridor. She could feel the thick walls closing in on her.

Lydia's blindfold was not removed until she was in-

side her cell. There was very little light—only a lantern
hanging beyond the grilled bars—but still it took time
for her vision to adjust.

The man with the annoying voice was speaking
softly to Scovile. He was short and wizened, clad in a
leather apron from which dangled a loop of keys. His
thinning hair clung in greasy strands to his pink scalp.
He was not very old, but he had the gray face of
a corpse.

My jailer, she thought dismally.

Redon locked her in the cell and then went out
behind Scovile and the guards, carrying the lantern
away with him. Lydia wanted to cry out for them to
leave it, but she would not give them the satisfaction
of hearing her plead. She'd sleep in the dark. There
was a small, rectangular window at the top of the cell.
Perhaps in the morning a bit of daylight would filter
through it. She could wait.

She lay down on the rude cot and pulled her cloak
over her. It was odd that she couldn't hear any other
prisoners. In her brief view of the outer area, she'd
seen no other cells, only granite walls rising up to a
vaulted ceiling. She had never seen the inside of a
prison—she was not one of those fashionable ladies
who went to gape at the unfortunates inside Newgate.
Nevertheless, her instincts told her this was not the
usual sort of prison. And that thought frightened her
beyond words.

Prisoners were usually kept in befouled communal
cells, where visitors and lawyers were occasionally allowed to mingle with them. This she knew from Sir
Robert, who often spoke about the wretched state of
English jails. Her cell, in comparison, was a desolate,
isolated space. There would be no visitors, certainly
no lawyers, no one she could entreat to pass a message
to the outside world. Only the wheezing, unctuous
jailer.

Lydia slept after a time—her distraught brain seeking the healing oblivion of sleep as it had done on her
journey. She dreamt of Matthew's strong, tanned

arms, his supple mouth and his laughing, moonstone eyes. He was dancing with her, whirling her through a crowd of faceless couples. He lifted her off her feet and cast her into the air. She flew high above the dance floor and could see only his lean face below her. There was blood on that face . . . and the light had gone out of his eyes. She plummeted down, falling and falling. . . .

She started awake, bathed in sweat with her hair clinging to her forehead in sticky tendrils. Only a dream, she told herself. Only a frightening dream. She soon fell back to sleep—and she was in Evionne Cove again, among the boys, laughing with Matthew.

She awoke for the second time, snuggling under the warmth of her cloak. She knew with certainty that her whole misadventure with Jean-Louis and the priest had been a nightmare—and that the creature Chabrier was only a figment of her imagination.

But when she sat up in the murky dawn and beheld the stark stone walls and the thick iron bars that confined her, she fell back onto her cot with a sob. God save her, it *was* true. The nightmare was real. Chabrier did exist. Jean-Louis was the son of a monster, and Matthew, her Matthew, was lost to her forever. It was all horribly true.

Some hours after daylight, Redon came in, his footsteps uneven as he progressed along the stone floor. Lydia saw that both his feet were badly misshapen. She could have found it in her heart to pity him, except for the way his ferretlike eyes scanned her body as he slid her breakfast plate into the cell. He licked his lips as she reached for the wooden charger.

"Nothing so dainty, I'm afraid," he wheezed. "Just bread and water. You'll lose your bloom down here, my lady. Not that there's any but me to notice."

"Where are the other prisoners?" Lydia asked biting into the crust of stale bread.

"The others?" He mulled this over, then motioned to the wooden door at the end of the corridor. "They're all beyond there."

"Can you carry a message for me? I fear there has been a dreadful mistake. My friends will pay you handsomely if you do this." .

His beady eyes brightened.

"I will also give you this emerald ring." Lydia held up her right hand.

"Let me see." He peered close to the bars. Lydia was careful to keep out of range as she displayed the impressive gem, recalling the captain's sleight of hand that first day.

Redon's eyes widened. "I'll definitely think about it."

Once he was gone, she dragged her iron cot beneath the high window. Standing on it, up on tiptoes, she could see outside. The walls of the cell were thick, so her range of vision was limited to objects at ground level. She yearned to view the sky, but could only see grass and hedge bottoms and, in the distance, a wrought-iron fence. She nearly ducked back as two pairs of gray-clad legs passed close by.

She slumped back down on her cot. Think, Lydia, she admonished herself. What would Matthew make of this situation? What would Gilbert deduce from what you have just seen?

She cataloged her information. A blindfold. No other prisoners within earshot. Pebbles underfoot. A wrought-iron fence. Gray uniform trousers.

She recalled the comte's words to Jean-Louis. *I promise you Miss Peartree will not leave this house.*

And that's exactly where she was, Lydia realized with a sinking heart. The wicked comte had not lied to his son. The guards had walked her about in the street to confuse her but had surely led her right back to the stone mansion. For all his guile, the comte had not realized how tall Lydia was, that she would be able to see out the window and identify the uniforms of his guards.

It made enormous sense. The comte could not risk placing her in a public prison—not with the number of Englishmen who were currently in Paris. Her identity would surely have been discovered. A beautiful young aristocrat with striking red hair was not your everyday prisoner. At least not since the Reign of Terror had decimated the ranks of the nobility.

No, she was truly cut off from any source of rescue. And if Matthew did come to Paris after her—not that she would blame him if he didn't—but if he came, he would never locate her in this underground cell. He was a clever man, but she had to admit that even he was not omniscient.

"I must get a message to him," she murmured aloud, "as I did in Father Boniface's study. Just in case he does follow me to Paris."

When the weaselly man appeared with her dinner plate, she had devised a fledgling plan.

"Have you thought about what I said this morning?" she asked him.

"I asked Scovile what I should do. We are old comrades in arms, he and I."

"You never did! He is the comte's man. Now they know you are thinking of betraying them. Oh, foolish wretch."

"No, no. You never know how the wind blows with Scovile. But he dares not cross the comte just yet. And he advised me not to either—for any price." He bent and slid her plate beneath the grill. Lydia let her right hand linger near the bars, while she poked at the gray-brown stew with her spoon.

"Not very promising." She looked up at her jailer through her lashes. His eyes were on the green ring. In an instant his hand had snaked through the bars and caught up her fingers in a painful grip.

"No," she cried, trying to pull away as he pried the ring from her finger. "It's all I have to bargain with."

"You've a deal more," he said, ogling her openly while he tucked the ring into the pocket of his soiled apron. "But this will do for now. It's a pretty bauble, but not so pretty as you, miss. Still, I've had my orders." His oily grin revealed several discolored teeth.

"Sell it," Lydia hissed softly as he lurched back

toward the door. "Pawn it, hock it, you foul insect. Flash it to all your lowly comrades, and then dispose of it. You'll get a good price, my larcenous little friend."

It was a large stone, a famous stone, in fact—the Orlov emerald—part of the Russian crown jewels. It had been Catherine the Great's gift to Lydia's grandfather for defeating the Prussian army. It was her fervent hope that the jewelers of Paris would recognize it and get word to the British embassy, who would trace it back to Redon. It was a slim chance, but it was the only card she had to play. She prayed that Redon's greed was greater than his need to gloat. If the ring languished for too long in his dirty pocket, she was lost.

Chapter Fourteen
The Prodigal and the Players

"*B*ut, Papa, can we not send to the embassy for her?" Jean-Louis complained to his father, who had come to visit him in his small bedroom.

"No," Chabrier responded curtly. "She told me before she departed last night that you must make your way without her. You are not a little child any longer, to be hanging on a woman's skirts."

The boy's lower lip trembled. "But she promised."

"She is back among her own kind now—the English *ton*—and is probably thinking of nothing but embassy balls and diplomatic parties. That is ever the way with women. It is time you learned it."

Jean-Louis looked up at his father resentfully. He remembered him vaguely from his childhood in Provence, and though he had loved him, he also recalled him making *Maman* cry a great deal. He had been too young to defend his mother but he would not let his father defame the *mam'selle*.

"You are wrong," he said staunchly. "Something has happened to keep her away. She does not break her promises. You do not know her as I do."

"Perhaps." The comte stroked his chin. "In the meantime, look what I have brought you." He took a covered plate from the dresser. "Bonbons from my chef."

Jean-Louis's eyes brightened only marginally. He was not to be so easily bribed out of his concern over Miss Peartree. "I am not very hungry," he said. "I'd like to go outside. I want to see Paris. Why am I kept locked in this room?"

"It's for your own safety. This is a large house with many dark corridors. I wouldn't want you to get lost. My offices are here, as well, and they are off limits to young scamps like you." He attempted a jocular laugh.

Jean-Louis looked perplexed. He'd had the complete run of the captain's Exeter house from the time he'd gone to live there. He could climb rigging and shoot a pistol and had even hit a French dog with a rock to save the *petit gris*. In the past weeks he'd faced far greater threats than getting lost in a corridor.

"When I have the time," his father was saying, "I will show you around the house. Perhaps this afternoon. Now eat your bonbons—my chef will be distraught if you don't finish every one."

After his father left, Jean-Louis threw himself upon his bed and sulked. He eyed the plate of glazed confections on the counterpane. Perhaps it wouldn't hurt to eat just one.

The candy was delicious, flavored with apricot and a bit of rum. Something about the scent reminded him of the *mam'selle*. He ate another and yet another, until the cloying sweetness began to make him queasy.

Jean-Louis went to the small window that overlooked the courtyard and opened the casement. He needed to breathe some fresh air. Pigeons strutted on the narrow ledge that ran below the window, their iridescent gray breasts afire in the morning light.

As he gazed down, he realized the window lay high above the street. How odd that he, the comte's son, had been given such a small room at the very top of the house. His sense of hierarchy was deeply offended. This was not the homecoming he had envisioned—

no doting father full of tender endearments, no
friendly servants to pet him and make him feel welcome. There was no brightly curtained bedchamber
with shelves of books and a chest full of toys and
amusing games.

No, there was only this stern gray-haired man who
had hugged him so stiffly the night before. Only the
remote, grizzled Scovile and the sour-faced maid who
had brought him his breakfast. Only this sparsely-
furnished garret room, with its one window and
empty dresser.

A strange, new sensation washed over Jean-Louis.
He probed his thoughts and discovered it was a feeling
of enormous relief. Even if the comte had offered the
world on a platter to his newfound son, he would not
have been able to replace Matthew Frobisher in Jean-
Louis's heart. Now, in the face of the meager gifts his
father *had* offered, the boy felt free to return all his
allegiance to the captain.

Jean-Louis placed three of the candies on the ledge
before partially closing the window. He settled back
on his bed, wondering what had happened to the
mam'selle. He had a fairly good notion of what it had
cost her to leave the *capitaine* behind, and Jean-Louis
doubted she would so quickly abandon him in Paris
after giving up so much to get him there. Something
was wrong. He was puzzling it out when he fell asleep.

It was long after noontime when he awoke. No one
had roused him for lunch and his father had obviously
not come to take him on the promised house tour.
Jean-Louis popped another of the bonbons into his
mouth as he crossed the room to reopen the window.
The bright sun had made the room stuffy.

Two dead pigeons lay just below his sill, the pecked-
at remains of one of the bonbons near their limp heads.

Jean-Louis turned abruptly and grabbed for the
china dish, choking out the piece he'd been chewing.
He ran for the chamber pot and fell to his knees as
his stomach emptied violently. Once his head stopped
spinning, he gathered up the half-eaten bonbon and

the remaining whole ones and wrapped them in the cloth that had covered the dish. He thought to throw the whole mess out the window, but then what if another poor creature found them? Maybe even a street child. He finally opted for placing them under his mattress. At least there no unsuspecting mouse would be able to nibble on them.

Because they'd been poisoned.

Jean-Louis was finally able to admit the truth to himself. He returned to sit, shivering, on his bed, trying to grapple with the knowledge that someone was trying to kill him. He had to tell his father, warn him that his son was in danger.

It seemed incomprehensible that someone wished him ill. Had his father remarried and begotten other children? Did he have a jealous stepmama who wanted him out of the way?

He fell into a fitful doze and was awakened by the maid with his dinner tray—fried fish and red potatoes. He eyed the plate warily.

"Did you watch the cook prepare this?" he asked the prune-faced woman.

"Why should you care?" she grumbled.

"I am interested in cooking," he said brightly. "Did he baste it in olive oil?"

"That he did—your fish and all the servants', as well. Now, if you'll let me go, so I can get back to my own supper before it's ice cold . . ."

She thrust the tray at him, and then locked the door.

No deference there, he thought as he wolfed down his meal. *I am the most unwelcome prodigal.*

"Papers," the uniformed guard called up to Gerardone. "You can't enter Paris without your papers."

The Gascon leaned down from his seat and proffered a sheaf of soiled documents.

"Six players," the man read aloud, "two women, four men."

"And a monkey," Gerardone laughed, holding up his pet, who clung to one brawny arm.

"Let's see them, then, these players."

"In the back." He motioned with his head as he climbed down.

The guard strode to the rear of the caravan and lifted the canvas scrim. He beheld a mixed group in the shadowed interior—a thin redheaded girl stood beside a tall, winsome brunette, who gave him a chip-toothed smile. A bruising young man sat upon a large wicker hamper, chewing on a turkey leg. Another man, not so young and a bit more elegant, with gleaming black hair and drooping mustachios, leaned languidly against one wall. The final occupant, a stooped, old man with straggling white hair, sat rocking himself on a wooden chest. He wore shaded spectacles.

"Come forward all of you," the guard called. "You too, grandfather."

As they shifted to the edge of the wagon, three other men, who'd been loitering behind the guard, moved in closer. They, too, studied each of the five faces.

"Take off your spectacles, grandfather," the guard ordered, not ungently.

The old man's lower lip trembled as he plucked at his glasses with shaking hands. The guard peered at his eyes. They were surprisingly youthful and bright blue. The trio of men who had gathered to watch now moved away.

"Pass through," the guard called out, standing back as Gerardone whipped up his piebald team and sent them trotting through the arched gate.

"We've gotten over the first hurdle," Matthew announced, watching the west gate of Paris—and the three men who'd been lurking there—recede in the distance. He pulled off the glossy black wig and tweaked away the long mustaches. "You all passed with flying colors, I might add."

"If I'd known I had to dress up like a girl, I'd have rethought this whole thing," Rowdy complained, trying to undo the laces of the boned taffeta gown.

"Oh, and who was it then that winked at the

guard?" Seamus inquired archly, pulling off the curly wig that was no redder than his own hair.

"I was just keeping in character," Rowdy protested as he helped Fripp from the wicker hamper. Oxer was assisting Tenpence from the captain's sea chest, where he had been forced to fold himself up like a pretzel.

"Next time I wear the dress," he carped to Seamus as he rubbed some feeling back into his arms, "and you go into the bloomin' chest!"

"Gad, I don't know how woman stand it!" Rowdy rolled his gown into a ball and tossed it into the wicker hamper.

Gilbert, who was wiping his face before a small mirror, remarked, "At least you don't have gallons of greasepaint all over you."

"That bit with the spectacles was inspired, Gil," the captain said. "Chabrier's watchers at the gate were sure they had found the man with the scarred eye."

As he spoke, Matthew wiped away the flesh-colored greasepaint that had obscured the white seam that marked his own eye. "You've all learned a valuable lesson. Half of what people perceive is nothing more than illusion. Magicians and actors know it, and now you know it as well."

Gerardone set his horses for the left bank. There was a gypsy camp near the river where his troupe had always been welcome. The captain, looking much more himself, climbed through the canvas partition and settled beside him. The monkey took umbrage at this and scurried away into the back of the wagon, chattering loudly.

"Curious," the captain mused. "I've an affinity for most animals, but that scamp of yours has taken me in total dislike."

"It's your hair, Captain. His previous owner was a white-haired villain who beat him when he didn't perform on cue. I was called upon to show the fellow the error of his ways . . . and relieve him of his pet."

"So tell me, Monsieur Gerardone, how does Paris these days? It looks to be the same as before—

crowded, dirty, buildings sprouting up every which
way with no thought to geometry. Beggars in the
street, footpads in the alleys—"

"Yes," the Gascon laughed. "A great city, Paris."

"Yes," Matthew agreed with a wistful look. "In
spite of the crowds and the dirt, Paris is a very great
city."

"It's the city of romance, as well. Have you ever
been in Paris and in love, Captain?"

Matthew was debating how truthfully to answer,
when he realized the Frenchman's question had
been rhetorical.

"There was a dancer once, Cosette of the *Comédie-
Française*. A sylph, my friend, a veritable sylph.
Courted by a hundred men. But it was humble Ge-
rardone—"

"Ah, yes. The humble Gascon." He grinned. "Go
on."

"She chose me above all the others. There was no
explaining it; I was but a fledgling actor and had not
yet penned my great opus—*Leovigild the Visigoth*. As
bloody and heroic a tale as ever a playwright set to
paper."

"I don't recall ever having seen it," Matthew said,
managing to keep a straight face.

"We've performed it mostly in the provinces. The
peasants love a good impalement scene, I can tell
you."

"And what of your Cosette?" the captain coaxed.

"She broke my Gascon heart. And that takes some
doing—we've hearts of forged steel. She swore to be
mine always and so we married. And then she ran off
with a defrocked priest."

Matthew eyed him warily. "You're not making
this up?"

"By the bones of St. Caradoc, patron saint of actors,
I swear it. You don't know what heartache is until
you've lost your wife. And I should know—I've lost
three at last count."

Matthew kept his voice purposely glib. "How careless of you to misplace them, Monsieur Gerardone."

He gave a loud guffaw and clapped Matthew on his back. "You are a decent fellow, Frobisher. And a master of disguise, as I saw at the city gate. Pity you never turned your hand to acting. Sailing's got nothing on it. A right proper villain you'd make—set the gentlemen to rattling their swords in the gallery and make the ladies all swoon with delicious fear."

"I'll bear it in mind," he said drily.

"And now I'd be interested in hearing why you needed to be smuggled into the city. You're British citizens and could enter Paris bold as brass. Are you merely eccentric, as the English are said to be, or are you playing a deeper game?"

The captain examined his companion. He wanted to trust the man; he probably needed to trust him. Yet still he held back.

"If it will help convince you," the Gascon said. "I could tell you of another English gentleman I knew back in '07, a man who called himself Macanée." Gerardone's face had lost its expression of affability. "He passed himself off as a cloth merchant from Chantilly. I wonder if you ever met him while you were here in Paris?"

Now, here was an interesting bit of news. "Perhaps . . . how did you know this man?"

"Macanée loved the theater and often came out drinking with us. He was another who should have taken to the stage—the commanding voice, the polished presence. It wasn't until he was murdered that we learned he was an English spy named McKinny. We drank to his soul, poor devil. We liked him all the more when we discovered his true profession. It takes a lot to fool an actor."

"Why do you think he and I were acquainted?"

"Just a guess. I believe you were engaged in a similar line of work. Any Englishman who was in France during those early days of the Empire was either a spy or a fool. And you are no fool. Besides, if you did know him, why, then you and I could do something to avenge his death."

"Even though he was working against your own country?"

Gerardone spat. "This caravan is my only country. Actors are whipped through the streets, wherever they live. I have no allegiance to France. So tell me, Captain, who killed McKinny?"

Matthew ran his knuckles over his chin. Back in Lempère he'd told the Gascon only enough to pique his curiosity. Now he had to make a choice. So many lives would be riding on the discretion of this towheaded giant.

"Your silence speaks volumes," Gerardone said, as he guided his horses across the Pont Marie. "I understand your reticence. Especially since there is a lady involved. I saw you with her the day you careened your ship. A bright angel."

He'd spoken of Lydia with reverence and near awe; it made up Matthew's mind for him.

"The man you seek is Lucien Chabrier," he said in a low voice. "He killed Alan McKinny. He is why I have had to come sneaking into Paris. And if you recognize the name, you will know not to bandy it about in strange company."

His companion gave a long, low whistle. "The asp in the bosom of France. You do aim high. Of course I know Chabrier. To every child he is the bogeyman who hides under the bed."

"You can drop us off anywhere along here. If you chose not to aid us, I will certainly understand."

"Understand this, my friend." Gerardone had grasped his arm with one huge hand. "I am a Gascon! Not some child to be frightened by bedtime tales."

"You should be frightened." Matthew shook off his grip with a strength that surprised the other man. "Chabrier is everything they whisper about him. Ruthless, bloodthirsty, hungry for power. And most importantly, he is a survivor. Did you know he conspired against Napoleon in '04? But he survived it—and rose even higher. Now you have a new king, and is Chabrier exiled? No, his power is unassailable. You should be very frightened, my friend. God knows I am."

"Then why do you seek him?" Gerardone had slowed his horses to a walk as they wove through the twisting warrens of the Faubourg St. Victor. "And what had the old priest to do with it?"

"The good father is a Bonapartist. His confederates in Paris ordered him to bring the woman and the boy here."

"What would these Bonapartists want with an English lady and an English boy? It makes no sense."

"The boy is not English, he is French." Matthew drew a breath. "He is Chabrier's son."

The horses reared in protest as their driver jabbed at their bits.

"Sweet Mother of God!" the Gascon cried. "You were cast up on the shores of France with Chabrier's son in tow?"

"Ironic, isn't it?" Matthew said. "It was only to be a day cruise off Exeter until a squall blew up. But an ill wind, as they say. Still want to throw your lot in with us?"

"Now more than ever. Chabrier has your lady, doesn't he?"

"I believe so. If she still lives."

Gerardone gaped at the nonchalant manner in which he uttered the words. "You're a cold-blooded one, Captain Frobisher. I think this lady deserves a man with more fire."

"This is not a play," Matthew said, the muscles in his cheek tightening. "Passion solves nothing. I think more clearly with my emotions kept in check." He gripped Gerardone's wrist, again surprising the Frenchman with his strength. "But mind you this—if he *has* harmed her in any way, he will feel my sword and die a slow, painful death . . . and all of Paris will hear his cries for oblivion."

The captain released Gerardone and pushed his way back into the belly of the wagon.

"*Jesu,*" the Gascon murmured, rubbing at his bruised skin. "I think this Englishman has enough fire in his veins for ten men."

The cobbled street before the comte's home was not brightly lit—the lantern from the small guardhouse threw only a feeble glow, not strong enough to reveal the man watching in the shadows from across the street. Matthew lit his pipe, cupping the bowl to hide the flame, and pulled the brimmed gypsy hat low over his brow. He leaned against a stone wall and studied the graceful lines of Chabrier's mansion. Twelve years ago he had danced there with his radiant Marianne and had made her brother Armand laugh at some quip over the punchbowl.

Even before he'd attained his present lofty stature in the government, Chabrier had lived in that impressive house. Not so heavily guarded back then, the captain recalled. He had been a welcome guest that night—a courtly young gentleman from the provinces—not yet perceived as a threat to Chabrier's marriage plans.

But after he'd held Marianne in his arms and seen the love glowing in her eyes, he knew he would do anything to keep her from the comte's hands, do anything to keep that adoring expression on her face. Including ignoring his orders to infiltrate Armand's offices. He had lost all thoughts of King and Country.

He'd often wondered afterward if neglect of duty was as treasonous as overt actions against the Crown.

That same night he'd made love to her on the seat of her family coach, long after the comte's party ended. She had crept down to meet him in the stable behind her home—the same stable where her brother hanged himself less than a month later. Marianne had been shy at first, but as passion took hold of her, she had blossomed under his touch and given herself completely, with almost frantic abandon.

They met often after that, frequently in public, in the park or at the theater, but even more frequently in private. She would come to his rooms, heavily veiled, and they would while away an afternoon in the blissful arms of Eros.

She may have loved him first, but by the second week of their trysts, he was mindlessly, violently, gut-wrenchingly in love with her. He had never experienced such razor-edged emotion in his life. The city of romance, Gerardone had called Paris. More like the city of reckless passion, Matthew mused.

Marianne pleaded with him to marry her; she couldn't understand his hesitation. She was the daughter of a venerable French family, surely a prize for a man of his background. But he knew it wasn't breeding that made him stay his hand, it was bloody politics. Could she, would she, still love him if it meant leaving her home and family and sailing across the Channel to the country of her enemy?

He was never to find out. Before he could steel himself to reveal his true identity, her brother had killed himself and she, his darling Marianne, had betrayed him to the French government.

Betrayal. He chewed on the word. Had Lydia betrayed him as well?

Then again, he was a fine one to be casting stones when he had lied to her about Jean-Louis's father being dead. If he'd trusted her enough to tell her the truth, she wouldn't have gone haring off to Paris and straight into the hands of his enemy. He could have made a case to her that the boy was better off with a stern schoolmaster than with a depraved, immoral bureaucrat.

Too late now for might-have-beens. They'd both suffered from his duplicity, but he swore that once she was safe in his arms, he would never lie to her again. Not even the smallest fib.

He knocked the ashes from his pipe against the wall and sauntered across the street, tugging his hat even lower over his eyes.

Time to go in for a closer look.

There were only two men in the guardhouse. One

sat at a narrow table cleaning a pistol, the other, a lanky fellow, lounged in the open doorway.

"Evening." He touched his hat as he addressed them. "I'm Pierre's cousin from Rouen."

"Pierre?" The lanky man's brow furrowed as Matthew held his breath.

"Pierre-Alain?" the other guard asked, looking up. "He's off duty tonight. Have you a message for him?"

"No, not really." Matthew examined the toes of his thick peasant brogues. "Just the matter of a small gaming debt. It's not important . . . hmm . . . My cousin spoke last night of a woman who was visiting here—the most beautiful woman he'd ever seen, he said. I was hoping to catch a glimpse of her. Thought she might be going out tonight—you know, attending a party, something like that." He looked expectantly at the two men.

"She was a looker, all right. Even under her cloak you could tell. Hair like spun copper." The lanky man nodded appreciatively, but the seated guard shot him a look of warning.

"She's not here any longer," he said curtly. "She left last night with an escort of the comte's guards. Now, you'd best be about your business."

The captain shuffled his feet and looked down the street. "The comte must be very pleased that his son is come home."

"Not so you would notice. What did you say your name was?" The guard was getting up now, coming toward the door.

"It doesn't matter." Matthew was drifting back into the shadows.

The guard snatched up his pistol and pushed past his cohort in the doorway. The street was empty. Not a movement, not a footfall. It was as though the man in the felt hat had never existed. The guard shivered unaccountably and turned back to his companion.

"Damned gypsies," he muttered.

"Funny eyes for a gypsy," the lanky man remarked. "Clear, like water."

"Bah! I've a mind to tell Pierre-Alain to keep his relatives away from here. Damned nosy gypsy."

The captain whistled tunelessly as he made his way back to the caravan. He always felt at home in Paris after dark. It was a dirty, crowded city, but no more so than London. And it possessed something that the English capital couldn't approach—an aura of mystery and intrigue, like an exotic courtesan. London was a plump dowager in comparison. Matthew's theory was that it had to do with the rivers. The doughty Thames rolled through London carrying commerce and travelers, giving London a very respectable character. But the raffish Seine, chuckling along its banks like quicksilver, carried very little traffic; it traversed the city and offered only its beauty and its rippling, liquid mystique.

God, I'm obsessed by water. He grinned in the dark. He wondered how the *Rook* was faring, if she'd been fitted with her new mast yet. He would sail her home to Devon, holding Lydia before him at the wheel, as he had done during the storm. For such a willowy woman she had a good deal of strength; he'd felt it in her shoulders and seen it in her arms as she mastered the ship's wheel. He only hoped she had enough fortitude to get through this ordeal.

At least he knew she was no longer in the comte's home. He debated his next move. He needed to call at the embassy to make sure she hadn't gone there— though it was unlikely. Chabrier would not have let her return to her English brethren so easily. And he wanted to pay a call on the good father once they had determined his whereabouts. Gerardone knew of a Franciscan hospice near the Invalides—it was as good a place as any to start.

The comte appeared in Jean-Louis's room the next morning accompanied by Scovile. The boy did not want to speak of the poisoning attempt with the other man present; he would bide his time until he was alone with his father.

"Monsieur Scovile is to take you walking on the grounds," the comte explained. "There is no time to show you around the house, so I'm afraid you will be locked in again."

"Can Monsieur Scovile not show me through the house? I grow so bored in here." He gazed up beseechingly.

"No, you need to be out in the air. Now look, I have more bonbons for you. I see you ate all I brought you yesterday."

"Yes, Papa. They were not like anything I have ever tasted."

"I'm pleased to hear it." The comte stepped into the hallway and motioned Scovile to join him.

"You understand," he said in a gruff whisper. "I want him to be seen. If Mattei is watching the house, I want him to know the child is here."

"I thought the woman was to be the bait?"

"No, she's too distinctive. I dare not let her be seen, not with the strong British presence here in Paris. Besides, I have other plans for her." He turned back to the room.

"Run along now, boy. If you behave, I will have some books sent up."

Jean-Louis went sullenly along with the grizzled man. As they descended the four flights of stairs, they passed a number of exquisitely decorated rooms. Jean-Louis thought again of his spartan bedroom and began to feel a wrenching ache in his chest.

He meandered a little way ahead of his companion as they made their way around the perimeter of the house, keeping to the grassy verge that separated the mansion from the high iron fence. The complex was U-shaped, the residence on the left, the offices on the right, and the kitchens and guards' quarters in the recessed center section. Jean-Louis made note of how the house was configured, noting where his own room was located high above the main entrance. He was playing the observation game that the *capitaine* had taught them.

Eventually Scovile returned him to his room with a promise to take him walking the following day. Jean-Louis found several books on his dresser and settled on the bed with a volume of Fontaigne's fables. He gave the cherry bonbons a wide berth; by the time the maid came with his luncheon, he had hidden them beneath his mattress with the others.

Lydia sang to keep her sanity. Softly—since the guard had warned her she would be gagged if she continued to make such a foul racket. She sang every song she had ever learned from childhood on—English ballads, French carols and even a few Russian folk songs. She sang until her voice was hoarse, and she had to swallow mouthfuls of the tepid water from the bucket on the floor.

Two nights had passed since she had been brought here. She wondered if she should ask for a piece of flint to mark the passing of the days on her wall. Her jailer rarely spoke to her. When she asked him what he had done with her ring, he had merely glared at her and wheezed, "What ring?"

No one came to see her. That morning she had thrown her shoes out the barred window in a fit of frustration. It had been a mistake—she suspected that late at night rats crept through her cell and feared her stockings would be poor protection.

When she heard church bells tolling the hour, she wondered if the comte's home was near the great cathedral of Notre Dame. This naturally reminded her of the perfidious Father Boniface, who had ranted about his sanctified mission and then turned her and the boy over to the most unholy creature in France, a man corrupted by vengeance and hatred. Whatever Matthew had done to keep the child out of his hands was surely justified. Even committing murder.

She knew the captain would be in Paris by now—if he had found her message in the priest's study and deigned to follow her. Would he even try to find her? Perhaps he only intended to steal back the boy as he had six years ago. If that were true, if he really had no concern over her whereabouts, then she wanted to die. Let them march her to the guillotine and execute her forthwith. Without Matthew Frobisher her life was over anyway.

Lydia, Lydia, the little voice chastened her, *he vowed that he would never let you go, as long as he lived. And remember, he called you intrepid. Where is that brave spirit now? You must have faith if you are to prevail over these wicked men. Hold tight to your faith—in yourself and in Matthew's love. He will come for you. He will.*

During their first full day in Paris, the boys, paired by age, one older and one younger boy, scoured the city for Lydia. Oxer and Tenpence kept watch before Chabrier's mansion, while Rowdy and Fripp monitored the comings and goings of Father Boniface. It had not been difficult to locate the priest—as the captain suspected, he was staying at the Franciscan hospice.

Gilbert and Seamus had a rather more curious assignment—they were to visit all the prisons and jails in the city, masquerading as two country boys seeking their red-haired sister who had been arrested for petty theft. The tears would well up in Seamus's eyes as he pleaded with the captain of the guard to let him walk through the jail. His plea was always accompanied by a small coin. It worked like a charm. But after they had been inside five different lockups, they were still no closer to finding Lydia. They did, however, carry away a grim impression of the French penal system.

That same morning the captain donned his elegant black suit and went off to the British embassy. An underling informed him that the ambassador would not be available for some time, and so he was fretting on a bench in the foyer when Sir Robert Poole stepped out of one of the adjoining rooms.

"Sir Robert!" he called out, rising to his feet.

The leonine statesman turned at the familiar voice, and his eyes grew wide.

"Matthew!" he cried in amazement. "Thank God you are safe." He wrung the captain's hand and then threw his arms around his shoulders and clasped him to his barrel chest. "I cannot say how glad I am to see you."

"You're a rather welcome sight, yourself, Sir Robert. We must talk. I came here to speak with the ambassador, but I'd much rather talk to you than that poncy nitwit."

Sir Robert's eyes twinkled. "Ah, I recall you were at Oxford together. You ever give short shrift to fools, Matthew."

The older man led him into the room he had just vacated and poured out a generous measure of brandy. "Now, sit, Matthew, sit. You're giving me a megrim pacing around like that." Sir Robert relaxed into a club chair and watched as his edgy friend finally came to roost on the arm of a delicate sofa.

"It's not good news," Matthew said. "I expect you've heard what happened to the *Rook*. I sent messages from Lempère to the embassy, through both the mayor and the local priest."

"The mayor's letter was received. There was nothing from a priest."

"Not surprising," the captain responded. "So how is it you are in Paris, Sir Robert?"

"Because of you, of course. I was notified of your message by diplomatic pouch, four, maybe five days ago. I cleared up some business in London, then posted here directly. You've saved me the journey to Finistère, Matthew. The ambassador couldn't spare anyone to see how you were faring, so I volunteered for the job."

Matthew was greatly honored. Next to the prime minister, Poole was arguably the busiest politician in England. The thought that he would give up his precious time to see to Matthew's welfare was humbling.

"We are not faring too well at present. Not unless you can tell me that Miss Peartree is here in the embassy."

"You've lost Lydia?" Sir Robert's voice held a touch of mirth, but the captain's grim expression quickly eradicated it. "Is it of such matter, Matthew? Paris isn't under the Reign of Terror any longer, and the Corsican is exiled. Britons are flocking here by the hundreds; it's an open city once again. But tell me how you came to misplace that tempestuous young woman. I'd think a man of your experience would have had no trouble keeping her to heel."

Matthew rolled his eye. "She is the most headstrong woman I've ever met. It would take a troop of dragoons to bring her to heel."

"I'm surprised, Matthew. Forgive the presumption, but I was sure you would find Miss Peartree irresistible. And I thought it wouldn't hurt you any to be around a lady of quality, if only for one day."

"It's been nearly three weeks—since the storm took us."

"I can't think of any man I'd rather have looking after her. And so I informed her cousin, Arkady, only today. But, come, man, you still haven't told me your tale. You know I will do all I can to help."

The captain quickly told Sir Robert what had transpired since the *Rook* foundered off the French coast.

"And now Chabrier believes that Jean-Louis is his son?"

"He *is* his son!" Matthew stated vehemently. "I told you, I abducted the child from Provence to save him from that jackal."

Sir Robert wrinkled his brow. He had a more than passing acquaintance with all of the captain's students. "Matthew, I know this is a delicate subject, but we are both men of the world, and so I can say this with some impunity. They might never have said this to your face, but a good many people back in Exeter believe Jean-Louis to be *your* son."

"My son?" He started back. "Impossible."

"Taunton Hardy swears that except for the color of his eyes Jean-Louis is the image of you at that age."

"The boy's hair is chestnut, mine is—or was, black."

"I recall when your father was a magistrate in Exeter years ago. His hair was a reddish brown, was it not?

"It was more brown than red. Besides, the boy's mother had russet hair exactly like his. And since we are treading in delicate waters here, I can tell you that Jean-Louis was born almost a year after I had last been with his mother. I hope I don't need to spell it out."

"I just can't credit that Chabrier sired such a child."

"What? Should Jean-Louis have sprouted horns and a long tail? He's half Marianne's, remember, and thank God for it."

"And so now we are left with this conundrum. Lydia and the boy are brought to Paris by the priest. The priest is a Bonapartist. He is in league with Chabrier, therefore Chabrier is a Bonapartist. The boy is returned to the comte, the priest earns the gratitude of the influential father, and life goes on. As long as the Corsican stays in exile, at any rate. These factions of Bonapartists are annoying but hardly a real threat. But I'm still wondering how Lydia enters into all of this."

The captain narrowed an eye at him. "Bait," he said succinctly. "There's a deal of unfinished business between Chabrier and myself. The jackal couldn't count on me coming to Paris to take back the boy. Jean-Louis is his own child, after all. But he knows somehow, damn his eyes, that I would go to the ends of the earth to rescue Lydia."

Sir Robert's mouth widened into a grin. "So that's the way of it? I wasn't wrong about Miss Peartree's allure."

Matthew looked away from his amused scrutiny. "We are . . . that is, she's . . . God, Sir Robert, you've seen her. All that beauty and such a gallant heart. I held her off as long as I could, but I'm only human."

"I'm sure you were a tower of strength."

"She made mincemeat of me if you want the truth."

"Farthingale will be despondent. I assume you'll marry her once you're back in England."

"You'll be invited to our church wedding, never fear. But I think it behooves me to retrieve her from Chabrier before I make any future plans."

Sir Robert got to his feet. "I'll save my felicitations until then. But I really couldn't be happier for you. And now, off to talk to that poncy nitwit; I'll let him know that he needs to get his spies out and about. Perhaps I'll visit Chabrier myself, shake the tree a little and see what falls out. You'll have all the assistance the Foreign Office can furnish, Matthew. We owe you that much."

"I appreciate it. I've set the lads to watching Chabrier's house and following the priest—"

Sir Robert appeared startled. "You've got your crew here? Aren't they a bit young to be gallivanting about Paris on their own?"

He smiled wryly. "They've been seasoned something uncommon. They're not the same lads who sailed out of Exeter."

"I trust you know best. We'll find her, Matthew." Sir Robert clasped his shoulder. "Hard to hide a woman like Lydia Peartree, even in a city this size."

After he'd gone, Matthew sat and reflected on his unlikely friendship with the indomitable Poole. Their conversation had left him with a lighter heart. He had a sure sense, for the first time since leaving the cove, that his quest would not fail.

He was making his way across the wide marble foyer toward the door, when he heard someone at the top of the staircase behind him. He turned to look up, out of curiosity—and because Paris was one city where he wanted no man at his back.

A gentleman gazed down at him with limpid green eyes. He was tricked out in a coat of amber satin embroidered with a riot of gold lace, his exaggerated shirt points reaching almost to his straight, wheat-colored hair.

Matthew regarded him with some wonder. "I know you, sir."

"Not in this lifetime, old lad," the blond gentleman replied genially as he made his languid way down to the foyer.

"Indeed I do." The captain stepped toward him. "And I've waited twelve years to thank you properly. And to learn your name."

The gentleman in amber looked bewildered. "Cambridge? If that's the case, I daresay we were a few years apart. Or perhaps you belong to one of my clubs. Pardon me if I don't recall your name—so difficult keeping the members straight."

There was the sound of a door opening on the upper floor, and the poncy nitwit stuck his head over the railing and warbled, "If you're coming in to lunch, Mitford, I wish you'd hurry it along. My lamb is turning to mutton."

"Mitford!" the captain crowed. "You're Lydia's cousin, Arkady. Come with me." He caught the dandy by one sleeve and propelled him out of the embassy under the stunned eyes of the ambassador.

"But my lunch," he protested as Matthew whistled up a hackney. "I quite adore lamb."

"I'll see you fed," he promised, virtually pushing him into the carriage.

They rode along in silence, the captain beaming uncharacteristically and the Marquess of Mitford adjusting his sadly rumpled cuffs.

"It *was* you, don't deny it," Matthew exclaimed at last. "You saved my bacon, rescuing me from that foul hole—and only days before I was to be executed. Though I never got a clear look at your face, I swore I'd never forget your eyes. It's odd—except for the color they're a dead match for Lydia's."

"People have observed that about us," his companion remarked. "As for this other—I'm afraid I've never been inside a French prison."

"Aha!" The captain shook a finger at him. "I never said it was a French prison."

"No, you have me there. I'm not thinking very clearly for lack of food."

"We'll dine on gypsy fare—it's not bad once you get past all the bones."

Mitford wrinkled his nose. "I can hardly wait."

"Did you come over with Sir Robert?"

"Mmm. I've been haunting Whitehall with the Earl of Monteith, trying to get news of the *Rook*. He'd have come with us but his lady is increasing. Finding out her brother Gilbert was safe was the best tonic. And I was delighted to learn that my errant cousin wasn't shipwrecked or taken by pirates."

The captain fidgeted.

"Was she?" the marquess asked incredulously.

"No, not pirates." Once again Frobisher explained how she had run off and all the events that followed.

"Let me get this straight—Lydia displayed her typical 'where-angels-fear-to-tread' foolishness and got caught in the middle of a jolly old case of revenge."

"That's certainly encapsulated it very well. Cambridge, did you say? I'm an Oxford man myself."

Mitford made a moue of distaste and then grinned. Matthew couldn't help grinning back.

For twelve years he had puzzled over the identity of the man who'd saved his life. What were the odds of his savior turning out to be first cousin to the woman he loved? No, not so strange, he decided, considering how lately his life kept revolving back on itself. And now here they sat, trading quips like two beaux on the strut in Pall Mall. Gad, he liked the man's style. In spite of his splendiferous coat and foolish face, Mitford was a remarkable fellow.

"Would you mind if I did a bit of poking around on my own, Captain? Only if you don't mind an amateur muddying up your pond." Arkady stroked his gilded lapel.

"You're no amateur, not if the way you smuggled me out of that prison was any indication."

"Oh, that was just a boyish lark. I've done unauthorized favors for the Foreign Office now and again. Very unauthorized. But I believe you were my first." He gave the captain a particularly sweet smile. "You went on to do some very good work after that. It's a pity they don't give out medals for spying." His eyes danced. "After spending two weeks marooned with my cousin that's the least you deserve."

"We managed to rub along fairly well. She's not a bad sort once you get past the red hair."

Mitford eyed him intently, but the captain stared back with total aplomb.

"I think we'd do well to pool our resources, my lord."

"You must call me Arkady," he insisted. "No one ever calls me by my title. Except for Lydia, when she wants to vex me."

"Well, vexatious or not, right now she needs to be rescued from the comte. Sir Robert is going to his house this afternoon to make inquiries. I've a gut feeling he's holding her there. If Chabrier fears a search, he's bound to move her. And that's when we'll get her back."

His companion mulled this over. "I hate to play devil's advocate, but what's to prevent Chabrier from killing her outright?"

"He wants me too badly to unbait his hook prematurely. There's still a deal of unfinished business between us."

"I've a number of relations visiting Paris I could enlist . . . Russian royalty and all that. Nobody knows how to ferret out gossip like a Romanov. If you'll just set me down here, I can get on with it."

"What about your gypsy luncheon?"

Arkady rolled his eyes. "I believe I can bear to forego it."

Later that afternoon the captain heard his crew's reports. He learned from Gilbert that Lydia was not in any of the city prisons. It increased his suspicions that she was somewhere in the comte's compound.

"Jean-Louis was walking in the comte's garden with an older man, someone called Scovile," Oxer pronounced. "I don't think Jean-Louis saw us."

The captain filed away one interesting part of Oxer's statement. "Go back tomorrow," he said. "And take the monkey. See if you can bring Jean-Louis to the fence. He needs to know he is in danger—and he may be able to tell you something of Lydia."

"The priest went to the comte's home this afternoon," Fripp reported. "We followed him right up to the gate."

"He must be seeking his reward." The captain stroked a forefinger over his lip. "I believe it's time I paid a call on the good father,"—he smiled slyly—"if only to remind him that confession is good for the soul."

Chapter Fifteen

Marianne

*T*he next morning another batch of bonbons appeared in Jean-Louis's room, carried in by the
sour-faced maid. She was followed shortly by Scovile.
The boy motioned to the fondant-glazed confections
on the dresser.

"My father must think I am too thin," he complained, thinking of Hansel being fattened up for the
witch's table. "He sends me these rich treats every
day."

"I wouldn't eat them," Scovile muttered. "Too
many sweets will make you sick."

He looked up sharply at the man. There seemed to
be an expression of concern on his grim, lined face.
Is he trying to warn me? he wondered. *Does he know
about the poison?*

Jean-Louis didn't bother to ask after his father; he
knew in his heart that the comte had no real desire
to see him. He had also deduced that he would never
be granted the freedom of the house. None of it made
any sense. He had been lured away from Finistère by
Father Boniface and brought to this house where he
had been promptly locked up, and now someone was
trying to kill him. Jean-Louis had a shivery suspicion
of who it might be.

But whether or not his father was responsible for the poisoned bonbons was immaterial. His only thoughts were of escape. Surely if he got past the gates of the house, he could find his way to the British embassy and prevail on the *mam'selle* to return him to Devon. *If* she was even still in Paris.

These bleak thoughts occupied his mind as he ambled along the rear section of the house, a little ahead of Monsieur Scovile. He was so distracted that he almost didn't see the slipper. It was lying beneath a hedge, near a recessed opening in the building's foundation. He crouched to picked it up, instantly noting the water stains on the toes, and the particles of sand wedged into the leather lining. It was the *mam'selle*'s slipper, he was sure of it. He had seen that shoe and its mate on her feet every day for two weeks. He'd stashed it in his coat pocket and was idly studying a sundial set on a marble column when Scovile caught up to him.

"What lies here beneath the house?" he asked. "Beyond that little window?"

"The wine cellar. Your father is known for his collection of rare vintages. It is kept under lock and key at all times."

Rather like me, he thought wretchedly.

"And who lives above the wine cellar—in those rooms?" Jean-Louis pointed to a gallery of windows on the ground floor.

"Those are the barracks for your father's guards."

"And above them?"

"A gymnasium. You are a curious one, young sir. Perhaps you've the makings of an architect."

Jean-Louis grinned and then, as his gaze moved past Scovile's shoulder, his mouth widened into an enormous smile.

"Look, Monsieur Scovile, a monkey!" Before the man could stop him, he dashed off to the fence, where two urchins were entertaining the passersby.

"*Zit!*" Jean-Louis hissed through the bars to Tenpence. "The *mam'selle*, she is here. Take this." Under the guise of reaching out to pet the monkey, Jean-Louis passed the slipper to his crewmate. Scovile came huffing up just as Tenpence whisked the shoe into his shirt.

"Come away, young sir. These are dirty street children. You might get bitten."

"I don't bite," Tenpence said in gutter Parisian, baring his teeth.

"I meant the monkey." Scovile was still tugging at his charge's sleeve.

Just then the tiny simian jumped from Ten's arm, clambered up the fence and launched himself into space. He narrowly cleared the top of Scovile's head before landing on the grass and scampering on all fours toward the house.

"We'll get you away soon," Oxer assured Jean-Louis while Scovile darted about in pursuit of the beast. "The Cap's got it all in hand. Thank God she's not dead. He will be that relieved!"

"Are you sure about Miss Lydia?" Tenpence asked. "That she's here."

"It's her shoe." Jean-Louis had lapsed into French. "I found it near the wine cellar. I think she's locked up in there. The comte keeps me locked in as well, but I'll find a way to get to her tonight, to let her know you're in Paris. Come back tomorrow."

Jean-Louis turned and ran toward the monkey, calling, "Let me help you, Monsieur Scovile."

But at a sharp whistle from Tenpence, the beast scampered back through the fence railing. The two boys moved quickly away.

Scovile, still breathless from the chase, huffed all the way up the stairs to the attic. After he'd been locked in again, Jean-Louis bowed his head and fought back tears of relief that he was to be rescued after all. No, it was time he stopped behaving like a baby. He would help them rescue the *mam'selle*, and the *capitaine* would see that he was not a weak little boy.

Jean-Louis thought again of Miss Peartree's kidskin slipper, certain proof that she had not gone away to the embassy. Poor *mam'selle*, to have come so far and given up so much and to now be a prisoner. He determined to get a message to her, to give her the same hope he was now feeling.

It was late at night, the fourth night of her imprisonment, and Lydia was dreaming again. Jean-Louis was speaking to her, telling her that the *capitaine* was coming to rescue her and that she should not be afrightened.

"Take my hand, *mam'selle*," he whispered. "Please, let me know you are in there."

Something dry and gritty showered down on her.

Lydia sat up abruptly. When a small shower of dirt cascaded from her hair, she realized it was no dream. Heart pounding, she quickly stood up on her cot and peered through the window. It was black as Hades outside. A small hand came snaking out of the darkness.

"*Mam'selle* Lydia?"

She grasped his hand and leaned her forehead against the slim fingers. "Jean-Louis!" she cried softly. "Thank God you are safe."

"I am sorry to throw dirt on you. I had to wake you. I cannot stay here very long. The guards will come by soon."

"Jean-Louis, listen to me. I have to warn you about your papa. I know you might not believe this, but he is a very wicked man."

The boy made a rude noise. "Me, I know this. He is a French dog, like those robbers who came for our horses. He gives me bonbons, and the pigeons eat them, and *pfft!* they are dead. He locks me in the attic, when there are beautiful rooms, too many to count, in his house. And he keeps you here in the wine cellar."

"How did you get out?"

"*Tres facile.* If I can climb up a ship's rigging, I can climb down a rain gutter. I go out my window and come here to see you. I found your shoe, *mam'selle*."

Lydia was stunned. After all her careful plotting with the emerald ring, it was the slipper hurled in anger that had brought her this hope of rescue.

"Can you get away, Jean-Louis? It's not safe for you to stay here. Think of the pigeons."

"I will be fine for now. I put the bonbons under the mattress. He does not poison my other food—I eat what the servants eat."

Lydia clung to the edge of the window, trying to see him. "Can you ever forgive me? For bringing you here—to this?"

"You, *mam'selle*? It is Jean-Louis who should say he is most sorry. I whine like a baby to be with my papa. This French dog. Bah! I will kiss the *capitaine*'s hand when I see him and call him master for the rest of my life."

Lydia sighed. "We might never see the captain again. I expect he is quite angry with us for running off without any word."

"*Non*, Oxer, he say the *capitaine* is not angry, only afrightened that you are dead. And Tenpence, he had such a *charmant* monkey with him."

Jean-Louis was making no sense. Lydia began to fear this might be just another dream after all.

"Oxer and Tenpence? When did you speak with them?"

"This morning, when I take my walk with Monsieur Scovile. They are in the street near the fence and I see the funny monkey. I run away from Monsieur Scovile, who is a bad man, I think, though not so wicked as my papa."

Lydia wanted to reach through the high window and give him a good shake. His convoluted manner of storytelling was maddening.

"Jean-Louis, please tell me right now—where is Captain Frobisher?"

"He is here in Paris. Oh, *mon dieu*, have I not said this to you?"

"No, not since I've been awake you haven't."

"But of course he is here. I give Tenpence your

shoe. He will show the *capitaine* and we will be saved. I must go now—I hear the guards. Tomorrow night I will come back. *Adieu, mam'selle.*"

Lydia leaned back against the stone wall and slid limply onto her cot.

He had come for her. He didn't hate her for running away. She wrapped her arms about her waist and breathed a prayer of thanks.

With very little effort she recalled how he had looked the last time they'd been alone together in the sea cave. So ardent, so compelling. And mellowed with happiness—as though only halcyon days in Evionne Cove stretched before them.

It had been a viciously hot afternoon. Too hot to work. Too hot to do anything but laze about in the water. Matthew coaxed her into the sea cave for a refreshing swim. Afterward he had coaxed her damp gown off her, pressing kisses on her warm, moist skin. She would never have a surfeit of his kisses, she had realized then, for each one left her hungering for the next. It was an appetite that was only sated when he finally thrust himself deep inside her and made her cry out in mindless completion.

It was a form of communion she had never sought, but having found it with her scarred captain, she valued it beyond price. There was so much more between them than the mere coupling of bodies. And now her greatest fear was dissolving away—that she would never again hold him to her in the quiet afterglow of lovemaking, never again feel his mouth laughing against hers as he teasingly kissed her. His supple body, his finely honed mind, his rarely given dimpled smile—they would not be lost to her.

"Till the heavens break asunder and the world is turned to dust," she murmured the vow he had spoken to her. "That is how long I will love you, Matthew Frobisher."

Lydia slept soundly for the first time since she came to Paris.

                    *   *   *

She was stirring on her cot the next morning when she heard voices in the corridor.

"Just give me the key, Redon. I won't need you to stand guard. She is but one woman alone."

Lydia rose quickly and straightened her twisted skirt. She was surprised to see the comte himself making his way to her cell. He unlocked the grilled door and entered. An aura of depravity seemed to emanate from him, and it took all her resolve for Lydia not to shrink back against the wall. Thankfully, her aristocratic Russian blood and steely English backbone came to the fore. She stepped toward him and said, with one hand raised languidly, "And to what do I owe this honor?"

"There's been a change of plans." His voice was curt. "We've had to move your execution up a few days—it's tomorrow."

Lydia threw her head back and regarded him without a visible tremor. She would at least deprive him of that satisfaction.

"Why such haste? Is the ambassador asking you uncomfortable questions? Have they petitioned to search your home? Oh, yes, I know this cellar is a part of your estate. It appears you forgot to block up the window." She waved a hand toward the opening. "And your guards do wear such distinctive uniforms."

"It doesn't matter now if anyone from the embassy knows you were kept here. They can't prevent your execution. And by the way, do not expect to see the boy tonight. He was discovered trying to sneak back into the house. He had to be whipped—it was most unpleasant—and is presently under guard. Though I don't think he'd get very far if he ran . . . considering the state of his back."

"I'm not surprised that you revenge yourself on a helpless boy. Held down by servants, no doubt, while he was whipped. What a petty tyrant you are."

She turned from him, clearly preferring to study the bleak stone wall rather than gaze upon his despicable person.

"I am not yet finished with you, Miss Peartree," he muttered. "You'd best attend me."

So, she had tweaked him with her snub. She felt a small frisson of victory.

"If I am to die, why should I show you the least consideration?" She folded her arms and refused to face him.

"I can still dictate the manner of your death. Quick and merciful or exceedingly slow and painful."

"You continue to frighten me with hobgoblins. You won't dare kill me once the English ambassador knows I am here. This is all sound and fury. You'd do better to release me and throw yourself on the mercy of the courts. And pray they show you more kindness than you showed your own son."

He growled low in his throat and spun her roughly around. His eyes, no longer remote, now blazed with fury. By God, she *had* roused him! Lydia almost smiled. Until he raised one hand and clouted her sharply across the cheek. She fell to one knee on the cot, nursing her face with her hand.

"That was pretty." She glared up at him. "Perhaps you can assault an old woman next. Or kick a crippled dog." He raised his hand again, but Lydia flew up at him, her temper finally roused. Her fingernails raked his eyes. He fell back toward the grill and then propelled himself forward, catching her arms and twisting them behind her.

Redon came lurching through the doorway. "I warned you, sir! She's strong for all that she's a woman."

"Leave us," he barked.

Lydia noted there was now a long, jagged scrape over the comte's left eye. "Sit down!" he commanded as he dabbed at the seeping wound with his handkerchief. "You will listen to me or you will be the worse for it."

Lydia perched on the edge of her cot, still trembling. "Some plain speaking, then, and no hobgoblins," she stated. "Then I will listen."

Chabrier wondered at her spirit. He had expected

cringing supplication and instead had received a lesson in manners. Gad, she was royalty to the tips of her fingers. But he would not be dissuaded from his course.

"I am sorry we have met under these circumstances, Miss Peartree. I encounter few woman with your courage. It would be entertaining to explore that part of your nature—"

"I said no hobgoblins," Lydia snapped.

"You are very bold with me today. And I believe I know why. The boy told you that Frobisher is in Paris, and you think yourself assured of rescue. Yes, I see the joy leap to your eyes at the mention of his name." He shook his head. "But he will not rescue you. My men will make sure of that. You will be taken under guard to the guillotine and beheaded."

"And you hope to trap him then, when he comes to save me?"

"No, I don't subscribe to such melodrama. What I desire is for Mattei to watch as you are sent to your death, standing by helplessly as the blade falls. I may not be able to see his face, but my imagination will suffice. The boy will be dead by the end of the week—he's been gobbling bonbons laced with arsenic—and then my revenge on François Mattei will be complete. He will go on living, as I have had to do, knowing that all he loved was taken from him."

Lydia shook her head to clear it of such unimaginable vice. Thank God Jean-Louis had discovered the poison.

"But why kill your own son? That would surely punish you, more than the captain."

"My own son?" Chabrier laughed bitterly. "He is no child of mine."

"But what of the portrait of his mother? The description on the handbill?"

"Oh, he is Marianne's child. But he is not the son of Chabrier."

Sweet heavens, could it be? Could Jean-Louis be Matthew's child?

"I see you anticipate me. Yes, he is the whelp of your English captain."

"How could Matthew not know it?"

The comte sighed. "I will tell you this only because you will never be able to reveal it to a soul. While your precious captain was here spying for the English, he tried to lure away the woman I intended to marry. His traitorous activities were discovered and he was betrayed by Marianne."

"Yes," she said impatiently. "I know all this."

"I went with the guards to arrest him. He drew his sword to resist and managed to wound me twice. One a trifling slice on the shoulder, the other a deeper cut, low down on my side. Of no consequence, I thought. They both healed fairly quickly, in time for me to wed Marianne, a week before Mattei was to be executed."

Chabrier took a breath. He had not told a living soul what he was about to tell this woman. "Afterward, we traveled to my chateau in Provence. But there was a problem. I could not consummate our marriage."

Lydia's eyes widened.

"I returned immediately to Paris, to consult with Napoleon's own physicians. The wound on my side had not healed as I thought. The infection had spread . . . and I was never the same man. No, don't gaze at me with pity in those blue eyes. I found other avenues for my energies—politics, espionage . . . revenge."

"But you still had the woman you loved. Surely other men have been so afflicted and found happiness with their chosen partner."

Chabrier continued as if she hadn't spoken. "Two months after our wedding, it was evident that my wife was increasing. She finally confessed to me that Mattei had been her lover. When the child was born in Provence his birth date was posted three months ahead.

"The boy was her only solace, and so I let him remain with her. I still cared for her, you see, in spite of her perfidy. But I eventually discovered her heart would always be closed to me, that she cared only for Mattei. She thought he had been executed and I never revealed the truth." His voice rose. "Let her think him dead! Let her not look for him to come to her in the night! It . . . it was only as she lay dying that Scovile told her the truth—that Mattei lived."

"Poor Marianne," Lydia whispered. "To discover on her deathbed that the man she loved and betrayed was still alive."

"He couldn't have her!" Chabrier growled. "She was mine! I banished Scovile from me for *his* betrayal. I knew he was besotted with her himself and so forbore not to kill him. I owed him that much."

"But he is here with you now. It was he who brought me to this cell."

"I allowed him back in return for a very great favor. Can you not guess? It was he who first brought me news of your captain."

"Oh," she said in a weak voice. "I was sure it was the letter Father Boniface sent for me that alerted you."

"No, we would have had you here without the good father. He only greased the wheels a bit."

"So there was no colleague in Paris as the priest told me? It was you?"

He nodded. "It has always been Chabrier guiding your course."

"And what of the newspaper story of the man who was murdered? The priest implied Matthew killed him to keep him quiet."

The comte smiled slowly. "I wanted you to feel a disgust for the captain, so that you could leave him more easily. In truth the man was killed by Scovile— he was another English spy."

Relief flooded over Lydia. Matthew had not taken an innocent life. She looked up at her captor, still trying to fathom how he had become so full of hate.

"After Marianne died could you not let go of your anger?"

"I am not angry, Miss Peartree. What I feel is a great deal deeper than anger. And after Marianne was gone there was still the child to deal with. How wise of your captain to steal the boy away when he did. I was already making plans for the brat to meet with an accident."

"This is infamous!" Lydia had risen to her feet. "Regardless of who fathered Jean-Louis, he was just a little boy—and the only heir you would ever have."

He glared at her thunderously as he flung one hand out. "You think I would leave all this to Mattei's bastard? Better it should go to the State. But now I am glad he lived; he has played nicely into my plans. What despair he shall feel when the boy is dead."

His inhuman expression of gloating made Lydia's gorge rise. Reeling back, she covered her face with her hands. The man was truly a monster, and it frightened her to be in the same city with him, let alone the same small cell.

"I hope you are not going to swoon," he purred.

"You are so twisted by hate," Lydia sobbed. "I cannot even imagine what it must be like. Is there no way to reach you, to make you see how foul this vengeance is?"

His face was a granite mask. Yet there was still a man, a tortured, wounded man, somewhere behind this creature's grim facade. She must try to appeal to that part of him. Lydia pulled herself upright, wiping away the traces of her tears. She recalled again the words Matthew had spoken to her in Evionne Cove— that the dead can surely affect the living.

"Look at me, my lord," she said softly, laying one hand on her breast. "Do you not recognize me? *I* am Marianne." His gaze darted to her face. "I am the young woman of good family, betrothed to another, who has fallen in love with the wrong man. I am at the mercy of my emotions and cannot turn away from the one I love, even though I betrayed him. Again you have separated us, my lord. My soul is gone from my body . . . it wanders through the dark streets of Paris seeking its mate."

The comte's complexion had taken on an ashy hue. In the dim light of the cell, with her auburn hair in a haze about her head and her face lit from within by an unearthly radiance, the woman might, in truth, have been his dead wife. There was such purity in that face. All his lost hopes for redemption shone there. *Marianne,* he keened silently.

His breath was coming in fits and starts as she continued. "You can resolve this now, my lord; it requires only a fragment of human kindness. Make your peace with Marianne, and let her have her love this time. She would die for him, and gladly, were it to save his life. But not to cause him harm. Not to be an instrument of revenge."

Chabrier was canted forward, his dark eyes never leaving her face.

"I entreat you not to destroy Jean-Louis, all that is left of Marianne on this earth. I believe you will be forgiven for the lies and deceits, if you would only heed me. Please, let the torment stop here—for Marianne, for the child and for you, most of all. Let the healing begin, my lord, before you are driven mad by your pain."

She reached toward him and his hand went out to her, as if drawn by a lodestone. His face had lost its knotted, bitter expression. His mouth opened, softened as if to speak an endearment.

Then he shuddered and drew back, raising one arm to ward off this red-haired specter.

"No!" he cried harshly. "You are not Marianne. She walks only in my dreams. And I have no need of forgiveness. Not now, when my vengeance is so close at hand."

He went from her abruptly, thrusting the cell door closed with dreadful finality. "In another century you would have been burned as a witch, Miss Peartree. Now we can only offer you the embrace of Madame la Guillotine." As he spoke, he rubbed absently at his eyelid where she had marked him.

"Then I will die," Lydia uttered vehemently. "But you, sir, who have turned your back on all that is wholesome, are destined for the asylum. Ponder who shall have the worse fate."

He faced her through the bars of the cell, gripping them so tightly the tendons in his hands stood out in sharp relief. "This *is* my asylum, Miss Peartree. Paris is a city full of madmen."

He was almost to the outer door when she saw him stagger slightly and heard him gasp, *"Marianne."*

Lydia paced in her cell, too agitated to sit.

She had affected him, she knew it. She had held the mirror up to him, and the jackal had at last been appalled by what he'd seen. For several seconds his face had taken on the aspect of a younger, more decent man. But the reflection of his dark nature she had furnished had not turned him from his course. Now it was only a matter of waiting, waiting to be taken from this cell by his guards.

Tears came unbidden to her eyes. Was she to die alone in the midst of her enemies and at the hands of this monster? She was suddenly very afraid, her stomach churning with rank, clutching terror. Questions raced through her disordered brain.

Even if Matthew was nearby, how could he possibly rescue her from the comte's guards with only a handful of boys? Had he enlisted the help of the British government, and if so, could they openly challenge a minister of France in the very streets of Paris?

She was still wrestling with her fears when the jailer came through the door. He was accompanied by a man dressed in a black cassock and wearing a wide-brimmed, black hat.

"There's a priest here—a Father Boniface. He insisted on seeing you." Redon nodded toward the tall, thin man who stood, head bowed, behind him. She could see a feathering of white hair above his clerical collar.

"My master is gone off to visit the king, so there was no use asking his permission. But I'll stay right here. That way Chabrier can't complain I didn't do my duty."

The jailer shifted aside as the priest approached the grill.

"You are not of my faith, Miss Peartree," said Father Boniface in his elegant Parisian French. "But I thought to comfort you, nonetheless. I fear I am partly responsible for your unfortunate situation."

"They used you to trap me," Lydia admonished him bitterly. "How can you, a man of God, live with that knowledge?"

The priest shrugged. "The Lord moves in mysterious ways."

"Will you not help me? And the boy?" Her eyes entreated him but his face remained obscured by the brim of his hat.

"Watch that!" Redon snarled. "He is here to console you, not to hear your foolish pleas."

"Be assured that I have done what I can," the priest said. "All else is in the hands of God."

"Will you at least take a message to Captain Frobisher?" Redon raised a hand to object, until Lydia added, "When this is all over, I mean."

"If it is within my power. Captain Frobisher is not an easy man to find."

"Tell him . . ." Lydia tried to stifle the sob that rose in her throat. "Tell Matthew that I am sorry I left him. Tell him it was my nature that was unsteady, not his, and that I was wrong not to trust him. He is not to blame himself for any of this. Do you understand, Father?"

The priest nodded and raised his head to gaze at her. In the poorly lit corridor his face was nothing more than a collection of shadows. Something glimmered in his pale eyes and then was gone.

"I promise I will find the captain and give him your message. Is that all you wish to say?"

"One thing more." Lydia thought furiously of how to relate this last, most vital piece of information without Redon getting wind of it. "Tell him this—he will understand its meaning—tell him the jackal's child is really the rook's son."

"Miss?" One of Father Boniface's gnarled hands was gripping the grill. "I cannot have heard you correctly. Your French is lacking perhaps?"

"No, you heard me. Please tell him exactly as I have said it."

"Time's up," Redon called out. "You'd best be away, Father, before my master returns."

The priest held up the book he carried. "May I leave Miss Peartree this Bible to comfort her?"

Redon took it and rifled quickly through the pages. "Looks harmless enough." He handed it back.

Father Boniface smoothed down the pages, then shut the book and slid it through the bars. As Lydia reached for it, his hand closed firmly over her wrist.

"Courage, Miss Peartree!" His eyes held hers for an instant before his hat brim was once again lowered.

Lydia nearly stopped breathing. It couldn't be! The priest's hands were twisted with arthritis, his cheeks lined with age, and no scar marred his face. *Oh, but his eyes . . .*

"I believe you will find great solace in the Psalms," he said quietly as he drifted back from the grill.

With her heart hammering in her breast, Lydia shifted to her cot. She opened the Bible near its center, thumbing swiftly through the poems of King David, until she came to the Twenty-third Psalm. A small square of paper had been tucked deep into the gutter. It bore only a drawing of a purple flower—a common weed.

"Matthew!" Lydia's heart sang out in exultation. It had been he—entering Chabrier's citadel in broad daylight to bring her this message of hope.

She carried the drawing of the nightshade to her

lips, and as she tucked it again into the book, she realized with stabbing regret the one message she had not given the priest.

"I never told him how much I loved him," she sighed. "But he must know it. And now he knows the truth about Jean-Louis, as well."

She raised the Bible and read aloud, " 'Yea, though I walk through the valley of the shadow of death, I will fear no evil, for Thou art with me.' "

"And you are with me, Matthew," she said, gazing with renewed hope at the sketch. "And I will fear no evil."

Chapter Sixteen
The Valley of the Shadow

*I*t was almost sundown when Scovile returned to his rooms near the Tuileries. The comte had been unexpectedly summoned to the palace, and Scovile had been forced to await his return for several hours. Chabrier had finally stalked in with a scowl on his face.

"We dare not send her to the guillotine," he muttered. "Louis's gotten wind of our guest in the wine cellar from the British ambassador. I cannot execute her in public now that the damned English have started an inquiry."

"Will the king back you up if you carry out the execution elsewhere?"

"He is not in a position to stop me from killing her. Louis will find a way to smooth things over with the British, once the deed is done. He'll offer more concessions—as if he hasn't bargained away most of France's rights already. God, Scovile, I pray that the emperor can be returned to power before our country becomes an insignificant dot on the map of Europe."

Scovile nodded but said nothing.

The comte threw himself into his chair and began shuffling through some papers.

"What's this?" He lifted a wrapped package from the desktop.

"Father Boniface left it for you with Redon. The priest came to offer his services to your prisoner. I would have prevented it, but I understand the jailer stayed with him the whole time, so no harm done."

Beneath the brown paper lay a small bound volume, a copy of Shakespeare's *Richard III*—in English. Chabrier's dark eyes bore into Scovile's.

"Now, why would the priest give me an English book?"

Scovile was about to suggest that there might be a message inside, when the comte himself opened it.

"Ah, no!" he cried out, leaping up and back from his desk. He pointed with a shaking finger to the purple flower that had been sketched upon the title page.

"He's been here, Scovile," he uttered hoarsely. "Inside this house. It wasn't Boniface visiting the English woman, it was Mattei." He glanced nervously around his office, as if the man might still be lurking nearby. "We must kill her now."

He rapidly skirted his desk and headed for the door.

"No, my lord!" Scovile threw himself upon the comte. "We dare not! Please calm yourself. We must go with caution. She is to be executed as a criminal. You will undo everything if she dies by your hand. Even the king himself can't save you if you murder her in cold blood."

"I'd risk prison to thwart Mattei," Chabrier muttered, trying to regain his composure. Smoothing down his rumpled coat, he returned to his chair. He picked up the book and hurled it into the cold hearth.

"Richard III." He laughed harshly. "I know the tale—the usurper king who held the young heirs captive in the Tower of London. Mattei has a sense of the ironic. But his humor will serve him ill when the woman lies dead."

"My lord, I must remind you again. The balance of power in Paris has shifted. Mattei is no longer operating alone in a city full of his enemies. We must find a way to kill her that complies with the new laws. If not the guillotine, then perhaps a firing squad. In one of the faubourgs beyond the city walls."

"Hmm? A military execution." The comte's thick fingers drummed softly on his blotter. "I believe that would suffice. I'll draw up new affidavits—we'll say she was caught stealing papers from my desk, that she was working for the emperor. The king can sign the new death warrant after the fact. Good work, old friend. My debt to you increases daily."

"I want only one thing in payment, Chabrier."

The comte's eyebrows rose. "And that is?"

"Let the boy live," Scovile said fervently. "He is all that remains of Marianne on this earth." Chabrier winced. Those were the exact words Miss Peartree had spoken. "You know I support you in all else that you do, but I cannot stand by and watch her child die."

"His existence is an offense to me."

"Then let me take him from you. Let Mattei think him dead, if you require it. But don't kill him. I will go from here and you will never see us again."

"He means so much to you then, that puling whelp, that you would give up all I can offer you—power and wealth?"

Scovile nodded. The comte looked amused.

"Getting soft in your old age, my friend. I'll think on it. For now, I've the matter of Miss Peartree's execution to set in motion. I think perhaps the Faubourg St. Antoine, out past that monstrous elephant statue. There's an abandoned military school there."

"The Academy of Sevraine. My brother taught there, before he died on the retreat from Moscow."

"Not our emperor's finest moment," the comte remarked in a low voice. "Very well, then. Select a squad of riflemen from the king's garrison. Bring them to the academy at eleven tomorrow morning. Oh, and hire me a cart and driver. I've a mind to see Miss Peartree driven through the streets like the

Widow Capet. I will escort her myself with a full guard."

Scovile went up the steps of his boarding house a troubled man. He wondered why it bothered him now to be an instrument of death, when for so long he had not balked at being the devil's henchman. Perhaps he *was* getting soft in his old age.

He made his way up the three flights of stairs, feeling an increasing weight on his shoulders as he climbed. He knew Chabrier would not give up the boy. Once set in motion, the comte's plans were never altered. Not for anyone.

The last rays of the setting sun were filtering through the faded curtains of his parlor window. He lit a candle and turned to place it on a deal table.

"*Bonsoir*, Scovile."

He started back with a muffled cry.

François Mattei was seated on a tattered armchair, aiming a long pistol at Scovile's belly. He was dressed all in black, a stark contrast to his silvery hair and gleaming gray eyes.

"Have you no words for an old friend?" One side of the captain's mouth was drawn up.

"Jesus!" Scovile breathed, and then hissed as the canted candle dropped hot tallow onto his fingers. He thrust it onto the table and then sidled backward toward the door.

Mattei shook his head reproachfully, motioning him further into the room with the gun's barrel. Scovile moved to a wooden chair and sat down heavily.

"We need to have a talk, you and I."

"It won't gain you anything," Scovile said sullenly. "The woman's as good as dead. You'd best focus on the boy."

"You mean my son?"

"So you do know. I've often wondered when you would discover the truth. You're such a clever fellow."

"Not so clever as that, it appears. I only learned of it this afternoon."

"Chabrier's been poisoning him with bonbons." Scovile saw the look of anguish flash across the captain's face. "But I've cautioned the boy not to eat them."

"Then I am in your debt, for that at least."

"The comte said those same words to me just now. It appears all this gratitude will not serve me in good stead."

"Poor Scovile." The captain sighed. "You cannot serve two masters. You are truly between Scylla and Charybdis." When a look of incomprehension crossed his face, the captain added, "I forget you've not had a classical education. Let us say then that you need to choose between two evils. Chabrier on one hand, who will only kill you if you betray him . . ." Mattei's voice was silken. "And me on the other hand, who can injure you in such a way that the rest of your life will be an endless torment. You decide, Scovile."

Scovile's face glistened with a fine sheen of sweat. "I've always suspected you were as twisted as Chabrier in your own way."

"I don't flinch from inflicting pain." His eyes narrowed. "But my causes are usually a bit more worthy than the jackal's. I plot to keep my country safe. Your master schemes his own petty vengeance and abuses the power of the state. I believe Chabrier may be the greatest traitor in this country, he, who courts the king, all the while plotting the return of Napoleon."

Scovile tugged at his neckcloth. "How did you—"

"Father Boniface," Mattei interrupted. "Who unfortunately has been imprisoned. He was unwise enough to leave a great many incriminating documents behind in Lempère."

"Boniface arrested?" Scovile's face crumpled.

"Yes, only a few hours ago. I only hope, for your sake, that the priest does not talk. Especially since he revealed to me that you were the leader of the brigands in Finistère. You could hang on several counts, it appears. So, would you care to bargain now?"

"Chabrier will protect me," he declared, leaning

from his chair. "He holds the king in the palm of his hand. Louis has already signed the woman's death warrant. What Chabrier does tomorrow will be completely legal; your government can protest it, but they cannot prevent it."

"Oh, but be assured *I* will." The captain smiled, but his eyes never lost their steely threat.

Scovile heartily wished he had stayed in Finistère. "If I decide to aid you, you must promise to free the boy."

"I intend to. But his peril is not as great as my lady's."

"I understand." He added after a moment, "She is very like Marianne, isn't she?"

"There is some resemblance." The captain's voice was clipped.

"It's rare that a man finds two such women in one lifetime. You always were a lucky devil, Mattei."

"Lucky?" He cocked his head. "Do I need to remind you that I lost the first to the jackal. But I'll make sure that he does not deprive me of the second."

"That is his intent—no, it's his obsession. He never had Marianne, Mattei. I believe it's been slowly driving him mad. Before she died she told me—the wound you inflicted on him, well . . . he was never a husband to her."

The captain flinched. "God, no wonder he seeks such a twisted vengeance. I can almost find it in me to pity him."

"Don't," Scovile snarled. "He brought it upon himself. I served him once out of duty . . . and to protect the emperor. But now I am sickened by his desire to punish an innocent child."

"The woman is innocent, as well," Mattei pointed out. "Help me to rescue her, Scovile, and all your past crimes will be forgotten. I have the ambassador's word on it."

The older man ran both hands over his lined face. His sins might be overlooked here in Paris, but they would not be so easily forgiven in another kingdom.

He had started on his path to perdition when he strangled Marianne's brother.

"Suppose I do help you. . . . What's to prevent me from returning to the comte and telling him he must alter his plans. How can you guarantee my loyalty?"

The captain pulled a folded paper from his pocket. "This is a note of commendation in Napoleon's own hand. If you betray me to Chabrier, the king's men will find it in your rooms."

"I'll claim I was framed. They will believe me—I have given years of service to France."

"*You* do not hold the king in the palm of your hand, my friend. And the guillotine has welcomed many former patriots, has she not?"

Scovile lowered his head. He felt like a rat in a mineshaft that offered only dead ends.

"You will answer my questions, and you will not give me away to your master. Agreed?"

Scovile nodded slowly.

"Swear it! On the memory of Marianne Dieudonne."

"I swear, by all I hold sacred—which is the love I bore for her. I will do as you command."

The captain offered him a mirthless smile. "Good. Now we can begin."

It was long before daybreak when Lydia awoke. She wondered with a hollow ache if this was the last dawn she would ever see.

Yesterday Matthew had called upon her courage. But now, in the shivery darkness of the cell, Lydia felt as though all her intrepid spirit had fled. It had been easy to be brave while the memory of his fingers, warm against her wrist, and the memory of his pale eyes, gleaming with love and a promise of rescue, both still lingered. Now all the specters of doubt rose up to assail her.

Then a vision surfaced, of a tall man battling his way through a tangle of cutthroats. That image offered Lydia all the comfort she needed. He would die himself before he let any harm come to her. He would rescue her, or he would perish in the attempt. And if that were the case, Lydia knew she would welcome her own death. She would find him again, in the afterlife, or if there was nothing beyond the grave, she would share the black oblivion with him. Whatever happened this fateful day, they would be together.

When she rose from her bed at last, it was to sit with almost serene acceptance on the edge of her cot. Her faith in Matthew would give her the courage to face whatever the next few hours brought.

She barely glanced at the comte when he appeared, accompanied by six uniformed guards. His dark blue coat was cut on military lines, embellished with orders and traversed by a bright sash the color of blood. His bicorne hat was reminiscent of those favored by the emperor.

Still holding the Bible, she was escorted from the cell. Not one word was spoken.

They marched her across the wine cellar, up the stairs and into daylight. Lydia blinked against the sudden glare. Along the back of the compound they went, through a gate in the iron fence which gave onto a cobbled alley. An open tumbrel, driven by a seedy man in a ragged straw hat, awaited her. Six mounted soldiers, each holding a riderless horse, were lined up behind it. After tossing the Bible into the cart, one of her guards tied her hands together in front of her with a piece of twine. "Not too tight?" he asked gently.

His kindness almost undid her. Tears welled up as she shook her head.

After the guards helped her into the cart, the driver craned around and mused lazily, "Nice day for a beheading."

Lydia had a fleeting image of a begrimed face and pale green eyes beneath the wide-brimmed hat, but then the comte rode up, distracting the driver.

"We're bound for the Academy of Sevraine," he pronounced. "It's to be a firing squad."

Lydia blocked out their voices—the manner of her

death did not interest her. She was trying to recall
where she'd seen the driver before.

The tumbrel made its creaking way along the cobbled streets, flanked on either side by a single guard.
Five more rode before the cart and another five
brought up the rear. The comte, sitting erect on a
glistening black stallion, rode at the head of the
procession.

Street children called out rude comments as they
passed. The adults merely lowered their eyes and went
on about their business. No one had forgotten the time
when daily executions were a form of entertainment
in Paris—when so many died that the gutters ran red
with blood. Now they preferred to look away.

As the procession moved out of the center of Paris,
the streets grew narrow, the roadbed uneven. Lydia
had to clutch the wooden cart rail with her pinioned
hands to keep from falling. The town houses and government buildings gave way to rougher dwellings, and
the people on the pavement wore the coarse home-
spun of the laboring classes.

"We turn here," the comte called out to her driver
as they came to an open square.

Lydia gasped at the sight looming before her—a
plaster elephant painted in gaudy colors standing at
least three stories high.

The driver shifted around. "One of Napoleon's
monuments. It was to have been in bronze, but he ran
out of money, poor blighter. The Bastille stood here,
you know. On this very spot." He flashed her a sweet
smile—and his green eyes lit up with mirth as she
recognized him.

Her cousin, the Marquess of Mitford—the toniest
dandy in all of Britain—sat before her with dirt on
his face and a tattered hat tugged over his elegant
blond locks.

"Arkady!" she whispered hoarsely.

"I was wondering when you'd notice," he drawled.
"Now, don't say another word, dear girl. Everything's
well in hand."

Lydia gave a dry swallow and nodded.

Several streets in from the square their progress was abruptly halted. A farmer's wagon loaded with melons had collided with a fishmonger's cart. Men were shouting in the street as children darted through the debris, plucking up melons and running off.

"We'll never get through there," a guard called out to Arkady. "We must find a side street."

"Blast," he muttered in English. "This has put the cat among the pigeons."

Up ahead, Chabrier was scanning the street nervously. "That way." He pointed with his whip to a shadowed lane.

When Arkady shook his head, he spurred his horse back to the cart.

"Not a good idea," Arkady stated laconically. "That street narrows something wicked at the end. If you're looking for an ambush, that's a likely place to find one."

The comte chewed his lip a minute, then ordered his guards to clear the debris.

Lydia would have thought it comical—the imposing soldiers rolling dozens of wobbling melons out of their path—if she had not been overcome by anxiety. Something was going to happen. An odd electricity hummed in the air, and her cousin's shoulders had tensed noticeably.

The procession threaded its way through the littered street and entered a wider boulevard. Up ahead, a crowd had gathered before an improvised stage that jutted from the back of a large caravan. Above it a banner flapped in the sultry breeze. LEOVIGILD THE VISIGOTH, SCOURGE OF PARIS, it proclaimed in a florid crimson script.

A giant of a man, dressed in a tunic and cross garters, was striding about on the stage wielding an enormous sword. His theatrical hair and long beard flew wildly about his head. Several other players, dwarfed by his incredible height, were also garbed as medieval vagabonds.

Again the procession halted as the guards tried to force the crowd aside.

"Hey, there!" the giant called down to them. "There's a show going on here, in case you haven't noticed, you ignorant swine. Leave my audience alone. It's hard enough to find people of discriminating taste in this city, without you fellows knocking them about."

"Silence!" the comte barked. "Let us pass, or I'll set my men on you."

The audience, misliking his tone, began to surge around the tumbrel. Lydia gasped as several swarthy men swung themselves up onto the cart's rails.

"Hold tight," Arkady said through his teeth as he stood up, tugging sharply on the reins. The horse danced in its traces, backing up erratically and swinging the cart until it was close to the lip of the stage.

The next instant something dark was thrust over Lydia's head. Strong arms lifted her, carried her. Suddenly, she was tumbled roughly to the ground. Woozy from the impact, nearly swooning, she tried to struggle her way out of the sack. She heard the comte roaring an order, and then the sharp report of a single gunshot.

Matthew! her brain screamed in terror as someone raised her up again and tossed her onto a hard wooden surface. Her last bleary thought before she passed out was that she was back in the tumbrel—and that the rescue attempt had failed.

The comte watched in impotent rage as the seething crowd closed in on his prisoner. He quickly spurred his horse into the mass of people, laying about him furiously with his whip as he tried to move up beside the cart. His guards, stranded at the perimeter, were likewise trying to force their way through the melee. Four or five gypsies had climbed onto the tumbrel, and he could no longer see Miss Peartree.

Chabrier's gaze flicked across the crowd. *He* was here somewhere . . . the comte could feel it in his bones. Yet he saw no one who resembled Mattei in height or coloring—until he caught sight of the tall, bearded actor at the edge of the crowd carrying a bulging sack over one shoulder.

"Stop!" Chabrier bellowed, riding toward the fleeing figure. "Stop, or my men will shoot!" He pulled his own pistol and fired into the air. The giant halted in midstride and turned to glare at him.

"Just getting a bit of my own back," he muttered sourly. "You ruined my spectacle, so I'm putting a damper on yours." He lowered the sack to the ground.

"Put her back in the cart, you meddling oaf."

The giant shrugged and pulled the sack along the ground for several feet.

"Lift her, you lummox! I want her alive."

The man hefted the sack again to his shoulder and then slung his burden over the side of the cart's rail. When the burlap fell away, the comte could see the top of Miss Peartree's head as she crouched there sobbing.

"Too bad, Mattei," Chabrier murmured as he returned to the head of his men. "It would appear your rescue attempt was badly botched."

The onlookers had been cowed into submission; they now parted to let the cart pass unimpeded. In a matter of minutes the procession reached the abandoned military academy. Its sandstone walls had been defaced with painted slogans, and the courtyard gate hung crookedly by one hinge.

A cloud of dust swirled around them as they marched onto the grounds. The comte peered through the reddish haze, his brows meshed in anger. There was not another soul in the courtyard. He had told Scovile to meet him at eleven, and it was already ten past the hour.

He didn't need the king's sharpshooters, he reminded himself. His own men would carry out the execution in their stead. He climbed from his horse and approached the tumbrel as his men dismounted and formed ranks on either side.

"A close call, Miss Peartree." He sneered. "What a pity your captain's plans came to naught."

She crouched in a corner of the cart, refusing to look up at him.

The driver, however, was observing the comte with a jaundiced eye. "Like to gloat, do you, my lord?"

"Just get her down from there," he snarled.

The driver swung over the seat. He gently drew Miss Peartree to her feet and tried to coax her from the cart. But after a few steps, her knees buckled.

"You'd better do it," the driver called out.

With a weary sigh, the comte heaved himself onto the cart. The woman was huddled before him, her red hair in a tangle over her face. "Please, sir, release me. Please!"

When she raised her hands to clutch at his coat, he recoiled slightly, his mouth twisting in distaste. How disappointing! He'd thought she would go to her death with a bit more dignity.

She was wailing "Aaaah! I beg you . . . do not do this to me," as he tried to thrust her away from him. *"A-a-a-a-h!"* she shrilled even louder.

"Enough!" Chabrier growled, reaching down and dragging her to her feet.

"More than enough," said a boyish voice as a pistol was thrust into the comte's belly.

A pair of bright blue eyes gazed limpidly back at him. They were, unfortunately, not Miss Peartree's eyes.

"Not a word, you festering cur." The tall boy's arm snaked around Chabrier's throat.

"Shoot him!" the comte bellowed to his thunderstruck guards as the driver leapt nimbly back to his seat and whipped up his horse. "Shoot him, you fools!"

"Follow us, and Chabrier is a dead man!" the boy cried.

"Kill him!" Chabrier roared again as the driver sent them rattling out of the courtyard.

They were out of sight by the time the comte's men roused themselves enough to remount and ride in pursuit.

"What shall we do with him now?" the marquess inquired urbanely as he guided the cart through the twisting lanes of the Faubourg St. Antoine.

"Gut him and throw him in the Seine?" Gilbert suggested, edging the pistol barrel up to the comte's throat. "He'd probably make good fish bait."

Chabrier's face had gone radish red, and his breath was coming in tortured gasps.

"Looks like he's having a fit of apoplexy," Arkady observed over his shoulder. "We'd best be rid of him, Gil. Don't want his death on our consciences."

Gilbert promptly knocked the comte's hat off and cracked him over the head with the butt of his pistol. As the cart slowed, he tumbled Chabrier's limp body out the back, onto a festering heap of refuse. "That's for Lydia!" he bit out as the great man's head sank into a pile of rotting tomatoes. "And for Jean-Louis."

"Well done, my dear chap." Arkady smiled gleefully. "He's going to have the devil of a headache when he wakes up—and, alas, that elegant coat will never be the same."

Chapter Seventeen

A Triumphal Return

*S*omeone had pulled the sack off Lydia; it was pooled on the floor beside the cot on which she lay. Once she had returned to consciousness—and pinched herself to make sure this wasn't just another dream—she realized she was in the belly of a moving gypsy wagon. The cluttered interior smelled of campfires and horses.

She wanted to laugh and sing in jubilation. Somehow, by some miracle, she had been whisked away from impending death. But at whose hands? Except for her cousin, she hadn't seen one familiar face in that milling crowd. Not that it mattered; even if these Roms were carrying her off to sell as a harem slave, it was still a reprieve.

Though she wouldn't fetch a very good price in her present condition. After days in a cell, her hair had lost its bright luster—and her blouse and skirt were grimy beyond words.

There were some garments hanging on the wall beside her. She eyed them speculatively and then quickly pulled off her soiled clothes, replacing them with a muslin blouse and a violet-colored skirt. As she slipped on a pair of hemp sandals, she silently thanked the absent owner.

She was standing in the middle of the lurching floor, looking for a hairbrush, when the wagon came to an abrupt halt, pitching her forward onto her hands and knees. The driver thrust open the curtains at the front of the wagon and stepped into the interior.

She swiped her tangled ringlets away from her brow, craning her head back to gaze up at the tall spare man in black. Her heart nearly stopped.

"Good day, Miss Peartree."

"I'm not Miss Peartree to you," she protested as she struggled to rise, desperate to close the gap between them.

"That's a fine distinction," he said as he flung himself to his knees in front of her. Their noses were barely six inches apart.

He kept his arms loose at his sides, and she did likewise, restraining herself from touching him. There were things that needed to be said first, hurts that needed to be soothed. They waited, studying each other intently, Lydia thinking he looked gaunt and yet surprisingly vital. Finally she decided that since her sin was of the most recent vintage, it was her duty make the first overture.

"I understand now why you lied to me and to Jean-Louis. Chabrier is a monster."

He drank in her words, nodding once. His eyes burned with emotion, but his mouth remained guarded. "And I understand why you ran off. I imagine Chabrier's pocket priest painted *me* as the monster."

"He did."

He caught her swiftly about the waist. "I'll let you be the judge of that," he said just before his mouth bore down on hers almost punishingly.

Lydia could hardly breathe, she was so shattered with relief and joy. But if she gave into her tears, Matthew would stop kissing her. She couldn't get enough of the taste of him on her lips or the feel of him, hard against her. Though his powerful arms nearly crushed her, it was the sweetest of pains.

"God, Lydia," he groaned at last. "I can't stop touching you. It was hell to be with you yesterday and not break open that cursed cell and take you out of there. My blessed girl, just tell me you are well; tell me you are not hurt."

"Oh, I am much more than well," she proclaimed. "I am beside myself with happiness."

Bending her back in the crook of his arm, he studied her face, deeply, probingly.

Lydia returned his searching gaze, noting the shadowed hollows beneath his gray eyes, which were only now beginning to lose their haunted expression.

"Ah, sweetheart," he crooned. "Promise you won't ever leave me again."

She turned away, unable to bear the raw pain in his voice. "I was such a fool to run off."

Matthew took her chin in his hand. "I was the bigger fool. I thought to keep you safe by keeping you ignorant of the truth. If you forgive me, I swear I'll never make that mistake again."

"No more deceptions, then. And no more talk of forgiveness. As I told Father Boniface yesterday, you have nothing to blame yourself for. I mean it, Matthew."

His tight, wary expression eased.

"In fact, I'd like to thank the good father for comforting me in my time of need," she said, stroking the hair that feathered his collar. "I never realized until yesterday what a very attractive man he is—for a priest."

"I think I can put you in his way," he drawled. "And just how would you express your gratitude?"

"Like this . . ." She pulled his face close and kissed him openmouthed, kissed away his wry grin until he was groaning and straining against her. He tumbled her onto the narrow bed and held her there, imprisoned by his arms.

"You'd be struck by lightning, my girl, if you ever kissed a priest like that," he taunted. "But I'd rescue you daily, if I could be assured of such a bonny reward."

"How *did* you rescue me, Matthew? All I remember is being tied up in the tumbrel and getting knocked about by gypsies."

The captain drew back from her and stood up. "I'll answer all your questions presently. But we need to keep moving—you're still not safe in the streets of Paris. I'm taking you to the embassy. I just wanted to, um, greet you properly before we got there."

"Afraid to be seen kissing me under the eyes of the embassy guards?"

"Exactly." He clasped her shoulder. "God, it was hell without you, Princess. You'll never know."

"I do know," she said softly, nuzzling his hand with her cheek. "I told Chabrier that my soul had gone from my body and was wandering Paris looking for its mate."

His eyes gleamed. "I see you do know, after all." He pulled her forward and pressed a kiss to her brow. "Now, wait in here for just a bit longer, my love, and we shall have our triumphal return."

The soldiers stationed outside the embassy didn't turn a hair when a brightly painted cart drew up before the stately granite building. They didn't bat an eye when a lean man who was dressed like a pirate handed down a flame-haired gypsy wench from the wagon's interior. It was only when the man laughingly kissed the woman under their very noses that they broke from their impassive reserve and grinned in appreciation.

Hand in hand, Matthew and Lydia went up the steps and into the marble foyer. Mitford was there, still dressed in his shabby clothes, holding court before a cluster of gentlemen. As they came through the door, he turned to them with a broad smile. "It went like clockwork, Frobisher. Scovile accomplished his mission, as well—"

"Arkady!" Lydia was hurrying toward her cousin, arms outspread, when one of the gentlemen, a strapping young man of thirty or so, stepped into her path.

Sir Robert Poole watched keenly as he intercepted her.

"Lydia! Thank God you are safe!"

"Donald!" she gasped and reeled back.

Matthew had come up behind her; he suspected his hand at her waist was all that prevented her from tumbling backward in a Tilda-like swoon.

"You must be Captain Frobisher," the young man exclaimed in a hearty voice. "I am Donald Farthingale of Exeter. Miss Peartree's intended, don't you know? You've got my eternal gratitude for bringin' her safely back to me. Not that it wasn't your fault for getting her stranded in this godforsaken country in the first place. Never could abide ships. The voyage across from Dover yesterday was hellish, I can tell you. But that's water under the dam."

"Over the dam," Arkady murmured. Gad, the fellow was worse than he was for talking nonsense.

Meanwhile, Lydia was gaping like a fish in a dry pond as she regarded her betrothed.

Farthingale didn't seem to notice. "I expect you'd like to be about your business, Captain, so I'll just take Miss Peartree off your hands. Come along, my dear, your room is waiting."

He reached for Lydia, who was wilting against Matthew, a look of dismayed disbelief quivering in her eyes.

"I'll take her up." Arkady slid his slim body in between the robust gentleman and the wary-eyed captain. "She's my cousin, after all."

Farthingale made a humphing noise. "True, Mitford, but she is *my* fiancée. I believe that gives me some precedence."

"Matthew," Lydia moaned over her shoulder as Farthingale reached for her again. "Do something."

"Yes, I can see I'd better."

He swept Lydia up in his arms, cradling her tight against his chest. She slid her arms around his neck and then looked up at him winsomely. "You'd best tell them."

"What do we have here?" Farthingale was glaring at Matthew, eye to eye, his hands clenched at his sides. "This is an outrage, sir! I demand that you put her down."

"Well, I will tell you what we have here," Matthew observed sanguinely. "Her cousin . . ." He nodded affably to Arkady. "And her fiancé." He squinted at Donald Farthingale. "Now, you two can brangle over her all you like, but it happens I outrank you both— I am the lady's husband."

He tightened his grip on Lydia as the two men took a startled step back.

"Married her secretly in Lempère, in front of the mayor . . . oh, weeks ago, it must be."

"I'm so sorry, Donald," Lydia cried. "It was that blasted storm . . ."

Matthew grinned crookedly. "Among other things. And now, if you gentlemen will excuse us, I'm taking my wife to bed."

And without another word—for really, what was there left to say?—he carried his lady up the wide, curving staircase.

"I can't believe you were going to marry that pompous, overgrown pup!"

Matthew was poking through a dish of fruit as he spoke, looking for a glossy, fat grape to pop into his wife's mouth.

After Lydia had availed herself of the commodious hip bath awaiting her in the royal suite, Matthew had dressed her in a lacy chemise and entreated her to sleep. She'd eyed the tray of tempting delicacies beside the bed and insisted she'd rather eat. From the heated expression simmering in his eyes, she decided it might be wise to fortify herself with food.

She rolled her eyes at him now. "If you must know, Donald was very amusing back in London. Everyone adored him. And he danced divinely."

"No . . . I can't believe it." He rolled half on top of her and captured her chin. "You would marry a man because he danced well?"

"Not well"—she squirmed out from under him and reached for an apricot—"divinely. And he was very attentive. He worshiped me, as a matter of fact."

"Fustian!"

"You do owe him some gratitude, Matthew. If he hadn't come down with measles, you and I would never have met. I trust *you've* had all your childhood illnesses."

"Yes, thank God. And even if I had the bubonic plague, I'd not let another man lure you away from me . . . Mrs. Frobisher."

"Mmm?"

"Nothing, I just like the sound of it. You're sure you wouldn't prefer to be Lady Frobisher? Sir Robert's always trying to heap honors on me, and I keep refusing."

"No," she said with conviction. "Titles are tiresome things. Arkady quite dislikes his."

"Your cousin is a surprising fellow, Lydia. He doesn't appear to be a man of action, but he's pluck to the backbone when it counts."

She grinned. "I don't think I was ever more shocked in my life when I realized he was driving the tumbrel. I thought I'd lost my mind. So, now will you tell me how you rescued me, since you're obviously done kissing me and such—"

"And such?" His hands were creeping up from her waist.

"I want to know how you managed to get me away. And you never explained how Jean-Louis was rescued. No, Matthew . . . I want . . . I . . ." Her protests ceased as his hands stroked her breasts.

"What do you want?" he murmured, his teeth against her throat.

"This," she sighed. "Always this."

"Mmm." Matthew gave a little hum of pleasure as she traced the center of his chest with her tongue. "That was very nice."

He leaned in close, nuzzling her delicate ear, blowing a whispery breath into the shell-pink whirl. When he felt her move restlessly beneath him, he kissed her there, his warm, moist mouth making her rise up against him.

"Tell me, again, what you desire," he commanded huskily.

"Touch me, Matthew. Everywhere . . ." Her fingers were urgent as she peeled him out of his shirt and then traced one velvet hand along his spine.

He had to shut his eyes against the waves of passion her caresses evoked. She was exhausted, traumatized, she needed the healing balm of sleep . . .

He had her chemise off in a matter of seconds. His boots and breeches followed. They had an eternity to sleep and only this one moment in time to recapture the magic they'd nearly lost. His sole thought now was to touch and be touched, to take and be taken—to let the potent power of consummation wipe away the darkness that had engulfed them for the past week.

He kissed her deeply, murmuring her name against her lips, an affirmation that he had never stopped saying it, never stopped thinking it. Her panting moans came to him as if from a great distance. But when at last he thrust inside her, his whole focus came roaring back—she was his life and his love, the only thing in his universe that had any meaning.

He plundered her slowly, arms extended taut on either side of her head, his pale eyes never leaving her face.

Lydia gazed back in wordless wonder, her thoughts a tangle of raw emotions. She felt tender and fierce, brazen and a little shy, overcome by her need, overcome by him—and yet so blessedly *certain* that he was equally helpless against her.

"Rise to me, sweetheart," he whispered as he shifted her upright, holding her with one steely arm.

Lydia responded eagerly, wrapping her legs about his waist, drawing him even further into her secret heart. She matched his increasingly powerful rhythm, growing bolder and more sure, meeting every lunge with a tightening, involuntary response. Breast to breast they plunged, heads thrown back, throats exposed in a straining arc. Arms entwined and bodies joined in tandem, they each drove the other toward a shuddering, spiraling release.

"Matthew!" she wailed, her hands tugging convulsively at his hair.

He gave one last throaty cry and arched back from her, his eyes blazing with a savage light.

Gasping her name, he fell forward, carrying her down with him to the mattress—and then for some time there was only the sound of their ragged breathing in the quiet room. The afternoon sunlight shifted on the patterned carpet, and still they did not move or speak.

"I've said you would kill me," Matthew murmured, when he was finally able to form coherent sentences. "Not a bad way to die, all things considered."

Lydia smiled against his throat. "Don't die yet, my love. I believe I'm finally getting the right of it. Just think what you'll miss."

"You had the right of things from the start." He abraded her smooth white shoulder with his chin. "Sweet Jesus, I do adore you, Lydia."

"Ah, but do you worship me?"

He leaned away from her slightly. "Don't you dare compare me to that bag-pudding downstairs. And, no, I don't worship you, little jade. You've had quite enough of that in your lifetime. I . . . well . . . I have a regard for you—"

"Oh, that's too bad of you. To think I gave up worship for mere regard."

"Let me finish, minx. I have a regard for you that is stronger than any friendship or any family affection. . . . You are my companion, Lydia, in every

way that two people can be together. I suppose that's
what love is, but it seems a puny word—"

"Hmm . . . puny again."

"—for what I feel for you. I will tell you one thing—
I loved Marianne, but it was a young man's infatuation, flaring up with fiery intensity and shaking my
world. Now that I'm older and a bit wiser, I see that
what you and I share is different—it endures and is
steady."

"A safe harbor?" Lydia said softly.

"Yes, exactly. We offer that to each other, don't
we? It didn't take a vow before the mayor of Lempère
to bind us forever, Lydia—I knew we were destined
to be together well before we wed."

"When, Matthew? When did you know it?"

He quirked up his mouth. "It was during the storm,
when you came staggering out onto the deck, soaked
to the skin, and proudly showed me your rope. 'This
is the only woman for me,' I said, 'Headstrong and
beautiful and brave.' You've a sailor's soul, Lydia—I
would have loved you even if you didn't return my
regard. And now, since we're sharing secrets, when
did you first know how it was between us?"

"That's easy. I recall the exact moment. It was our
second day in the cove, when you came riding back
from Lempère and your horse reared up in front of
me. My heart stopped for an instant—and when it
started up again it beat only for you."

"Ah. So I knew before you did," he taunted her.

She sniffed and sat up. "That's because men are
victims of their base desires. We women know how to
control our natures—"

He gave a shout of disbelieving laughter and tumbled her onto her back. "You were the most uncon-
trolled baggage I've ever met."

She smiled up at him. "Not until I met you. You
made me feel quite predatory." She drew him down
beside her. "And now I want to hear about the rescue.
I told you I hate a mystery."

"Aye, you did."

He stroked her bright hair absently with one hand as he explained how she'd been whisked away under the very nose of the fearful comte.

"Gilbert was hidden beneath the stage in a burlap sack. He was dressed to resemble you and wore a fetching red wig—my lads could have done Elizabethan theater, for all the female geegaws they've had to wear this week. Anyway, after the gypsies put another sack over you, they lifted you from the cart, and then Gerardone, my giant friend, rolled you under the stage. He picked up Gilbert and made as if to carry him off."

"No wonder I was getting bounced about so badly."

"Happily, the comte was completely taken in by our . . . red-haired herring."

"And where were you during all this?"

"I was watching from below the stage, waiting for the switch to be made. I pulled you along beneath the Gascon's caravan to the gypsy cart, and lifted you into the back. You had swooned, poor angel, but since I needed to get away, I didn't have time to revive you."

"I fainted because I couldn't breathe," Lydia said quickly. She certainly didn't want him to think it was from fear.

He then explained how Gilbert and Arkady used the comte as hostage to get away from the guards at the academy.

"I'd like to get all the details from your cousin," he added. "I suppose I'll have to go down and speak with him . . . eventually."

"We'll both go down," she said. "I need to tease him for his dreadful taste in hats."

"Ah, no. You can bait your cousin in the morning. I want you to spend today resting."

She started to pout but then was distracted by another question. "What of Jean-Louis? All you told me was that he was being brought here?"

He nodded. "We checkmated the comte rather

neatly today. While he was off trying to execute you, Scovile fetched the boy from his room and escorted him to a waiting carriage. No one dared question him—the comte had given him carte blanche." He hesitated, and then said softly, "My son is safe."

Lydia's eyes brightened. "Then you did understand my message yesterday?"

"The rook's son," he mused. "Maybe I've always known it, somewhere deep inside. Even though his birth records proved he couldn't be mine."

"The comte told me he'd had the records altered—to avoid scandal. He told me a great many things, Matthew. I'll be a long time forgetting some of them."

He tugged her against his shoulder. Memories were the one thing he couldn't protect her from.

"If no one's said anything to Jean-Louis yet, I'd like to be the one to tell him." He set his chin on her curls. "Gad, Lydia, I'm still trying to credit that I have a son. I thought to die childless—"

"I'm not *that* old," she protested.

"—and now this news has turned my world around. I've been very hard on the boy, trying to compensate for his wretched patrimony. Now we'll have to begin again."

"You've already begun, Matthew. You were so much gentler with him that last week in Evionne. And it's very clear he loves you."

"Does he?" He twisted around, his eyes seeking hers. "I seem to have spent my life holding everyone who loves me at bay."

"Not any longer." She leaned forward and brushed her lips over his cheek. "We've worn you down."

"Aye." He smiled ruefully. "That you have."

"But tell me one thing more. Scovile is Chabrier's man. However did you convince him—or even come to trust him?"

"The man's a ruffian, but he has a care for Jean-Louis. I just added a little blackmail to turn him to our side. I can be very . . . persuasive. It was Scovile who revealed where the execution was to take place and the route the comte intended to follow."

"Chabrier never had a chance going up against you, did he?"

"It wasn't only me. We have some gallant friends— that rascal Gerardone, the gypsies, your cousin. And my young crew. I once told you that I worked best alone. The past week's events have proven me very wrong."

Lydia pondered all he'd told her. So much had depended on chance, and yet, miraculously, here she was, back in her husband's arms. Jean-Louis was safe, and the fearsome comte had been rolled up, horse, foot and guns.

"Matthew, my head is spinning. There were so many threads in this plot you wove, any one of them could have unraveled at any time."

"I had one ace up my sleeve. A rather grubby Cockney ace."

"Tenpence?"

"Exactly. He and Rowdy were inside the abandoned academy with a brace of dueling pistols. If we'd been unable to make the switch, he would have picked off Chabrier from the windows. Your cousin was also armed. By the way, that nag Arkady was driving once belonged to the comte—won a great many races for him. I thought it a nice touch."

Lydia's eyes narrowed accusingly. "You enjoyed planning this, didn't you?"

"Not enjoyed, precisely. Still, it sharpens the brain to go against a man like Chabrier. It was . . . stimulating. You had the hard part—the waiting part. As you once pointed out, women always get to play that role. Not fair, but there you have it."

"I wish I could be in the thick of things for once. All I got to do was throw my shoe out the window and cozen the jailer into stealing my ring. Not very stimulating."

"Which reminds me . . ." He was leaning half off

the bed, fishing in the pocket of his discarded breeches. He sat upright, took Lydia's hand and slipped the emerald onto her finger.

"It worked!" she exclaimed. "That horrid little man did sell it. Oh, but I'm delighted to have it back."

"Thank Arkady. Apparently the jeweler recognized the stone and tried to peddle it to the Princess Ouspenskya,"

"Aunt Olga's here?"

"The princess contacted your cousin, who was able to trace the ring back to the comte's crippled jailer. It corroborated what we already knew from Jean-Louis. That you were being held inside Chabrier's house."

"I can't believe it worked. I felt so foolish at the time—like I was grasping at straws. What a . . . puny creature you must think me."

Matthew ran his thumb along the line of her jaw. "No, Lydia. You might have been the bravest one of all. I've been in prison myself; I know how it chips away at your strength and your courage. You kept your stout heart and your clear head. When I saw you in your cell yesterday, I couldn't credit how composed you looked. I may have foiled Chabrier's plans for revenge with all my spying and plotting, but you, Princess, bested him with nothing more than your unquenchable spirit."

The sunlight was fading beyond the brocaded draperies when Matthew announced he was heading down to find Arkady.

"I need to make sure my boys got back to the gypsy camp. And I want to spend some time with Jean-Louis," he added, tugging on his breeches.

He'd tugged his shirt carelessly over his head, and Lydia reached to smooth his hair.

"Will you grow it long again? For me?"

He chuckled. "Ah, you prefer the pirate."

"It suited you, Matthew. You're not a fashionable fribble like my cousin—"

"Speaking of whom . . . I've really got to go. I promise I won't let Arkady talk circles around me."

"Matthew?" she called out as he opened the door. "Chabrier isn't any threat to us now, is he?"

He leaned against the frame. "He wouldn't dare come after us in the embassy. The comte's days in the sun are waning—only today the king was informed that he's been plotting the return of the emperor. The jackal had better look to his laurels."

He cast a last admiring glance at Lydia, lounging naked amid the rumpled sheets—like a high-priced courtesan. He realized this was the first time he'd been with her in a proper bed. It hadn't seemed to impede them any.

"You'd better rest now, sweetheart. I don't expect we'll get much sleep tonight." He leered at her wickedly, and she heaved a pillow at the closing door. His laughter echoed down the hall.

"Insufferable man." She grinned lazily as she lay back, thinking of all the delightful things the night would bring.

She tried to sleep, but her restless desire for Matthew kept her tossing and turning. Finally, she drew on her chemise and went to stand before the floor-length window. The remains of a vivid sunset streaked the horizon beyond the spires and domes of the Paris skyline. She watched, leaning against the heavy draperies, as the pinks and golds faded to a cool, deep azure. Odd, that she had been in Paris for nearly a week and was only now seeing it as a beautiful, captivating city. She wondered if every place she shared with Matthew would seem enchanted to her.

Once the sky had darkened to a deep, even blue, Lydia drew away from the window, stifling a yawn. She padded back to the bed, tucked herself under the covers and was soon fast asleep.

Chapter Eighteen

Nemesis

*L*ydia felt the pistol barrel against her throat before she was even aware that someone had entered the dark room.

"Up," a man's voice whispered gruffly in English. "Get up and get dressed. If you make a noise, you're dead."

She crawled out from under the bedclothes and stooped, trembling, to search for her skirt and blouse. Some part of her was still deep in sleep, secure and untroubled. But the alert part of her mind keened in wordless terror.

Once she was dressed, a cloak was thrown over her shoulders. The man grasped her arm and dragged her from the room. In the light from the hallway tapers, her abductor was revealed as a tall, fleshy man wearing the wine-colored livery of the embassy staff.

Lydia's gaze darted frantically up and down the deserted hallway. Where were the guards? Where in God's name was Matthew?

The man forced her down a narrow servants' staircase and through the deserted scullery to a service door that opened into a cobbled yard. They had not encountered one other soul during their rapid, silent passage.

Her abductor propelled her relentlessly through an iron gate and along the lane toward a closed carriage. Another man waited there, muffled in a long cape, his hat pulled low over his brow. Lydia had no trouble recognizing Chabrier.

I must run or I'm doomed, she thought frantically. As if anticipating her thoughts, Chabrier stepped forward and caught her wrist in an iron grasp, his eyes glittering feverishly beneath the brim of his hat. The liveried man opened the carriage door, and he thrust Lydia inside. A slight figure huddled in the far corner—Jean-Louis.

The comte climbed in after her and then leaned out the window.

"You can consider your debt to me repaid, Delacourt. You've done well."

As the carriage drew away, Lydia curled herself protectively around Jean-Louis. "No one will hurt you," she said softly. "I promise."

His eyes gazed up at her blankly. There was a mark on his face, a fresh bruise. Something dark surged inside Lydia. In that instant she knew she was fully capable of killing the man who sat gloating silently beside them.

Once again, she and the boy were taken to his office, a nightmarish reprise of their first night in Paris. She sank onto the settee, holding Jean-Louis close beside her. The comte began pacing before his hearth, his wide face a mottled gray and red. No longer the composed aristocrat, he now looked like a man nearing the end of his endurance. When the tension in the room grew intolerable, Lydia burst out, "He won't come!"

The comte hissed as he turned, his eyes like those of a wild beast. "How can he not, with such an inducement?"

"Why should he?" she replied tartly. "I'm finished with him after today. My fiancé Donald Farthingale has come for me from Exeter."

"Delacourt swore you were with the captain."

"My betrothed is a tall, fair-haired man. It would be easy to mistake the two. I expect Captain Frobisher wants nothing more to do with me now."

"He came for you this morning," Chabrier muttered.

She gave a delicate shrug. "He was merely fulfilling his responsibility to me. But he is a commoner—and one can hardly expect such a man's chivalry to be boundless."

"If not for you, then, he will surely come for the boy."

"I wouldn't count on that either. When I told him at the embassy that the boy was his son, he raged about the room in a rare temper. Claimed he'd never had, um, congress with your late wife. He insisted that Jean-Louis must be another man's child. Perhaps even Scovile's. I seriously doubt the captain will risk his neck to save either of us."

Jean-Louis was glaring at her as though she were a viper.

"He will come!" Chabrier snarled. "You are merely trying to save your own skin."

No, I'm just trying to keep you off balance, you loathsome reptile!

She folded her hands in her lap so he wouldn't see them trembling. "The one thing I do know is that Father Boniface betrayed you to the Crown. Your plans for a new empire will soon be dust. I might suggest your time would be better spent packing up and getting out of Paris than in holding hostages who haven't any expectation of being rescued."

Chabrier approached her, his hands behind his back.

"I would have enjoyed crossing swords with you in the old days. You are quite convincing as the heartless coquette playing two men against each other. And this tale of Jean-Louis's mysterious father—most ingenious. I might even credit it, if I hadn't heard from my wife's own lips that Mattei fathered her child."

"The captain was an easy scapegoat—since your wife thought him dead."

"Yes, I can almost believe he won't come," Chabrier purred. "Except for one thing." He drew his hand from behind him and held up the paperweight. "Mattei would never refuse a challenge from me. He may send you and the boy to blazes, but he will come to me for his own reasons—because this meeting was ordained twelve years ago when I marked him with his own sword."

Lydia observed the clear globe with the image of her husband's namesake at its center.

Nightshade, her heart whispered. *The purple flower is blooming again . . . its poison will spread.*

"Then why keep us here?" she cried. "I beg you, don't make Jean-Louis a witness to your vendetta."

"Oh, he's seen murder done once tonight. I spitted Scovile in the boy's room at the embassy."

This was too much for Jean-Louis, who cried out, "Monsieur Scovile tried to protect me, and this evil one stabbed him in the heart."

"Quiet, you little upstart, or I'll have you whipped again."

Lydia felt a ripple of lightheadedness. So the comte had left a trail of blood behind him. Matthew must be mad with anguish. But, please God, she prayed, let him go cautiously, tonight of all nights.

The captain had been closeted with Arkady for nearly an hour. He was just heading back to Lydia when Sir Robert hailed him and drew him into a council room, where the ambassador and his aides were seated.

"The king has refused our petition against Chabrier," Sir Robert told him dolefully. "Louis will not hear a word spoken against him, even though we know from the priest that Chabrier is at the head of the Bonapartist network."

Matthew nodded grimly. "Yesterday Scovile bragged that his master holds the king in the palm of his hand. I thought he was exaggerating, but perhaps it is true. The comte's never been averse to a little blackmail in exalted circles. Is Scovile still in the embassy?"

"He was keeping your boy company," Sir Robert said.

"Then let's bring him down here so we can discover just what Chabrier is holding over Louis's head."

One of the aides was sent to fetch him. Not three minutes later, he came flinging back into the council chamber.

"The boy is missing!" he panted. "And Scovile's been wounded. I met Mitford in the hall—he's gone to check on the lady."

Arkady met them on the staircase, his face ashen. "He's got Lydia, Matthew. I checked her bedroom and found this note on the pillow."

The captain scanned the message. *Come to my office alone and unarmed.*

He cursed himself for leaving her, for believing her safe inside the embassy. The jackal had clearly not been cowed by his defeat that morning. Matthew suspected it had only increased his hunger for vengeance.

He immediately tried to draw on his mantle of cool detachment—and failed. His gut burned with fury and his heart was icy with apprehension.

"Take me to Scovile." His hand was like iron on Arkady's wrist.

The grizzled man lay sprawled upon Jean-Louis's bed, the handle of a dagger protruding from his ribs. He looked up at the captain, his eyes glassy and unfocused. "Mattei," he gasped out. "Hear my confession, please. I . . . I want to die in peace."

Matthew knelt down. "I'm here."

"I m-murdered Armand Dieudonne . . ." he began haltingly, "at Chabrier's command. He forged a note . . . made Marianne think you had betrayed her brother. He forced her to turn you in. She never got over it . . . never."

Matthew nearly reeled back. All those years he had

suffered, thinking Marianne had callously sent him to prison—to his death—to avenge her dead brother. He should have guessed it was the handiwork of Chabrier.

"If you want absolution," he said with quiet intent, "then you must help us defeat the comte. What hold does he have on the king?"

"Papers," Scovile rasped. "Papers and letters in his safe . . . foolish promises Louis made before he was returned to the throne. Behind Rousseau in his office. Burn them, Mattei . . . let France be free again."

He clutched Matthew's hand. "One thing more . . . you must save Marianne's son."

"I will," he said. "Die assured that I will."

He watched the light fade from his former enemy's eyes. "And may God have mercy on your soul."

Matthew thought furiously as he made his way down the staircase and then sketched out his plan to Sir Robert and Arkady.

"Are you really going inside that house alone, Matthew?" Sir Robert asked

He gave a low chuckle. "In truth, how can I be alone with seven lads in tow?"

"You've only got six now," his friend reminded him. "Chabrier's got Jean-Louis."

"I'll be the seventh," Arkady offered and then grinned ruefully. "Lydia's always complaining that I never stopped behaving like a lad."

As the two men raced toward the gypsy camp, Matthew honed his plan. He would exact a revenge that would be sublime and lasting—and if it worked, he would avoid staining his hands with the jackal's blood.

Once again he was going to be indebted to the giant Gascon.

The room had subsided again into a tense silence. Chabrier was at his desk, watching the candlelight dance on the paperweight. Lydia sat unmoving on the settee, rigid with anxiety, with Jean-Louis curled up beside her. It felt as though time was standing still, though according to the mantel clock over an hour had passed.

When a knock sounded abruptly at the door, she almost came off her seat.

A man's voice spoke from the hallway. "He's here."

Chabrier called out, "He's alone? Unarmed?"

"Yes, my lord. We searched him thoroughly. He had a knife hidden in his boot."

"Well done. Send him in."

Lydia held her breath. There was a brisk tread on the hallway tiles and then Matthew strode into the room. He wore a tailored black coat over a deep gray waistcoat, his shirt a blazing white, though no brighter than his neatly cropped hair, and he carried a bicorne hat under one arm. His face was almost gaunt, jaw taut, pale eyes burning with a martial light. He had never appeared more elegant—or more dangerous.

He didn't even glance at Lydia as he crossed to the desk. "You're looking fit, Lucien," he pronounced evenly, "for a greedy toad who's been feeding off the people of France."

The comte stood up slowly, one hand resting on the desk, the other aiming a pistol at the captain's chest. "Ah, Mattei, ever the gracious guest. As I recall, the last time you were in this house, you stole my bride-to-be."

"Not precisely. I was in this house yesterday. I paid a call on this lady." He motioned to Lydia but never took his eyes from the comte.

"How remiss of me to have overlooked that visit. And you left me a gift, did you not?"

"I trust the meaning was not obscure." The captain toyed with his hat as he spoke.

"I was never fond of Shakespeare." His gaze shifted to the hearth, where the copy of *Richard III* lay.

"A pity. The Bard had a talent for portraying black-guards. I thought you could use a few pointers, since you appear to have grown lax."

"Not so lax, Mattei. You are here, after all. I've waited so very long for this moment." He shifted the pistol to Jean-Louis. "I was going to kill them both and let you live. But now I will have it all—they will die before your eyes, and then I will have the pleasure of putting an end to you myself." He cocked the hammer.

"Wait!" the captain commanded. "You think I will stand by and do nothing while you murder them. No, I know how your mind works, Chabrier. You want something from me."

"Clever fellow. I want Boniface's papers. It was very remiss of the good father to leave such valuables behind in Lempère. He made the mistake of underestimating you."

"It's too late. They're in Louis's hands. Not enough to incriminate you, but it's a start."

The comte was scowling as he came around the desk. "Then you've nothing to bargain with."

Matthew held his hands out, palms up. "I have myself. Let the woman and the boy go free, and then we will settle things between us. Or aren't you man enough to take me on yourself? Scovile's no longer here to do your dirty work—like killing Armand Dieudonne."

Chabrier's eyes darkened. "Armand's death was necessary," he growled.

"You know, Lucien, I actually pitied you when I learned of your . . . affliction." There was undisguised scorn in Matthew's voice. "But not now, not after I discovered how you murdered Marianne's brother. You're a contemptible beast and not fit to live."

"If I die, it won't be at your hands." The comte raised his pistol.

"Gutless bastard," the captain hissed. "Shoot me down unarmed and where's your victory? Where's your manhood, Lucien?" Chabrier's face twisted as Matthew entreated him softly, "Let us finish what was begun twelve years ago. Let us bring this to a close like men of honor."

The two were now only an armspan apart. Lydia drew back further onto the settee, shaken by the seething hatred that filled the room. Jean-Louis had covered his face with one arm.

The comte drew a deep breath and then spun away. He set his pistol on the mantel before moving to a tall armoire. Matthew backed up two steps to where Lydia sat shivering. He put one hand behind him, seeking her touch, and then murmured in English, "Stout heart, Princess. And don't believe everything you see."

The comte had returned to the center of the room cradling a pair of dueling swords. Matthew took the blade that was offered, whipping it through the air several times. "You used to be quite good with a sword, Lucien. Kept up your skills?"

"There's not a swordsman in Paris who can beat me."

"We'll see," Frobisher muttered. "Lydia, take Jean-Louis behind the desk."

She drew the boy to safety, watching breathlessly as the men circled each other, the comte's face wearing a look of murderous intent.

When they engaged at last, it was with astonishing speed. Chabrier's sword leaped forward, and Matthew blocked it with one fluid motion, then immediately countered with a low riposte. They thrust, parried and thrust again in such rapid sequence that Lydia saw only a blur of steel. There was only the staccato clang of blade striking blade and the muted thud of their booted feet upon the carpet.

Chabrier's initial attack had forced the captain back against the door.

"Impressive." Matthew made a mocking bow. "Still all brute force, I see. You could learn a little delicacy, Lucien"—his tone was silken—"in all things."

"I'll give you delicacy—"

Matthew's sword flashed repeatedly as he pressed forward, forcing the comte to retreat until he was backed up against the bookshelves. They grappled

there, blades crossed. Chabrier finally thrust Matthew
away from him with one burly arm, sending him reeling until his chest came up hard against the mantel-
piece. When the captain sprang away, Chabrier
renewed his attack.

The captain now seemed completely on the defen-
sive as Chabrier continued his ruthless assault. Lydia
nearly cried out. It was like watching a thick-necked
bull pitted against a lithe stag.

"Had enough, Mattei?" the comte taunted. "I can
make the end painless for you. Just lower your
sword."

"I'll see you in hell first!"

To Lydia's amazement, the captain flew at him,
driving him rapidly back with more fury and force
than Chabrier had any ability to counter. When the
Frenchman finally came to a halt, he was arched back
over the edge of his desk, the captain's sword point
pricking the base of his throat.

"Drop it!" Frobisher commanded.

The length of steel fell from Chabrier's nerveless
fingers. The captain raised the hilt of his own sword,
angling the blade down in the classic duelist's stance
for the coup de grace.

"No, Matthew!" Lydia entreated him, meeting his
fevered eyes. Demons danced there in the pewter
depths. "Hasn't there been enough killing?"

"Yes," he muttered, lowering the sword. "I need
some clean air. There's a stench in this room."

He had turned away, intent on gathering up Lydia's
cloak, when she screamed his name. The comte had
plucked his pistol off the mantel, and as Matthew spun
around at her belated warning, Chabrier shot him
from across the room, square in the chest.

He staggered to his knees, and then fell backward
onto the rug, still holding the cloak. Lydia watched in
horror as a bright red stain spread across his chest.
Chabrier stood unmoving, eyes blazing with dark victory, the smoking pistol dangling from one hand.

She sank down and threw her arms around Matthew. "Matthew!" she cried, raising his head. "Oh, God, no!"

"Steady, lass," he breathed, his voice barely a whisper. "I'm not really shot." He held her firm as she recoiled. "Stage pistol," he murmured. "And fake blood. But heed me, Lydia—you must get Chabrier out of this room. There's something I need to do. Lock him in your cell and go out the back gate. And remember, he must think me dead. Here—" From under the cloak, he slid a pistol into her hand. "Use this."

He looked up into her shocked eyes, and drawled, "You said you wanted to be in the thick of things." Then with a dry rattling sigh, his head fell back.

Lydia swore his face took on an ashen pallor.

She climbed shakily to her feet, holding the pistol in a fold of her skirt. She was very tempted to use it on her husband instead of the comte. How dare he put her through such torture? Well, he *had* warned her, but that didn't alter the fact that she would be forever haunted by the sight of that scarlet stain blossoming on his breast.

She squared her shoulders and turned to the comte. "He's dead," she said in a sullen monotone.

"And I thought him immortal," he murmured contemptuously.

Jean-Louis had gotten over his initial shock and began pummeling the comte's chest.

"Monster!" he wailed. "You killed my master! Bastard!"

"No, you're the bastard, little man," Chabrier said, holding him away. "I am merely the son of one."

He was bending to retrieve his sword when Lydia stepped forward and laid the gun barrel against his temple.

"Stand up slowly. And no noise or you're dead." At least she knew the right words. "I can't kill you in here," she observed with cold-blooded detachment. "So I think we had better take a walk."

He sneered. "Put that thing down before you injure yourself."

"I can shatter a bottle at fifty feet, sir. I think I can hit you from this distance."

"She killed many brigands on the beach," said Jean-Louis through his tears. "You should do as she says."

"Get my cloak," Lydia said to the boy. "And put it over my shoulders."

Jean-Louis crouched beside Matthew's prone body and gently tugged the garment from under his limp hand.

"Au revoir, mon capitaine."

Matthew counted to twenty before he climbed to his feet. He opened the door a crack and watched Lydia march the comte along the corridor, waiting until he knew they'd made it safely outside before he closed it and set the lock. He crossed to the window just as Tenpence came easing through it, dragging a leather satchel behind him.

He sketched a salute. "Nice wound, Captain." His eyes crinkled. "You got the gun past the guards?"

"I smuggled it inside my hat as you suggested. And then slipped it into my waistcoat while I got reacquainted with my old friend."

Ten nodded. "I saw you switch the pistols on the mantel while you were dueling."

Matthew was already scanning the bookshelves. "Mmm . . . I had a hunch the jackal would fire at me. Chabrier can always be counted on to attack an unarmed man."

"I got a bit edgy when 'e kept waving 'is gun around. Thought I'd have to shoot 'im through the window." The boy stroked the butt of Lydia's small pistol tucked inside his shirt.

"You *are* a bloodthirsty little rogue." Matthew grinned down at him and then went back to his search. When he found the section he sought, he traced his fingers over the spines, murmuring, "Rabelais, Racine, Richelieu . . . ah, Rousseau."

He quickly pried a cluster of books away from the wall; behind them lay a metal plate. Ten shifted a chair beside the bookcase, climbed up and began fiddling with the lock.

Matthew watched, stony-faced, praying Lydia wasn't having any trouble with the comte. He wouldn't have considered placing her in danger if retrieving the documents hadn't been imperative. He'd been derelict in his duty to England once before because of a woman, and he hoped Lydia would understand how much he needed to rectify that rent in his honor.

Of course, he could have simply killed Chabrier out of hand. But this way he'd land his enemy a more devilish blow. As Lydia pointed out, enough blood had been shed.

Tenpence gave a crow of victory as he tugged open the safe. " 'Eres's a fine mess o' papers."

They quickly bundled them into the leather satchel. Matthew then went to the cavernous fireplace and plucked up the copy of *Richard III*. "No use wasting good literature on philistines."

" 'Now is the winter of our discontent made glorious summer . . .' " Ten quoted in a lordly voice.

"Just so," the captain said as he straddled the sill.

He gazed one last time at the chamber where so much evil had been done. Even without the comte's malevolent presence it seethed with ill humors. He decided it was long past time he turned his back on this room with all its hovering ghosts.

Without another word, he followed Tenpence out the window.

Lydia and her hostage proceeded along the guarded corridor, Jean-Louis trailing behind them. She prodded Chabrier with the pistol occasionally through the cloak, but he seemed almost resigned. Still, she wasn't able to take a decent breath until they were outside in the courtyard.

With Jean-Louis scouting ahead, they made· their way to the wine cellar. No one else was moving about inside the iron fence.

"Here, it's this door." She pulled the comte into the

shadows while the boy tugged at the latch. When the door wouldn't open, she nudged Chabrier with the pistol. "The key, if you please."

With a grumbling sigh, he held out a gold chain with several keys. Jean-Louis quickly found the right one, but when the door opened into darkness, he murmured, "We have no candle."

"I know the way," she said tersely, forcing Chabrier down the stairs. "And so does the comte."

She coaxed him through the wine cellar until they reached her former cell, where a slight spill of light came through the high window. Unfortunately, the cell door was locked and none of the comte's keys would open it.

"Jean-Louis, run back to the entrance, and see if the jailer's keys are there."

Chabrier's voice came slithering out of the shadows. "What you do to me now is of small moment, Miss Peartree. I have destroyed my enemy, and so even if you shoot me, I die contented."

Lydia smiled to herself. "I am not Miss Peartree any longer. I am the wife of Matthew Frobisher."

"He was your husband?" His tone was hushed.

"I gather your informants left out that little detail."

For the first time Chabrier felt the stirrings of real fear. This was no coquette who'd lost a chance-met lover, but a bereaved widow with vengeance in her heart.

"*Mam'selle!* I can't find it!"

Jean-Louis's voice was urgent; Lydia turned without thinking.

The comte lashed out swiftly, forcing her arm up as he grappled for the pistol, his fingers biting cruelly into her wrist. As her grip began to weaken, Lydia fired into the air—vowing he would not use the gun against her. The explosive shot echoed painfully in the small chamber. Chabrier snarled in frustration, knocking the gun away just before his hands closed over her throat.

Lydia battled back, writhing, twisting, clawing at his

face, tearing at the fingers that gouged her flesh. She kicked out hard, catching him upon both shins.

"Jean-Louis!" she wailed as the comte thrust her against the cell, pinning her to the bars. Again she kicked, higher this time, her knee connecting with his groin. He staggered back, hunched over and cursing. She braced herself as he straightened, his eyes promising a terrible retribution. Then, unaccountably, he gave a low grunt, his eyes rolled up . . . and with a rasping, guttural groan he slid to the floor.

Jean-Louis was standing behind him, wearing a triumphant smile. He held up the pistol by its barrel. "I tripped on it in the dark. And then I hit this French dog with it, *splat*, on his ugly head." He prodded the comte's slumped body with his toe. "That is for shooting my master—and for those disgusting bonbons—you son of Satan."

Lydia was clinging to the grill, trying to regain her breath, trying to ignore the pain in her bruised windpipe. Why in God's name did they always go for her throat?

"Jean-Louis," she rasped, "the captain isn't dead."

The boy chuckled. "Of course he is not dead."

"You knew?"

"Oui. When I take the cloak from him, he wink at me. Very clever, my *capitaine*." His voice lowered. "But, *mam'selle*, why did this evil one say that I am my master's son?"

Lydia crouched down, clasping his narrow shoulders. "The captain wanted to tell you himself, but I think you've gone long enough without hearing the truth. Matthew Frobisher is your real father, Jean-Louis."

"Mais non!" She saw his eyes brighten even in the stygian darkness of the cellar. "My father," he breathed. "I so much wanted it to be true. But why did you say to the comte that the *capitaine* denied me?"

"I wanted him to think you meant nothing to the captain, so he would let you go. But you truly are his son." She hugged him. "And my son now, as well, because I am the captain's wife." Jean-Louis gave a low cry. "Yes, it's true. We were wed in Lempère."

"But why did you not tell us?"

"We agreed to keep it a secret . . . because you boys all had enough to worry about, and we didn't want you to feel that the captain was . . . distracted."

"This is a thing most wonderful! I am so happy! Ah, don't cry . . . *Maman*."

"I'm not," she sniffled, holding his head against her shoulder.

She was still clinging to him when there was a rustling at the end of the hallway. Tenpence, carrying a small lantern, poked his head through the doorway. He whispered sharply, "They're in here, Cap'n. And that rascal Chabrier, 'e's out like a light."

"Well, I'll be damned. Run back to Arkady now. Tell him we'll be along in a minute."

The boy set the lantern down and scurried away as the captain came along the corridor. With a crow of delight, Jean-Louis flung himself forward.

"Johnny!" Matthew cried, swinging him off his feet.

"*Capitaine!* The *mam'selle* says I am to be your son. I will not have a father who is a French dog."

"No, you get an English dog, instead. You're sure you don't mind?"

"Mind? That I have gotten a father and a mother all in one night?" Jean-Louis pulled back and said in a clear, earnest voice, "Father, I will try very hard to make you proud of me."

"Ah, Johnny, you already have."

Lydia watched her husband embrace his son, and her spirit soared—Matthew's homesick child had found his true family at last.

"My *maman*," the boy whispered, "she has been crying."

Matthew nodded and put his son aside gently. When he approached Lydia, it was almost tentatively. He went down on one knee and murmured, "Can you ever forgive me for causing you such grief? It was impossible to warn you properly . . . he needed to think me dead. And I needed to get at his safe. It was something I owed England. It was . . . necessary." He winced when he realized he'd used the comte's own words. "Oh, sweetheart," his voice throbbed, "please don't cry—"

"I'm crying because I'm so happy," she gurgled as she tugged him to his feet. "Because it's finally all come right."

"Still, I'm sorry for frightening you and for placing you in danger."

"I'm not made of glass, Captain. And I did vow to help you in every endeavor, did I not? Besides, the comte was fairly docile . . . at least until the end."

"It looks like he gave you a rough time."

"Not nearly as rough as the time Jean-Louis gave him." She looked up at him impishly. "Matthew, when you told me we wouldn't get much sleep tonight, this isn't exactly what I was expecting."

His startled laughter rang through the stone chamber.

"Ah, Lydia, there's not another like you," he declared as he tugged her against him. "Kiss me, jade, and then we'll be gone from this accursed place. And leave his lordship to his unholy dreams."

Lydia kissed him tenderly, holding his face between her hands . . . this man with the courage to forsake that which he loved for something he believed in.

In truth, there was not another like Matthew Frobisher.

Chabrier staggered out of his wine cellar, one hand cradling the back of his throbbing head. He called out hoarsely several times and was soon surrounded by his men.

"Find them!" he ranted. "Set fire to the embassy if you must. I want that red-haired baggage! And the little cur, as well!"

Still clutching his crown, he made his unsteady way to his office, shaking off the men who tried to aid him. They followed behind, muttering to themselves.

His progress was impeded when he reached the door to his office. It was locked—and that red-haired she-witch had his keys.

"Break it down!" he barked to his men.

They stared at him in confusion; it was made of oak and very thick.

"Are you all deaf?" he roared.

Snatching a rifle from the nearest guard, he fired point-blank at the lock. It still refused to open. He commandeered three more rifles, firing in rapid sequence, standing like a wild-eyed beast in a cloud of acrid smoke. As the echoes of the final volley reverberated through the hallway, he gave a mighty kick—and the door yawned wide.

He lurched forward and stood gaping, gazing with stunned disbelief at the bloodied spot on his carpet where the body of François Mattei had lain. The man was dead, and dead men did not walk away. He had seen the body, seen the blood . . . as he had once before, in a burned-out Paris boarding house. His thoughts reeled as he staggered against the doorframe.

From his vantage point he could see the emptied safe, its door left boldly open.

He drove his fist into his chest, as if to restart a heart frozen with terror. They would come for him now, the countless enemies whom he had held in check with weapons forged of paper. Flight was his only option.

I must get away tonight, away from Paris, away from France. His thoughts raced, and still he could not move, could only stand and stare in bewildered incoherence at the telltale patch of blood.

Nightshade! His unraveling mind screamed. *Nightshade . . .*

And over his shoulder, amid the carvings on the splintered door, a demon with the face of an English sea captain had its final, triumphant laugh.

Epilogue

*T*he *Rook* floated in stately splendor upon the aquamarine waters of Evionne Cove. Her sails were reefed and her new mast rose up straight and true from the deck. The captain gazed out across the water as he drove the gypsy cart down the bumpy path, and remarked to Lydia that his ship had never looked more beautiful.

"It's my curse," she bemoaned softly, "to be married to a man who thinks his ship beautiful and his wife merely intrepid."

"Aye," he laughed, "but it's true."

The French sailors and the actors greeted them joyfully. Tilda and Sebastian announced that they had been married by the mayor of Lempère, and then Sebastian asked the captain in halting English if he might accompany them back to Devon.

Gerardone and the captain's crew followed shortly in their wake, having stopped off in Lempère to attend to some mysterious business. The Gascon now called Matthew to his side, and Lydia watched in puzzlement as he handed down a large wrapped parcel.

"Your wedding present," the captain told her.

She immediately crouched on the sand to unwrap it. It was a painting of the Virgin, full of rich, deep

Renaissance hues. She gazed down at the lovely, tranquil face and then up at the man who never ceased to amaze her.

"It looks like Titian," she crooned, running her hands along the gilt frame. "Wherever did you find it?"

"It belonged to the priest. The mayor had impounded his property, and I asked Gerardone to convince him to part with it. Which he did, for a rather astonishing sum. I hope you like it."

"Oh, Matthew . . . it's beyond anything."

"I always admired Titian," he drawled, leaning forward and kissing the top of her head. "Even if he did insist on painting red-haired women."

They remained two more days in the cove. The crew of the *Rook* lazed about on the beach and explored the cliffs. Jean-Louis discovered the secret path the brigands had used and was greatly lauded by his crewmates. He grew more confident with each passing day, basking in the fond smiles of his newfound father.

On their last night, Gerardone's troupe gave a performance of *Leovigild the Visigoth* for the people of Lempère. When the cruel invader Leovigild was at last impaled by the White Prince, the crowd rose up from the sand with hearty applause. Gerardone bowed repeatedly and then came to the edge of the stage, quieting the tumult with one enormous hand.

"My friends," he began, "it has been my pleasure to know many good men—soldiers and statesmen, farmers and shopkeepers, and of course actors. But I have never met a man I esteem as highly as this English captain. A teacher, a sailor, a swordsman, a lover—" There were scattered titters. "—and a damn fine actor. This man came to our country through the hand of God—a mighty squall that cast him up on our coast."

"Fellow should go into politics," Matthew hissed into Lydia's ear. "He's windier than the mayor."

"I bless the storm that blew him to our shore.

Where once there was want and fear, there is now prosperity and security. He came before to our country as an enemy; he leaves tomorrow a comrade and a friend. I have learned many things from him, but most importantly, I now believe that it is possible to stand fast against tyranny and prevail. He has awakened in me the true spirit of France. People of Evionne Cove, I give you Matthew Frobisher."

Lydia prodded him to his feet to acknowledge the cheering. He looked almost sheepish as he turned about and smiled at the sea of admiring faces. He was about to resume his seat, when a thin figure came toward him through the crowd—an exotically dressed old woman. She came right up to him and put a wizened hand on his arm. Her eyes held his an instant, and then she placed the coiled lock of his hair into his hand.

"You *are* the one, sir," was all she said in her strange Provençal accent. And then she disappeared back into the throng.

"What . . . ?" He gazed after her with a peculiar expression.

" 'More things under heaven and earth,' Matthew," Lydia whispered.

He turned to her, his eyes full of strange musings. She reached out to hold him, felt him trembling in her arms. They sat together, heads touching, until the crowd dispersed. Soon the beach was empty except for the shadowy presence of Gerardone's caravan.

As he gazed out across the water, Lydia watched the emotions play over his angular face. Something had shaken him to the core. Still she said nothing, holding his hand against her waist and remembering the night he had wept in her arms.

"Lydia, I am not larger than life," he said at last in a strained voice. "I am not some demigod. I do not enjoy all this attention."

"Oh, you know Gerardone—he can't resist playing to his audience."

"Lydia, what did the gypsy woman mean? I am not the one, whatever she says. I am just a scarred old sinner who happens to know his way around intrigue."

Lydia cupped his cheek. "Don't you see it, Matthew? They need heroes in this country. Even English ones. This is the land of Charlemagne, of Roland and Joan of Arc. They've lost this century's hero—exiled to Elba. And even if he was a bit monstrous at times, there was greatness in him, for all that.

"You brought only good things to these people— gold for their markets, safety to their roads. It hasn't all been intrigue and deception, my love. There has been change for the better. With Napoleon gone, France will be our ally now. And once Chabrier and his confederates are banished, he will not rise again. Or not for very long, if we English have any say. The two countries can exist in amity—oh, until the heavens rip asunder and the world turns to dust. And you helped bring that about. You *are* the one, Matthew. Their hero. And mine, as well."

"How did you get so wise, little jade?" He nuzzled her nose.

"I had a very good teacher." She tipped him back on the soft sand and kissed him. Kissed all the pained perplexity from his stern face. She felt the muscles of his cheek relax beneath her lips.

"My safe harbor," he whispered, turning his mouth up to hers.

"Mmm. Always."

They lay together on the shingled beach, watching the ship rock hypnotically in the shifting tide. Then without a word the captain pulled Lydia to her feet and led her along the water's edge to the darkened sea cave.

"For old time's sake," he said as he drew off her gown and lowered her to the place their bodies had carved in the sand weeks before. "And because I can't resist the siren's call."

They made love beside the enchanted pool, without any urgency, taking their time to awaken the sensations that hummed always near the surface whenever they were together. Lydia delighted in the languid quality of their play—so at home with each other's wants and desires they felt no need for haste. Somewhere on the road from Paris, she and Matthew had discovered that with familiarity came only a stronger, richer union.

At last they lay inert and breathless, entwined in each other's arms and in the sweet glimmer of passion spent. Lydia felt a rush of regret that they would never again take their pleasure in Evionne Cove. She, like the Gascon, blessed the storm that had sent them to this magical place.

Soon the cooling night air roused her. Lydia leaned on one arm and traced her fingers along his throat. "Wake up, Matthew, I have something to tell you."

"Mmm?"

"I got a letter from Arkady today, from Paris— you're not going to like it."

"It would take a lot to sour me at this particular moment, Princess." He gave her a mellow smile.

"King Louis has written to the Prince Regent, informing him of your service. My cousin says you'll be lucky to escape with a knighthood, but he thinks a barony is more likely."

Matthew groaned. "Damn." He shifted away from her and sat up. "That will play havoc with my family motto—*No honors but my own.* We Frobishers have always been simple sailing men. Now it'll be Lord This and Lady That. Stop grinning, Lydia. I thought you didn't want a title."

"I'm simply jealous. The Peartrees don't have a family motto. Only a crest. My mother designed it when my father was made a baron. A golden shield with a flowering pear tree at its center, full of white blossoms—" Lydia's eyes widened as she recalled the words the gypsy had spoken the day of the careening.

The captain stopped her mouth with his hand. "No. Don't even say it. I want no more of gypsies or baronies or Gerardone's Gasconneries—what I want, all

that I want, is here in this blessed little cove. My ship,
my lads, my son . . . and the woman who makes it all
come right. You, Lydia, are all that I want."

The next morning dawned gloriously fair, with a
freshening wind and not a cloud in the azure sky. The
only hitch in their departure had been Jean-Louis's
refusal to leave the little donkey behind.

"But, Father," he had implored. "The *petit gris* is
my friend. We must take him with us."

"Most boys want a dog," the captain growled to
Lydia.

"Let him come along, Matthew," she coaxed gently.
"You can raise him over the side with the hoist."

"I'll have no livestock on my ship," he pronounced
sternly. "Women are bad enough."

Lydia had given him a look of amused reproach
until he relented, remarking drily that he could foresee
a future where he would be completely at the mercy
of a red-haired doxy and a young French scamp.

They now stood together at the ship's wheel, Lydia
again behind him as he guided the *Rook* through the
narrow channel and out into the open sea. He drew
her to the wheel then and coached her in the ways of
the wind. The *Rook* heeled over, leaving a trail of
foam where her prow thrust back the sea. Lydia felt
her heart soar as the sails bellied out, promising a fair,
swift crossing.

"I trust you have enjoyed your cruise, my lady." He
spoke against her wind-tossed curls.

She laughed and nuzzled his cheek. "I only hope
we'll be home in time for tea."

"I make no promises. We could always run into
another squall. Remember, my love, the sea takes us
on some remarkable journeys."

He left her on her own and went to recline against
the ship's rail, lighting his pipe. The wind caught at
his silvery hair and tumbled it about his lean face.
Lydia wondered if she would ever find that face less
than compelling.

"Where did your journey take you, Matthew?" she asked.

His mouth quirked around his pipestem. "It feels like I've sailed all seven seas, this voyage. Let me think . . . I've found a son, I've gotten a new crew member—"

"I should hope I'm more than that to you."

"I was talking about Sebastian, minx. I've also acquired a lop-eared ship's mascot, and now I'm heading home with a truly rare prize."

Lydia was preening at the wheel, when he added wickedly, "Never thought to own a painting by Titian."

"Matthew," she rebuked him.

"Oh—" His eyes widened guilelessly. "Did I forget something?"

"Yes," she said. "You forgot your wife."

"How remiss of me." He knocked the ashes from his pipe and returned to her side. "Gerardone lost three wives, you know, poor fellow. I think I'll take good care to hold onto my one." He snaked his arms loosely about her waist and rested his chin on her shoulder.

They stood so for some time, the east wind at their backs.

Around them the crew of the *Rook*—boys once, but now young men tested and found true—were busy with their chores. All except Jean-Louis, who was just emerging from the hatchway with a large pot, trying to fend off his pet.

"Soup!" he called out.

"Soup?" the captain echoed against Lydia's ear.

"No, I'd rather stay right here."

"Mmm. Me too."

She leaned into him, feeling his arms tighten around her as she held the wheel steady. She thought of the painting he had given her, now resting on the sideboard below the silver sword. The Titian Madonna. Lydia had her own wedding gift for the captain—something she knew he would like very much. There was a new life growing within her, just below where his hands rested at her waist. Another Frobisher to grace the world with moonstone eyes and a secret dimple.

The life she was returning to would bear little resemblance to the one she had sailed away from on that hot summer day. No fawning dandies, no whirl of social engagements—only a school full of rascally boys, and a stern, scarred schoolmaster to fill her days.

She would be his helpmate, his companion and the mother of his children. And in the soft, deep shadows of night, she would be his lover. Well, maybe not only at night, she reflected wryly, considering their appetite for each other.

The captain noted her revery. "And where did your journey take you, Princess?"

"Here, Matthew," she said, shifting one hand from the ship's wheel and pressing it over his heart. "Right here."

He smiled deeply and covered her hand with his own.

"Sail us back to Devon, Lydia," he commanded softly, his joyful eyes on the far horizon. "Take us home."

With a mischievous grin she said, "Aye, Captain." And squinted.

Matthew Frobisher threw back his head and laughed, and then he kissed her, reaching out to hold the wheel so she could turn full against him and surrender up her rosy mouth.

Gilbert Marriott gazed down at them from the foretop spar where he perched next to Rowdy.

"I saw from the first how it was between those two," he pronounced, his boy's heart at last banishing all thoughts of the delectable Miss Peartree. "It just took a while for them to see it."

He grinned and his blue eyes brightened. "Now, look sharp, Rowdy, and let's get this sail lowered. We'll be back in England by nightfall, and then maybe we can scare up an adventure or two of our own."